ODIN'S SHADOW

Sons of Odin Series

ERIN S. RILEY

SOUL MATE PUBLISHING

New York

ODIN'S SHADOW

Published in the United States of America by
Soul Mate Publishing
P.O. Box 24
Macedon, New York, 14502

ISBN: 978-1-68291-041-2

ebook ISBN: 978-1-61935-768-6

www.SoulMatePublishing.com

For my daughter Savannah—

A beautiful young woman with

an even more beautiful spirit.

I love you more than all the stars in the sky.

Acknowledgements

Thank you to my husband and children for supporting my need to write, including a willingness to eat ramen noodles for supper without complaint whenever I'm on a roll. A special thanks to Carmen Vanscyoc, Nicole Armstrong, and Kelley Franks, three wonderful friends who were my first readers and are still my biggest supporters, and to Kim Freeman, a dear friend who never tires of discussing story ideas with me. Thank you to fellow writers Susan Ward and Terry Wilson for their positive feedback and encouragement through this sometimes overwhelming journey. Thank you to Regan Walker and Carol Cork for their support. And a heartfelt thank you to Diana Deyo, a friend who refused to let me give up. Above all, thank you to my mother, Karen S. Ward, who was taken from this world too soon but taught me what unconditional love truly is. Everything I am and everything I will be, I owe to her.

I am so grateful to Debby Gilbert from Soul Mate Publishing for providing the opportunity for me to pursue my dreams. A special thanks goes to Victoria Vane, cover designer extraordinaire. And finally, thank you to my brilliant editor, Char Chaffin, who understood my vision from the beginning and who polished my story with unwavering patience.

Prologue

Ireland, 860 A.D.

Niall Ó Murchú opened the door to the house he had not been inside for nearly a year. The interior was very still. Very quiet. He gazed at the familiar surroundings as a nauseating wave of loneliness gripped his belly. Specks of dust caught in a sunbeam that streamed in through the open door. Silence enveloped him like Sile's shroud.

But if he closed his eyes he could almost imagine she still dwelled inside. Maybe she was in the kitchen and any moment would come to greet him, then chide him for tracking in mud on his boots. He smiled, remembering how she would settle into his embrace, tucking her head under his chin. Her hair always smelled so sweet.

Niall stood in the doorway for a long time, as though to enter the house would make Sile's death real.

No. He wasn't ready to go inside yet. Niall turned to set the horse to graze. He unloaded his goods from the wagon, stacking the crates of fabric into neat piles next to the front door, then trudged to the stream behind the house. As he dipped his pitcher into the water, he heard a noise on the other side and glanced up. What he saw made the hackles rise on the back of his neck.

There, sitting across the stream, were two small, dark headed children. They were wearing the genderless smocks of youth so it was impossible to tell if they were male or female. Their gaze was as silvery and fathomless as those of changelings.

"Hello," he said, feeling foolish. "Where is your mother?"

Not surprisingly given their age, they didn't reply, but

only blinked at him like tiny owls. One of them, even from this distance, appeared to have two blackened eyes in the late stages of healing. Niall shivered.

"Hello!" He called louder, hoping to alert whoever they were with. He didn't have much experience with children, but even he knew that the combination of a moving body of water and small children was an invitation for disaster. Who would have left them unattended?

The woods were quiet, and the children didn't move. Neither did they take their eyes off him. Changelings, *a voice whispered in his head, but he pushed the thought away. He was not a superstitious man.*

Niall splashed across the stream toward the children. They scrambled to their feet and toddled off, with Niall following them until the children stopped next to the still figure of a woman lying on the ground. They looked at her, then back up at him, as if expecting him to do something. One of the children made an unintelligible chattering sound and the other child nodded. For the second time the gooseflesh rose on Niall's neck, and he felt an almost overwhelming urge to run.

The woman was dead, but judging from the appearance of the body, hadn't been dead for long. Her clothing was filthy, and her slack mouth revealed that she was missing most of her teeth. Most likely a peasant. Niall knelt down next to her. There was a puddle of blood on the rock behind her head. Had the poor woman slipped on the wet undergrowth and struck her head when she fell? Niall looked again at the two children who knelt beside the woman.

"Is this your mamai?" he asked.

Their faces brightened at the word. "Mamai?" one of them repeated, looking at him with hopeful eyes.

Niall took the children into Baile Átha Cliath to search for someone who might know their identity. He felt uneasy about leaving the body in the woods, but if he could find the woman's husband or family they would want to bury her themselves. However, no one in the village had any idea who the strange children belonged to, and he was faced with the dilemma of what to do with them as darkness fell. He was tired and hungry, and the unwashed smell emanating from the children was overpowering. He wanted very much to be rid of them.

"Niall Ó Murchú." A familiar voice spoke from behind him, and he turned to find his former servant, Eithne, walking up to him. He had let her go after Sile's death and had not expected to ever see her again. Niall had not, in fact, expected to see anyone again. He had instead hoped his long sea voyage would prove deadly.

Eithne had a worried expression on her homely face as she took in the sight of the children in Niall's wagon. A deep groove always settled in between her eyebrows when she was worried. He had forgotten about that. That groove had gotten progressively deeper during Sile's agonizing three days of labor.

Niall shook his head to clear it, and smiled at his former servant. She would know what to do.

Eithne lived with her sister's family. This arrangement was not to her liking, as she was quick to offer to go home with Niall to care for the children until he could find out who they belonged to. Niall would have preferred to simply leave them with Eithne and go home alone, but took the offer as probably the best he would get. And so while Eithne went to find her sister to tell her of her plans, Niall bought some food and provisions to last a few days, then they took the children home.

The days stretched into a fortnight and still Niall was no closer to finding the family of the children. After the first two days he had resigned himself and buried the mother's body in the woods. If someone wanted to dig up the woman and move her, they would be welcome to do so.

Eithne was childless herself and seemed to take great

delight in caring for the children. She washed them, fed them, and sewed them tiny clothes. She made the girl's smock in blue wool and the boy's in green, to more easily tell them apart. Clean, the children were even more beautiful than Niall had at first imagined. The longer it took to find their family, the more the rumors would spread that he had two dangerous fairy children in his home.

In desperation, he had even gone to Dubhlinn in search of someone who might know who they belonged to. He didn't bring the children this time—the Finngalls had a distasteful habit of selling Irish captives into slavery. Niall was growing fond of the twins despite himself, and couldn't stomach the thought of them being hurt in any way.

But Dubhlinn had proved pointless, and he had finally been forced to face the situation for what it was. The children were orphaned, their mother buried in the woods, and Niall was the only thing standing between them and an uncertain future. He needed to make a decision.

The following day he brought the twins to the priest and had them baptized. He called the boy Ainnileas and the girl Selia, a variation of the name of his beloved wife. And then it was done; they were his.

God had given him the family that had been robbed from him with Sile's death.

Chapter 1

Ireland, 876 AD

The butcher ran a hand through his lank blond hair, studying Selia until her cheeks grew hot. His thumb brushed her hand as he handed her a wrapped parcel. She took a quick step back.

"Anything else, Miss?" His Norse accent was so strong she had difficulty understanding him. She blinked at him for a moment too long and he smiled, obviously enjoying her confusion. His teeth were worn down to rotten brown nubs.

He continued gawking at her as though she were the type of woman who would welcome his crude attention. Unpleasant little man. Selia averted her gaze and managed to keep her face expressionless. According to Eithne, it was almost an art to keep one's face arranged in a look of distant politeness that served to discourage any unwanted advances. No direct eye contact and no smiling. Men thought a smile meant so much more than it did.

"Willow bark," she said, too low to be heard over the crowd. She couldn't contain a shudder as the man leaned in closer. She spoke louder. "Where can I find an herb seller?"

He stroked the coarse hair of his beard, smiling, and finally cocked his head in the direction of the river. "Last stall. Don't let the hag sell you weeds."

Selia nodded as she hurried away. She made her way through the rough crowd, keeping her head down and the hood of her cloak up. Dubhlinn was large, and congested with a surprising assortment of people—native Irish, of course, and Norse, but also others of nationalities she was unfamiliar with. Men with strange clothing and smooth, honey-colored skin, speaking in a rapid language that sounded loud and angry. Other men who by dress and physical appearance seemed to be Irish, but those conversations were just as unintelligible as the shouters.

It was easy to become mesmerized by the rhythm of the words. If she had more time she would slow her pace and savor the exotic sounds. But if she dallied too long, Eithne would become suspicious.

The herb woman—neither a hag nor a seller of weeds—was native Irish. At least Selia wouldn't have to try to string Norse words into a sentence again as she had with the butcher, who had let her struggle for a few moments before revealing he spoke Irish. She bought a large packet of willow bark, then turned to go on her way.

The woman put a hand on her arm to stop her. "Surely you're not going toward the harbor."

"Why?"

"Why?" The woman's voice sounded too loud, and several people turned to look.

Selia winced. The last thing she needed was to draw attention to herself.

"Don't you know what's at the docks? A girl like you shouldn't even be out this far, alone," the woman said.

"I'm meeting my father. His ship is at the docks."

"Well . . ." the herb woman seemed uncertain. "Mind you stay away from the dragonships, then."

So they were still there—she wasn't too late. Selia managed an expression of appropriate concern. "I thought they were gone."

"No. The market's been crawling with Finngalls today.

Two went by just a few moments ago, as a matter of fact. I'm surprised your father didn't keep you at home until after they sailed." The woman frowned as Selia turned once again to leave. "Put your hood up, at least, child."

Selia hesitated for a moment before pulling up her hood. When had she lowered it? She mentally retraced her steps through the market, willing herself to remember, but there was nothing. This was exactly the reason her father and Eithne were reluctant to let her out of the house alone.

Coming to Dubhlinn had been a mistake, after all.

Selia straightened resolutely. She hadn't made it this far only to turn around now. She would do what she had come here to do, and wipe the smug look from her brother's face once and for all. She saw Ainnileas in her mind's eye, jaw agape, struck dumb by her boldness when he learned of her adventure. She had to bite her lip to keep from smiling.

Several days ago their father had warned Ainnileas about the dragonships in Dubhlinn and forbidden him to venture there, and although Selia was present for the warning she hadn't been included in it. The mere thought of *her* sneaking away to Dubhlinn was preposterous.

Ainnileas, of course, had gone to the harbor yesterday morning, watching the Finngalls for several hours as they unloaded cargo from their ships to trade at the market. One of the foreigners had spoken directly to him. The man had either ordered him to get out of his way, or had called him a skinny dog—Ainnileas was unsure about that part, since his grasp of the Norse language was limited. But it hadn't stopped him from coming home to gloat.

A year or two ago Selia would not have hesitated to hit him. But she was a young woman now, much too old to strike the smirk from her brother's face. Seething, she had assaulted the bread dough with such vigor that Eithne made her stop before she ruined their supper.

But her luck had changed this morning with the maid's female troubles. Eithne had planned to go to the market at Baile Átha Cliath, the village only a mile or so from their home, to buy a sausage for supper. But after a long hour of listening to the maid moan and mutter under her breath, cursing her womanhood, Selia offered to go to the market and buy fixings for the evening meal. She kept the offer as nonchalant as possible, for although Eithne was a servant, she was not a stupid woman.

Eithne had given her a sharp look as though assessing her options. Selia was not known to be particularly helpful or selfless, so she knew any such offer made would be regarded with suspicion. She kept to her spinning and willed her face to remain impassive.

The maid grimaced. "Don't know if your father would like that, my girl."

Selia shrugged and continued working. "All right. Go yourself, then."

A half hour later, Eithne called on the saints for mercy, and Selia took this as a sign in her favor. She suggested a cup of willow bark tea as she deftly pulled the wool.

The woman moaned. Selia had put her spinning down to rummage through the cupboards, pretending to look for the packet of willow bark. She'd used the last of it days ago for a headache, but Eithne didn't know that.

"Oh . . . I'm sorry. We don't have any." Selia gave her a look of deep sympathy. Eithne's eyes flashed and Selia feared she had pushed her too far, but then the woman doubled over with a gasp.

"All right! All right, little miss. But you go straight to the market and straight back—no dallying. Stay away from the crowds and don't speak to anyone. Do you understand me, Selia?"

"Of course." Selia had been careful to hide her smile as she donned her cloak and collected her basket. She *would* go straight to the market.

In Dubhlinn.

Selia left the main road and climbed to the top of a grassy hill close enough to the harbor to provide a good view. The hill had several mature trees that would protect her from any prying eyes who might notice her presence, namely her father or his acquaintances. She was not foolish enough to go directly to the docks as her brother had.

Characteristic of the eastern coast of Ireland, the weather had shifted from winter to spring seemingly overnight. The air was warm and fragrant, and the grass soft beneath her feet. She sat down, a bit out of breath from the climb. She *would* see a Finngall today, and wait on this hill until she did.

Selia and Ainnileas had been raised listening to stories of the Finngalls. Although their father was not much of a storyteller, Eithne had a talent for it, and the more horrific and brutal the account the more her eyes would sparkle with the telling. Of course the woman had never actually *seen* a Finngall face to face, as she found the walk to Dubhlinn very tiresome and had only been there a handful of times when she was much younger. Now the maid could barely make it to Baile Átha Cliath without wheezing and sweating so badly, Selia feared Eithne would collapse and die on the road.

According to Eithne, Ireland had been breached and raided countless times by various foreigners, but only the Finngalls had stayed. Several decades before, a group of them had recognized Dubhlinn to be a desirable trading center and had overtaken and claimed it as their own. Now, most of the inhabitants of the city were second-generation Northmen, no longer considered Finngalls by the native Irish, and yet not quite Irish either. There was an uneasy understanding between them and the Irish people who lived in Dubhlinn. Most of the native Irish still lived in Baile Átha Cliath, the outlying village where Selia and her family lived.

These settled Northmen had been in Dubhlinn for so long that they spoke both languages and had adopted many Irish customs—including for some, Christianity. Many of them had intermarried with the native Irish. They were therefore no longer a threat, or at least not a pressing one. The butcher was one such an example.

The Finngalls—or Vikingers, as they called themselves—were an altogether different story. It was the tales of these men that the maid spun, and it was these tales Selia never tired of hearing.

The word Finngall meant "white foreigner," and Eithne claimed the Finngalls to be indeed as pale and bloodless as the ice from which they emerged. They came from a land of darkness far to the north, a land where the sun remained hidden for most of the year and where no green thing could grow. Even in the summer the sun was too weak to melt the thick layer of ice that covered the land as far as the eye could see.

Food was scarce in this savage land, and the Finngalls hunted all sorts of beasts for their meat—their favorite was that of a white bear that stood so tall, even the giant Finngalls themselves were dwarfed by the creature. In the winter, when the snow was too deep to allow the men to hunt, Eithne claimed the Finngalls killed their Irish slaves and ate them.

The women of this land were as fierce as the men. At birth, each child was carried by its mother into a den of wolves to be laid down for inspection. The wolves would sniff and scrutinize the child, and if it was found lacking in any way they would tear it apart on the spot. An infant who found favor with the beasts would be suckled by a she-wolf, and only then would the human mother put the child to her

own breast and raise it. Therefore every living Finngall had the essence of the wolf flowing through his veins.

Eithne whispered that some of them—perhaps those who were nursed too long by the she-wolves—could actually shape shift into the form of the beasts, and would tear an opponent apart in battle with fang and claw instead of sword and axe.

The Finngalls came several times a year to raid the smaller villages along the coast of Ireland, leaving nothing behind but acrid smoke and the bodies of the dead. They would then spend several days in Dubhlinn to trade their stolen goods and celebrate their victories. The ale houses would do a brisk business, and there would be an increase in the number of murders and rapes. And, typically, every year, a young woman or two would disappear, never to be seen or heard from again.

According to most accounts, these missing girls had been taken as concubines for the Finngall chieftains. But Eithne had heard other, darker stories of human sacrifice. The northern gods demanded blood, and the blood of a beautiful Irish maiden was their preference. Eithne's gaze would always wander over to Selia whenever she recounted this, as though at that moment she had come to the horrible realization Selia would make a lovely sacrifice. Then she would break into laughter, and Selia would laugh too, even as a shiver of fear traveled up her spine. The woman was an excellent storyteller.

Selia loved the stories, and would have the maid tell them again and again. Although Eithne meant the tales to be cautionary, Selia found they had the opposite effect on her, for the thought of the wild Finngalls made her pulse quicken and her breath catch in her throat.

It wasn't proper for a good Irish girl to be so enamored of foreign men who had carved a bloody trail through the coast of Ireland, so for the most part Selia kept silent about it. But her brother knew.

Ainnileas, as he got older, had the opportunity to see Finngalls up close when he was with their father, and even to speak to them on occasion. He had outgrown whatever childish allure he had once felt for the foreigners. Selia knew Ainnileas hadn't gone to the harbor yesterday to satisfy his own curiosity, but instead to do what gave him endless delight—provoke the wrath of his sister.

Selia lowered the hood of her cloak and peered down at the harbor. There was only one ship docked—Ainnileas said he had seen three. Thankfully Eithne's female troubles had come today instead of tomorrow, or Selia might have missed the ships altogether.

The day was warm, and several Finngalls had stripped to their breeches. Sweat glistened on their pale torsos as they worked to transfer cargo from the ship to the docks. They called out to each other, but she wasn't close enough to hear what they were saying. And even if she could, the odds were scarce they were using words she knew.

Two of the men appeared to be arguing. One gestured to an item being loaded onto the ship, as though laying claim to it. Selia giggled as the other man stomped about, yelling to the crew as if trying to sway them to his side. He finally shoved the first man over the side of the ship and into the sea, bringing an immediate round of cheers from the rest of the crew.

The Finngall came up sputtering, shaking his fist, while the second man untied his breeches and aimed a perfect stream of urine down on the man in the water. The bay rang with the laughter of the Finngalls, until an older man pushed the urinator aside. He reached over the rail of the ship to pull the disgraced Finngall back up.

Selia snorted with laughter. This story would be *much* better than Ainnileas' account of being called a skinny dog.

She would make that infuriating boy green with envy before she was finished with him.

There was a deep male chuckle behind her, much too close, and every hair on the nape of her neck stood at sudden, panicked attention. She leapt to her feet and knocked over the basket. The sausage parcel rolled out into the dirt toward the man who was leaning against a tree behind her.

Where had he come from? How long had he been there? She was sure she had been alone when she sat down.

Selia turned to run but hesitated at the thought of the sausage. Would being raped or abducted be worse than going home without food and thus facing the wrath of Eithne? She grabbed the basket, stupidly holding it to her chest like a shield, as she gaped at the man.

The stranger was a Finngall, and bigger than any Selia had ever seen. She had to take another step back and crane her neck to get a clear view of his face. It was startling in its foreignness, with angular bones and bright blue eyes. Eithne had always maintained that Finngalls had the cloudy eyes of a corpse, but this man's eyes were so intense they seemed to glow.

His pale hair was loose around his shoulders, his beard braided into two plaits. The Finngall's clothing was cut in an unfamiliar style, but the red wool was of high quality and trimmed with silk. She saw the hilt of a sword at his hip, peeking out from the edge of his cloak, as well as a dagger hanging from his belt. He was smiling at her, but it was a peculiar smile—not the type that would put anyone at ease.

Don't look at him. Don't smile at him. Her gaze again flickered to the sausage, and she flushed at the absurdity of it all. But if she didn't bring it home, what could she tell Eithne that wouldn't raise her suspicions?

"Go on, get it. I won't hurt you," the Finngall said in Norse.

Selia clutched her basket in a grip so tight she could hear the twigs creaking with her every breath. If she ran, how many strides would it take him to reach her? She was a fast runner but the giant had very long legs. She looked up at him, once, and quickly away. Did all Finngalls have eyes that blue? *Don't look at him.*

"You don't speak Norse?" he asked after her silence. He paused for a moment and then continued in Irish with some difficulty. "Bad . . . no." He pointed to his chest.

Selia wavered. The man stared at her with obvious interest, but not in a leering manner like the butcher had. And he didn't move toward her or make any threatening gestures as she assumed a rapist would. Maybe Eithne's stories about the Finngalls weren't true after all.

She snatched the parcel from the ground, then shoved it back into her basket without brushing the dirt off. The man laughed. She ignored him, and instead turned to run down the hill. When she looked back up he was still watching her. The Finngall put his hand up in a wry wave, and despite herself, Selia smiled. What a story she would have to tell Ainnileas.

The sun was nearly setting when she finally reached home. Eithne's snores could be heard from outside the house, and Selia pushed down a twinge of guilt. The woman must have given up on the promise of willow bark tea and had moved on to the ale, or worse, to the wine—the cask her father saved for special occasions only. What would he do to Eithne if he learned she had allowed Selia to go to the market alone? Though cantankerous, Eithne was the closest thing Selia had to a mother, and she loved her. Usually.

But the encounter with the Finngall had flustered her more than she cared to admit, and at the moment she had no patience for the woman's questioning. She needed time to think about it, to savor it in her mind, before any mundane conversation with Eithne had a chance to dull the memory.

The house consisted of three circular rooms. The main room in the front was where most of the daily living took place, and included the sleeping areas along the walls that could be curtained off for privacy. Through this main room the kitchen could be accessed, as well as a storage room for her father's wares. Following the sound of snoring, she found Eithne leaning against a wall in the kitchen, mouth slack, with a wooden cup of wine next to her on the floor. Selia rinsed out the nearly empty cup and put it back in the cupboard, then stirred the hearth coals for preparing supper.

Her thoughts wandered again to the encounter with the Finngall. How handsome he had been. And his eyes . . . she had never seen eyes quite that color. Did he gaze at everyone so intently or had he also found her pleasing to look at? Maybe not, since he hadn't tried to touch her and Finngalls were well known to be rapists. Maybe they preferred a sturdier sort of woman.

Just because the men of Baile Átha Cliath found her beautiful didn't mean a Finngall would. The shy youths of the village were usually struck dumb in her presence, while the bolder ones would sometimes preen and banter with their friends as though that would impress her. She found this amusing since she and Ainnileas had grown up with these boys, and they had seemed oblivious to her existence until a few years ago.

The men, however, were different. She had first noticed in church, the way one senses another's regard, and had looked up from her clasped hands to find the priest staring at her. After that it seemed the eyes of men were always on her, in the street, in the market, even in her home when her father's colleagues dined with them. Old ones, married ones. At Eithne's instruction, Selia learned to keep her eyes lowered and her face expressionless.

Unfortunately this only served to fuel the fire for many of them, as her demure behavior seemed proof of her piety and virtue. Ainnileas thought this ridiculously funny, and would mime the old men after they left, mocking their moon eyes.

Many of these men, and even a few of the boys, had approached her father with an offer of marriage; some, more than once. Niall had considered each suitor with care but always refused, stating she was too young yet. Maybe in a year or two he would reconsider. But she was by now well past the typical age of betrothal, so this line of reasoning wouldn't work for much longer.

She only learned of the proposals, and of Niall's responses, from Ainnileas. Selia knew she would have little to no input into the final decision. Although her consent to her eventual marriage was necessary, to refuse her father's choice of husband for her would be considered the worst form of disrespect.

Most other girls her age—unless destined for the convent—had been married for several years and had a child or two. So the fact that her father had not accepted an offer by now was suspicious. Ainnileas, of course had his own theory; their father wanted her to marry Buadhach Ó Donnagain, who had been a close friend of their now-deceased grandfather.

Old Buadhach was nearly eighty, with a hump on his back and not a tooth in his head. His hands were as dry as dead leaves and they shook when he clasped Selia's hand. As much as her brother liked to tease her about this possibility, she knew there was a grain of truth to it. The old man had been widowed this past winter, and had spent a good deal of time at their home since then. And there seemed to be more of a spring to his aged step of late.

None of the perspective suitors appeared to mind that Selia was not Niall Ó Murchú's daughter by birth. As a trader of fine fabrics, Niall was in the merchant class, and most of the suitors thus far were also men of comfortable means. But it was no secret that Selia and Ainnileas were not his natural children. There had been whispers early on, rumors they were actually changelings; fairy children. One would think any prospective husband might have some concern over this, but apparently youth and beauty won out over better judgment.

What would it be like to be married to the Finngall? Or not him, specifically, since it was nonsense to consider marrying a foreigner, and a heathen at that. But no, someone *like* him. Tall, handsome, and in the prime of his life, with eyes the color of a cloudless sky.

Someone whose hands didn't shake with palsy when he touched her. Someone her brother couldn't laugh at.

Selia's reverie was interrupted as her brother and father entered, shaking the dust from their cloaks. Ainnileas laughed to see her cooking. He gave the air a cautious sniff as though expecting the worst.

Selia pushed him out of the kitchen before he noticed Eithne asleep on the floor. As the men settled around the table, she brought them mugs of warmed ale and plates of sausages, crusty bread and goat cheese. They both startled as a loud, guttural snore emanated from the kitchen.

Niall raised an eyebrow.

"She's ill," Selia said. She felt a bit responsible for Eithne's present condition, and tried to distract her father with a larger helping of sausage.

Ainnileas took a bite, grimacing as he chewed. "The sausage tastes of dirt."

Selia glared at him. Was he simply mocking her culinary skills or did he really know something about the encounter with the Finngall? His clear gray eyes were all innocence as he smiled at her.

Ainnileas was much too handsome for his own good. His black hair curled around his face in a rather girlish fashion, despite his attempt to keep it secured at the nape of his neck. His eyes—which, when the light caught them appeared to be silver rather than gray—glittered behind their dark frame of lashes. His top lip was slightly fuller than the bottom and his mouth arched up at the corners, which caused him to perpetually look as though he was about to burst out laughing. And he was, usually at Selia's expense.

He and Selia had always been small and fine boned, but she had stopped growing several years ago and he hadn't. Now, for the first time in their lives, Ainnileas was significantly taller than she was. Black hairs sprouted from his chin and upper lip, and his voice would still crack at the most inopportune moments.

These things gave Ainnileas admission into the world of men that Selia would never have. Sometimes she hated him for it.

"Did you enjoy yourself today, working with *Dadai*?" she asked sweetly. As a textile merchant, their father was gone frequently, but when he was home he would occasionally bring Ainnileas along while he transacted business. These occasions were now happening more often and becoming more formalized as he prepared to join Niall in the business. Selia knew her brother found the trade of fine fabrics excruciatingly dull, and she smiled to herself as she poured her father another cup of ale.

"Yes, as a matter of fact I did. We actually had quite an interesting day."

"Did you now?"

Ainnileas gave her a smug look. "Three of the Finngalls approached us looking for silk. We're lucky to have escaped with our lives after Father insulted them."

She nearly splashed the remainder of the ale on the table. "*Dadai*," she asked, "Is this true?"

Niall gave her hand a pat. "Ainnileas is exaggerating as usual, my lass. No blood was spilled."

Ainnileas laughed. "The heathens said they wanted silk

to bring home to their wives, but Father didn't understand the Norse, and thought they said they wanted it for themselves—"

"I understood the Norse well enough. What you don't know, boy, is that the Finngalls are the vainest race of men and would wear silk every day if they could. Their men are even worse than their women. Why, they probably bathe and wash their hair more than our lass here."

Selia raised her eyebrows at him. Eithne had always claimed Finngalls bathed only once a year, in ice water, and never washed their clothes. But the Finngall today had been dressed very agreeably. His hair had looked soft and clean. Selia shot a dark look in the direction of the kitchen. How many more of the maid's tales had been fabricated?

"So, what happened?" she asked.

Her father scowled. "I just told you—did you hear nothing of what I said?"

Selia blushed, shaking her head. As usual, she had missed a chunk of the conversation.

Niall sighed. "Nothing more happened, my girl. They wanted silk, we had none to trade, so they left. Not quite as exciting as Ainnileas would lead you to believe." He belched as he pushed his plate away.

Selia knew full well her father had plenty of silk to trade—there were a dozen or more bolts of it in their storage room. Niall clearly had not wanted to do business with the Finngalls. He didn't like them, and he didn't trust them.

Silly, to imagine men wanting silk for their own clothing, such as the foreign princes their father had once told them about. What would the handsome Finngall on the hill look like dressed head to toe in silk? She bit back a giggle and felt her brother's gaze on her as she cleared the table.

Selia gave him a sly smile, savoring the knowledge that for once her day had been more exciting than his.

Chapter 2

She waited for her brother in the darkness, listening to the slow, regular breathing coming from her father's sleeping bench across the room. Eithne's snores still rattled from the kitchen. Selia had covered her with a blanket but otherwise left her alone. The woman would be sore in the morning, and most likely in a foul mood.

Where was Ainnileas? Surely he hadn't stolen away again to see the fishmonger's daughter. Not when he knew his sister had a secret. Though he would always make her wait when it was *he* who had an interesting tidbit to tell her, away from their father's ears. The boy enjoyed teasing her, drawing out her impatience until she was in tears. Selia smiled a little at the unaccustomed feeling of power she felt as she waited.

A bit later, Selia heard the soft sound of the door closing, followed by Ainnileas' footsteps. He shoved her over as he climbed onto the bench with her. She wrinkled her nose at the smell of him—obviously he had been passing time with the fishmonger's daughter. If he wasn't careful he would end up having to marry the girl. She feigned sleep to punish him for making her wait so long.

"Selia," Ainnileas whispered, shaking her. "I know you're awake."

"Go away."

"Not until you tell me what you've been grinning about all night."

She smiled but didn't answer. Ainnileas pinched her and she squealed.

There was a sound of rustling straw as their father rolled over on his bench. They lay very quietly, waiting until Niall's breathing returned to normal, and then Selia elbowed her brother. "Leave me alone," she hissed. "I'm tired. And you smell like a rotten fish."

"Well, I did have something important to tell you. But since you're being cross . . ."

Selia turned over and gave him a sharp look. Was he telling the truth? One never knew with Ainnileas.

"All right," she said finally. "I'll tell you. But you have to promise not to tell *Dadai*."

In a whisper, Selia told him of her visit to Dubhlinn. She blushed as she spoke of the unexpected encounter with the Finngall on the hill. It was good that Ainnileas couldn't see her face clearly in the darkness. Just the thought of the big foreigner made her heart beat faster and brought a flush to her cheeks, and she had difficulty hiding her excitement from her brother.

But Ainnileas gripped her arm. "Selia," he said in a tight, hard voice, "*never* do that again. Do you understand?"

She tried to shake him off, but he refused to let go. "You're lucky you didn't get killed," he chastised. "Or worse."

She snorted. "Worse than killed?"

"It's nothing to joke about. You know as well as I do what those men are capable of. Promise me you won't go back there."

She glared up at him. "Fine . . . yes, I promise. Now let go, you stupid boy."

He did, and lay on his back, staring at the rafters, uncharacteristically quiet. Selia rubbed her arm and refused to look at him. Who did he think he was, talking to her like that? He was letting the silly wisps of hair above his lip fool him into believing he was already a man.

Finally Ainnileas spoke. "Father met with Old Buadhach today."

His voice was serious—he didn't sound as though he was teasing about Buadhach this time. She sat up. "That doesn't amuse me, Ainnileas."

His eyes looked sad. "Buadhach made a fine offer. Father even told him . . . about you . . . and Buadhach said he wasn't concerned about it."

The bile rose in Selia's throat. Why hadn't her brother stood up for her? How could he let this happen? With the strength of fury, she shoved Ainnileas off the bench. He landed hard on the dirt floor.

"Stay away from me," she managed to choke out. He reached for her in a rare expression of tenderness but she slapped his hand away.

Ainnileas slinked back to his bench, then lay in silence. She didn't attempt to muffle her tears, hoping her brother found satisfaction in being right.

Selia opened her eyes, blinking at the unfamiliar, pale light of morning. On a typical day the family would be up and at their chores before dawn. Why had Eithne allowed her to sleep so late? Unless she was feeling guilty. The woman must be in on her father's plan to marry her off to Buadhach.

Selia's suspicion was confirmed as she rose from her bed and reached for her gown hanging from a hook on the wall. Her old one was missing, and in its place was the new lavender gown Eithne had been sewing for her. The woman was wonderfully skilled at needlework, and had embroidered tiny purple and white flowers on the bodice and sleeves. Selia fingered the delicate embroidery, torn between a desire to wear the beautiful gown as well as shred it to pieces.

The door shut and Selia turned to find Eithne watching her. "You've been crying." The maid tisked at the sight of Selia's puffy eyes.

Eithne looked more contrite than Selia had ever seen her, but she refused to be pacified. Did Eithne actually think a new gown could distract her from knowing her father schemed to marry her off to a feeble old man?

She glared until Eithne dropped her gaze.

"How could you let him do this to me?" Selia's voice sounded raw. She had cried for most of the night and would have thought she had no tears left, but she could feel them building up again, thick in the back of her throat.

Eithne sighed and opened her arms. "Oh, my girl . . ."

Selia's strength of will broke and she ran to the woman, throwing her arms around her ample body. Eithne was nearly as wide as she was tall, and her embrace enveloped Selia. The maid stroked Selia's hair until her sobs turned into hiccups.

"Why, Eithne?" she whimpered. "Why would he marry me to Buadhach? I can't do it. I *won't* do it."

Eithne didn't answer immediately, but instead drew Selia to the table and sat her down. She brought a bowl and a pitcher of water to the table, then soaked a cloth in the cool water, which she used to press against Selia's eyes.

"You know about your father's wife?" Eithne asked quietly.

"Sile? Of course."

"I was there when she died, mind you. It was the most horrible thing I have ever seen, the suffering of that poor woman. Enough to make your blood run cold. Your father loved her very much. As he loves you."

"What does that have to do with—"

"It has everything to do with it," Eithne cut her off. "He's protecting you."

Selia snorted. "Protecting me? Giving me to a disgusting old man is *protecting* me?"

Eithne dropped the cloth and gripped her shoulders. "Selia, you are of an age to be married. The fact that your father hasn't accepted an offer for you yet has begun to raise suspicions. If things weren't as they are, you could enter into a convent. But of course that's not possible. So your father *must* choose a husband for you."

"But why does it have to be Buadhach? I know there have been other offers."

The woman flushed, shifting uncomfortably in her chair. "Old Buadhach is unable to fulfill the obligations of the marriage bed. Do you understand?"

Selia frowned as she considered the question. Of course she knew how babies were conceived—it would be impossible not to know, living in close quarters with animals—yet she didn't quite understand what Eithne was getting at. She shook her head.

Eithne sighed. "Well. Um . . . you've seen the horses, then?"

"Yes."

"The stallions cannot mount the mares unless their members are erect. The same is true for men. Old men sometimes . . . just cannot, I don't know why. Old Buadhach is unable. Your father has made sure of this."

Selia was thoughtful for a moment. She wouldn't be expected to lie with the old man, thankfully. "So . . . I'll never have children?"

"Not as long as you're married to Buadhach."

No children. According to the priest, it was the sacred duty of a wife to bear her husband's children. For Selia's entire life she had expected to become a mother. Now she contemplated the loss of that and nearly choked up again.

"But why would he want to marry me, then?"

Eithne shook her head with a rueful smile. "Well. I suppose even a man of his age can't be blamed for wanting what he can't have, my girl."

Eithne sent Selia out to collect firewood for the day. She headed toward the woods behind their house, taking her time, thinking about this new predicament.

Buadhach. *Marriage* to Buadhach. Even if she didn't have to lie with him, she would still be his wife. She would still be expected to cook his meals—boiled to a pulp and then mashed so he could gum his food down. She would still be expected to converse with him. Buadhach was stone deaf in one ear, so whenever anyone spoke to him they either had to shout or lean in very close to his good ear. And after Ainnileas had pointed out that Buadhach had white hairs sprouting from his ears, Selia had been unable to force herself to get close enough for the old man to hear her. So she shouted.

Niall's reasoning was sound, even if Selia didn't agree with it. Women with her slender build typically did not fare well in childbirth. And Niall had watched the woman he loved die an agonizing death, a death he himself must feel somewhat responsible for. But it was quite a leap to go from understanding Niall's protective fatherly instincts to her acceptance of marriage to a man sixty years her senior.

Entering a convent would be much preferable to marrying Buadhach, and she already knew a good deal of Latin simply from listening in church. She had never learned to read or write, however—in any language—even though Niall had attempted to teach both the children some rudimentary skills. Ainnileas had picked up enough to satisfy their father, but to Selia the markings looked like gibberish.

No amount of practice could make her mind memorize the letters or her hand to make the strokes. And only nuns who could read and write were exempt from the most menial labor in a convent. Selia would end up emptying slop buckets and mucking out the stables.

But this wasn't the reason Niall wouldn't send her to a convent. The real reason was his reluctance for anyone—the church in particular—to discover Selia's shameful secret. Although Niall was not a superstitious man, she knew her problem made him uncomfortable, and he feared for her safety if anyone found out. So a life as a nun was out of the question.

And that left Buadhach. According to Ainnileas, the old man knew her secret and was still willing to marry her. That meant something, at least. And how bad would it be to be married to Buadhach, after all? The old man was affluent. She would live in a large home with numerous servants to help her run the household. When he died, she would be left a wealthy widow with much more freedom and independence than she would ever know as a daughter or a wife. Or a nun. She would finally be able to make her own decisions. She could walk into Dubhlinn without a second thought, her hood down and her head held high.

Selia pushed the uncharitable thought from her mind. What kind of a person looked forward to the day she would be made a widow?

She heard the rustle of footsteps behind her and turned to scowl at Eithne. "I'm going as fast as I can—"

She stopped in mid sentence. It was the Finngall from the hill, not Eithne, coming toward her. The sheer size of the man was startling, and the way the morning sun glinted off his pale hair and the breeze stirred his deep red cloak around his body made him appear not quite human. Almost like one of the heathen gods the Finngalls worshipped. She stared, unable to move or speak. Shallow breaths seemed almost more than she could manage.

The Finngall met her gaze and smiled. He had a beautiful smile—a flash of white teeth and a boyish dimple on his left cheek—but as yesterday, something about it struck her as unusual. What was it?

Then she knew. His smile didn't reach his eyes, and they looked hard.

Selia shook herself back into reality. The Finngall stood between her and the house, so there was no way she could get around him and home quickly enough to bolt the door. And outrunning him was unlikely in any case. She could scream for help to bring Eithne to her aid. But what could their maid do against a man such as this? If the Finngall was bent on violence, she could not bring herself to put Eithne in harm's way.

Making her decision, she dropped the firewood save for one stout stick, which she held at the ready, then glared at the huge man with a fierceness she didn't feel. "What you want?" She demanded in broken Norse.

The Finngall's eyebrows went up in surprise. "So you do speak Norse." He took another step toward her, and she raised the stick threateningly.

He looked amused at this, but remained still, at least. "What's your name, little one?"

How had this stranger found out where she lived? Had he been watching the house so as to approach her when she was alone? And what could he possibly want with her? No man of honorable intentions would approach a woman in this manner. Surely even a Finngall would know that. But if he were bent on rape, would he stand here asking her name?

Frustrated with her own limited grasp of the Norse language, she repeated her original question. "What you want?"

"My ship sails in the morning. I wanted to see you again."

He moved toward her. Selia tried to sidestep to avoid him, but he grabbed her arm. She whacked him hard with the stick. Instead of letting go, he just looked annoyed. He pried the stick from her fingers, then threw it aside.

The man gripped her shoulders and leaned in close. Selia found herself again mesmerized as he locked his gaze with hers. She smelled him, wood smoke and fresh male sweat . . . and something else, like flowers. His hair fell around his face and shoulders, clean and shiny, and a silvery lock of it was inches from her nose. So her father had been right about the Finngalls' peculiar grooming habits, after all. The realization would have been amusing if the situation were different.

"Don't be afraid," he said. "I don't want to hurt you. I want to take you with me."

Selia absorbed the Norse words, translating what she knew and inferring the rest. What kind of a woman did he think she was? Did this Finngall regard himself so highly that he expected her to leave her home and family, and be his whore?

Anger superseded her fear for the moment, and her words spilled out in Irish. "I will be no man's concubine, you Finngall bastard—let go of me!"

He held her as she fought to get away. His eyes narrowed to slits and his fingers dug into her flesh.

"I could take you, little one. As my thrall." He slid one large hand up to grip the base of her skull. His fingers felt like rough wood against her skin as his thumb stroked her cheek. He leaned closer, and she realized he was about to kiss her.

Selia had never been kissed before. In her imagination a kiss from a suitor would be a gentle pressure of lips on hers in a brief moment of tenderness. This kiss was neither gentle nor brief. The Finngall's mouth was hard, bruising. When she felt his tongue she tried to turn her head away, but he held her still.

Her knees began to buckle, and he lifted her to crush her body against his chest. Her feet dangled above the ground. She had the irrational thought that she was being kissed by a barely-restrained animal, as though at any moment he could break his tether and kill her with tooth and claw.

Her senses overwhelmed, everything else seemed to fade away. She was acutely aware of the scent of him, the taste of his mouth, and the hardness of his large body against hers. Her flesh responded to him in a way she had never felt before, with an unfamiliar ache deep in her belly and a sense of urgency that was almost painful.

The Finngall groaned. He pressed Selia against a tree, pinning her between him and the rough bark. He parted her legs with his knee, and when she felt the sudden coolness of the breeze on her bare limbs she realized he was lifting her skirts.

She gave a strangled scream and shoved at his chest, until he finally pulled back. Again, she sensed the beast that raged within him as he lowered her to the ground, his hands clenching convulsively on her arms.

It was several moments before he spoke. "Tell me your name."

She didn't take her eyes from his. "Selia."

"Selia." His Norse accent made her name sound strange, foreign. "My little Selia, will you come with me?"

She was shivering with fear, desire, even some anticipation of the decision she was about to make. Selia wanted this man, this beautiful, glorious, dangerous Finngall. She wanted him more than she had ever wanted anything in her life.

"As wife," she whispered. Buadhach be damned.

He released her so suddenly that she stumbled, and had to brace her hand against the tree to keep from falling.

The Finngall's face hardened. "You do know who I am, then." It was more a statement than a question.

What was he talking about? "No," she said, rubbing her arms to bring the feeling back where he had gripped her so tightly. She was sure she would have bruises.

He crossed his arms and frowned. "Don't trifle with me, child."

She didn't understand the Norse word 'trifle,' but from his tone and facial expression the meaning was clear. He thought she was lying. And he didn't want to marry her—he was only looking for a concubine. Not a wife. Arrogant Finngall bastard.

What had she been thinking? This man only wanted to bed her, and she had been on the brink of giving him exactly what he wanted. After just a few minutes with him she had nearly been willing to shame herself as well as bring embarrassment to her entire family.

"Stay away from me," Selia spat at him in Irish. She turned and ran.

He didn't follow her.

She arrived home out of breath and bolted the door behind her. She brushed the tears from her face, pushing past Eithne as the woman emerged from the kitchen. Selia dove onto her bench and pulled the covers over her head.

"Where is the firewood?" Eithne asked.

Selia's face crumpled and she burst into fresh tears.

Eithne most likely assumed she was still upset about Old Buadhach. The woman sat on the edge of the bench to pull Selia close, comforting her again as she sobbed. Selia couldn't bring herself to tell her about the encounter with the Finngall.

What would Eithne think of her? Just speaking to a Finngall would be considered disgraceful enough. It was common knowledge no honest woman was safe around a Finngall man. To admit she had been alone with him— *twice*—was tantamount to announcing he had spoiled her maidenhood. She would bring disgrace to her family. No decent Irish man would want her, not even Old Buadhach.

Selia drew in a shaky breath. No, she couldn't admit what happened. And after Ainnileas' reaction last night, she obviously couldn't trust him anymore. She was on her own.

What had come over her, to so boldly suggest the Finngall make her his wife? As if her father would ever agree. Did she even want such a thing herself? Now, away from the man and his curious effect on her, the idea of leaving her family to live in a strange land with a foreign husband, speaking a foreign tongue, was madness.

But the memory of him, of his big rough hands and piercing eyes, shook her to the very core. Even after he had humiliated her, she couldn't deny she desired him still.

What is wrong with me?

The rest of the day dragged on, with Selia agitated and out of sorts. Eithne seemed constantly vexed with her. Every sound, no matter how mundane, made Selia jump as if it were a thunderclap. And she ruined everything she touched; the bread wouldn't rise, the stew scorched, and she snapped the thread during her mending. The maid attempted to harness her restless energy by setting her to sweep out the house, for which she was promptly thanked with a broken broom.

"For the love of Mary, child, whatever is the matter with you?" Eithne huffed. She placed the water pitcher in Selia's hand and steered her toward the door. "Go. And don't come back empty handed this time!"

Eithne shut the door and Selia heard the bolt fall into the latch. She was actually locked out of her own house. Selia glared at the door, muttering a curse under her breath. Hateful woman.

She scanned the woods, searching for a flash of red cape. She saw nothing. Honestly, did she think the Finngall had nothing better to do than to lurk outside her house, waiting for her to emerge? He had probably grabbed another pretty Irish girl and gone home.

Feeling rather silly, she picked her way toward the stream. She headed to a small pool where the water was still, then knelt down with caution. Like most women, she couldn't swim, but she had to be even more careful around water than the average woman.

She caught the blurry reflection of herself in the water, and as usual thought of Ainnileas. But while his face was taking on a more masculine form, hers still retained the gentle contours of their childhood. Niall joked that when he had found them, he had made Eithne sew their clothing in different colors because he couldn't tell the twins apart otherwise. No longer was this the case.

Her brother was growing away from her. Whether Selia married Old Buadhach, a Finngall, or no one at all, the fact remained that she and Ainnileas would eventually lose their closeness. If last night were any indication, it was already happening.

Tears stung at her swollen eyes. She blinked them back— she would not cry yet again today. Tears were for children.

She took a deep breath. If only she had someone to talk to, someone to confide in. But there was no one. All of the girls she had grown up with were already married, and were mothers themselves now. Selia often spied self-satisfied pity in their eyes whenever they spoke to her. *Poor, unbetrothed Selia. She doesn't even have a mother to talk to about important matters such as this.*

Her gaze wandered to the other side of the stream. Her mother's grave was there, just past the gnarled oak tree. Her own mother, lying forgotten in the ground. Selia had no memories of the woman, which only served to make her feel worse about the situation. A mother *should* be mourned by her children, regardless.

She was a neglectful daughter. Selia added that to the growing list of everything else wrong with her, before crossing herself and saying a prayer for the soul of the stranger who had given birth to her.

Chapter 3

Selia's stomach was in knots as dusk came and went. Her father and Ainnileas would be home soon, and she fully expected Niall to announce her betrothal to Old Buadhach tonight. Combined with the memory of her disgraceful behavior with the Finngall this morning, it was enough to make her want to crawl back to her bench and feign illness.

She hadn't eaten all day but had no appetite as she stirred the stew. Eithne had scraped out the burned bits as best she could, but the scorched smell was still thick in the air. Selia grimaced at the teasing she would surely have to endure from her brother tonight. One of the greatest enjoyments of his life was poking fun at her culinary skills.

She heard the faint sound of hooves in the distance and she took in a shaking breath to brace herself. But the sound grew louder—much louder than usual. There was more than just the wagon coming this way. Surely her father hadn't brought Old Buadhach home with him?

She opened the door, and clapped a hand over her mouth to keep from screaming. Her father and Ainnileas were indeed approaching in the wagon but were surrounded by a group of Finngalls, one of whom was leading the wagon's horses by the reins. The big Finngall rode in front and was followed by another man who resembled him in size and appearance. The remaining three Finngalls had a roughness about them, an edge of sorts. Two of them seemed familiar. Were they the men she had seen arguing on the dragonship?

Her breath caught in her throat to see Ainnileas' and her father's hands tied in front of them. Eithne came up behind her and screamed. The big Finngall turned his head in their direction, catching Selia's gaze with his own. He smiled then, a smile of such cold calculation that the blood chilled in her veins.

Eithne grabbed her wrist, pulled her to the storage room, and shoved her inside. Then slammed the door. "*Bolt it,*" she ordered. Selia, moving as if in a dream, slid the bolt into the latch.

The room was in shadows. Selia stumbled over wooden crates of cloth as she pushed her way to the back. She sat against the wall, clasping her trembling hands around her knees. Was the Finngall here to take her for his concubine? Or had she angered him to the point where he no longer wanted to bed her, but intended to cut her heart out and offer it up to his gods as a bloody sacrifice?

She heard the sound of wood splintering, then the clamor of the men as they entered the house with their loud voices and thumping boots. Shouting in both Norse and Irish, and sounds of things being overturned and broken, were interspersed by Eithne's shrieks. Selia covered her ears but she couldn't block it out.

A dreamlike quality enveloped her, a profound sense that this had all happened before. She, huddled in a corner, making herself as small and quiet as possible to hide from foreign invaders with bloodlust in their eyes. She began to sniffle, and a voice in her head told her to shush, but the name it called her wasn't Selia . . .

The door rattled. "Selia," the deep Finngall voice called to her. "Open the door."

"No!" her father yelled. Selia cringed as she heard the smacking sound of fist on flesh and Niall's heavy grunt.

"*Dadai!*" Selia threw the door open. Her eyes quickly scanned the room and locked on her father, his hands still tied as he crouched on his knees. Blood streamed from his nose. There was a laughing, red-faced Finngall standing over him. The man did not seem to be much older than Selia, and though shorter than the others, had a thick, muscular torso and fists as large as hams.

Niall was a gentle man, never one to resort to violence. To see him on the floor, helpless and bleeding, was too much for Selia to bear. Her eyes narrowed in fury.

The big Finngall reached for her. She ducked under his arm, then launched herself at the one who had hurt her father. Taken by surprise, the man stumbled and fell backward with Selia on top of him. She struck him and scratched at his face, intent on ripping his eyes from his skull.

The man bellowed like a wounded bull and threw Selia off. The back of her head struck the stout wooden table leg, and the room went dark for a moment.

"Irish bitch," the wounded Finngall snarled, glaring murderously at Selia as she blinked at him. There were deep, angry scratches running from his eyebrow to his cheek. But a shadow of fear crossed his face as he shifted his gaze to the larger Finngall. The wounded man mumbled a quick apology.

The big one scooped Selia to her feet, holding her close. He turned to Niall, then motioned for one of the Finngalls to help him rise.

"Niall Ó Murchú," he said in a formal voice, bowing slightly. "I am Alrik Ragnarson, and I am here to ask for your daughter's hand in marriage."

Selia's jaw dropped as she looked up at the Finngall. Did he actually think her father would agree to such a thing after they had brutalized him?

Niall's face flashed with anger. He opened his mouth to speak, but Alrik held up his hand. "Think carefully before you answer. I will take Selia either way, as my wife or my thrall. It makes no difference to me. You, however, may care a bit more about the honor of your daughter than I do. You choose."

Niall's face went purple. He sputtered in incoherent rage as he lunged toward Alrik, but was jerked back by the

Finngall behind him. Eithne burst into fresh sobs. Ainnileas stood still and pale, his eyes riveted on Selia.

Niall's body sagged in defeat. He was quiet for a moment. "My Selia, daughter of my heart," he finally whispered in Irish. "I'm sorry." Then he looked up at the Finngall and spoke in Norse. "Take her as a wife."

Selia uttered a faltering gasp as she dropped her gaze from her father's. She had never seen that look on his face before, a look of utter heartbreak. Did he know she had set this entire nightmare in motion by sneaking off to Dubhlinn? Had Ainnileas told him?

Alrik pulled a small sack from his belt, spilling its contents onto the table. Silver, more than Selia had ever seen in her life. "The bride price," he said.

"Tainted with the blood of Irish souls," Niall retorted in Irish.

Alrik turned to one of the Finngalls—the oldest of the three, who by appearance might be the father of the two younger ones—and whispered to him. Then he inclined his head toward Niall.

"I thank you, Father-in-law," he said. Niall spat on the ground in response, and Alrik's lips turned up in a cynical smile. He grasped Selia's arm and headed for the door.

Eithne's screams escalated as Selia was pulled from the house. She looked over her shoulder for one last glimpse of her family, and caught Ainnileas' gaze. Time stood still for a moment as she despaired of ever seeing him again.

He murmured her name, then spoke in the language that was theirs alone. "Selia . . . *I will find you.*"

Alrik hoisted her in front of him on horseback. Selia shook so hard her teeth chattered, and he removed his cloak to wrap around her. Were the three other Finngalls still in the house with her family?

She turned to Alrik in a panic, forcing her mind to form the Norse words. "They not . . . hurt?"

"No." His arm tightened around her as they rode off into the night.

The moon, round and bright, gave the objects they rode past a surreal quality. Selia had a good view of the other Finngall as they rode. The man looked very much like Alrik. Were they brothers?

They traveled in silence. Where were they going? They weren't headed toward Dubhlinn, where the ship was docked. In fact, they were going in the opposite direction, toward Baile Átha Cliath.

They reined the horses to a stop in front of a small, unassuming house. She recognized Father Coinneach's cottage.

The other Finngall looked over at Alrik. "You're sure this is the house?"

Alrik nodded, motioning for him to take her while he dismounted.

The Finngall's gaze met Selia's as he helped her down. "This is madness, Alrik."

Alrik regarded him coldly as he reached for Selia. "Then go," he said over his shoulder as he pulled her toward the door. The other man shook his head, but followed behind them.

Alrik gave the door a sharp rap. There was no response from inside. He pounded harder, and after what seemed an eternity Father Coinneach answered the door.

The young priest blinked as he recognized Selia. He looked up at the two giant Finngalls, then back to her.

"Selia." His voice cracked over the word. "What is the meaning of this?"

Alrik pushed past the priest with Selia in tow. The other Finngall followed, shutting the door behind them. "You are a priest of the White Christ?" Alrik asked in Norse. Father Coinneach looked confused. The other man stepped forward, translating in Irish. Obviously the Finngall wasn't a native speaker, but his Irish was much better than Selia's Norse.

Father Coinneach finally replied, "Yes."

The Finngall continued in his careful, somewhat stilted Irish. "I am Ulfrik Ragnarson and this man is my brother, Alrik Ragnarson. He wishes to marry this woman. A priest of the White Christ must watch."

The priest turned to Selia, eyes wide. "Your father has consented to this?"

She nodded, feeling sick.

Ulfrik spoke again. "He has given consent, and accepted the . . . silver," he shook his head as though unsure of the correct word.

"Bride price," Selia said quietly.

Father Coinneach stepped back, his prominent Adam's apple bobbing as he swallowed. "Your brother is not a Christian. If he desires a marriage, my observation isn't necessary."

Ulfrik motioned toward Selia. "This woman is a Christian. Alrik wishes for her to be pleased."

"But he isn't baptized. I can't observe a marriage between a Christian and a heathen. I'm sorry."

Ulfrik looked at the man for a long moment before translating for his brother. Alrik's face hardened, his eyes narrowing to flinty slits. Selia cringed. He would not be happy that the priest refused to marry them. Would he take her as a thrall instead?

Father Coinneach appeared visibly shaken as he looked up at Alrik. He reached for Selia as though to protect her from the big Finngall.

There was a sudden blur of motion as Alrik sprang toward the priest. He grabbed the smaller man and spun him around, drawing his dagger across his throat.

Selia screamed.

For long seconds nothing happened, and she felt faint with relief. Maybe Alrik was only attempting to scare the man. Then a dark red line appeared on the priest's throat as Alrik dropped him to the ground with a snarl. Father Coinneach held his throat; blood bubbled over his fingers and onto the floor.

He was dying. Father Coinneach was dying, bleeding to death at her feet. His eyes rolled up to Selia's and he stretched out trembling fingers as if to implore her to help him.

There was a terrible noise in her head, an overpowering rushing sound, which made her screams seem quiet in comparison.

Run! Selia turned but Alrik caught her wrist. She pulled and twisted, frantic to get free. His hand, slippery with blood, lost its grip on her and she wriggled away, running toward the door with Alrik shouting to his brother to stop her.

Ulfrik grabbed her and they fell to the floor together. Selia fought him with every ounce of strength she had. She landed a solid punch to his jaw that sent shock waves of pain up her own arm, but he didn't so much as flinch.

Selia pleaded with him in Irish. "Let me go . . . He's a monster! Let me go . . ."

He shook his head. "I'm sorry."

Alrik shoved his brother aside, then dragged Selia to her feet. She struggled wildly but he carried her to where the priest lay on the floor. The Father's breath came in a slow, gurgling rattle. Selia sobbed. She had known Father Coinneach for as long as she could remember. He was dying because of her.

Alrik's hands gripped her shoulders. His eyes were so fierce and murderous she couldn't bring herself to meet his gaze for longer than a second. "I, Alrik Ragnarson, take you, Selia Niallsdottir, as my wife."

Selia stared down at the fading priest. Alrik shook her. "*Say it*. Say it before he dies."

She pushed the halting vow past her lips.

The priest took one last, ragged breath, his eyes fixed on her in accusation.

Chapter 4

Alrik's laugh was triumphant. Selia tore her gaze from the body of the priest to gape up at him. His eyes blazed even in the dim light, making him look like the devil himself. He turned to Ulfrik and motioned to the door.

"Get out, brother."

Ulfrik didn't move. "What? Here?"

The edges of Selia's vision went dark as she realized what was about to happen. Her marriage would be consummated with the eyes of a dead priest staring at her. She couldn't breathe, couldn't focus on anything but the body of Father Coinneach. She looked around, panicking, and caught the gaze of Ulfrik.

He took his cloak off and shook it out over the body of the priest. Alrik smirked at him. "You're soft, Ulfrik. You always have been. Like a woman."

"Look at her. Look at your wife. She's terrified."

Alrik shrugged. "She got what she wanted." He pushed Ulfrik through the door, then turned to Selia. His smile looked feral.

"Come here, my little wife."

She hesitated, still staring at the body of Father Coinneach, now covered by Ulfrik's blue cloak. Selia had an irrational thought of Ulfrik sitting outside without it, cold and shivering in the night air. She felt her lip tremble.

Selia knew full well what was about to happen. She had wanted Alrik, indeed had been so carried away with desire for him that she had nearly given him her maidenhead this morning in the woods. She had brought this nightmare upon herself.

This man's rage, what happened when the animal inside him was unleashed . . . she had no wish to experience it again. But she couldn't bear thought of his murderous hands on her. What to do? Fight, or allow the marriage to be consummated? Fighting might make him angry enough to hurt her. Perhaps kill her. And his brother was most likely just outside the door, to catch her if she ran. She was trapped.

Selia blew out a breath, steadying herself. If he wanted to kill her he would have done it already. He was calmer now, but the rage had come upon him so quickly. To refuse him now would only anger him further. She approached her husband, keeping her gaze to the floor.

Shaking, she pointed to the kitchen area in the back of the house. "There," she said. Selia could not commit the sacrilege of allowing her marriage to be consummated in the same room with the body of her priest. Would Alrik understand that? Or even care?

He studied her for a moment. Then he smiled the same hard smile he had given her in the woods, and led her through the doorway into the kitchen. Selia nearly sobbed with relief. He had a trace of compassion, after all.

Alrik took her to a nearby table, then lifted her at the waist and sat her upon it. He hooked a finger under her chin to tilt her face, and brought his mouth down upon hers in a deep, rough kiss.

He kept one hand on the small of her back while his other wandered down her body. Pulling her gown up with an impatient grunt, he ran his hand over her bare leg, nudging her knees farther apart with his own.

Selia jumped when she felt his hand on her thigh. He wound his other hand in her hair to force her head back as his lips moved down her neck. She shivered to feel his breath against her flesh.

"I have no wish to hurt you, little one," he whispered.

The words might have been kind coming from someone else. But the man she had found so handsome now seemed like nothing more than a terrifying stranger—hard, angry, and devoid of compassion. She had married a Finngall, a wicked heathen. His hands could snap her neck so quickly she would be dead before she even realized it. Like Father Coinneach.

Selia didn't struggle as he leaned her back against the table. She took a deep breath, gripped the edge of the table with both hands, and braced herself. She prayed it would be over quickly.

Although she sensed gentleness did not come easily to this Finngall, he had been truthful, at least, in his desire not to hurt her. His body was large and heavy, and Selia closed her eyes so she wouldn't have to look at him as he entered her. There was a moment of pain but she refused to cry out. She bit her lip hard and tasted blood, willing her mind to drift.

Just when she thought she could take no more, Alrik groaned, then finally collapsed on top of her in a heap of muscle and sweat. It was over.

Selia opened her eyes. Pinned to the table, she couldn't move under his suffocating weight. She felt numb from the waist down. Was it supposed to feel like this? Maybe she would bleed to death on the table.

He shifted to look down at her, his silky hair falling around them like a curtain. "Next time won't be so bad." He gave her a sly smile. "You might even come to enjoy it."

He obviously meant to do this to her often. She sniffled and wiped her eyes. Alrik pulled away from her to refasten his breeches, looking very pleased with himself. At least his mood had lightened.

Selia brought her legs together. Her hips felt odd, loose and disjointed. She tried to get down from the table and instead fell to the floor.

He laughed as he pulled her to her feet. "Can you walk? Or do you need me to carry you?"

She flushed. "I walk."

They had to step over the priest's body once again to get outside. Alrik did it without pause, as if he maneuvered over a rain puddle. Selia crossed herself when Alrik's back was turned.

Holding in a sob, she stepped around the body of the man whose death she was responsible for.

They rode for what seemed like hours, every jolt of the horse a fresh assault to Selia's aching body. She smelled the sea and heard the sound of water in the distance, so it seemed they were following the coastline. But she couldn't see anything past Alrik's arm when she tried to look.

Finally, the men turned the horses toward the sound of the sea. A group of about two dozen Finngalls sat around a blazing campfire in a small cove, with the dragonship beached behind them. Alrik called out as they approached. A few men began to cheer, then the others joined in. The cove rang with their harsh Norse voices.

Alrik dismounted, tall and proud, and lifted Selia from the horse. She was suddenly surrounded by large, loud men, peering down at her in blatant curiosity. Although she didn't understand all of their words, by tone and body language she deduced that her husband was the leader of this rough group of men.

The musky male scent of the Finngalls was sharp in the air. They all seemed to be speaking at once in their guttural language, which, if she closed her eyes, sounded almost like dogs barking. Or wolves. She remembered Eithne's story and shivered.

Selia took a few steps backward and tripped on someone's foot. Ulfrik. He patted her on the shoulder, just once, then dropped his hand back to his side.

A bald, ruddy-faced man with a blond moustache introduced himself as Olaf Egilson. He pressed a cup of something into Selia's hands which she accepted with gratitude, and gulped. Unfortunately it wasn't water, but very strong ale. She coughed and sputtered, bringing a round of laughter from the men.

The Finngalls continued to congratulate Alrik, commenting on Selia's beauty as well as her diminutive size.

"Is she even as old as Ingrid?" someone called out with a laugh.

Alrik frowned at Selia. "How old are you?"

She hesitated, not knowing the Norse counting words. She turned to his brother. "I'm eighteen," she said in Irish. Ulfrik looked at her for a long moment before translating.

The men laughed about this, and she heard the name 'Ingrid' mentioned again. Who was this Ingrid? A girl at home Alrik was already betrothed to? Selia swallowed the rest of her ale and didn't resist when the bald man refilled it.

The group moved back to the fire as another man asked Alrik to tell the story of what had happened after leaving Niall's house. Selia recognized him as the eldest of the three Finngalls who had been with Alrik and Ulfrik when they had taken her. Those three were the last to see her family.

She turned to Ulfrik and studied him for a moment until he looked down at her. He seemed kind enough, knocking her to the ground notwithstanding. And he spoke Irish.

"I'm sorry I hit you," she said.

He rubbed his jaw with a wry smile. "So am I."

She smiled back at him. "Will you ask that man if my family is all right?"

Ulfrik motioned her to a spot away from the group of men. Selia sat with Alrik's cloak wrapped around her against the night air while she waited for his brother to return. The ale was making a warm spot in her belly and she began to feel drowsy.

Ulfrik returned and sat down next to her with his own cup of ale. He took a long drink before speaking to her. "They are unharmed."

Selia sighed in relief. "Thank you."

Ulfrik nodded and they both watched Alrik regale the men with the tale of Selia's capture and the visit to the priest. She looked away as he described Father Coinneach's ghastly death throes. Shouting and cheers erupted from the men, and Selia shuddered.

"He'll be congratulating himself all night," Ulfrik muttered under his breath.

Selia didn't understand the Norse word 'congratulating.' "What do you mean?"

By his reaction it was clear he hadn't meant for Selia to hear him. After a brief hesitation he replied, "I don't know the Irish word." Ulfrik glanced over at the group of men to be sure he wasn't being observed, then mimicked Alrik, puffing his chest out and patting himself on the back.

Selia giggled as she watched him. She suddenly missed Ainnileas very much. It was something he would do, and Ulfrik's playacting was a harsh reminder that she would never see her brother again. Her laugh turned into a stifled sob and Ulfrik stopped.

"What is it?" he asked in Irish.

"I miss my brother. You . . . you are like him, a bit."

"You are twins, are you not?"

Selia nodded as she drained her cup. She hadn't eaten all day and the strong ale was going to her head.

Ulfrik paused again. He seemed to be the sort of person who thought things through very carefully before speaking. "What did your father mean when he called you the 'daughter of his heart?'"

"He's not my real father," Selia explained. Her own heart contracted at the thought of the man she called '*Dadai*.' She would never see him again. "My brother and I were orphaned when we were very young. Niall found us wandering in the woods, and he took us in."

Ulfrik's face remained expressionless. "How old were you when Niall found you?"

Selia shook her head. "About two years old, he believed."

The firelight flickered in Ulfrik's eyes. Selia hesitated when she saw the muscle in his jaw tighten.

Why had she told him so much? Tipsy or not, she had to be more careful. This man—no matter how kind he seemed—was Alrik's brother. His loyalties would lie with him. Alrik had paid an absurdly large bride price for her, with the expectation of obtaining the daughter of a merchant, not of an Irish peasant.

"Will Alrik be angry that Niall is not my real father?"

Ulfrik's face was unreadable. "You might not want to tell him."

Selia swallowed. Yet another secret to keep from her new husband. She and Ulfrik sat in silence for a moment, watching the drama unfold across the fire.

She turned back to him. "Who is Ingrid?"

"Ingrid is Alrik's daughter," he replied, draining the remains of his ale.

Chapter 5

Selia woke just before dawn. Unaccustomed to sleeping outside on the cold ground, her night had been restless. She had been acutely aware of Alrik's large body pressed next to hers. He slept on his side with one arm pillowed under his head and the other thrown across Selia's body, the red cloak covering them both. She peeked at him to make sure he was still asleep.

Relaxed in slumber, there was a peace about him. Her gaze wandered over him in curiosity, taking in the pleasing outline of cheekbone and jaw, the full mouth, and the thick sweep of his brows. He was an undeniably handsome man.

His eyelashes were darker than his hair, golden blond, the same shade as his beard. Unlike most Irishmen, Alrik's cheeks were as smooth and hairless as that of a boy. His braided beard began only at the edges of his moustache. How old was he? Ulfrik had informed her that Ingrid was fifteen years old, so Alrik must be older than he looked.

Her first impression of his size had been correct, for he was by far the largest of the Finngalls in this group. Last night she had noticed he stood half a head taller than his brother Ulfrik and nearly a full head taller than any of the rest. And he wasn't gangly in the way of some tall men—Alrik was thickly muscled, lean and hard, with a latent power that was evident even as he slept.

One of his enormous hands was thrown possessively over her belly. His hands were weathered to a darker color, with rough, calloused skin and short nails. The little finger on his right hand was crooked, as though it had been broken and not set correctly. There was a scar on his hand which began at the base of the broken finger, snaking through the golden hairs up to his wrist. How many more scars were on his body, covered by his clothing? Violence begat violence, and Alrik was the most volatile person she had ever met.

This was her husband. No matter what misgivings she had about their marriage, she was bound to him for life. Why, *why* had she gone to Dubhlinn alone? It had only been two days since she had made that fateful decision, but it felt like a lifetime ago.

Alrik mumbled in his sleep. His hand shifted, landing heavily on her bladder. Selia gasped and decided she couldn't wait any longer. She lifted the hand to slip out.

He rolled over onto his back but didn't awaken. All of the men had been drinking heavily last night, and all were still asleep. Selia headed toward the forest for privacy.

There was an uncomfortable sensation on the skin of her thighs as she walked, and as she finally squatted down to relieve herself she found she was covered in dried blood. She unsuccessfully attempted to scrub the blood off with a handful of dew-covered leaves. She needed water.

She headed toward the sea and within a few minutes of walking found a small, shallow inlet, partially secluded by rocks. As private a space for bathing as any she was likely to find. The water was icy, and Selia drew in her breath as she tested it with her hand.

Suppressing her natural fear of the water, she undressed and left her clothes on a massive chunk of driftwood, then wound her hair in a knot atop her head. Selia waded into the frigid water, waist deep, and scrubbed herself clean with wet sand. She splashed her face and rinsed her mouth, and then, gasping, crouched down in the water to rinse the sand off.

"Are you trying to drown yourself so soon?" Alrik's voice came from behind her.

She jumped, surprised how quietly he moved for such a large man. How long had he been watching her bathe?

He sat down on the log next to her clothes and held out the red cloak. "Come out before you freeze to death."

Selia *was* shivering, so hard her teeth chattered, but she balked at the thought of walking out to him completely naked. She met his gaze. His smile was thin and hard, and she sensed anger behind it. At all costs, his anger must be avoided.

She lowered her gaze and walked to him, acutely aware of his eyes on her. Selia heard the sharp intake of Alrik's breath.

Selia did not consider herself shapely. Her breasts and hips were small, with a slender waist and limbs. There was a fragile quality to her body which she knew not all men appreciated. Alrik appeared to be one who did.

He wrapped the cloak around her to pull her to him. With him sitting and her standing, they were face to face, which seemed strangely intimate. His bright eyes burned into hers as she shivered.

"Your lips are blue," he murmured, rubbing his thumb across them. "What were you thinking?"

"Blood," Selia said through her chattering teeth. She looked down in the direction of the area in question, and felt herself flush even deeper.

"Yes, I imagine there was." He didn't sound the least bit remorseful. In fact, if the way he was looking at her was any indication, he wanted to repeat the act that had caused the blood in the first place. She blinked away the tears that welled up in her eyes.

Alrik put a hand on the small of her back to pull her closer. He let her hair loose, then slid his other hand up to cup her breast. His fingers dug in a bit too hard, and she cried out. He smiled his angry smile.

"Selia. Under no circumstances are you to wander away without me. Ever." His eyes narrowed darkly. "Do you understand what I'm saying?"

She looked at him with uncertainty, interpreting that he was angry at her but not comprehending all the words. It was of the utmost importance to know what she had done wrong so she could avoid doing it again.

Alrik gripped her shoulders. "You stay with me. *You stay with me,*" he said, shaking her slightly with each word for emphasis.

Selia nodded.

Relaxing his hold on her shoulders, he slid both hands under her buttocks and pulled her into his lap. Her legs dangled as she straddled him. She squirmed at the position, but he kept her still as he brought his mouth upon hers in a kiss, hard and possessive.

Selia sensed the animal within him coming to life. The heat rising from Alrik's skin warmed her cold body where he touched her. His hand was on her breast again, each tweak of his fingers causing an unexpected jolt of pleasure to course through her veins. Then he broke the kiss to lift her, bringing her breast up to his mouth, and suckled roughly.

The sensation was overwhelming. Despite her fear, there was an ache deep in her belly, a heaviness that called for release. How could her body desire him, how could *she* desire him, knowing what he had done last night?

Yet she gripped his shoulders, feeling the ripple of his muscles as he held her. His hair glittered like spun silk in the sun. She had a sudden urge to touch the silvery strands, to feel its texture. She did, cautiously at first, then with a moan twined her fingers into it and pressed his head to her breast.

Alrik looked up at her. She shivered at the beauty of his face, the beauty that masked the shadow inside him. But Selia's fear was gone for the moment, and she gave him a hesitant smile. Maybe he had been right last night . . . maybe she could grow to enjoy this after all.

He shifted her body and pushed his breeches down over his hips. She felt the hard, naked length of him as he pulled her back into his lap. She took in a shaky breath. His eyes were so blue, so mesmerizing. She tried to look away, but he held her chin so she couldn't.

He filled her completely in one long, slow movement, then remained still for a moment as he watched her. She gasped, flushing. She had to close her eyes to steady herself.

Alrik brought his mouth to hers. The kiss deepened as he began to move inside her. His large hands tightened around her hips, digging into her flesh, and Selia held on as his thrusts intensified. He seemed to be everywhere at once, taking her, claiming her, overpowering her.

The sensation was extraordinary. Her fear and desire forged into a powerful, molten need that was unlike anything she had felt before. A current of pleasure rippled through her body with every thrust, and she bit her lip to keep from crying out. He moved faster. She gripped his arms, digging in with her fingernails. There was a buildup of tension in her belly, a feeling both terrifying and exhilarating, then a sudden release that shook her to the very core. With a sob, she pressed her face into his shoulder.

Alrik groaned. He crushed her against him as he thrust a last time. She melted into him, confused and exhausted. She could feel his heartbeat hammering in his chest.

He finally grasped her shoulders so she was forced to look at him. He was achingly beautiful, face and lips flushed, eyes slightly hooded. She lowered her gaze. Looking at Alrik was like looking into the sun.

"I told you next time would be better," he said.

Chapter 6

Selia had never been on a moving ship before. Being a non-swimmer, she had a natural aversion to the open sea, and she gripped the side of the dragonship with both hands as the prow cut through the water with surprising speed. The wind whipped her hair around her face and she longed to braid it, but couldn't bring herself to let go of the side long enough to do so.

Alrik had the men erect a small tent for Selia for her to be able to relieve herself in privacy, as they wouldn't stop until nightfall. She could climb in there now, to rest and try to get the knots out of her hair, but Ulfrik had warned her that since she wasn't accustomed to being on a ship she might sicken if she stayed in the tent too long. So she kept her eyes fixed on the horizon as he had suggested.

The vessel contained no hull for transporting goods as her father's ship had. Instead, each man possessed a large sea chest which served both as a seat for rowing as well as a place to store his weapons and personal cache of treasures. Before they left, Alrik had rummaged through his own chest and pulled out a cloak for Selia. It was made of felted wool in a beautiful deep blue, lined with white fox fur and trimmed with bands of silk brocade. He fastened it around her shoulders and seemed pleased with how it looked on her. Selia had pushed down another flash of jealousy as she thanked him. Who had the cloak been meant for? Some other woman he was courting at home, or his daughter?

Alrik gave her firm instructions to stay as far away from the men as possible. Selia wasn't sure if he simply wanted her out from under their feet, or sought to guard her from them. If it was the latter, he needn't bother; the men seemed in awe of her and looked away quickly if she met their gaze. Not one of them spoke to Alrik about his new wife. Odd, after the good-natured ribbing of the night before.

He stood at the helm of the dragonship, arms crossed, deep in conversation with Ulfrik and the bald man, Olaf. Selia studied the brothers as the wind blew their hair back. Ulfrik's beard was short, cropped close to his face, and his jaw was slightly wider than Alrik's. She had noticed a small scar through one of Ulfrik's eyebrows, cutting it in two. His nose was narrower, his frame a bit leaner than his brother's. Other than that they looked remarkably alike.

The difference was in their presentation. Alrik stood with bold self-assurance, his size intensifying his immense physical presence rather than causing it. He walked with a swagger and spoke with the conviction of one who expected to be obeyed. And the ship of Finngalls deferred to him without question.

Even Ulfrik, his brother and equal, seemed not to dare defy him. He had obviously been against Alrik's marriage, had recognized Selia's fear and unwillingness, but in the end had not tried to prevent it. Indeed, he had restrained her from running and had all but handed her over to his brother despite his own misgivings. And then Selia, only a few hours later, had blithely confided a secret to the man that could have dangerous consequences.

She should have known better than to drink strong ale on an empty stomach. With her eyes on her new husband, she pulled the cloak tighter around her shoulders. Alrik was either a very important man or simply *thought* he was, but regardless might not be pleased to learn he had married a peasant. He was so volatile, so unpredictable. Keeping him happy would be wise.

But she needed to be able to converse with him. Whenever he spoke to her, she took in the words she knew, placed them in context with his tone and facial expression, then made a guess as to his meaning. But what if she guessed incorrectly? She didn't want to do anything to bring his wrath upon her. And even more frustrating than not understanding much of what he said, was not having the words to explain herself to him.

Above the wind, she heard the Finngalls calling out to each other and she understood one word out of every three or four. She had to learn the language as quickly as possible. To do that she would need Ulfrik's help. Although a few of the other men also spoke Irish, he seemed to be the most fluent. He had already shown her a bit of kindness, and he didn't stare at her the way other men did.

Surely he would be willing to teach her. Whether or not her husband would allow it was the more important question. She would have to tread very carefully to ensure Alrik wouldn't think she had an ulterior interest in his brother.

Selia made her way toward them. She squeezed past the two horses that pawed at the deck with nervous hooves, keeping her gaze lowered as she passed the men. Ulfrik saw her first and motioned to Alrik, who turned as she approached.

His scowl looked like a thundercloud. "Didn't I tell you to stay out of the way?"

Selia ignored her impulse to run back to her tent. Instead she looked Alrik directly in the eye and forced herself to smile. It worked, surprisingly enough; his face relaxed and he chuckled. Eithne had been right about that after all.

Selia turned to Ulfrik. "Tell him I want to be a good wife to him, so I need to learn Norse. Ask him if it would be all right if you taught me."

Alrik smirked down at Selia as his brother translated. "You don't have to speak to be a good wife, little one."

Ulfrik appeared hesitant to translate this, but she understood Alrik's meaning from the way he was looking at her. She flushed. But then Alrik waved his hand, effectively dismissing them. "Teach her, brother. Just stay where I can see you."

Selia spent the remainder of the day with Ulfrik, on the deck in front of her little tent. Wary of his brother's jealousy, Ulfrik sat as far from her as he could while still being able to hear her over the wind.

He was a good choice of teachers, patient with her even when she lost focus, and Selia liked his dry sense of humor. She found she enjoyed his company. But it was impossible to tell if Ulfrik enjoyed the lessons himself or if he was indifferent, since he revealed very little emotion on his face. So unlike his brother.

The hours flew by as Selia willed herself to soak up every word he spoke. They had begun with simple things but moved on quickly to more complex thoughts and difficult sentence structures. It was as though Ulfrik also understood the urgency of her request to improve her Norse.

However, the more tired she became, the more her mind wandered away from the lessons, and for the third time she found herself snapping back to attention. Had he noticed? Feigning a headache, she closed her eyes for a moment and rubbed her temples. When she opened them again Ulfrik was watching her.

"We should stop for today," he said in Irish.

She shook her head. "Speak Norse to me," she reminded him. "I must learn."

"Selia . . . how is it that you spoke some Norse already? You did not live close enough to Dubhlinn to have heard much of it."

"Ainnileas taught me. My brother," she explained. He had been a terrible teacher, nothing like Ulfrik. "He would go to Dubhlinn with our father and whenever he learned a new word he would teach me."

"But I spoke to your brother. I'm sure he did not know as much Norse as you do."

Selia made a face. "That's because he doesn't remember anything. I would make him tell me as soon as he came home because he would forget by the next day."

"But you would not?"

"No," she said in Norse. "I remember all."

"'Everything,'" he corrected. "'I remember everything.'" Ulfrik studied her as he continued in Irish. "What language was your brother speaking to you the night we came to your house? It did not sound like anything I have ever heard."

"That isn't a real language—Ainnileas and I made it up when we were children."

"What did he say to you?"

"Nothing." Selia gazed out at the horizon. She liked Ulfrik, but had again said too much. He seemed to have a way of drawing things out of her. "He said goodbye."

He scrutinized her as though he knew she was lying. She changed the subject, switching back to her stilted Norse.

"And you, Ulfrik? Why you speak Irish and Alrik not?" Other than a few commands, and words related to trading, Alrik's grasp of the language seemed very limited.

"I guess I pay attention more than he does."

"What means, 'pay attention?'"

"To listen, to give focus to something. As you're doing now." She nodded. "Ulfrik. What means 'trifle?'"

"Trifle?"

"Yes. 'Don't trifle with me, child.' It means lie?"

"In a way, I suppose." He looked out at the water. "Alrik said that to you?"

"Yes. I would not trifle." The accusation still smarted. "He thinks . . ." she trailed off, not knowing the correct Norse words, and finished in Irish. "He thought I was trying to trick him into marrying me."

Ulfrik did not seem surprised at this.

"You think I trifle?"

"No. And he married you anyway, didn't he?"

Selia was unconvinced. Her gaze wandered over to where her husband stood in conversation with several of his men. Alrik clapped a large hand on a man's shoulder, laughing, and her breath caught in her throat at the sudden flash of white teeth. It would be much easier to despise him if he wasn't so handsome.

She knew very little about her husband, but what she had learned so far was frightening. He was arrogant, moody; possessive. He had no respect for any opinion other than his own, and seemed to think of Selia as a prize or a plaything, not a person. Not a wife. And worst of all, he was a murderer-he had killed a priest in cold blood, without any apparent remorse, and laughed about it with his men.

Niall was a strict but gentle father who had protected her from the wickedness of men. Not even for a king's ransom would he have considered a man such as Alrik Ragnarson for his daughter. Why then, when she looked at her husband, did her body grow warm and her belly squirm with excitement? She had found pleasure in his touch this morning. She desired him even now.

That bothered her more than the rest of it, more than being taken from her family, more even than the murder of Father Coinneach. That was the worst; despite her knowledge of what kind of man Alrik was, she *wanted* him. What sort of wickedness must then reside in her own soul?

Her father and Eithne had been right to keep her secluded at home. There was something truly wrong with her.

Something perhaps out of her control.

Chapter 7

As the light changed and the shadow of the mast lengthened across the deck of the ship, Ulfrik informed Selia they would soon stop for the night. Her stomach had been rumbling with hunger for quite some time. But a moment later a shout arose from one of the men who pointed out to sea with excitement. There was another ship on the water.

The energy of the crew changed immediately as they all looked to Alrik in anticipation of his orders. His gaze scanned the ship for a moment. Apparently satisfied, he nodded, giving the order to pursue.

A fierce shout arose in unison from the men, a terrifying battle cry, and Selia cringed at the sound. Ulfrik turned to her, his cheeks as flushed with excitement as the rest of them. So he was capable of emotion after all.

"When we reach the ship, you must stay in your tent. Don't look out. Do you understand?"

She nodded, and he left her to join the others.

The men turned the sail to pursue the ship, then everyone threw open their sea chests to pull out their battle raiment. Most of the men donned only a simple leather helmet and a thick tunic that appeared to be padded. Alrik, Ulfrik, and Olaf, however, had metal helmets with eyeholes and a nose guard, as well as mail tunics.

Alrik turned to look at Selia, just once, and she took a step backward at the sight of him—a Finngall warlord in full battle array, with his sword at his hip and his axe over his shoulder, preparing to plunder a ship and most likely murder its crew.

She had a momentary sense of recognition, as though remembering a dream. An icy wave of fear shot through her body and she felt an overwhelming urge to run away. But there was nowhere to go other than overboard.

They were approaching the other ship at a shocking speed. It was fat and solid, a direct contrast to Alrik's lean, predatory dragonship. Most likely a merchant vessel such as the one her father owned, the crew of that ship would be sailors, not warriors, and completely unprepared to fight the fierce Vikingers.

She was wrong. Sailors or not, the men from the merchant ship were not going to sit and wait for the dragonship to overtake them. One of the Finngalls cried out—a word she didn't know—and they all looked upward and raised their shields. She looked up as well and saw what appeared to be dozens of sticks flying through the air. Why would the sailors be throwing sticks at them?

Arrows. She crouched down and covered her head. Seconds later she felt an arm go around her just before she heard the sound of something thumping against wood, directly above her body.

Selia opened her eyes. A shield blocked her from the arrows, and she recognized the forearm around her waist as Alrik's. He picked her up and deposited her in the stern of the ship, with the rail at her back.

The look on his face bespoke fury as he gave his men orders to ready their bows. They notched their arrows, awaiting Alrik's signal. He called it out, and the Finngalls let their arrows fly to rain down upon the merchant ship.

Alrik turned back to Selia, his eyes glittering behind his helmet, as she shrank against the side of the ship. He cursed as he set the massive shield in front of her.

When she made no move to reach for it, he grabbed her arm, nearly pulling it out of its socket. "Hold this, and do not move from here." Then he left her.

The shield was made of a thick slab of painted wood, with a metal band around the perimeter. It was too heavy for her to carry—she couldn't have moved from the spot even if she wanted to. There were two arrows sticking out of the shield on the other side, and she tried to pull one out with which to defend herself if necessary. But they were sunk deeply into the wood. Those arrows would have killed her if Alrik hadn't blocked them. But now that she had his shield, he had nothing to protect himself.

Should she even care if he died? His death would free her, after all.

She cowered behind the shield as another volley of arrows rained down upon the deck. The ship lurched against a wave, causing a loose arrow to roll close to Selia. She grabbed it, but found she couldn't hold the shield upright with only one hand. She wedged the arrow between her knees where she could reach it quickly if she had to.

The dragonship pitched again, harder this time, and she nearly lost her grip on the shield. She peered over the top and saw they were alongside the merchant ship. The Finngalls had thrown grappling hooks onto the larger ship to board it.

The merchant ship sat higher in the water, and she spotted several of its crew members above. They had dark hair and dusky complexions, and were speaking a language she had never heard before. But the fear in their voices was unmistakable. One of them made eye contact with her, then shouted something to the others. She ducked back behind the shield with her heart pounding in her ears.

There was an explosion of noise and movement as the battle began. The very air seemed to shake with the clanging of metal and the thudding of shields, along with the grunts, curses, and screaming of men. The screams were the worst—although Selia refused to look at the carnage, her imagination provided the horrible image of men being run through with a sword or hacked to pieces with an axe. Her trembling hands caused the shield to rattle against the deck of the ship.

Through her haze of fear she thought she heard Alrik call her name, and the urgency in his voice coaxed her to again peek over the edge of the shield. He was on the other ship, swinging his axe like a madman. Selia felt the bile rise in her throat as he brought the axe down on the shoulder of a dark-headed man, nearly cleaving him in two. The man's body crumpled onto the deck. Alrik put his foot on the man's chest and freed the weapon with a sickening jerk, then dashed to the side of the ship and threw his leg over to clamber down.

"*Run,*" he yelled. She was confused for a moment until she saw one of the men from the merchant ship had already climbed over and stalked toward her with determination, gripping a dagger in his hand.

She screamed, dropping the shield, and ran as fast as she could in her husband's direction. He was back on the dragonship, and she was only a dozen steps away from him when someone grabbed her from behind and pulled her off her feet. She was still carrying the arrow, and she stabbed blindly with it, feeling an unexpected sense of satisfaction as the point made contact with the man's thigh. He yelled at her, jerking the arrow from her hand, and threw it onto the deck of the ship.

The blade of the dagger pricked against her throat, and she stopped struggling. Her captor called out to Alrik in a threatening voice. The man probably did not intend to kill her, but instead to hold her hostage as a way to free his ship and the remaining lives of his crew. Unless he panicked and pressed too hard with the dagger. Selia held still, barely breathing.

Alrik stopped mid-stride with the axe over his head. "Do not move," he said to her. His voice sounded ragged, as though his fury made it difficult to speak. The pressure of the dagger bit deeper into her flesh, and she knew she couldn't move even if she wanted to. The sailor spoke to Alrik again, louder this time, and there was fear in his voice.

Alrik nodded at the man, then bent as if to lay his axe on the deck. The tension of the blade against Selia's throat eased somewhat. Then with a movement so quick Selia would have missed it if she had blinked, Alrik pulled something from his boot and threw it at them.

There was a rush of wind, then the awful sound of metal sinking into flesh, just above her head. The man's body shuddered behind her. He staggered backward a few steps before he collapsed onto the deck of the ship, dragging her with him.

Alrik reached them in three long strides. He pulled her free, forcing her head back to peer down at her throat. "Are you hurt?"

Selia shook her head. She saw the man out of the corner of her eye, lying on the deck with a dagger protruding from his face. He was still alive, making a gurgling noise she knew she would never be able to extract from her memory. She wanted nothing more than to close her eyes and cover her ears until the battle was over.

But Alrik wiped at her neck, rubbing a droplet of blood between his fingers where the blade had nicked her, and bellowed with incoherent fury as he grabbed his axe. He ran for the dying man, then with one brutal swing chopped off his head. He held the severed head up by the hair and roared, causing the Finngalls—still fighting on the merchant ship—to shriek out their battle cry.

Blood spurted from the headless body as the dead man's hand twitched against the deck of the ship. The foul stink of his blood and excrement filled Selia's nostrils.

Her field of vision narrowed and faded to black, with the war cry of thirty Vikingers ringing in her head.

She awoke to a scraping sound, long and persistent, vibrating the floorboards of the ship beneath her. Judging by the voices and laughter outside, the battle seemed to be over. Had she fainted? She had never fainted in her life, but perhaps witnessing one's husband lop a man's head off was a legitimate reason to do so.

Would she ever become accustomed to the violence of these Finngalls?

She peeked outside her tent and saw the men loading numerous large vats from the merchant ship onto the dragonship. The Finngalls had rigged up ropes to lower the unwieldy vats onto the ship, where several men waited to roll and push them into the middle. One of the ropes slipped, causing the vat they were lowering to hit the deck with a thud. The horses, already skittish from the smells of battle, reared away as the vat cracked open, spilling its blood-red contents over the planks of the ship. A vision of the foreigner's spurting blood arose in Selia's mind, and she averted her gaze with a shudder.

Wine. The merchant ship had been carrying wine. Those men had left their wives and families to trade their goods in Ireland, but instead had found a brutal death at the hands of Alrik's band of Finngalls. The families of the foreigners would be awaiting the return of their loved ones, as she herself had waited for Niall's return from a long voyage. But these men would never make it home. Their final resting place would be at the bottom of the sea, and no one would ever learn of their fate.

Selia watched as Alrik supervised the transfer of cargo from one ship to the other. He was covered with blood—the front of his mail shirt was slick with it, his face and beard spattered with it, and even the ends of his hair appeared to have been dipped in red. There was blood everywhere, the men slipping in it; part of the reason they were having so much trouble with the vats.

She counted to determine how many had fallen to the foreign sailors' weapons. Then, unbelievingly, she counted again. All of the Finngalls had survived. Although a few of them had a bandage here and there, no one appeared to have more than a superficial wound.

No wonder her people lived in dread of the Finngalls' return each year. The crew of the merchant ship had been well armed and prepared to defend themselves against attack. They had outnumbered the Finngalls two to one. Yet they had died, every one of them, and all of Alrik's men had lived. Clearly the Finngalls were not only physically larger and stronger than other men, but were also much more skilled in battle. How could a village hope to ever defend itself from such invaders?

And she was married to the leader of this war band. A man who could frighten her beyond belief, yet the next moment look at her in a way that made her lose all reason. He had saved her life twice today, once from the arrows and once from the man with the dagger. Yet he had been the one who had put her life in danger in the first place by ordering his men to attack the merchant ship.

Should she be angry with Alrik, or grateful?

Selia wrapped her cloak tighter around herself. Alrik noticed the movement and met her gaze. His lips curved in a flinty smile. He was on the far end of the ship, but even from that distance she could sense his restless energy, could feel his desire for her. She stared at her blood-covered husband, and a sudden, unexpected surge of heat coursed through her body, as though answering his call. It felt like the very flames of hell.

They beached the ship in another deserted cove. The men knew what to do with very little direction from Alrik; several went in search of firewood while another unpacked dried meat from the ship. While one man busied himself with the makings of a fire, another cleaned a string of fish they had caught earlier that afternoon. Others took buckets of seawater and scrubbed the blood from the deck of the ship. It all seemed very efficient to Selia, more accustomed to men who were helpless when it came to basic housekeeping tasks.

Alrik had perched her on a large boulder away from the men, with orders not to move from the spot. She felt rather like a dog, sitting obediently and waiting for its master, but did as she was told. He would occasionally glance up from what he was doing as if to assure himself she was still there, and each time a surge of excitement would course through her veins.

Was that the human equivalent of wagging her tail?

Then Alrik and his men stripped off their clothes, and dove into the sea. They bobbed up, laughing and splashing each other in the moonlight, more like playful little boys than grown men. But the smoky fire of the merchant ship burning in the distance behind them was a harsh reminder that these boys were deadly.

Many of the men, Alrik included, had curious dark drawings on their torsos. Were they tattoos? Some of the men were nearly covered with the markings but she could only see one on Alrik, a small mark on his chest. She would have to look at it later when they were alone.

The men washed themselves, scrubbed the blood from their clothes, and finally climbed back onto the ship to lay their clothing out to dry. Selia averted her gaze. Did that mean she would be surrounded by a group of nearly-naked men tonight, wrapped only in their cloaks? But the Finngalls pulled out a change of clothes, clean and dry, from their sea chests. These men were prepared for the possibility of being drenched in blood on occasion.

Scrubbed clean, Alrik returned to her carrying two cups of wine. Selia was a bit ashamed at how much she enjoyed the way the tight muscles of his thighs moved under his breeches as he walked. He had a glint in his eye as he handed her a cup, and she blushed.

She took a delicate sip, mindful of her alcohol-induced confession to his brother the night before. She would not make that mistake again. She had only tasted wine twice before in her life when her father had attempted to impress a high status guest. This wine was delicious, much better than she'd had at home. But again the memory flashed of blood spurting from the foreign sailor's headless body. Selia's throat contracted, causing her to sputter and nearly choke.

Alrik frowned as he rubbed his thumb across the mark on her neck left by the tip of the dagger. Selia's heart did a strange flip-flop inside her chest. Was he actually concerned for her wellbeing? No, he was more likely angry at the idea of someone damaging his property. Or maybe he wasn't interested in having a wife whose beauty was flawed by a scar.

He dragged his thumb against her flesh, down her throat and across her collarbone. His hand was hot against her skin. "So," he said slowly, "What did you and Ulfrik find to talk about all day?"

She drew her brows together as she translated the words. Her own mind had been consumed by thoughts of the battle at sea and her brief stint as a hostage, and she had assumed his would be as well. But no, he had obviously moved on to the more important issue of whether or not his wife and his brother were overly interested in each other.

Selia wasn't sure how to answer. "Norse . . . words," she said hesitantly.

After a moment, Alrik threw his head back and laughed. She released a relieved breath.

"Ulfrik says you're quite the quick learner." He took a long drink, watching her over the rim of his cup.

Selia smiled. "I want to speak . . . for you happy—happiness."

He put his hand on her thigh, and she could feel the heat of it even through the fabric of her gown. Again he drew her in with his hypnotic gaze. She was still more than a bit afraid of him, but when he was this close to her she felt so strange, completely overwhelmed by his physical presence. Like a bug caught in a spider's web, waiting for the inevitable, poison bite. No, not just waiting for it.

Wanting it.

Alrik leaned in close to her. She smelled the briny scent of seawater on him, and she shivered when the damp strands of his hair brushed her cheek.

"There are many things I can teach you, little one," he whispered. "Things that will make me very happy."

Chapter 8

The next several days passed pleasantly enough as they sailed along the Irish coastline, stopping to trade at ports along the way whenever the mood struck Alrik. He seemed in no great hurry to get home. Selia kept herself occupied learning Norse from Ulfrik during the day, and learning the intricacies of intimate expression from Alrik at night. Just a short time ago she would have been shocked and repulsed at the various ways two people could join their bodies. How quickly Alrik had changed her opinion on the unavoidable necessity of bedding one's husband.

Selia had made a vital discovery as well; Alrik's desire for her gave her a surprising power over him. Her marriage had made her the property of her husband. But she learned she could bring the big man to his knees with just a word or a touch. Selia took a wicked satisfaction in it.

Her lessons in Norse were also coming along well, and she now understood most of the conversations she heard aboard the ship. As a consequence of spending so much time together, Ulfrik's Irish had also greatly improved. They had fallen into an easy and unexpected friendship, and Selia looked forward to the time she spent with her husband's brother. The other men were still uncomfortable around her, however. Most of them wouldn't even look at her, much less speak to her.

On the morning she had wandered off to bathe, Alrik had gone into a jealous rage, convinced one of the men had taken her into the woods. Ulfrik had calmed his brother down, but not before Alrik threatened to kill any man who so much as looked at his wife. The Finngalls took this threat seriously, and they now avoided Selia at all cost. But they couldn't stop the wind from carrying their words to her ears.

She learned quite a bit about her new husband and his brother from these snippets of conversations.

From the way the men talked, it was clear Alrik's jealous behavior made them uneasy. They thought he was besotted with his wife, which she could only conclude was not befitting a man of his standing. There seemed to be more to it than that though, from the way they spoke in hushed whispers of Alrik's father, Ragnarr.

She also heard the word 'curse' mentioned more than once. She didn't know what this word meant but had a strong suspicion it wasn't a compliment. She didn't dare ask Ulfrik about it, in case he took offense at the disparagement of his and Alrik's father, if indeed it was meant as such.

Ulfrik seemed to be genuinely well liked among the men, although the nickname they called him, 'Ulfrik Child Lover,' gave her pause. It was always said behind his back, and always with a slight snicker. Many of the men had a nickname, and she was not surprised to learn Alrik's was 'Blood Axe.' Most of the nicknames had to do with either the person's prowess in battle, or a unique physical characteristic.

Except for Ulfrik.

At first, Selia worried the men had the wrong idea about her Norse lessons with Ulfrik, but after hearing the nickname several times in reference to things other than her, she decided it must be related to something else. Again she was hesitant to ask Ulfrik about it directly, as it appeared to be an insult. How exasperating that the only source of her information was also the subject of the gossip she wanted to ask about.

She found Ulfrik to be an interesting person. During battle he had been as much a bloodthirsty Finngall as the other men, yet otherwise he seemed slightly removed from them. Different, although she couldn't put her finger on the reason. He worked beside them, he slept beside them, and he killed beside them. He made jokes with them and laughed at theirs. Why couldn't she shake the suspicion that Ulfrik felt like an outsider?

"Selia. Do you want to stop?"

She blinked at him. How long had her mind been wandering? "No," she said. "I'm sorry, I was . . ." She trailed off, not knowing the correct Norse word.

"Daydreaming," he offered. "Wool gathering."

She turned away, laughing, and out of the corner of her eye saw Mani Nefbjornson picking his nose. Selia nudged Ulfrik with her foot, eager to change the subject. "Mani Nose-Picker," she whispered.

His gaze was dispassionate as he took in the sight of his comrade, but she wasn't fooled. She had discovered his sense of humor early on, quite by accident, when he had made a quiet reference to Rodrek Sialfson as 'Rodrek the Fragrant.' Rodrek was one of the few men on the ship who didn't bathe on a regular basis. The smell of his crusty boots caused her eyes to water whenever he walked past.

Selia was in awe of Ulfrik's ability to keep his face expressionless when he wanted to, and it took her several seconds to grasp he was joking. She had bitten her lip to keep from laughing out loud, but a strangled snort escaped anyway. He did smile at her then, and since then they had been secretly making up silly nicknames for the men. He was better at it than she was. Somehow the fact he could keep his face completely straight while saying something ridiculous made it even funnier.

"You can do better than that, Selia Wool-Gatherer," Ulfrik said now, without taking his eyes from Mani. "Try again."

She thought hard. It was unfair to do this in Norse. She *could* do better if she wasn't trying to make jokes in a foreign language. Selia broke the rules by speaking in Irish.

"Mani Cavern-Explorer." She leveled him with a smug smile, and it was Ulfrik's turn to laugh so hard he nearly choked. Triumph at last.

The evening was clear and mild. After their nightly sojourn into the woods, Selia and Alrik returned to the beach. They lay on his cloak under the stars, a good distance away from the rest of the group as the men drank and prepared supper. She heard their disembodied voices as they spoke to each other, but it was too dark to see anyone clearly.

Alrik was in a foul temper which even the use of her body had not dissipated. She didn't like the way he was looking at her. She had hoped to return to the group but he refused, grumbling he was not in the mood to be sociable.

Gazing up into the inky darkness, she nudged him as she saw a shooting star. "Look!" She pointed, hoping to distract him.

He rose up on his elbow but looked at her instead of the night sky. "Selia. What were you and Ulfrik laughing about today?"

So that was it; he was jealous. She should have known better than to make Ulfrik laugh so hard. She had taken his unflappability as a personal challenge, and had been so pleased with herself when he had broken. Now she would pay for it, it seemed.

"Nicknames," she told Alrik, too afraid to lie to him.

"Nicknames?"

"Yes. I saw Mani pick his nose, and I called him 'Mani Nose-Picker," she whispered.

Alrik gave her a look of disdain. "Did anyone else hear you?"

"No."

"Mani is one of my best warriors. He has brought great honor to my war band. You disrespect him with your laughter."

She swallowed. "I'm sorry."

"I should have known better than to think Ulfrik Child Lover could be trusted to teach a *child* anything but jokes."

Selia felt a hot flush creep over her face. It was several seconds before she was able to speak. "I'm sorry," she said again. "It is . . . my fault."

His face still looked stony, so she stroked his hand until he met her gaze.

Alrik's expression didn't soften as expected. "Your Norse is much improved, Selia, and Ulfrik is needed on the ship—"

She cut him off quickly with a kiss. "Forgive me, Alrik. Do not be angry. I cannot stand it." She smiled at him, slow and sweet.

"Selia—"

"Why do they call Ulfrik 'Child Lover?' Does he have childs?"

"Children," he corrected her. She had used the incorrect word on purpose in an attempt to distract him. She nodded in innocence as he continued. "He doesn't have children. He just likes them too much."

Selia's jaw dropped. A man who lived on the outskirts of Baile Átha Cliath had been burned alive inside his house because it was rumored he had a sinful attraction to young boys.

Surely not Ulfrik—?

Alrik burst into laughter. "No, not that. He's just squeamish about killing them. In battle."

Selia blinked in confusion. She sat up with her heart hammering in her chest, unable to take a deep breath.

"You, you are Alrik Blood Axe. You kill . . . children?"

His hesitation told her it was true. He frowned as he reached for her, but she smacked his hand away. She tried to stand but Alrik grabbed her.

His face was very close to hers as he spoke. "Yes, I kill children." His eyes narrowed to slits. "Everyone does but Ulfrik. You kill the ones you have no use for—the old ones, the sick ones, and the children. There is a word for a man who cannot kill, and it is 'woman.' Would you rather be married to a woman, Selia?"

The bile rose in her throat. If she needed a reminder of what she had married, this was it. She had watched Alrik kill grown men, had seen him drenched in blood as he severed a man's head from his body. Although she would never be able to condone such brutality, she had reluctantly accepted it as part of the Finngalls' violent culture. But Selia had not allowed herself to consider the possibility that her new husband's savage nature would be equally applied to women. Or children.

She turned her back on Alrik Blood Axe and curled up into a fetal position, choking back her tears. More than anything, she wanted to be home.

Alrik's mood remained foul that night. He kept his distance from the men, clenching his hands and muttering to himself. Selia sat with her knees drawn up and her cloak wrapped tightly around her body in an attempt to fade into the background. She held her gaze on Alrik as he paced like a caged animal. Someone was going to get hurt tonight, and she could only pray it wouldn't be her.

The men were restless as well; they too could sense Alrik's volatile temperament had reached a dangerous level. They gave him a wide berth and lowered their eyes. The normally raucous laughter and bawdy jokes of the evenings were subdued this night. No one wanted to be the man who pushed Alrik beyond the pale.

Only Ulfrik dared approach him. He did so with an air of indifference, sipping from his cup, as if accustomed to the task of having to talk his brother back from the brink.

"What is wrong?" he asked quietly, looking at the fire instead of directly at Alrik.

"That's none of your concern."

Alrik's voice had an edge to it that made Selia fear for Ulfrik's safety. He wouldn't hurt his own brother, would he?

Ulfrik took a few steps away from the fire, motioning for him to follow. He pulled out his sword and raised his eyebrows questioningly at Alrik.

Selia stared, openmouthed. Surely Ulfrik didn't mean to fight him? No one in their right mind would even consider doing such a thing with Alrik in the state he was in.

Alrik grunted, turning away, but then Ulfrik held out his broadsword and pressed the tip of it into his brother's shoulder. Alrik whirled and pulled out his sword in one quick, angry motion.

Selia clapped a hand over her own mouth to keep from screaming. She had no desire to watch Ulfrik die tonight.

Apparently, he had the same thought. "Left hand, Alrik," he said. "Unless you do want me dead."

Alrik's eyes blazed like the devil incarnate. He ripped off his cloak, slung it aside, then tossed the sword over to his left hand. "Ulfrik Child Lover," he snarled as he picked up his shield.

"So this is about me, then?" Ulfrik eyed his brother warily.

Alrik lunged toward Ulfrik without answering. Ulfrik parried the blow with his shield, pushing him back. And again. And again. They did this over and over, like a perilous dance, until they were both sweating and grunting with exertion. Was this Ulfrik's plan, then—to exhaust Alrik until his anger dissipated?

The brothers circled each other, eyes locked. Alrik abruptly spun, sword raised, and slammed it into Ulfrik's shield with such force that the clearing rang with the impact.

The wooden shield splintered apart, and a large chunk of it fell away from the metal band that encircled it. The edge of Alrik's sword met Ulfrik's shoulder, drawing a dark line of blood against his blue shirt.

Selia could take no more. She ran to them, grabbing Alrik's arm in an attempt to restrain him, but he shook her free and she fell on her backside. He stood over her with his sword in his hand, eyes so wild she feared he didn't even know it was her.

"Stop! Don't hurt him because you're angry at me," she cried out in Irish, too distressed to remember to speak in Norse.

A murmur went through the men, as several quietly inquired what she had said, and someone translated, just as quietly. A man laughed. His rough whisper could just be heard above the others.

"I think she's bedding them both."

A stunned silence spread over the group. The joke, meant for only one or two men, had been heard by all.

Alrik turned to face them and his gaze locked onto Skagi Ketilson, the man who had spoken. The color drained from Skagi's face, causing the red scratch marks left by Selia's fingernails on the day of her abduction to stand out in stark contrast against his white skin.

Alrik lunged toward Skagi with his sword still drawn. Ulfrik tackled his brother, and at his urging several men were able to disarm Alrik while he was down. But Alrik somehow managed to pull Skagi to the ground by the legs.

The men unsuccessfully tried to restrain their leader as he climbed on top of Skagi and began pummeling him with his fists, to the sickening sound of cracking bone.

An uproar exploded, the men trying to pull Alrik away. Skagi screamed and his father, Ketill, implored Alrik to stop. But he was a man possessed. As Selia scrambled to her feet, Alrik continued to hammer away at Skagi and at anyone else within distance. Several of the men, including Ulfrik, suffered a bloody nose or a rapidly-swelling eye.

Selia gasped as she caught a glimpse of Alrik's face. The whites of his eyes were visible all around the irises, like a mad dog. He looked wild, feral . . . inhuman. *Berserker,* a voice whispered in her head.

Eithne's stories were true, after all.

No. *No.*

Berserkers were what the Finngalls called the 'shape-shifters.' These warriors would be struck with fits of uncontrollable rage that caused them to kill anything in their path, including their own kinsmen, until their lust for blood had been slaked. Although some stories asserted these men could actually turn into wolves at will, other tales claimed they instead channeled the spirit of the animals—retaining the form of a man but possessing the strength and soulless ferocity of the wolf.

Every Irish child knew the Norse word *berserker*. Parents used it frequently to ensure their children's compliance. 'Stay on the path lest there is a berserker in the woods,' was a common warning in Irish households. Niall had never stooped to such tactics, but Eithne had been known to on occasion. Selia and Ainnileas had also heard the stories from other children.

As Selia had grown older she had begun to suspect these tales were exaggerated. A berserker was a made-up creature meant to scare children. Nothing more.

But now she could see it with her own eyes—there was such a thing as a berserker. And she was married to it.

Skagi sprawled limply on the ground as his leader continued to pummel him. Suddenly, Olaf Egilson came up behind Alrik with a bucket of seawater and dumped it over his head. Alrik gasped, and the pause was just long enough for the men to restrain him. Six men picked him up, carried him bodily to the sea, and threw him in.

Selia was overcome with a wave of nausea as she looked at Skagi. The young man's face was mangled beyond recognition. His slack mouth revealed a row of newly missing teeth, his nose was smashed to one side, both eyes swollen shut. His head was in his father's lap, and he didn't appear to be breathing.

She had harbored an intense dislike for Skagi since the moment she had met him, but she hadn't wished *this* horrible fate upon him.

"This is your fault," someone spat at her, and she jumped as if he had been reading her thoughts.

"Riki, stop," Ketill commanded. Riki was his other son, Skagi's brother, and the third Finngall who had been at Niall's farm the night Selia was taken.

"Irish whore," Riki continued, undeterred. "You know what Ragnarr Geirson did to his wife, don't you? You won't last long."

"That's *enough.*" Ketill grabbed his son by the shirt and looked him in the eye. "I'll have you remember you swore an oath to Alrik Ragnarson, boy. Hold your tongue."

Riki glared at Selia and she took a few steps backward. Ragnarr Geirson was Alrik's father. What in the name of all that was holy had he done to his wife?

Alrik, Ulfrik, and the other five men emerged from the sea. Alrik was stripped to the waist, dripping wet, but did not seem to be affected by the night air. He strode to the group of men surrounding Skagi.

"Is he dead?" Alrik's voice sounded hoarse, as if he had been the one screaming, instead of Skagi.

"No," Ketill replied.

Alrik looked at Skagi's bloody face for a long moment, then back to Ketill. He ignored Selia completely. "You are a good friend, Ketill Brunason. But if Skagi insults my wife again, I will run him through."

Chapter 9

Selia slept poorly that night. She was anxious, lying close to Alrik, and when she did manage to drift into a fitful sleep it was fraught with visions of him coming toward her with his sword drawn, intent on gutting her with it.

She woke screaming, with Alrik shaking her shoulders.

Olaf's voice came from the other side of the fire. "Everything all right?"

"Fine." Alrik was gruff. "Go back to sleep." He pulled Selia to him in a tight embrace, tucking her head into the crook of his arm. The gesture seemed more to keep her quiet than it was to offer comfort, for clearly the man possessed no such womanish instinct.

And so she lay quietly. She listened to her husband's heartbeat as it slowed to a more gentle rhythm, feeling his warm breath in her hair, and hated the fact that his heart beat and his lungs breathed. He was a bad man, an *evil* man. He should not be suffered to live.

Alrik slept with his sword by his side, but kept his dagger strapped to his belt at all times, even when he slept. It lay on his hip just inches away from Selia's hand, the hilt a bronze blur against his red cloak.

A brave woman would do it. A brave woman would pull the dagger out and plunge it into Alrik's heart without a second's hesitation. She imagined herself doing it, rehearsed it in her mind, over and over. The sibilant hiss as she pulled the dagger from its sheath, the exact spot on his chest she would need to aim for, the resistance of his body as she plunged the cold metal through meat and bone.

His eyes opening in surprise, looking up at her as he felt the blade, knowing he was to die by her hand. And the blood; the blood that spurted out as his heart beat its final, jerky rhythm.

A brave woman would do it, but a coward would only think about it. And so she was a coward.

Selia did not want to die. For die she would. He'd stop her hand before the deadly plunge and turn the dagger on her, or, if she did manage to do it, his men would avenge their leader against his murderer. Either way, she wouldn't survive the night.

Yet how long did she expect to live, married to Alrik? He was a brutal man, mad with power, and prone to fits of rage. It was only a matter of time before he turned that rage on her. As perhaps his father had done to his mother.

If she were being completely honest, she was equally angry with herself. She had let herself care for Alrik despite knowing what kind of man he was; had allowed her desire for him to cloud her better judgment. She had deluded herself that he also cared for her, and might even one day come to love her. What a fool she was.

Now she knew the truth about him. The man was incapable of any emotion other than those which fulfilled his own selfish desires.

But the crux of the matter remained that even through her anger, her fear, she still had a tiny stirring of tenderness for him. To admit it cut to the bone. She was a person of such questionable character and low morals, she could still care for a man such as Alrik Ragnarson. That, she couldn't live with.

Selia moved quickly, her heartbeat pounding in her ears. She slipped out from under Alrik's arm, ready with a story about needing to empty her bladder if he stirred. He didn't. She gazed down at him one last time, then crept away and didn't look back.

She began to run as soon as she got to the tree line. Not aimlessly—she had to be clever if she had any hope of eluding him. Instead of heading down the coastline, toward home, she instead traversed inland. The dragonships were built shallowly to forge through rivers and streams where deeper, heavier boats couldn't venture. This gave the Finngalls the ability to attack villages further inland than the coast, villages caught completely unaware. Selia would move away from the coastline, staying clear of any body of water large enough to allow passage of a longship.

Alrik had sold the horses to make more room on the ship for the wine, so if they came inland to follow her, it would have to be on foot.

She would sell her beautiful cloak at the first village she found, then buy clothing and food. But she would wear boy's clothing, and she would cut her hair. Selia knew she could pass for a boy; she could easily model Ainnileas' walk and mannerisms. It would be safer to travel as a boy, and her disguise would help throw the Finngalls off her trail. With any luck she would make it home without a second glance from anyone.

Home. Would her father take her back, ruined as she was? She was the wife of a Finngall. The marriage had been consummated. Only death—either hers or Alrik's—could set her free.

And was it even safe to go home? Would he be waiting there for her, ready to carry her off again, or—more likely—kill her for defying him? No, if she were to stay alive, she would need to outsmart him. Go as deep inland as possible, and look for somewhere safe to hide. She could find work, keep to herself, and eventually send word to her family. How long this would take, Selia didn't allow herself to contemplate.

The day dawned cold and rainy. Exhausted and soaked to the bone, still she kept moving. The men always rose early. Alrik would be awake by now, looking for her. The thought of his big hands wrapped around her neck gave her the boost of fear she needed to press on.

How long had she been running? Two hours, maybe three? Her legs were so tired. Rain dripped in her eyes, and she had already fallen twice. But Selia pushed on blindly, keeping the diffuse light of the rising sun to her back, always running west.

She lost her footing again, stumbled, and landed on the edge of an embankment. She slipped in the mud as she tried to rise, then slid even further. Her arms flailed, grasping for roots or branches, but everything she managed to clutch on to slipped free from the wet soil. She dug her toes into the mud in an attempt to stop sliding.

Suddenly the earth gave way beneath her feet. For a few confusing seconds, her body rolled and gained momentum.

Then, blackness.

Ulfrik had rarely seen his brother so angry. He seemed to be lit from the inside with it. But it wasn't a blind rage as it had been last night; this had a clarity and focus that Alrik's anger usually lacked. So when the men split up to look for Selia, Ulfrik made sure to go with his brother. None of the men would be disappointed to see the Hersir snap his new wife's neck and be done with it.

If she hadn't gotten in between them last night, the situation with Skagi would never have happened. Ulfrik knew if his brother's anger continued to build unchecked, someone would end up hurt. But if provided with an intense physical release early enough, Alrik's fury could be diffused.

A few more minutes of sparring last night would have been enough to calm him, but Selia had jumped in. The embarrassment of his wife leaping to his brother's defense would have been enough to fan the flames of the anger that still burned in Alrik's belly, but then Skagi's ill-timed joke had been too much. It was a wonder the man wasn't dead this morning.

And even if Alrik didn't intend to kill Selia, with the mood he was in he was likely to do so, if only accidentally.

He was a very strong man under normal circumstances, but when enraged, his strength was legendary. If he touched his wife in his current mood, things would not end well for her.

Selia was so small. Much too fragile for an unpredictable man like Alrik. The night he had killed the priest she had tried to run, too, and he had ordered Ulfrik to stop her. Ulfrik hadn't meant to knock Selia down—he had barely touched her, really—but hurt her he had. Her body had felt so insubstantial under his, her eyes so terrified as she had begged him to help her. Why hadn't he done something? Why hadn't he stopped it?

Once when they were young children, Ulfrik had found a tiny bird on the ground beneath a tree. He had tried to climb the tree to return the hatchling to its nest, but found he couldn't do so with one hand. Alrik had watched his attempts with amusement for a while, then offered to hold the bird while his brother climbed the tree.

When Ulfrik reached the nest he had stretched his hand down carefully for the bird, only to have a mangled ball of blood and feathers handed to him. The crushed bones looked like tiny twigs emerging from the ball, and the small orange beak was slightly open, as if in surprise.

Alrik had insisted he had killed the bird on accident— he had only tried to hold on as the creature attempted to wriggle out of his hand. Ulfrik hadn't thought of the little bird in years, but now the image of those crushed bones refused to leave his mind.

Ulfrik sensed Alrik's growing anger, minute by minute, as they tracked Selia, made worse by having to pursue her on foot. She was a clever girl, going inland. But obviously too panicked to attempt to hide her tracks. They had followed her trail easily by the footprints she left in the damp earth.

The rain was a blessing in that sense, but the mud continued to slow them down. Ulfrik cursed under his breath as he once again lost his footing and nearly fell.

"Keep up or I'll leave you behind," Alrik growled over his shoulder. He abruptly stopped as the footprints ended.

He backtracked as he scanned the brush, wiping his wet hair out of his eyes with an impatient hand. "There." Alrik pointed to something in the distance, then disappeared from sight as he made his way down the embankment.

Ulfrik squinted in the direction his brother had been pointing. His gaze rested on a small figure lying next to a rock, unmoving.

Selia.

Sliding down the bank, he approached Alrik who cradled his wife's lifeless body in his arms. Her head lolled back to reveal a substantial trail of blood that had dripped down her forehead and cheek. Selia's face, usually so animated, was waxy and still, the lips a delicate shade of blue.

Ulfrik held his breath. Was she dead? Would he be surprised if she were? Since meeting her, Alrik had been more jealous and volatile than Ulfrik had ever seen him. The poor girl never had a chance.

Alrik's face was stony as he looked down at his wife. Did he feel anything? Did he know—or care—that he was responsible for this?

Selia took in a small breath, and Alrik jumped. "Selia." He patted her cheek.

She moaned, so quietly it could have been imagined, and Alrik's lip turned up in a smile. Maybe he did feel something for her after all. He held her head with one hand while pressing her skull with the other, searching for the wound to staunch the bleeding.

Alrik paused, then felt again. Confusion lanced his face.

"What is it?" Ulfrik asked, although he suspected it was pointless to prevaricate.

"Her head. The bleeding is on this side, but there is something over here. A dent," Alrik said. "Feel this."

Ulfrik studied his brother. It would have been only a matter of time before he figured out who he had married. The bigger question was what he would do about it now that he knew. Ulfrik knelt to run his hand over the spot Alrik indicated. There, hidden by Selia's hair, was a small but unmistakable divot in the bone of her skull. He parted her hair, seeking the area in question, and revealed an old, thickened scar.

Alrik's face drained of color as he met his brother's gaze over Selia's head. He thrust Selia's limp body into Ulfrik's arms, then stood as if he had been burned. "No," he whispered.

Ulfrik was careful to keep his face neutral, but his brother's eyes narrowed in suspicion. "Did you know this?" Alrik demanded.

Ulfrik looked down at Selia as the drizzling rain pattered against her skin. He leaned over her slightly, trying to keep her dry with his body. "I suspected, yes."

"You suspected." Alrik's voice rose in timbre. "But you didn't think to share your suspicions with me?"

"You had already married her. What was I to do?"

"Did you tell her?"

"Of course not."

Alrik grunted, unconvinced. "Why else would she have run?"

Ulfrik stared at him for several seconds. "Why else. *Why else, Alrik.* You don't think you've given her any other reason to be afraid of you?"

Alrik swallowed as he reached out to brush a muddy lock of hair from Selia's forehead. "Those eyes . . . I should have known her from her eyes. I kept thinking there was something familiar about her."

Ulfrik again kept his face expressionless. "What are you going to do?"

Alrik didn't answer immediately. "When we saw her in Dubhlinn I knew I had to have her. There was something about her that drew me. Now I know she came back to me for a reason."

"A reason?"

"She is meant for me. She is a gift from Odin. He has placed her in my path twice."

Ulfrik turned the thought over in his mind. His brother was not known to have pangs of conscience, so it was doubtful this was his guilt speaking. But Alrik had never been one to think deeply about spiritual matters. To claim divine intervention in meeting Selia again was almost as out of character as the guilty conscience would be.

Selia moaned. Ulfrik shifted her, and her head rolled and settled against his chest. She weighed nothing in his arms, like a child, yet there seemed a strength to this girl that defied her size. The blow to her head that had caused the dent in her skull should have killed her. The fall from the embankment and a second head wound, not to mention lying insensate in the cold rain for hours, should have killed her. And yet she lived.

But truly, how long would she last as Alrik's wife? How long would it be before he snapped again?

Ulfrik's memories of his father were fraught with Ragnarr's delusions and paranoia, and his eventual descent into madness. At the end, his ranting had taken a decidedly religious turn. It would be dangerous to encourage this line of thinking in his brother, but what other way was there to keep Selia from getting hurt?

Ulfrik chose his words with care. "I think you're right." The quickest way to appease Alrik was to let him think you were agreeing with him. "Odin is testing you."

Alrik drew his brows together in a scowl.

"Odin gave you a second chance. Why else would she have survived that?" Ulfrik motioned to Selia's head.

As Alrik studied his wife, Ulfrik moved in for the kill. "If you keep Odin's gift safe you'll prove yourself worthy of his favor."

Alrik reached his arms out for her, and Ulfrik transferred Selia's limp body back to his brother. *Little bird.* He had done all he could for her. For now.

He turned to go but Alrik called out to him.

"Wait. Swear to me you'll never tell her," Alrik commanded.

Ulfrik met his brother's gaze and nodded, but it wasn't enough for Alrik. "*Swear* it, right now."

He hesitated, and Alrik's face grew hard. "This is not the time to defy me, Ulfrik. Swear it or I'll run Muirin through the second we step off the ship."

It was all Ulfrik could do to maintain his mask of impassivity. He breathed through his nose, then let it out slowly, forcing his hands to unclench. "I swear it."

He had been very young when his father died, yet his recollections of that time were clear. If it was true that fear burned memories into the mind more indelibly than any other emotion, he would be able to remember Ragnarr's face for the rest of his life.

There had been a few occasions since the death of their father when a look would come over Alrik's face that was so like Ragnarr, it froze the blood in Ulfrik's veins. It was always brief, a sudden interplay of light and shadow that was gone as quickly as it came. His imagination, perhaps, or a buried memory. But now, standing in the rain in an Irish forest, the mad ghost of Ragnarr again smiled from Alrik's face as he gazed down at Selia's unconscious form. The vision was as clear and chilling as if the man had clawed his way out of his grave and stood before him.

This would end badly. And Ulfrik was powerless to stop it.

Chapter 10

Selia woke to the churning of a rough sea and a pounding head. The pain was excruciating, a sharp hammer strike with every beat of her pulse. What was wrong with her head?

She lay still for a long time, just breathing. She cracked open her eyes, saw she was in a tent, and shut them again.

The ship pitched sharply to one side. She rolled, but was stopped by something tied around her waist. A length of rope. She was clad only in her shift but was in too much pain to be concerned with modesty.

She heard footsteps outside, then felt blinded as the tent flap was flung open by a bald man whose name she couldn't remember. She threw an arm over her eyes to protect them from the light. The man shouted with surprise, and Selia groaned at the answering shot of pain in her head. There were more quick footsteps outside, and voices. After a moment someone crawled into the tent, whispering her name.

She opened her eyes again and saw Ulfrik smiling down at her. He stroked her cheek, and she recoiled. What did he think he was doing?

"Selia," he said again, but the voice wasn't Ulfrik's. *Alrik*? She blinked and forced her eyes to focus on his beard, braided instead of cropped. Her gaze wandered up to his eyes, which looked . . . kind. If this was Alrik, he was acting so unlike himself. Was she dreaming?

She would not be in this much pain in a dream, and her throat wouldn't be as dry as dust. "Do you have any water?" she rasped. Her tongue felt twice its normal size.

Alrik furrowed his eyebrows and said something she didn't understand. Norse, he was speaking Norse. Did she speak Norse, too? What on earth was the word for water?

Groaning with the effort, she raised a hand to her lips to make a drinking motion. He said something unintelligible, then left the tent. After a moment he returned with a cup, holding it to her lips with one hand while he lifted her head with the other.

White-hot pain exploded through her head, paralyzing in its intensity. Selia felt the water dribble down her chin before she succumbed to the sweet relief of the blackness once again. She had been here before, floating weightless among the stars in the night sky . . .

When she next woke it was dark, which didn't make sense because she was still in her tent. As long as she had been with the Finngalls, they had always made their camp on land, only sailing in the daytime. She could hear the sound of quiet breathing next to her. Instead of trying to turn her throbbing head, Selia reached out, fumbling, until she made contact with a large hand. The little finger was crooked.

Alrik stirred. "You're awake?"

It took several seconds, but she understood what he said. She raised her hand to her head, touching the source of the pain with careful fingers, and forced her lips to form the Norse words.

"My head hurts," she whispered.

"You fell. You hit your head on a rock."

She blinked for a moment, then closed her eyes and saw a flash of something bloody. Something mangled. Skagi's face. Suddenly everything rushed back to her.

Alrik.

He was a berserker, he had beaten Skagi nearly to death. She had run away—

He was here, lying next to her. Why was he being so kind, so seemingly concerned with her welfare after she had attempted to flee? It had to be a ruse—he must be planning something horrible to make her pay for what she'd done.

Selia whimpered and tried to move away from him.

"Shh," he murmured, shifting his body to put his arm under her head. She gasped in agony at the movement, but didn't lose consciousness this time. He put his other arm around her, stroking her bare shoulder with gentle fingers.

The rope around her waist had become uncomfortably snug when he shifted her, and she tugged on it to get some slack. He didn't trust her or he wouldn't have tied her up, but where did he think she would try to go? Overboard?

"I will not jump, Alrik," Selia gasped. "I cannot swim."

"The rope was to keep you from flopping around on the deck like a fish, little one. The sea's been choppy for days."

Days? Just how long had she had been unconscious? Selia slipped back into sleep before she could ask him.

She felt well enough to emerge from the tent the next evening. She bathed herself as best she could with a bucket of seawater, then dressed in her gown. Someone had washed it—she doubted it was Alrik—but it was stained, one sleeve ripped. The beautiful gown Eithne had worked so hard on was ruined.

Her legs felt disjointed and her head wobbly as she walked. Although she kept a firm grip on Alrik's arm, she was out of breath before she had taken more than five steps. He sat her down on one of the chests, calling for food and ale, then sat across from her.

Despite the uncommon kindness Alrik had shown to her since her fall, she still harbored a dark suspicion he would punish her for running away. But since he didn't mention it, she was reluctant to bring it up herself. And so it had remained between them, unspoken.

The rays of the setting sun enveloped Alrik in a halo of dazzling gold. How could a man be so beautiful? The sight of him made Selia's heart flutter in her chest, and she couldn't look away. He was a murderer, a berserker. Yet she still ached for him—ached to touch him, to feel his powerful body against hers. She couldn't stop the rush of desire that flooded her senses, or the hot flush that crept over her cheeks.

He met her gaze, and her blush deepened. Alrik's lips turned up in a smile. He hadn't touched her since the fateful night of her fall, and she knew from the short time she had been married to him, he didn't tolerate lustful frustration well.

Alrik watched her as she picked at her food. "Finish that," he urged. "You look like a bag of bones."

They had been at sea for some time. The bread was stale and the dried meat so tough Selia could hardly chew it. She flicked off a spot of mold with her fingernail, then forced herself to take another bite of the hard, dry bread. She had to drink deeply of the ale to swallow the yeasty lump.

"We will be in Norway tomorrow," he continued. "The food will be better then, little one."

Norway. "To your home?"

He shook his head. "No, not yet. We will stop at Bjorgvin first, to trade. But we won't stay long. The men are anxious to get home."

Alrik was probably also anxious for his home, and for Ingrid. How excited Selia had always been when Niall would return from a long voyage. He would throw his strong arms around her, exclaiming how she had grown in his absence, then give her a trinket or two he had bought for her in some foreign port.

But how would she have felt if Niall had returned from a trip with a new stepmother in tow—a stepmother who was nearly her own age?

Her stomach tightened in an uncomfortable knot and she pushed the remainder of the food away.

"Alrik," she said hesitantly. "Will Ingrid be angry about me?"

He didn't respond for a moment. "Yes, I suppose she will. Ingrid is always angry, though."

"Why?"

He looked out to the horizon as he answered. "Her mother died last year. Ingrid blames me for her death."

The chunk of bread in her stomach threatened to come back up. Dear God, had he killed his wife?

She stared at him, unable to move.

Alrik scowled at her. "I didn't kill her, Selia. She died of an illness, and my two other daughters died with her."

She breathed out shakily. But why would Ingrid blame Alrik for her mother's illness? That didn't make sense. Before she could ask, Ulfrik approached them. He sat down next to Alrik and smiled at Selia. Unlike that of his brother, the smile reached his eyes.

"How are you feeling?"

She raised a hand to her head. "It hurts a little bit."

Ulfrik nodded. "You're lucky to be alive. That was quite a fall."

Selia flushed again, afraid of where this conversation was headed. Maybe she should apologize to Alrik now while Ulfrik was here as a buffer. He might be less apt to punish her in front of his brother.

"Yes," she said quietly. Her eyes fluttered to her husband and quickly away. "I am sorry I ran away, Alrik. I was afraid of you."

"Why?"

She gaped at him for a moment. Was he jesting? He and Ulfrik were both watching her very intently, awaiting her answer.

"Skagi," she said, and Alrik looked oddly relieved. As usual, she couldn't read Ulfrik.

"Skagi insulted your honor. If I had done nothing about it, I would have lost all respect from my men," Alrik retorted. "I should have killed him, but Ketill is a friend. I would not like to deprive him of a son."

Selia's gaze wandered over to the other end of the ship where Skagi sat with the men, a scowl across his distorted features. Although the swelling had gone down, his face was still covered with greenish bruises, and his shattered nose was packed with wool in an attempt to set it. His left cheek appeared to be sunken, and she knew it was where his teeth no longer filled out that side of his face.

She looked away. "I am sorry," she repeated. Were her words for Alrik or for Skagi?

Alrik leaned in closer to her, locking her gaze with his. "You must never run away from me again, Selia. You must never disobey me in front of my men. What will they think of me if I can't control my own wife? A man who doesn't respect his Hersir will hesitate in battle. And a man who hesitates in battle is dead."

Her lip quivered at the thought of being responsible for any more deaths.

She nodded as Alrik continued in a softer tone, "I didn't mean to scare you."

Selia swallowed. Was he apologizing? Was he not going to punish her after all? Perhaps he wasn't a berserker. Or maybe the stories about berserkers weren't true.

Or perhaps he did care for her.

Regardless, she was safe. At least for now. The relief that flooded her body was sudden and absolute, and Selia closed her eyes for a moment. She felt as though she could melt into the floorboards of the ship.

The brilliant light behind Alrik extinguished as the sun slipped over the horizon. He stood, holding out a hand to her, and led her back to the tent.

Chapter 11

Once again on dry land when they arrived in Bjorgvin the next afternoon, Selia's senses were overwhelmed by the noise and crowds, much larger than in Dubhlinn. It didn't help that the bustling town seemed to be inhabited by giants. She had not been the smallest person in Baile Átha Cliath, but she was positively dwarfed by most of the residents of Bjorgvin.

Alrik and Olaf moved through the crowd with Selia in tow, and she was soon out of breath trying to keep up with their long strides. Since her fall from the embankment she had felt vaguely disoriented at odd moments, as if she were floating. She still tired very easily. She breathed a sigh of relief as Alrik made his way toward one of the larger buildings, then pulled her inside.

The cavernous, smoky room was dimly lit but loud with the voices and laughter of dozens of people. When her eyes adjusted to the light, she realized she stood in a tavern. A serving girl walked past them carrying a large kettle of something that smelled delightful, and Selia's stomach gave an answering growl. She had eaten enough stale, moldy food to last a lifetime.

Alrik stopped the girl and leaned over to speak to her. Selia couldn't hear what he said. The girl motioned in the direction of what must have been the kitchen, judging by the smells and commotion, and went on her way.

Alrik pulled a chair out from an empty table in a dark corner of the room, and Selia sat on it. "Stay here," he ordered. Then he nodded to Olaf and disappeared into the kitchen.

She settled in to wait. Hopefully Alrik had at least told the serving girl to bring them some food. Olaf stood next to Selia's chair with his arms crossed, as though expecting to have to defend her honor from one of the tavern patrons at any moment. Now that Alrik was out of sight, she could definitely feel their curious stares.

Tired, her head aching, the smoke in the air made her cough. If only she could just lie down while she was waiting.

She smiled as Alrik ducked back into the room, but her smile faded when she saw that a woman followed him—a very pretty, buxom redhead, with an annoyed expression on her face.

The pair stopped in front of Selia, and Alrik motioned for her to stand. She did, keeping her eye on the redhead, who looked askance at Selia.

"I don't believe it," she said to Alrik, after a long, critical perusal down her nose at Selia. "You married this girl?"

Selia bristled. She pulled herself up to her full height, which was somewhere at the level of the redhead's shoulder. Who was she?

"Gudrun." Alrik addressed the woman in a patient, almost coaxing tone, and Selia frowned. He had been so concerned with Skagi insulting her, yet he was willing to allow this woman to speak to her with disrespect?

Gudrun huffed loudly, then gave a curt nod in Alrik's direction. She put her hands around Selia's waist in a very businesslike fashion, and Selia gasped as she took a step back.

"What are you doing—" she started to ask, but Alrik shushed her.

"Hold still." He grasped her arm to keep her from backing away. "Gudrun is going to make you a new gown."

Selia flushed as the woman touched her familiarly, measuring her with her hands at bosom and waist. Olaf had his broad back to her to block the women from the inquisitive eyes of the tavern patrons, but the serving girls were still walking in and out of the kitchen. They tittered as they saw Selia with Gudrun.

Gudrun wrapped her fingers around Selia's upper arm to judge its circumference. She tisked with displeasure in Alrik's direction, and he smirked back at her. Selia studied the redhead. Just what was this woman's connection with her husband?

Gudrun's hands moved down to Selia's hips. She patted them mockingly, making a show as if finding nothing there. "I hope you didn't pay too great a bride price for her," Gudrun remarked. "Because this girl will not be able to birth any child of yours, Alrik Ragnarson. You threw your silver away."

Selia had had enough. "*Stop.*" She took a step back. "Alrik, I do not want her to make my gown. I will make it."

Alrik ignored her and spoke to Gudrun. "Can you have it ready by tomorrow evening? We sail the morning after next." He squeezed Gudrun's hand, smiling at her. "And have the girl bring some food to our room, and water for washing."

Selia followed him through the tavern. "I do not like her, Alrik." She glared over her shoulder at Gudrun, who was still watching them.

He frowned as he led her into a back room. "You don't have to like her, little one. Gudrun is the best seamstress in Bjorgvin. I won't bring you home dressed in that." He motioned dismissively to her gown.

He was ashamed of her. She turned away, feeling her lip begin to quiver, but he caught her wrist. "Stay here and get some rest—I'll be back soon." He chucked her under the chin as though she were a child. "Olaf will be outside the door if you need anything."

Olaf's charge was more likely to keep her from running away, but Selia kept silent as she watched Alrik shut the door behind him. She looked around at the small, dim room, furnished with nothing but a table and a narrow bed.

There was one tiny window, set very high in the wall. She could just reach up to open it but was unable to see out. The fresh air helped though.

The bed was nothing more than a wooden bench topped with a straw mattress and several blankets of indeterminate cleanliness, but to Selia it looked heavenly. It had been a long time since she had slept on anything other than the hard ground or the deck of the ship, and the idea of a nap was very tempting.

She was removing her shoes when she heard a knock at the door. Without waiting for a reply, the serving girl entered carrying a covered dish. Another girl followed behind her with a bucket of water and a basin. They looked her over with brazen curiosity, whispering to each other. One of them pealed with laughter as they walked out.

Stupid girls. Selia glared at the door for a moment but was too hungry to sulk for long. She lifted the lid of the platter to find a sizeable bowl of stew and a chunk of fresh bread, which she tore into immediately.

With her belly full, she sniffed at the cake of soap inside the basin. Underneath the strong scent of lye there was something else—an essence of herbs and flowers that reminded her of the scent of Alrik's hair. Her own hair was in need of a wash. She was still picking out chunks of dried blood from her scalp.

She stripped off her gown and shift to wash her hair, soaping carefully around the wound on her head. It was still very tender, and she would get a blinding flash of pain behind her eyes occasionally. But all in all, it was healing well. If Ainnileas were here he would surely have a joke or two about the hardness of her head.

She shivered as she washed her body in the cold water, but could not bring herself to put her shift back on. It was filthy from traveling. She scrubbed it with the soap, wringing it out as best she could, then draped it over the window shutter in hopes it would dry by morning.

There, that was enough. When was the last time she had been this tired? Selia finally crawled naked into the narrow bed, wrapped the coarse wool blanket around her, and fell almost immediately asleep.

She awoke later to the faint sounds of water dripping. The room was dark, lit only by a flickering candle, and Alrik was washing himself at the table.

He ran the soapy rag across his broad chest and shoulders. Her body grew warm as she watched him. She felt brazen for staring, but couldn't force herself to avert her eyes. Droplets of water trickled down from his wet hair onto his chest. A glistening drop dribbled over the tattoo, clinging momentarily to his erect nipple before making its way down his body.

The memories of Skagi's beating were fading, and so were those of the merchant ship and Father Coinneach. And Selia simply refused to think about Alrik killing children. The shadow inside her husband was like a hole-deep and treacherous, yes, but ultimately avoidable if one remained alert. Now that Selia had fallen into it, she could learn to step around it. There were days the hole seemed like a cavern, and those where it was more of a dimple. To look at him now, it didn't seem possible he could harbor such darkness inside of him.

"You are beautiful, Alrik," she whispered.

He paused, meeting her gaze. "'Beautiful' is for women, little one."

"What is for men?"

"Handsome, I suppose."

"Handsome." Selia smiled at him. "You are very handsome."

Alrik chuckled as he toweled the last drops of water from his hair, moving slowly as though he knew how the sight of him affected her. She drew her breath in as she watched him. He pulled out a comb, and Selia rose from the bed, wrapping the blanket around herself against the chill. Alrik had not closed the window.

"Sit," she said, and he did, on the edge of the narrow bed. She began to comb through his hair. As she moved around to the front of him, she ran her fingers over the curious markings on his chest, just above his heart. Even up close, the tattoo appeared to be nothing more than faded lines and squiggles. And misshapen, as if it had been put on long ago when he had been considerably smaller.

"What does this mean?" she asked.

He shrugged. "It's nothing. It's for battle." He grasped her waist to pull her close, her face now on a level with his, and buried his nose in her hair, breathing deeply. "Mmm . . . you smell delicious."

"What is delicious?"

"Good enough to eat."

Delicious. He smelled delicious himself. Alrik the Delicious—she liked that much better than Alrik Blood Axe. But she didn't dare tell him of the nickname after the scolding she had received about Mani. Alrik's good moods were too rare to waste.

She pushed aside his damp hair to kiss his neck, nicking him with her teeth in the way he liked. Alrik shivered. Selia ran her lips over his flesh as her hand slid along his torso, the tautness of his chest, and belly. Her hand went lower, and she looked him in the eye and smiled.

Eithne had always warned her never to smile at a man, since it would give him the wrong idea about what kind of woman she was. But the maid hadn't explained how powerful a smile was when provoking the desire of one's husband. If Selia did it just right, she found it could make Alrik stop speaking in the middle of a sentence.

He stared at her, his mouth slightly open and his breath shallow. She leaned in again to press her lips against the base of his throat, then worked her way down his body with slow, soft kisses.

He hadn't touched her last night, even though she had wanted him to. She found his restraint confusing at first, but then realized he was afraid he would hurt her so soon after her injury. She *had* nearly died, after all. But the familiar abyss of exhaustion had pulled her under before she could let him know his self-control was unnecessary, and she had awoken this morning alone in her tent.

She was his wife. She belonged to him. Whether Selia cared to be thought of as a possession or not made no difference. Alrik could have chosen to take her last night, regardless of her injury. He could have forced himself upon her when she was lying helpless and half dead. But he had not. Surely that meant something. It *must* mean something.

He did care for her. Perhaps almost losing her had made him realize how much. Her breath caught in her throat at the thought, and she was glad Alrik couldn't see her face.

"You . . . you are feeling better?" His voice was tight with restraint.

"Yes." Selia whispered. "Much better. I miss you, Alrik."

She stood, letting the blanket fall to the floor. She saw the glint of desire in his eyes as he leaned in to kiss her. But his kiss was gentle, and his hands remained fisted at his sides. He was holding back, as though afraid he would hurt her. Selia gripped his face and kissed him hard.

Alrik eyed her warily. She laughed as she climbed into his lap, moving close to kiss him again. His hands slipped up her thighs to the swell of her hips, gripping harder as Selia gently sank her teeth into his bottom lip.

He made a noise that sounded like a growl as he laid her on the bed. His mouth and hands seemed to be everywhere at once, but still so gentle. Selia cried out when he finally parted her thighs and entered her. He moved carefully, but Selia arched up to meet his every thrust.

The familiar buildup began deep in her core, driving

her mad with need, refusing to let go. "Please, Alrik," she whispered, digging her fingernails into his back.

He groaned and began the relentless rhythm she was accustomed to. Selia nearly sobbed in relief as her body shattered with pleasure.

As he finished she lay still, replete but exhausted.

Alrik shifted his body to look down at her. "Are you all right?"

The concern in his voice made her heart stop for a moment.

"Yes," she whispered, hiding her face in his shoulder.

Chapter 12

The morning seemed to come very early, and Selia covered her head with the blanket as Alrik shook her awake.

"Get up, little one." He pulled down a corner of the wool to nibble on her shoulder. "We're going to the market."

She rolled over. "I am asleep, Alrik."

In response, he yanked the blanket completely off. Selia gasped as the cold air hit her skin. Alrik pulled her to her feet, handing her the shift, still slightly damp. She didn't bother arguing with him, but put it on with a glare in his direction.

"Are you awake now?" He was smiling, teasing her as she shivered. She couldn't stop herself from returning his smile through her chattering teeth.

"You are a bad man."

Alrik held her gown out to her. "So I've been told."

After a quick meal of porridge at the tavern, they ventured into the teeming marketplace of Bjorgvin. The morning was cold and misty, and she regretted her decision to wash her shift the night before. A dirty but dry shift seemed much preferable to a clean, clammy one that clung to her body.

Alrik, as usual, didn't seem to notice the cold. With Selia's icy hand tucked into his arm, he moved through the maze of wooden stalls. He was clearly searching for something, and she had to nearly run to keep up with his long strides. When they finally stopped in front of one of the stalls, she was dizzy and out of breath.

The silversmith glanced up, looked them over, and smiled in anticipation. Alrik was obviously a man of means.

"Do you desire something in particular for your beautiful lady, sir?" He rummaged through a box of necklaces, then pulled one out. "Perhaps an opal, to set off her eyes?"

"A ring." Alrik waved the necklace away.

"Ah." The silversmith set the box of necklaces down in front of Selia, then brought out another, smaller box. He squinted at her hands, muttering as he searched through the box, and finally drew out a tiny ring. He held it out to Alrik for inspection before handing it to Selia.

She slipped on the silver ring and smiled. It fit perfectly. She held her hand out, admiring it, but Alrik took her hand to remove the ring.

"We'll come back for it later," he promised her, then bent and whispered to the silversmith for what seemed like quite a while.

Frowning, she returned to the box of necklaces. One at the bottom caught her eye and she lifted it out. Made of twisted silver with dozens of glittering stones of a deep violet blue, she gasped at its beauty as she held it up to the sunlight.

Alrik watched her. "Do you like that one?"

She nodded.

"All right," he said to the silversmith. "The necklace, too."

Selia didn't want to hand it over. "We will come back later?"

"No," he laughed. "You can have that one now."

Alrik and Selia stopped at several different booths as they wandered through the marketplace. He bought a pair of brooches for the gown Gudrun was making for her, as well as a fillet for her hair. Selia had been taking careful note of the dress and hairstyles worn by the women of Bjorgvin, and she was determined not to embarrass Alrik tomorrow when they returned to his home.

She spent the rest of the afternoon back at the ship. The men unloaded cargo, took it to the market, and then came back with yet more cargo. It was exhausting to watch and seemed rather pointless, so she finally crawled into her tent and fell asleep. Toward dusk Alrik woke her to return to the tavern. Selia was still tired and her head ached. The thought of food and bed sounded very inviting.

She forgot about her headache as she entered their little room to find a folded parcel lying neatly on the table. It was her new gown-or more accurately, gowns, as the women of Bjorgvin wore two gowns, one over the other.

The ensemble consisted of a pale blue, fitted gown with a wide neckline, and a sleeveless apron dress in a complementary shade of darker blue. It was embellished with silk trim, intricately woven in shades of blue and white. The craftsmanship was exquisite, with tiny, perfect stitches, and Selia had to admit she could not have constructed anything so beautiful in such a short time. Gudrun must truly be the best seamstress in Bjorgvin.

She pulled off the stained violet gown, dropping it to the floor without hesitation, glad now that she had washed her shift the night before. It would have been a shame to spoil the pristine new gown with a dirty undergarment.

She slipped on the gown and the apron-dress. Alrik got out the brooches he had bought for her, then showed her how to secure the narrow straps of the apron-dress with them. Selia smoothed the fine wool over her hips as she looked up at her husband. Was she now presentable enough to bring home to his family?

"All right?"

He gave a slow nod. "Yes."

She released her breath on a smile, just as there was a knock at the door. Gudrun entered, peering toward the bed.

"I left the gown—" she began, then stopped as she saw Selia. "Oh. I see you found it." Her nostrils flared as though she smelled something foul.

Gudrun approached her, examining the gown critically. She raised and lowered Selia's arms, then knelt to check the hem. "Well, it's a bit long, but it'll do." She stood again, towering over Selia. "I suppose I didn't trust my own measurements. You could hem it yourself. You do know how to sew, don't you, child?"

Selia gritted her teeth at the hateful woman. Alrik moved in between them, pulling out a bag of silver.

Gudrun gave him an affronted look. "Put your silver away, Alrik. Do you think I'd let you pay me? Consider it a wedding present."

Smiling, she stepped to him and reached up to hold his face in both hands. As she brought his head closer, she rose on tiptoe, then kissed him smartly on the mouth. "Just come to see me a bit more often. I miss you."

Selia was too stunned to speak for a moment. Obviously Gudrun was on very familiar terms with her husband, and neither she nor Alrik had any qualms about revealing that fact in Selia's presence. Was she to stand idly by as he consorted with loose women? Was this the expectation in a marriage to a Finngall man?

Too furious to form words in Norse, she spat in Irish, "*Get your hands off my husband.*"

Alrik and Gudrun turned to look at her blankly. Gudrun interpreted the expression on her face first, and snorted with laughter.

"Alrik is my brother, child," she said with more than a hint of condescension in her voice. "Surely you knew that."

Oh. *Oh.* That explained everything. Selia's cheeks burned and she wanted to sink into the floor. There *was* a resemblance in their bone structure, although the woman had red hair and her eyes were a different shade of blue. And then of course, there was the height . . .

"Why did you not tell me?" she asked Alrik.

He studied her with a puzzled expression. "I did."

Had he told her? She had no memory of such a thing. If she had missed that conversation, how many others had she also missed? Her flush deepened and she avoided Alrik's gaze. If he suspected anything out of the ordinary, he hadn't said as much.

But time was running out. He would find out sooner or later whether she wanted him to or not. Selia swallowed. Niall had told Buadhach her secret, and the old man apparently hadn't been deterred by the knowledge. Would Alrik be as accepting?

The expression on Gudrun's face made it painfully clear she suspected her brother had married a simpleton. Turning away, she took Alrik by the arm. "Come, enough of this nonsense. The feast I've had prepared for you is growing cold."

It certainly was a feast. All the men from the ship were in the tavern, enjoying large cups of ale. One of the serving girls dipped the ale from a huge tankard, refilling the cups as quickly as they were drained. Several other girls carried out steaming trays of meats, stew, bread, and a variety of cheeses. The noise was deafening, and Selia's ears rang with it as they sat down at a table next to Ulfrik and Olaf.

Gudrun bent to kiss Alrik on the top of the head, ignoring Ulfrik completely, before moving into the kitchen to oversee the workers.

Selia eyed the woman as she walked away. What kind of a sister so obviously favored one brother over the other? It made her like Gudrun even less, if that were possible.

Ulfrik had a way of studying her that made her feel as if he were inside her head. He was looking at her now in a watchful way, as though he sensed the uncharitable loathing she bore his sister. Or worse, as though he knew she was hiding something. How could he possibly know that?

Selia wiped her hands on her gown as she turned back to Alrik. "Do you have more brothers and sisters?"

"Another sister," he said. "Dagrun."

"That is all?"

Alrik's expression was cynical as he drained his cup. "That's all we know of."

"How many years have you, Alrik?" she asked.

He seemed puzzled for a moment. "How old am I," he corrected. "I'm thirty-one."

Selia struggled to hide her surprise as she did the mental calculations. Thirty-one? That meant he had only been sixteen when Ingrid was born. Although a typical age for a woman to have a child, most Irishmen didn't wed for the first time until they were quite a bit older.

She looked over at Ulfrik. She assumed he was younger than his brother, but only because Alrik was the leader of the war band and Ulfrik was not. He had a few lines around his eyes from squinting into the sun, just as Alrik did. The rest of his face was smooth and unlined, and he boasted a mouthful of white teeth. Still, he somehow seemed older than his brother. There was a maturity to Ulfrik that Alrik lacked.

Ulfrik appeared a bit uneasy at her scrutiny. Odd, for him to show it. Why was he so wary? He rearranged his face into his typical bland expression before he spoke. "We're the same age, Selia."

That was the obvious explanation—they were twins. She brightened. "Like me and Ainnileas . . . what is the Norse word?"

The brothers exchanged a glance. Ulfrik leaned over the table as the serving girl came around with the full dipper of ale, holding out his cup. The girl blushed and smiled at him as she filled it. There was a definite swing to her hips as she walked away.

Ulfrik took a long drag of ale before he set the cup down. He leveled his gaze at Selia. "Alrik and I aren't twins. We have the same father but different mothers. I was born a moon's span before Alrik."

That meant their mothers had carried them at the same time. She felt sick. "Finngalls can have two wives?" she whispered.

As Alrik smiled and drained his cup, Ulfrik threw him a narrowed frown. "My mother was a slave. Our father freed me after she died."

"An Irish slave," Alrik pointed out. "Why else would he speak Irish so well?"

She sat for a moment, too stunned to say anything. A slave. How awful. No wonder she'd had the distinct feeling Ulfrik was different than the other men. He actually was.

So Gudrun's coolness toward her brother—*half-brother*—had not been Selia's imagination. Poor Ulfrik. Had anyone loved him, growing up? Family awaited them at the end of this journey. Would they claim Ulfrik as one of their own, or ignore him as his sister did? She longed to question him further, but she sensed his discomfort in discussing the situation. Maybe another time.

Selia spoke to Ulfrik in Irish. "I'm sorry if I embarrassed you. Thank you for telling me."

He looked at her for a moment, then nodded and stood up, mumbling something about finding the serving girl for another quaff of ale.

Alrik laughed and thumped Ulfrik's arm. "Be a man, brother, and ask her to do more than fill your cup."

The drinking and feasting continued for hours, with the behavior of the men deteriorating as the night wore on. The loud laughter, shouting, and clattering of several dozen drunken men seemed overwhelming. But even as tired as she was, Selia wouldn't leave Alrik's side at the feast. Such quantity of drink caused the men to grow bold with the serving girls.

Selia averted her gaze as they pinched the girls' buttocks and even pulled them into their laps to fondle their breasts. Alrik was as drunk as the rest of them, and there was no telling what he would do if she went to bed and left him to his own devices.

The difference in his personality from one day to the next—and sometimes one minute to the next—could be striking. He was in a remarkably good mood now, laughing and joking with the men, and whispering ribald comments in Selia's ear that made her blush. When he was like this she could almost forget about the shadow that resided in his soul.

Skagi sat with his father and brother on the other side of the tavern. He seemed to have a permanent scowl on his face now. The few times she had accidentally caught his eye, she had been flung a look of such hatred that it chilled the blood in her veins. She wasn't sure if Skagi's anger was directed at Alrik or at her, but she kept her distance from him.

The rest of the men, for the most part, avoided her as much as possible, and only spoke to her out of necessity. Everyone but Olaf, who seemed to like Selia well enough, behaving in a rather fatherly way toward her. She had suspected early on that he was some sort of kinsman to Alrik by the familiar way they treated each other, and she had been correct. Ulfrik had mentioned Olaf was married to their aunt, and the only one of the Finngalls other than Ulfrik who didn't seem to be afraid of the Hersir.

Olaf, every bit of sixty years old, currently had a serving girl on his lap who was no more than twenty. The light from the torch flickered on his bald head as he kissed her. Selia turned away with a flush creeping over her face. The fact that Alrik and Ulfrik did not bat an eye at his behavior told her more about the Finngalls' view of infidelity than any words could.

A sudden sound, like the flapping of wings, caused her to duck instinctively. Alrik turned to her, still laughing at something one of the men had said. "What's wrong?"

His face and voice were very far away. Her heart beat too fast; she could hear the *whoosh-whoosh, whoosh-whoosh* as it pounded in her ears. Everything else seemed quiet and distant. She stared down at what appeared to be her hands holding her cup, but she felt no connection to them.

No, not here . . . not in front of Alrik.

The cup she'd been holding fell from her numb fingers as she rose to her feet. Its contents pooled on the edge of the table, then spilled onto the floor in a slow, steady drip. She blinked, struggling to focus on the puddle of ale.

"I've had too much to drink—I need to lie down," she mumbled.

Alrik stared at her in confusion.

Wasn't she supposed to speak a different language when conversing with him?

Hurry—

There was another flapping, much closer this time. A putrid odor rose in the wake of that hushed, gentle whisper of sound—

Hide—

She stumbled through the tables of drunken men until she found herself in a little room. As she tried to close the door behind her, an arm shot through the crack and a man pushed his way in, yelling at her in a strange language.

Recognizing him, she opened her mouth to warn her brother, but nothing came out except a shrill scream.

She was trapped with the bad man.

Chapter 13

Selia's scream brought Ulfrik running, the chilling cry, clear and sharp; the sound a woman made as she was run through. One scream and then silence.

Why hadn't he done something before now? He was a fool to think his brother could be trusted with her, a fool to believe a ridiculous delusion about Odin could prevent the inevitable from happening.

He burst into the room, fully expecting to find Selia's body on the floor. He stopped short as he saw her-very much alive-standing in the middle of the room with Alrik. She stared blankly ahead of her as a blind person might. Although her mouth was moving, all Ulfrik could hear was a mumbling, incoherent whisper. Her restless hands picked at her gown, and Alrik grabbed them to hold them still.

"Selia!" He called her name in the stern voice he used when giving orders, yet she remained unresponsive.

Ulfrik sheathed his sword. He hadn't remembered drawing it-what had he been planning to do, kill his brother? "What's wrong with her?"

Alrik's face was hard as he turned in accusation. "You told her, didn't you?"

"What? Of course not—"

"She *knows,* Ulfrik. The way she looked at me . . ."

"If she knows, it's not because I told her. She's clever enough to have figured it out for herself."

Selia's mumbling intensified and Ulfrik took a step closer to listen. He drew back and shook his head at his brother. "She's not speaking Irish."

A look of fear crossed Alrik's face. Ulfrik knew from experience that fear made his brother angry. Alrik shook her, hard. "*Selia, stop it.* Stop it right now."

Her head wobbled dangerously, and Ulfrik pushed between them to tug her unresisting body away. "You're going to snap her neck, shaking her like that." He sat her down on the edge of the bed.

She stayed there, continuing to mumble and pick at her dress. Suddenly she ducked, crying out in her strange language.

Alrik gaped, then narrowed his eyes at his wife. "Maybe it's some sort of magic. One of Gudrun's girls could be a cunning-woman."

Magic? Evidently such an excuse was easier for Alrik to believe than the cold truth, that his wife had discovered who he was and slipped into madness as a result.

"Perhaps," Ulfrik replied.

"Or they could have poisoned her. Gudrun said Helga wasn't pleased I married—"

Both men spun as Selia suddenly leapt to her feet. Her faraway eyes had regained their focus, and she stared at them as a startled child might when caught in some forbidden act. A deep flush rose to her cheeks as she lowered her gaze.

The expression on her face was not what Ulfrik would expect—yes, he spotted fear, but more than that was embarrassment. Shame.

This had nothing to do with Selia finding out who Alrik was.

Selia took a step backward as they watched her. No. *No.* Had they both witnessed her humiliation? Had anyone else seen; any of the men, or Gudrun? Alrik regarded her with such confusion, such doubt. She couldn't even bring herself to look at Ulfrik and his mind-reading gaze.

"I . . . I'm sorry," she whispered. She stared at the floor, but both men were quiet for so long that she finally looked up.

"You're sorry?" Alrik appeared even more uncertain.

"I did not want you to know . . . I thought you would hate me."

Ulfrik studied her. "This has happened before?"

Her lip quivered as she nodded. The last time had been two days before she had gone to Dubhlinn. She knew it was the only reason Eithne had even considered sending her to the market alone, since there was typically a good span of time between one spell and the next.

"My father said . . ." she began, but trailed off with a shake of her head. Her mind was always a bit sluggish afterward, and now the Norse words eluded her. She continued in Irish. "He said that any suitor needed to know about my spells before he married me . . . because some people think it's a mark of the devil."

She swallowed as she looked at Ulfrik, but his face was impossible to read. What did he think of her? Would he be able to stop Alrik if he snapped? Would he even try?

Ulfrik hesitated for quite some time before he translated for his brother. He stumbled on the translation of 'devil,' finally deciding on 'dark magic.' Alrik blinked and sat on the edge of the table. He wouldn't even look at her.

When his brother said nothing, Ulfrik turned back to Selia and spoke to her in Irish. "How long has this been happening?"

"I don't know . . . always."

"Before Niall?"

She drew her breath in. As far as she knew, Alrik knew nothing concerning Niall's adoption of her. Unless Ulfrik had told him.

"Perhaps. I don't remember."

"That language you were speaking—is it what you and your brother made up?"

Selia nodded.

"What were you saying?"

"Ainnileas said it is gibberish. I mostly speak of birds. I never remember any of it."

"Birds." He drew his brows together.

Birds that peck people's eyes out. She shivered. Ainnileas had told her that detail only once, but she had been so disturbed by it, she couldn't sleep for days. After that her brother had kept quiet about what she said during her spells.

Ulfrik appeared to be deep in thought. "And the staring you do, is that a part of this as well?"

So he *had* noticed. Most people didn't. If they did, they simply assumed she was daydreaming. Selia had no warning of the staring spells before they came over her, and so had no way to hide them. Thankfully they only lasted a few seconds.

Her other spells—the 'bird spells,' she had named them—although more severe, could be felt coming on. As soon as she sensed the birds, she knew she had but a few short moments to hide from any unsympathetic eyes.

She nodded. "I just . . . fade away. It's as though I go to sleep but my body is still awake."

Ulfrik translated everything for his brother. He left out the reference to Niall, and Alrik didn't appear to pick up on it. Selia watched her husband carefully. His eyes flickered a bit as he listened, and she saw the muscle in his jaw clench.

Ulfrik stepped in between her and Alrik as though preparing for the inevitable outburst of temper. At least he would try to protect her.

Alrik stood. "Leave us."

When Ulfrik didn't move immediately, Alrik crossed the room to open the door. His face was stony. "Leave."

Ulfrik met Selia's gaze as he walked past his brother and through the doorway, shutting it behind him. Was he waiting just outside, or had he gone back to the feast? Her one ally.

Or was he?

She turned back to her husband, who had begun to pace back and forth in the small room. The shadowy hole was growing. Soon it would pull her in.

"I'm sorry," she repeated.

"You should have told me, Selia. A man has a right to know if his wife is under a spell of dark magic."

"I was afraid to tell you."

"Did you think I wouldn't find out? What if my men saw that—they would think I married a witch! And we're going home tomorrow. What am I supposed to do with you?"

Her eyes filled with tears. "I do not know how to stop it, Alrik. I do not want to be like this." She took in a trembling breath. "I hate it . . . I *hate* it. If I could cut it out of me, I would."

He stopped pacing and looked at her for a long moment. Alrik didn't possess his brother's inscrutability, and Selia could read his face. Fear, suspicion, and anger played across his features. But perhaps a flicker of understanding as well? He too had something inside of him that was out of his control.

Silently Alrik rifled through the leather pouch attached to his belt, and pulled out a small object. "Here." He held out his hand to her. "Perhaps this will stop it."

She cupped her palm and he dropped the ring into it, pulling his fingers away quickly as though he feared the witchcraft would infect him if he touched her. Selia cringed. "Alrik . . ." she whispered.

"Put it on," he ordered, "and leave it on."

As she slipped it on her finger, she noticed strange carvings in the metal, all the way around the ring. "What does this mean?" She squinted down at the tiny markings.

"They're runes. For protection."

She blinked, not understanding. He must have collected the ring earlier that afternoon when he left her at the ship to go back to the market. But if that were true, how would he have known then she would need protection from the spells?

"Protection from what?" she asked. Perhaps she had misunderstood the word.

"Protection from me, Selia. Sometimes, when I get angry—" He shook his head. "I don't want to hurt you. And perhaps it will protect you from . . . *that*, as well." He gestured as if to indicate the aura of malevolence surrounding her.

She shivered at the necessity of needing protection from the rages of her own husband. But she was oddly pleased with the ring, as well as the thought he had put into it. He must still care for her, even after discovering her darkest secret.

She looked up at him with a cautious smile, but his scowl only deepened. Selia dropped her gaze. "You think it will make—"she paused, searching for the words he had used earlier"—the dark magic go away?"

"I don't know."

"Thank you," she whispered, and rubbed her finger over the small band of silver that could prove to be her deliverance.

Selia awoke before dawn. The tiny window had been left open, and she was cold. Alrik hadn't thrown his warm body over hers as usual. Instead, he lay next to her in the narrow bed, but as far away as possible. One of his shoulders hung over the edge of the mattress, and it would only take a strong shove to push him onto the floor.

She sat up, gazing at him in the dim light. She enjoyed watching Alrik sleep; with his face relaxed he looked so peaceful, almost angelic. His mouth was soft now, the lips full and sensuous, and she was overcome with an urge to kiss him.

She cared about this man more than she wanted to. Their marital compatibility had taken her by surprise, and Selia didn't attempt to fight her desire for him any longer. She suspected other women had been afraid of the intensity of his needs, and Alrik had assumed she would be as well. But her fear played into her hunger for him in a way that defied explanation. She had learned to simply accept it as part of her new life with Alrik.

She had done her best to separate her lust for her husband from her general wariness of him. Moreover, her status with the Finngall war band still seemed uncertain, as her marriage to their leader had not gone over well with the majority. Alrik was very intent on maintaining the esteem of his men.

What would they do if they learned her secret? Her father and Eithne had been so concerned about how others would react to her strange spells that they had kept her secluded at home as much as possible. She didn't understand enough about Finngall society to know if they would feel the same way. But judging by Alrik's reaction last night, the fear of her spells might be shared by all.

And now here she was, in a foreign land, married to a foreigner who knew something about her that could potentially get her killed. Alrik was not the kind of man who might simply send her back to her family. No, he would be much more apt to wring her neck and throw her overboard. Or, if he wanted to regain some of the bride price he had paid for her, to sell her into slavery.

And while Ulfrik had seemed somewhat more sympathetic to Selia's situation, he had already proven himself unwilling-or unable-to stand up to his brother. She had let herself become too complacent with these Finngalls. Whether she liked it or not, Alrik was the only thing standing between her and a violent death.

She would do well to remember that.

Chapter 14

They left the tavern to board the ship just after dawn. Selia kept out of the way of the men as they made their final preparations. Looking out to sea, she observed another ship trolling into the harbor, a longship like Alrik's, but much bigger. Even from a distance it seemed to be overflowing with people.

As the ship approached to dock alongside them, she heard voices, mostly Norse. But her heart contracted as she heard Irish being spoken as well.

The ship contained a group of Finngalls and several dozen of the Irish, as well as an assortment of animals. The Irish clustered together, looking grubby and dazed. Selia saw only a few men and the rest women, but none over the age of forty or younger than eight or ten.

One of the Finngalls called out roughly, and the group began moving toward the dock with painful slowness. She cringed as she saw they were hobbled together, with chains attaching each Irish to the next.

A slave ship. These were her people, her kin, and they were being brought to Bjorgvin to be sold at the market like cattle. The aged, the sick, and the very young were conspicuously missing from the group.

Because they had been killed. *By men like Alrik.*

One of the women who appeared to be around Selia's age glanced up and saw her staring. Their eyes locked. The silent exchange lasted for only a few seconds, but time seemed to stand still as Selia gazed at the pretty, dark-haired woman, shuffling toward her fate. She had damp stains on the front of her gown, and her breasts strained against the taut fabric.

Selia had seen something similar when a neighbor's babe had died, leaving the mother with engorged breasts. This woman on the slave ship had obviously had an abrupt cessation of breastfeeding.

Feeling suddenly sick to her stomach, Selia gripped the rail and closed her eyes. When she looked up again the woman was out of sight, a part of the nameless Irish huddle moving up the dock.

The dragonship ploughed through the water, following the jagged coastline of Norway. Selia gaped at the rocky cliffs rising almost vertically from the sea, hundreds of feet above the ship. The quality of the light was different here, the colors crisp and sharp. The occasional glimpse of pasture was a fresh, bright green, the blue of the water the same brilliant shade as Alrik's eyes.

They stopped numerous times along the coast, pulling the ship into clefts in the cliffs to drop off a few men at a time. Families would run out of their homes, children bounding down the hills, wives holding up their skirts as they hurried toward their husbands with joy on their faces. And each time Alrik and the remaining crew would be invited in for food or ale, but Alrik would graciously refuse, saying they needed to be on their way.

At each stop Selia was introduced as Alrik's wife, and noted how a flicker of surprise would register over the faces of the women. She studied them during these brief encounters. They were mostly blonds and redheads, with a few brown heads thrown in for good measure, all with the striking Nordic bone structure she found both beautiful and intimidating. Like the women of Bjorgvin, most were nearly as tall as an average-sized Irish man, but even those who were relatively short appeared strong and capable-looking. There was nothing timid or subservient about these women-it was almost as though they thought themselves the equal of their husbands.

The slaves would gather quietly behind the women, awaiting orders to unload cargo. They were dressed in plain, undyed garments, and both the males and females had cropped hair. They did not make eye contact. No one seemed to even notice them except for Selia.

As if the short hair and rough clothing didn't make the slave's status clear enough, each also wore a thick metal ring around his or her neck. Like the collar on an animal.

Her hand crept up to finger the jeweled necklace that adorned her own throat, and she looked away. She had much more in common with the slaves than she did with any assertive Norse women. Alrik was a Hersir, a warlord, and if he had been intent on finding a wife he could have done a great deal better than the daughter of an Irish merchant.

It was easy to see now why he had hesitated to marry her. But the fact remained that he *had* married her. He eschewed the opportunity to take her as a slave, and instead chosen her for marriage. If he wanted a wife, why hadn't he married one of these strong, beautiful Finngall women with good breeding hips?

There could be only two reasons for this. Either Alrik didn't want one of these women for a wife, or they didn't want him.

Ulfrik approached Selia at the side of the ship. She hadn't a chance to speak with him since the awful events of the previous night, so she was reluctant to meet his gaze now. Even though he would keep his face neutral as he always did, the *thought* of what might be going through his head at any given moment could be maddening.

"No one expects you to be like them, Selia." He nodded in the direction of a group of Norse women.

She scowled. "Stop doing that."

"Doing what?"

"Reading my mind. It's rude."

He smiled at her. "Then be more careful of your face."

"Not everyone is like you, Ulfrik. Not everyone *hides* what they're feeling." The words came out more sharply than she meant them to. Why was she acting like such a child? She flushed and turned away.

Ulfrik studied her quietly. "I wish you would have told me about your problem before last night. You can trust me, you know."

"Can I? I don't know anything when it comes to you. I want to believe you're my friend, but . . ." She trailed off as she felt tears pricking at the back of her eyes. It was silly to consider Ulfrik her friend. He thought of her as his brother's wife, nothing more.

"I am your friend. Never doubt that."

Sniffling, she looked out to sea and watched a bird skim across the water, flying away with a fish in its mouth. "I'm afraid, Ulfrik. I'm afraid Alrik will never forgive me for lying to him. I'm afraid your family will hate me. I'm never going to fit in here."

He looked down at her. "You'll fit in. Hrefna will love having you around-she's been pestering Alrik to remarry."

Hrefna was Olaf's wife. Ulfrik had only told her bits and pieces of the family dynamics, but nevertheless Hrefna sounded like someone to be reckoned with. If she had wanted Alrik to wed again, Selia was relatively certain she wasn't the type of woman Hrefna had in mind for her nephew.

"Why did Alrik marry me? Why didn't he choose a Finngall woman?" Selia asked.

When Ulfrik took too long to answer, she narrowed her eyes. "They're all afraid of him, aren't they? None would have him."

"Probably not. Not one of any family or wealth, that is. Even Eydis-that was Alrik's wife-was not from a noble family. She was the younger sister of Ketill Brunason."

"Skagi's father?"

"Yes. Ketill's father was dead, so it was up to Ketill to make suitable marriages for his sisters. Alrik asked for Eydis' hand several times, but Ketill continued to turn him away. Alrik wasn't the Hersir then, of course. Only when she became with child did Ketill finally agree to the marriage. We were very young then, even younger than you are now, so that was before anyone knew the full extent of Alrik's temperament. Ketill's unwillingness was still about the curse of Ragnarr."

She nodded. They had dropped Ketill and his sons off at the previous farmstead, small and dilapidated. Only a handful of slaves had come to the docks to greet them. It had all been rather sad. "And then when Eydis died, it made everything worse?"

"Yes, but by then it was clear Alrik had inherited Ragnarr's instability. Even though Eydis didn't die by his hand, I think many people still held him in suspicion."

Like Ingrid. Selia twirled the ring on her finger, feeling for the rune carvings. For all her hesitation to put her faith into a heathen object, the ring's presence did ease her mind somewhat. But was it powerful enough to protect her from the curse of Ragnarr and his son?

She held up her hand to show Ulfrik the ring. "Alrik gave this to me last night. He said it would protect me from him, and maybe from my spells, too."

He gave the ring a cursory glance, paused, then looked again. He twisted the ring around on her finger as he read the runes.

"What does it say?" she asked, after Ulfrik remained silent. He appeared to be deep in thought.

"It is as he told you-it's for protection."

"But you don't think it will work?"

Ulfrik hesitated. "I'm sure you know by now that Ragnarr killed his wife. But I think it's time you knew the whole story, Selia, for your own safety. I hadn't wanted to tell you the details. But after last night, it's more dangerous for you not to know."

She nodded as Ulfrik continued. "Ragnarr was a devotee of Odin. Some say those Odin bestows his gifts upon, he also casts his shadow over. I believe those of an unbalanced nature are drawn to him. Regardless, Ragnarr was suspicious of everyone. He felt others were trying to deceive him, to trick him with magical delusions. The more anyone tried to reason with him, the more distrustful he would become.

"Ragnarr believed Alrik's mother, Evja, was a cunning-woman. A witch who uses dark magic to cloud the mind." Ulfrik's gaze locked on the horizon. "When he killed her, there was nothing anyone could do to stop him, but our brother Jorulf tried. And so Ragnarr killed him, too. Dagrun was able to get Alrik and me away, or I have no doubt he would have slain us as well."

Struck speechless, Selia shivered as she pulled her cloak around her shoulders. "You're telling me this because you think Alrik will hurt me? Because of my spells?"

"He has always been wary of magic, so your spells make him nervous. I think he does care for you, but whatever good intentions he has are lost when he's enraged."

There would be no repercussions for Alrik if he did end up hurting her. No consequences. Her father and brother lived across the sea, too far away to intervene on her behalf. Had he chosen her for that very reason? Marrying Selia was a safer option than marrying the sister or daughter of one of his men, who might complain to their families about his unpredictable behavior.

Or had he chosen her because her small stature and inexperience allowed for easy intimidation? Because he thought her to be a young woman whom he could keep under his thumb-and by default, would be too timid to fuel the fire of his rage? If this were indeed the case, Alrik must be furious to know his new wife was significantly more complicated than he could have imagined.

She shivered again despite the warmth of the day. Ulfrik's belief that Alrik might kill her had confirmed her own worst fear. He knew his brother better than anyone, and understood exactly what he was capable of.

Ulfrik kept his voice low. "You tried to run away when we were in Ireland. You were afraid of him. Are you still afraid? Enough to leave?"

She searched his face. Did she trust him enough to answer the question honestly? "I don't know. Sometimes I am. Sometimes I want to go home and forget I ever met him. But other times, when he's kind to me . . . it's as though he's a different person. Then I don't want to leave."

He nodded. "He's been that way since we were children. I used to think it would be easier if he were cruel all the time. I would always know what to expect."

Although his face remained stoic, Ulfrik's voice held a hint of sadness. He did understand, then, very well. He had been playing this exhausting game his entire life. Ulfrik was a grown man, strong and self-reliant, yet Selia had a sudden urge to comfort him as though he were still a motherless slave boy. She patted his hand where it gripped the rail.

He turned and locked his gaze with hers. "If you are ever that afraid again, come to me first before you do anything reckless. I'll help you."

The sun was still high as Alrik, Ulfrik, and Olaf steered the dragonship through the cliffs and into a wide blue bay of breathtaking beauty, the water so tranquil and clear that Selia could see a mirror image of the ship reflected on the surface. There was a good sized village ahead of them, silhouetted by steep, heavily forested hills.

This was to be her new home. As they made their way toward the docks, her anxious belly lurched and she again fought back an urge to vomit.

There was a shout from someone on land, then within a few moments people began to emerge from the dwellings-hurrying, but not running in joy as most of the previous families had. It seemed for a village of this size, there were remarkably few people in it.

One female did break into a run, which Selia assumed was Ingrid. She steeled herself for the meeting. But the woman threw herself into the arms of Olaf, and as they embraced Selia realized she was older than she appeared from a distance. Hrefna, most likely.

Selia liked Olaf. He was pleasant and generally good natured, which wasn't the case with many of the Finngalls. If only she could erase from her mind the memory of him kissing the serving girl in Bjorgvin.

Alrik took Selia's hand to lead her over to them. He bussed the redheaded woman's cheek, but all the while her puzzled eyes remained on Selia. "Hrefna, this is my wife, Selia Niallsdottir. Selia, my aunt, Hrefna Erlandsdottir."

Hrefna's jaw dropped. Selia took in a shaky breath as she smiled. "I am happy to meet you," she said to the woman who bore a strong resemblance to Gudrun. She could only pray they didn't share the same caustic personality.

Hrefna looked shocked, clearly taking in all that was wrong with her nephew's new Irish wife. She leveled her gaze at Alrik for several long seconds. Finally, she let out a breath, turning back to Selia with a smile. "Welcome, Selia." Her voice held warmth. "Welcome to our family."

There was a noise behind Hrefna, then a high, angry voice. "Who is that?"

They all turned, and Selia found herself face to face with a young woman who could only be Ingrid. During the journey, whenever she had thought of Alrik's child, she had seen in her mind's eye a girl barely out of childhood-a lonely, misunderstood soul, distraught over the loss of her mother and her sisters. Of course the girl would be shy and hesitant around her at first. But with any luck, she hoped Ingrid would warm up to her and they might become friends.

Selia blinked at the girl who stood in front of her. Ingrid was taller than most of the full grown Finngall woman she had seen so far in Norway. The top of Selia's head didn't even reach the girl's chin. Alrik's daughter stood with an arrogance that Selia hadn't seen in any other woman but Gudrun.

And like her Aunt Gudrun, Ingrid had quite an impressive bustline.

But Ingrid's face was the very picture of her father; fierce blue eyes, sharp cheekbones, full mouth. Her hair was the same silvery blond shade as Alrik's-although it hung in a disheveled mess, whereas Alrik was very particular about his hair.

Selia stared as the girl drew herself up, crossed her arms, and looked down her nose in an expression of superiority. She was a perfect female version of Alrik Ragnarson. It was uncanny.

But Ingrid's beauty was marred by a deep, scowling glare. "I *said*, who is this?"

Alrik stepped forward and gave his daughter a scowl that mirrored her own. "Watch your tongue, child. This is my wife."

Ingrid turned her unholy gaze back to Selia with the same restless energy that seemed to dwell in Alrik. The girl looked as though she were about to strike. Selia forced her shoulders back and tilted her head to look Ingrid in the eye. She must not let her think she could be intimidated.

A muscle twitched in Ingrid's jaw as they stared at each other. Finally, she spat at Selia's feet, then ran back toward the village. A collective sigh went through the group on the dock.

"That went better than I expected," Olaf chuckled.

Alrik's face hardened. He moved to go after Ingrid, but Hrefna stopped him. "Let her be, my boy," she whispered. "It's a bit of a shock for her-she'll come around soon enough."

Linking her arm with Selia's, she called back over her shoulder to the men. "The thralls can handle unloading the ship. Come to your supper." She headed toward the village without waiting for a reply.

Selia liked the woman more and more by the minute, and her earlier nausea began to subside. Maybe Ulfrik had been right, at least about Hrefna. "Which one belongs to Alrik?" she whispered, motioning to the group of buildings in the distance.

Hrefna regarded her with surprise. "Why my dear, they all do."

Chapter 15

They made their way toward the largest of the buildings on the farmstead-a massive, windowless longhouse with two plumes of smoke rising up from the roof. The house appeared to have been dug into the ground several feet, made of solid logs stacked one atop the other. The simple design consisted of one large rectangle with several smaller rectangles jutting out from the longer, non-gabled sides. They headed toward the carved wooden door.

Selia's heart hammered in her chest. Alrik's house was huge; large enough to fit several of Niall's houses inside. And there were other buildings everywhere. Some appeared to be barns, and others were much smaller versions of the longhouse. It was anyone's guess as to their purpose. But it all belonged to Alrik, and now she was mistress of this farmstead.

How long it would take these Finngalls to realize she had absolutely no idea what she was doing?

They stopped several feet in front of the door, then Hrefna turned to wait for the men to catch up. "Alrik will want to walk you through," the woman explained, as though Selia was supposed to understand what she was talking about.

Selia smiled and nodded. Doubtless she would be doing quite a bit of that until she learned what was expected of her in this new land.

She watched the men approach. The sun glinted off the pale hair of Alrik and Ulfrik, as well as from Olaf's bald pate. Alrik appeared more relaxed than he had all day-he must be glad to be home. He had barely spoken to her after the events of the previous night, but now he met her gaze and smiled.

Was she forgiven, then? Selia's heart swelled in her chest as she returned his smile.

Alrik passed the women to open the door. He stepped inside the house, ducking to avoid hitting his head on the lintel, and turned to Selia with his hand extended. "Welcome, my little wife."

As she reached for his hand, Selia saw something rushing toward her from the corner of her eye. *Ingrid.* The girl looked deranged, fully capable of committing murder. Selia screamed and turned to run, but before she had taken a step she was pulled off her feet from behind in a grasp so strong it expelled the air from her lungs.

Ulfrik kept one arm around her and held the other out to block the impact. Ingrid ran straight into his hand, bouncing backward into the dirt.

Alrik leapt from the doorway, grabbing his daughter by the hair, and yanked Ingrid into the house. Ulfrik didn't release Selia until the door slammed shut on her attacker.

She winced, but refrained from rubbing her bruised ribs.

Through the thick walls of the house, she heard Alrik and Ingrid screaming at each other, along with a range of thuds and smacking sounds. Olaf and Hrefna exchanged embarrassed glances but didn't look at Selia.

As a horrible wail emerged from the house, she moved a step closer to Ulfrik. "Alrik is going to kill her," she whispered.

Ulfrik did not deny this possibility. "Ingrid is too old to be acting like a spoiled child. I don't know if she was trying to hurt you, or just end your marriage. You never know with her."

"End my marriage?"

"It's a bad omen if a wife stumbles over the threshold the first time she enters her husband's house."

Selia's breath caught in her throat. "Did I stumble?"

"No."

The door flew open. Alrik came out, dragging his daughter behind him. Her hair was even wilder than before, and there was a clear outline of a handprint on her tearstained face. Yet her eyes were still defiant as her father pulled her in front of Selia.

Ingrid's lips curled into a sneer as she spoke. "I apologize for my behavior, Stepmother. Welcome to our home."

Selia eyed the girl. That apology wasn't fooling anyone. "Thank you, Ingrid."

Alrik gave his daughter a dismissive shove, and she slunk off toward the woods. Selia could tell he was furious, nearly to his breaking point. Maybe he would decide to finish this Finngall threshold ritual later, after he had calmed.

But he took Selia by the shoulder, wrapping his other hand around her upper arm like a vise, and practically lifted her as he steered her through the doorway and into the house.

Selia didn't stumble. She smiled hesitantly up at Alrik, but he was too angry to notice. He muttered something about chopping wood as he pushed past Ulfrik, Olaf, and Hrefna to get outside.

She started to go after him, but Hrefna hurried over to stop her. "We'll just give him a moment, my dear. How about if I show you the house?"

Selia tore her eyes from Alrik's retreating back and followed the woman.

The longhouse was even larger on the inside than it appeared from the outside, if that were possible. The cavernous main room was divided into sections, with several looms set up to the right, a massive hearth in the middle, and a dozen long wooden tables pushed against the walls to the left. Being partially underground, the house was as cool as a root cellar except for the area directly next to the hearth.

All around the room were spacious sleeping benches built into the walls, with curtains on either side of each bench that could be pulled closed for privacy. The room was lit by rows of torches as well as the large hearth. Since there were no windows in the house, the only fresh air came from two holes in the gabled ends of the roof, from which twin streams of pale daylight cut their way through the smoke.

Selia politely choked back a cough.

She followed the echo of Hrefna's voice as the woman led her through the rest of the house. There were three rooms attached to the back of the main room. A kitchen to the right boasted another smoky hearth as well as a door to the outside, then Hrefna and Olaf's bedroom to the left, and Alrik's bedroom in the middle.

Selia hid her surprise at the realization this house had private bedrooms. Even those of relative wealth in Ireland had bed closets only, not an actual room with no other purpose than sleeping. Alrik's massive bed frame was intricately carved with snakes, dragons and other fearsome beasts. It was piled high with furs and fine wool bedding, with a mattress so level and thick she suspected it was stuffed with feathers instead of straw. She would examine more closely later, when Hrefna wasn't watching her.

The only other furniture in the room was a table and two chairs in the corner, and several chests of various sizes. At the foot of the bed was a hide that had once belonged to a gigantic white animal. The deadly black claws were still attached to the fur.

She followed Alrik's aunt back to the kitchen. A slave was stirring a large pot of stew, and Hrefna waved the girl aside to taste it. Selia studied her. "How many people live here?" she asked.

Hrefna turned to her. "You mean, in this house?"

"Yes."

"Well, Alrik and Ingrid, Olaf and me, and Ulfrik, whenever the mood strikes him. And now you." Hrefna smiled.

It seemed strange to have a house this large with so few people residing in it. "What about the other people?" Selia motioned to the outside.

"The thralls? Most of them stay in the slave quarters. The other buildings you saw are the barns, the dairy, the smokehouse, and the bathhouse. I can show you later."

She nodded at Hrefna, although some of the Norse words the woman used were unfamiliar. But Selia dedicated them to memory to later ask Ulfrik what they meant. Surely these people didn't devote an entire house to bathing? Even for Finngalls this seemed excessive.

She had seen at least twenty-five to thirty people approach the boat as they docked. These people weren't villagers, as she had assumed, but slaves. *Thralls.* And they all belonged to Alrik.

"This looks to be finished." Hrefna gestured toward the stew.

Selia's stomach growled and she blushed. "Should I get Alrik?"

His aunt hesitated. "I'm not sure how well you knew Alrik before you married him. Have you seen him when he's angry like this?"

"Yes."

"Then I'm sure you understand it's best to leave him alone for a while. He can eat later, when he's . . . better."

Selia smiled at the woman. "I will check," she said tactfully. "I will come back if he is still angry."

Hrefna's expression seemed to reflect a struggle to stay out of the business of her nephew and his new wife. "Be careful," she finally cautioned, turning back to the stew.

Selia followed the sound of chopping wood to the rear of the house until she came upon Alrik. He had his back to her, so she watched for a few minutes as he worked his way through the pile of wood. Stripped to the waist, his skin dripped with sweat, and her own body grew warm as she watched the powerful muscles of his back and arms tighten with each blow.

It seemed like a very dangerous dance. Alrik quickly chose a log, placed it on its end, raised the axe high above his head, then swung down on the log with such force that the two pieces flew apart with a splintering snap.

Although she had often observed her father and Ainnileas chop wood, she had never seen them do it with such unwavering intensity. Each blow of the axe ended just inches from Alrik's feet, and she was reluctant to distract him. She waited until he finished the pile of logs before she called his name, softly.

When he turned to her, the look on his face was almost enough to make her run back to the house. He was as wild-eyed as he had been when he was attacking Skagi. She took a step backward.

"Hrefna said it is time to eat," she whispered.

He wiped his arm across his brow, still holding the axe. "I'm not hungry." His voice was harsh. "Get away from me."

Selia swallowed but didn't turn away. Could she help him when he was this far gone? Her heart pounded as she stepped closer, putting a hand on his arm. She could feel the energy resonating through his body before he snatched his arm away.

"Alrik, I want to take a walk . . . up there." She nodded toward the woods. "Is that all right?"

He didn't answer, only glared at her.

"You can come with me if you like," she said. Without another word she walked away from him toward the woods.

She had gained the tree line when she heard him behind her. It sounded as though a large animal was charging her, and she braced herself for the impact. Alrik grabbed her, dragging her deeper into the woods, and she stumbled. Suddenly she was on the ground with him on top of her. His face was feral, inhuman, and when he looked down at her it was as if he stared not at his wife, but at his prey.

This was the beast. Alrik *had* been holding himself in

check, all this time. But now the leash had snapped and the animal within him was completely out of control.

He dragged Selia's skirts up and she gasped as he pushed himself inside her. He gripped her hard, jerking her body upward to meet each thrust, and his hipbones ground into her flesh. His face was that of a stranger, and although Selia wanted to look away she found she could not. Her heart ached for him, longing to ease the madness of his mind. She would take this pain from him if she could.

It was over quickly, in a matter of moments. Alrik made an odd guttural noise she had never heard before, then collapsed on top of her, completely spent.

Selia pushed out a breath as her husband's pounding heartbeat slowed in her ear. He carried most of his weight on his elbows, but his chest was crushing her face. She squirmed as a droplet of his sweat ran down her cheek.

He lifted himself up slightly to look at her. "Selia . . ."

The beast was gone, and she had never seen Alrik so contrite. He rolled away, sitting with his elbows on his knees, and kept his head lowered as if too ashamed to make eye contact with her. He looked like a sad little boy.

"It is all right," she said quietly.

"It's not all right." He ran his fingers through his hair. "Did I hurt you?"

"No."

Alrik shook his head at her. "Selia, why did you do that?"

She paused, not quite sure herself. "I wanted to help you. I wanted you to feel better," she admitted.

"Don't ever do that again. I could have hurt you. I could have *killed* you."

"But you feel better now?"

He didn't answer.

She stared at him until he looked at her. "Do people think you have dark magic inside of you?"

He busied himself fastening his breeches. "I don't care what people think."

Selia gave him a tentative smile. "We are the same, Alrik. We are both . . ." she searched for a Norse word that would convey her meaning, ". . . broken, a little bit. Maybe we are made to be together."

Alrik went pale, and she squeezed his hand.

Spells such as Selia's were thought to be a mark of the devil, a sign that her good Christian body was possessed by darkness. Every time she had been overtaken by one of her spells, she knew it had been like a slap in the face to her family-a clear indication of the innate evil inside her.

Now she knew it to be true, herself. Her fascination with the Finngalls and their heathen ways had gotten her abducted by the wickedest of men, a man who could not control his baser desires; his lust for blood, for power, and for her body. And she desired him as well-she wanted him, *craved* him, no matter what he did.

Alrik was as imperfect a creature as she; deeply flawed, damaged beyond repair. And despite that—or perhaps because of it—she was in love with him.

As a child she had wondered what being in love might feel like, but this was nothing like the romance of her imagination. Her love for Alrik was a shadowy, desperate thing clawing up from the depths of her soul. And whatever he felt for her, whether he claimed it as love or not, was as dark and as unnatural. But what else could be expected for a husband and wife such as they, one as wicked as the other?

Selia reached to touch Alrik's face. He looked so scared, so vulnerable. She leaned in and placed a tender kiss on his lips.

He smiled at her, slow and soft, unbearably beautiful. The smile of an angel. Selia's breath caught in her throat. At last she had made him truly smile with his eyes as well as his mouth, and it was the loveliest thing she had ever seen.

She would be willing to put up with quite a lot to be the recipient of Alrik's smile again.

They walked back to the house hand in hand, stopping long enough to get his shirt from the woodpile, then entered through the kitchen door. Hrefna jumped, nearly dropping the spoon she was holding.

Hrefna gaped at them for several long seconds as her gaze focused on the disheveled state of Selia's hair, and the angry red mark—the size of Alrik's thumb—clearly visible on her collarbone. She looked up at her nephew and opened her mouth to scold him.

He flashed his beautiful smile at her, then bent to kiss Hrefna on the top of the head.

"I am starving." He walked past her toward the main room, pulling Selia by the hand behind him.

Selia glanced over her shoulder at the woman, who stared back at her, openmouthed and speechless.

Hrefna looked as surprised as if Selia had just stopped a bull from charging . . . and was now leading it around by the nose.

Chapter 16

Ulfrik and Olaf played some sort of board game as they waited for their supper. They sat facing each other with a painted wooden board balanced on their knees between them.

When Alrik and Selia entered the room they both looked up, and Ulfrik started, just as Hrefna had. Carved pieces of the game fell from the board and hit the floor. His eyes went to the mark on her shoulder, then he turned his gaze toward his brother.

Alrik ignored him, sitting with a satisfied thud, and Selia blushed and giggled as he pulled her into his lap. Ulfrik looked away, leaving Olaf to pick up the game pieces.

Ingrid was nowhere to be seen. Selia had to admit she was relieved the ill-tempered girl kept her distance.

Hrefna sat at the table, followed by two slave girls who carried in the food and ale. There was stew, bread, and cheese, and two types of roasted meat. Selia was so hungry, she felt as though she hadn't eaten in days.

Alrik let her climb down from his lap to sit next to him so she could eat her supper. He led the conversation almost completely, questioning Hrefna about the crops and the livestock, and any general news that had occurred in their absence. He listened to her answers, but he would stop occasionally and feed Selia a choice bit of food from his plate, flashing a devilish grin as she took each morsel from his fingers.

No one spoke of Ingrid.

Ulfrik was drinking heavily and not eating much. She tried to catch his eye but he wouldn't look at her, instead keeping his gaze on one of the slave girls. The slave's cropped hair was the color of honey, and her flawless skin reminded Selia of fresh cream. Under her shapeless smock was the outline of a voluptuous body, and Ulfrik seemed fascinated by her hips as she walked.

The girl appeared to be interested in him as well. She kept her hand on his cup just a moment longer than necessary as she filled it for him, and her eyes rested on him more than once before she realized her slip and lowered her gaze to the floor.

So Ulfrik did have someone who cared about him, someone who didn't mind that he had once been a slave. Although Hrefna had greeted him with a warm embrace, nevertheless Selia noticed an almost imperceptible difference in the way the woman treated the two brothers. Nothing like the pronounced coolness she had sensed from Gudrun, but still a difference. She was a bit surprised at how angry it made her.

Ulfrik was a good man. A much better man than Alrik was, truth be told. And yet due to the fate of his birth, he was forced to defer to his brother and live in the margins of his family, not quite fitting in.

Alrik and Olaf began setting up the board for another game as the slave girls cleared the table. Ulfrik excused himself, his plate barely touched. He walked with the deliberate gait of the very drunk as he followed the pretty slave into the kitchen.

Hrefna watched him for a moment before turning back to Selia. "Selia, my dear, your gown is beautiful. Did you make it yourself?"

"No," she admitted. "Gudrun made it, when we were in Bjorgvin."

"Oh, I should have recognized her handiwork. There never was a better seamstress, save possibly my sister."

She nodded, looking down at the tiny, perfect stitches on her sleeve. There was a grass stain on her elbow and she shifted her arm to hide it. "I—I can sew, Hrefna," she said, in case the woman thought Alrik had married a simpleton who was incapable of doing the most menial of household tasks. "I can spin and weave. And I can cook."

Hrefna's smile was kind. "Oh, my dear, I'm sure you can do all of those things. Myself, I'm a decent seamstress, but if I had my choice I would weave all day."

Selia brightened. "Me too."

The woman leaned in closer, picking up Selia's hand, and her smile deepened. "I knew you were a kindred spirit, child," she said as she rubbed the weaving callous on Selia's finger. Hrefna showed her the hard bump of skin on her own finger, and they both laughed.

"Would you like to look at my looms?" Hrefna asked. Selia followed her to where the three looms leaned against the wall of the house, each set up with a project in various stages of completion.

"We used to have a house full of women," Hrefna explained. "Now it's just me. And Ingrid too, of course, but she has no patience for weaving."

Selia nodded in understanding. How lonely Hrefna must be without the companionship of Alrik's first wife. She gave Hrefna a sympathetic smile, and Hrefna patted Selia's arm.

"What part of Ireland are you from, Selia?" she asked.

"Baile Átha Cliath." At the woman's blank look, Selia added, "Near Dubhlinn."

Hrefna perked up. "Oh yes, my niece lives there. Alrik's sister."

"Dagrun?"

The woman raised her eyebrows in surprise. "Yes, did you meet her?"

"No. I only met Gudrun." She tried to keep her face neutral, but Hrefna chuckled anyway.

The woman motioned to the looms. "Are these the same as you used in Ireland?"

Selia ran her hand up the stout wooden post. "This is bigger, and has more . . ." she stopped, not knowing the Norse word, and held up one of the weights.

"Weights," Hrefna supplied.

Selia repeated the word and turned back to the loom, eager to try it. But suddenly she felt Hrefna's hand in her hair, and she jerked as the woman pulled out a small stick from her curls. Alrik had brushed the dirt from her gown the best he could, and picked out an assortment of twigs and leaves from her hair, but he had apparently missed one. Selia's cheeks heated.

From the look on Hrefna's face it was clear she knew how the stick had come to be in her hair. How wanton the woman must think her to lie with Alrik in the woods less than an hour after arriving home. But when she met Hrefna's gaze she saw amusement there. The woman attempted to suppress a laugh, but it burst out, loud enough to echo through the room.

Selia giggled.

The men looked up from their game to be let in on the joke. "Never mind," Hrefna said to them, as she led Selia into her bedroom.

"Now, my dear." Hrefna rummaged through one of the smaller chests in the room. "I'm going to re-dress your hair, if that's all right with you. You're a bit disheveled." She pulled out a comb.

Thank goodness Hrefna was able to find humor in the situation. Selia sat on the chair as the woman began combing through her hair, starting at the bottom and working her way up. Eventually she placed three more twigs on the table.

"Alrik seems quite smitten with you," Hrefna commented. "I don't think I've ever seen him smile as much as I have today."

"What is 'smitten?'"

"Hmm . . . it means he cares for you very much."

On the ship, she had heard other words the men had used to describe Alrik's feelings for her. Besotted. Infatuated. Derogatory whispers that Ulfrik had been hesitant to translate. But smitten . . . that sounded almost like *love.* A lovely warmth spread through Selia's body, and she smiled.

Then she heard Hrefna's startled gasp as the woman found the depression in her skull.

"What . . . what is this?" Hrefna choked out. By the look on her face it was obvious she suspected the worst.

"It is nothing. It happened when I was a tot. It does not hurt," Selia assured her.

"But how did it happen? How did you survive such a thing?"

Selia laughed, which seemed to surprise Hrefna. "My brother says our mother dropped me on my head."

The woman chuckled a bit too, probably in relief that her nephew wasn't responsible for the dent in his new wife's skull. "Well, what did your mother say about it?"

"Nothing. She died a long time ago."

"Oh, I'm sorry, my dear."

"It is all right. I do not remember her. It is a good thing my head is very hard."

Hrefna finished with Selia's hair and stood back to observe her work. The woman's own blazing red hair was twisted into numerous tiny braids at the temples, pulled into a partial knot at the crown of her head, with the remainder of her hair hanging down past her shoulders. Her fillet was wrapped around her forehead and attached beneath the thick locks.

Selia had admired Hrefna's intricate hairstyle from the moment she had set eyes on the woman, and she now patted her own head carefully, pleased that Hrefna had styled her hair the same.

"How does it look?" Selia fingered the elaborate braids.

"See for yourself." The woman again rifled through the chest. She pulled out a looking glass and handed it to her.

Selia gasped, nearly dropping it. The image was so perfect she found it disorienting, almost as if there were suddenly two of her. She stared into the glass and her gray eyes stared back at her, the reflection so clear she could count her eyelashes if she wanted to.

"What's wrong?" Hrefna asked.

"I have never had . . . this."

"You've never had a looking glass? Why?"

Selia shook her head. "My father said it was better to be good, not to be beautiful." She didn't know if Niall had an aversion to looking glasses in general, or if he had been trying to keep his daughter's already compromised soul from being stricken with the sin of vanity as well.

"Humph," Hrefna grunted, as though she thought this line of reasoning rather foolish. "So you didn't even know what you looked like, until now?"

"Oh yes, I did. From the water. And from my brother Ainnileas. We look the same—everyone said so." She looked into the glass again, searching for differences in their features. The eyes and mouth were identical, as well as the shape of their faces. The only real difference she could see was Ainnileas' bushier eyebrows and bigger nose.

She stared into what looked like her brother's eyes. *I miss you. It's hard to be without you, but you must not try to find me. I need to stay here.*

Selia and Ainnileas had shared a bond that went much deeper than most siblings. Not that they could read each other's thoughts, but more as if they could share their feelings-strong emotions especially. Or pain. When Ainnileas had fallen out of a tree and broken his arm several years before, Selia felt the flash of his pain as if it had happened to her. She had left the house in a blind run, straight to where her brother was, nearly a mile away. She had no explanation for how she knew where to find him; she simply did.

Niall and Eithne had found the connection between the siblings disconcerting, to say the least. So the twins kept it to themselves as they got older. But it was still there, just under the surface. Selia missed her brother with an overwhelming intensity if she allowed herself to think about it, and she blinked back tears now as she lowered the looking glass into her lap.

"Oh, my dear child." Hrefna gave her a hug. "You miss your family, don't you?"

Selia nodded, sniffling into the older woman's shoulder. Hrefna seemed very kind, and in a way she reminded Selia of Eithne. Or at least the good parts of Eithne, without all the scolding. Was this what it would feel like to have a mother? A real mother, not a servant who took care of you because it was her job to do so? She inhaled deeply, enjoying the warm scent of Hrefna's neck.

"Selia." The woman pulled back to look at her. "How old are you?"

"Eighteen."

Hrefna grunted. "Well, I will say that's older than I thought you were. I feared you were younger than Ingrid. You are very small." She sat next to Selia, patting her hand. "It's hard to have to leave your family no matter what age you are, I know. I married Olaf when I was fourteen. I cried for a long time when I had to move away."

Selia drew her eyebrows together. "But . . . you live here," she said, not understanding. It was rather odd for Alrik's maternal aunt and her husband to live here, with him. In a typical Irish family, the wife went with her husband upon their marriage. If they ended up living with relatives, it would be with his, not hers. The custom must be different here.

Hrefna hesitated, perhaps unsure how much of the family's secrets Selia was aware of. "After my sister and her husband died, Dagrun and the boys went to live with their grandfather, Geirr. But he was in poor health, and after a few years he could no longer care for them. Geirr married Dagrun off, but before he died he sent for us to see if we could take care of the boys. There was no one else who could do it," she finished.

Selia could easily understand how no one else *would* have done it. Certainly no one who was willing to risk the curse of Ragnarr. Yet Hrefna had felt sorry enough for her nephew and his half-brother that she agreed to raise them. And moved into the farmstead where her sister had been murdered to do so. If that didn't say something about the strength and compassion of this woman, nothing did.

"Do you have any children, Hrefna?" Selia asked.

"Yes. Olaf and I have a daughter, Kolgrima, and she has five children of her own. I don't see them as often as I'd like. But that is the way of women, isn't it?" There was a tinge of sadness in her voice as she pulled Selia to her feet. "You look lovely, my dear. Now, let's see what those men are up to."

Both glanced up from their game as the women entered the room. Alrik stared, holding a game piece in his hand, mid-move. A slow smile spread across his face at the sight of Selia's proper Norse hairstyle.

"Come here," he said.

She walked over to him, blushing. Why did she suddenly feel so shy? Alrik reached for her wrist to pull her closer, but his movement caused the board to shift. A few of the pieces hit the floor.

"Am I actually going to get to finish a game tonight, or not?" Olaf protested.

Alrik was still looking at Selia. "Sit down here." He motioned to one of the benches built into the wall. "And watch me beat Olaf."

She made herself comfortable amongst the furs and pillows on the bench. Curious about the game they were playing, she asked a few hesitant questions. Alrik was in a fine mood, and he and Olaf patiently explained the rules of the game.

Tafl was a game of strategy. The black pieces represented the king and his men, and the white pieces the attackers. The object of the game was for Alrik to get his king to the other side of the board before Olaf could surround and capture the king with his own men. The smaller pieces were called knobs, which were unimportant and could be sacrificed to keep the king safe, or to eventually capture him.

Alrik made bold, impulsive moves. It seemed as though he played tafl exactly the way he lived his life; with overconfidence. Selia could see how Olaf might take advantage of Alrik's strategy, but Olaf's moves were consistently mediocre. Was he not a good tafl player, or did he simply know better than to beat Alrik?

The Hersir probably wasn't a gracious loser.

They were all drinking rather heavily, and after a while Selia began to feel warm and drowsy. One of the slave girls, the plainer of the twosome who had served them at dinner, sat in the corner out of the way but scurried to refill their cups of ale as soon as they were emptied.

Still unaccustomed to the strength of the ale they drank, Selia found it went to her head very quickly.

Hrefna sat by the hearth spinning a length of wool. Did she think Selia an idle girl, relaxing on the bench like a princess? She should get up and do something useful as well. But her body felt warm and heavy, and she couldn't bring herself to move. She had already nodded off twice despite her best intentions to stay awake.

Traces of lingering daylight filtered in through the smoke holes in the gables. How silly, falling asleep like a child while the adults laughed and enjoyed themselves.

The days had seemed to grow longer and longer the farther north they sailed. Had anything Eithne told her about the Finngalls been true? The woman had always asserted the blond giants came from a land of darkness. But here the sun rose at what was surely the middle of the night, and finally set hours after it would have been already dark at home.

Selia must have drifted off again, because she awoke bemusedly to the sound of Hrefna's disembodied voice.

"What do you think you're doing, Alrik?" Hrefna asked in a rough whisper. She sounded angry. Selia opened her eyes a crack, enough to see them through her eyelashes.

"I don't know what you're talking about," he replied.

Alrik's aunt blew her breath out as she dropped the spinning into her lap. "Oh, you don't, do you? Marrying that girl, for one thing. You look ridiculous with her, you know. What exactly were you thinking?"

Obviously Selia was not meant to hear this. Her breathing even, as if asleep, she remained still and unashamedly eavesdropped.

"Hrefna—" Olaf began, but she cut him off.

"You just hush. You had the chance to talk sense into him, and you didn't," she hissed at her husband, then turned back to Alrik. "There are bruises on her shoulder, Alrik. I saw them while I was dressing her hair. I won't stay here and watch you hurt that poor girl, I tell you—I had my fill of *that* with Ragnarr."

"She bruises easily. I didn't hurt her on purpose." Alrik's voice was gruff.

The woman refused to back down. "On purpose or not, it doesn't matter. She is too small for you-she will end up hurt one way or the other. And what will happen when you get her with child? Do you actually think she could birth a babe of yours? That girl will be dead in a year, mark my words."

Alrik stood abruptly, causing the tafl pieces to fly across the room. His jaw clenched as he glared down at his aunt. "I'll thank you to stay out of my business, Hrefna. If you want to go, then go. It is no concern of mine."

He bent to pick Selia up from the bench, then carried her to the bedroom, slamming the door behind him with his foot.

Selia could feel the tautness of his body as he laid her on the bed. She stared up at him.

"How long have you been awake?" He looked furious.

She averted her gaze, and he cursed, probably realizing she had overheard the entire conversation.

"Alrik," she said cautiously, "Do you think I will die . . . from your babe?" She had heard this prediction twice now, once from Gudrun and once from Hrefna. That, coupled with Niall's willingness to marry her off to Old Buadhach because he couldn't get her with child, had not left her with much confidence.

"No," he said, undressing. He threw his clothes in a heap on the floor. "I do not."

Selia wasn't accustomed to seeing her husband completely naked. Aside from their grisly nuptials at the priest's house and their brief time at the tavern, their lovemaking had always been conducted in the woods. And so he usually just unfastened his breeches, did his business with her, and fastened himself back up.

Now he stood in front of her in all his naked glory; a massive man, thickly muscled, achingly beautiful. She sucked in her breath at the sight of him.

Alrik bent to kiss her, hard and unrelenting, and she wrapped her arms around his neck and returned the kiss with fierce intensity. He pulled back with a thin smile, pausing just long enough to undress her, then he was on top of her again.

She shivered as the cool air brushed her skin, still a bit sore from earlier, but also throbbing with need. She found the longer she was with Alrik, the less foreplay was necessary for her to be ready for him-her body responded to him quickly, sometimes with just a look or brief touch.

Now she felt ready to explode. "Please," she moaned.

But surprisingly, he didn't pierce her just yet. His lips moved over her body with maddening precision, kissing and licking his way downward. The softness of his mouth was in direct contrast to the scratchy, rough feeling of his beard on her sensitive skin, and it was almost too much to bear. Selia had to bite her lip to keep from screaming. She tasted blood, but she didn't care.

Nothing mattered but what he was doing with his tongue . . .

They lay for a moment, breathing hard as their damp bodies chilled in the cool air. She smiled up at Alrik but he still looked angry. He must have held back quite a bit, keeping the beast firmly in check, and so had not allowed the tension in his body to fully dissipate.

He rose from the bed, then began to dress. "Sleep," he said as he bent to kiss her. The pressure of his hand on her shoulder caused her to flinch, and Alrik drew back. He hesitated for a moment, then stroked the bruise with his thumb. Without looking at her again, he walked out of the room, closing the door behind him.

Was this an apology? Did he feel remorse for his earlier behavior, and was trying to make it up to her? Or perhaps-more likely-he wanted to prove Hrefna wrong, to prove that he *could* be with Selia without hurting her. If that were the case, it must not have been quite enough for him, his victory therefore hollow.

Selia slipped into her shift, and turned the blankets down to climb into bed. She paused as her hand touched the unexpected softness of the sheet below. Silk. Alrik's bed not only had a feather mattress, but sheets made of silk. She pondered the extravagance of such a thing, but had to admit as she settled into bed that silk felt much nicer than wool against the skin.

Finngalls. Such curious people.

She covered herself with the blankets and furs, rolling over in the bed that seemed much too large without her husband in it.

As she drifted off to sleep she distinctly heard the splintering sound of wood being chopped.

Chapter 17

When Selia awoke, she wasn't quite sure if it was morning. Daylight streamed in from the smoke hole, but that meant nothing. Alrik slept on his side, away from her. She touched his bare shoulder but he didn't move.

She watched him sleep for a few moments. If the lingering scent of sour ale surrounding him was any indication, he wouldn't be up for quite some time. She might as well rise from the bed to see if anyone else was awake. Perhaps she could help Hrefna with something to prove to the woman she wasn't the lazy girl she had appeared to be yesterday.

She pulled on her gown, then slipped from the bedroom. The house was quiet as she followed her nose to the kitchen. There were several loaves of bread rising on the work table. Evidently someone was awake, but the kitchen and main room were deserted. The curtains on Ulfrik's bench were drawn tight. Was the pretty slave girl sharing his bed?

She made her way outside to the privy, holding her breath at the smell as she relieved herself. Her stomach had been more sensitive than usual recently, probably from the unfamiliar spices the Finngalls used in their food. Perhaps she would not break her fast this morning.

On her way back to the house, she passed one of the barns and heard the bleating of sheep coming from inside. She smiled as she lifted the latch to the barn door. A pail of fresh sheep's milk would be a suitable offering to Hrefna to make up for last night.

The interior of the barn was warm and dark, smelling strongly of sheep excrement. Selia wrinkled her nose, but nevertheless set out to find a pail.

"Is someone there?" a female voice asked, and Selia squinted into the darkness. She could just make out the shape of a human head leaning around one of the sheep.

"Yes." She tried to hide the disappointment in her voice. Now she would need to find some other way to please Hrefna.

"I've already done the first three. You can finish up here if you like, so I can check on the bread."

Selia walked over to the figure, prepared to do as she was asked. The woman looked up at her, then dropped to her knees with a cry of fear.

"Mistress," she said, "please forgive me . . . I did not know it was you."

Selia blinked down at the woman's lowered head for several seconds. How was she to respond to this? Judging from the woman's cropped hair, she was a slave. Her Norse had a slightly different quality to it than Selia was accustomed to hearing. Was she Irish?

"Stand up," she said in Irish. "I'm not going to hurt you."

The woman's cautious gaze met Selia's as she rose to her feet. It was the slave who had served them at supper last night, the one in whom Ulfrik had been so interested. She was young, tall and well-formed, and even in the semi-darkness Selia could see she had lovely green eyes. No wonder Ulfrik was so taken with her.

"I'm sorry, Mistress."

Her heart leapt at the sound of the girl's perfect Irish. It seemed a lifetime since she had conversed with someone who spoke her native tongue. Ulfrik didn't count-although his Irish had improved greatly since she had met him, he still had a Norse accent. This girl, however, spoke so clearly and so perfectly that for a moment Selia felt as though she were home.

"It's all right," she assured her with a smile. She couldn't restrain herself from reaching out to touch the girl's arm.

The slave flinched. "No one is ever awake this early except me . . . it's my job to prepare the bread."

"What's your name?"

"Muirin."

"Muirin." Selia let the fine Irish name roll from her tongue. "You have no reason to fear me. I came out here to milk the sheep, but since you're here we can do it together." Now that she had someone to converse with in Irish she was reluctant to stop. The bread could be damned.

She patted the stool. Muirin sat down rather hesitantly as Selia went to find another pail and stool. She returned, sitting before the next sheep in line, and began to work its teats.

After a while the girl seemed to relax a bit, and finally opened up to Selia's relentless questioning. Muirin was nineteen, and from a fishing village on the southwestern coast of Ireland. She had been nine years old when the Finngalls had come and taken her. A Hersir named Gunnar One-Eye had raided her village, selling her to a slave trader in Bjorgvin. She had only been here at this farmstead for less than a year.

Selia did her best to hide her shock at the story. Although Muirin was shy, she spoke matter-of-factly about the events of her early life, seeming almost numb as she told Selia of the raid on her village and the deaths of her parents and her younger brothers. Her sister was three years older than she and had been taken as well. Both girls had been sold to a brothel.

"What is a brothel?" Selia asked.

Muirin kept her gaze fixed on the udder in front of her. "It is a place where men pay for pleasure. They pick out a woman and she must do whatever he asks of her."

Selia stopped milking for a moment. What a terrible tragedy. Muirin had seen her family murdered, then had been torn from her home to be sold into slavery in a foreign land. She had been forced to service strangers with her body. But how had Muirin come here to this farmstead? Had Ulfrik been a patron of the brothel? There seemed no polite way to ask that question.

"Are you treated well here?" Selia asked.

She heard nothing but the sound of milk streams hitting the bucket for several long seconds.

"Yes, Mistress," Muirin finally responded.

A gnawing ache began to grow in Selia's belly. Both she and Muirin were silent as they finished milking.

They walked to the house, carrying their pails. The scent of porridge and freshly baked bread wafted to them as they entered the kitchen together. Apparently Hrefna had cooked the morning meal herself, as there was no one else in the room.

They stopped short at the look on Hrefna's face. "Where have you been?" she demanded of Muirin.

Muirin blushed and stammered, clearly reluctant to blame Selia, but unable to explain herself otherwise. Selia stepped forward. "It is my fault, Hrefna," she said. "I was talking to her. I went to milk the sheep." She held out her pail for inspection.

The woman turned to her with a strained smile. "Of course, my dear," she said, taking the milk from her. "But you don't have to—"

Selia startled as she heard Alrik's voice behind her. "Next time tell me where you're going." He leaned against the doorway, arms crossed.

"I did not want to wake you, Alrik."

He grunted, unwilling to be appeased. His eyes narrowed on Muirin, who shifted like a frightened rabbit under his blue gaze.

Hrefna gave her nephew a hard look as she waved him out of the kitchen. "Go sit down," she ordered, and she took Selia by the arm to follow Alrik to the table in the main room.

Ulfrik and Olaf were at the table, looking quite worse for wear after the night's hard drinking. They both gave Selia a weak greeting. Ulfrik's gaze followed Muirin as she and the other slave-whom Selia heard Hrefna call Keir-dished up their food, but Muirin did not look at him or anyone else.

Selia smiled up at her in thanks as the girl placed a bowl of porridge in front of her, yet the slave's face remained expressionless. It was as though the conversation in the barn had never occurred.

The front door slammed shut. Ingrid walked in, scowling at everyone around the table as she sat down. She ignored Selia completely as she tore into her food.

"And where have *you* been?" Hrefna inquired.

"At Bjorn's, of course," Ingrid said, her mouth full.

Selia studied her new stepdaughter. Who was Bjorn? Judging from the lack of reaction from the others at the table, it must be somewhere she went regularly. Apparently she could come and go as she pleased. How remarkable for an unmarried girl of her age to have so much freedom.

Muirin placed another platter of bread in front of Ingrid. The girl glanced up, and as her eyes registered on the slave she nearly choked on her food. She dropped her chunk of bread on the table and burst into laughter, looking from Muirin to Selia.

"Ingrid," Hrefna warned.

Alrik scowled at his daughter as if daring her to speak, but the look on Ingrid's face was triumphant. She turned to Selia. "Stepmother," she said sweetly. "Did they tell you this thrall is with child, and she doesn't know if it's by Ulfrik or my father?"

Time seemed to stand still as Selia gaped at those seated around the table. Ingrid was grinning like a fool, and Hrefna and Olaf looked mortified. Ulfrik's face drained of color as he pushed his plate away. Muirin stood frozen, her gaze to the floor.

Alrik, however, leapt from the table, knocking over his bench in his rush to get at his daughter. He grabbed her by the neck, lifting her high into the air, and her fingers clawed at his arm as her feet kicked helplessly beneath her.

Olaf and Ulfrik jumped up to restrain Alrik, but he shoved them aside. He threw Ingrid against the wall, and her body smacked hard before collapsing in a boneless heap on the floor. She moaned but didn't move.

As Hrefna screamed and blocked Ingrid's body with her own, Olaf and Ulfrik stood between him and the two females, prepared to leap on him. Alrik's hands clenched convulsively as he glared at his family with his wild, white-ringed eyes.

Then he snarled something unintelligible and stormed from the house, slamming the door so hard the log walls reverberated.

Chapter 18

Alrik had been gone for several days. Only Selia seemed surprised or upset by such behavior. He told no one where he was going, or when to expect him to return. She was almost as angry over this as she was about the babe growing in the slave girl's belly.

To avoid a difficult conversation her husband had left, revealing more than a few flaws in his personality.

She hadn't expected cowardice to be among those flaws.

Hrefna filled their days with Selia's preferred housekeeping duties in an apparent attempt to distract her from her anger. It wasn't working. They stood at the looms together, weaving, but she found the rhythmic movement she typically found so soothing could not ease her mind. Her work looked as though a child had done it, and she ripped it out to start over.

Hrefna watched her as she continued with her own flawless weaving. "Selia," she began, "how much do you know about Ragnarr?"

Selia turned to the woman. "He killed his wife and his own son. I think he was . . ." She couldn't think of a Norse word to describe what she had gathered about Ragnarr; that he was mad, impaired, deranged. "A berserker," she murmured. That was a word she definitely knew.

Hrefna raised her brows, nodding. "Yes. He was. Of course no one was sure of that at the beginning. He was too young when he married my sister . . . sixteen, perhaps seventeen. Ragnarr was charming and very handsome. Evja was completely enamored of him. She told our father she would have no other for a husband, and would throw herself into the sea if he refused the match."

Selia swallowed, understanding exactly. Poor Evja, smoldering with desire for a man who blazed brighter than the sun. A man who was also deeply, irreparably flawed.

Hrefna continued. "I didn't live here then, of course. After they were married I would come to visit my sister occasionally to help her with the children, for she had her twins, Jorulf and Gudrun, only a year later. I was five years younger than Evja and it boded well that I practice for my own eventual household.

"As I came on these visits I saw a change in my sister. She was afraid of Ragnarr, and I saw bruises on her body. But she would never admit to me that he hurt her."

Hrefna looked over at her as if expecting a reaction to this, but Selia went on with her weaving even as she listened closely.

"Ragnarr had made quite a name for himself as a warlord by that time. He built this house, and he had riches and slaves beyond imagination." Hrefna dismissed the current situation of the farmstead with a wave of her hand. "This is nothing compared to how it was in Ragnarr's time. But he was never satisfied. He always needed more.

"By the time Dagrun was born, I was married to Olaf. I was busy with my household and soon had a child of my own. But the year Kolgrima turned five I received word Evja was ill and needed me to come. So I left Kolgrima with Olaf and I went that very day."

Closing her eyes, she breathed deeply, as if to center herself. "Evja was carrying Alrik and had taken to her bed. My sister was ill, but not in body. She was sick in her spirit, sick with what Ragnarr had done to her. She spoke to me of her desire to die, just climb to the top of the highest cliff and throw herself off, taking the child with her. But in her next sentence she would speak of killing Ragnarr, or killing his whore. She rambled on, and it took me quite a while to understand what had happened."

"His whore?"

"Ulfrik's mother, the slave girl Treasa. She was the daughter of an Irish lord Ragnarr had captured in a raid. He brought her home with the idea he would ransom her back to her father for a fortune. But he fell in love with the girl. Or became obsessed with her. I think those things were one and the same with Ragnarr. When Treasa's father and his men came to ransom her, Ragnarr killed them all, as he would not give the girl up."

Selia crossed herself, turning her body a bit so Hrefna wouldn't see the gesture. She said a silent prayer of thanks that her own family had been spared the wrath of Ragnarr's son.

Hrefna frowned, chewing her lip as she worked her loom. "Evja had accepted that Ragnarr consorted with thralls. It is a common occurrence, one that many wives overlook. But the way he treated this girl was different, as if not a slave at all, but more of a second wife. Her hair remained uncut, beautiful golden hair that fell nearly to her knees. She wore fine gowns and jewelry that he gave to her. He refused to allow her to sleep with the other thralls, and so had a room built on to the house for her."

Selia's eyes widened at this. How would she herself feel if Alrik built a bedroom on to the house for him to have convenient access to Muirin? She broke out in a clammy sweat.

"Which room?" she managed to squeak out.

"The room that Alrik now sleeps in. When Olaf and I came to take care of the boys, much later, I could only sleep in my sister's room. The thought of sleeping in the bedroom where Ragnarr had kept his concubine, causing my sister so much pain . . . well, I would have rather slept on the floor." Hrefna shuddered.

The massive bed Selia assumed had been constructed for Alrik had not been built for him after all, but for Ragnarr, and Treasa, his concubine. Ulfrik might have been conceived in that bed.

"What did Evja do?" Selia asked.

"There wasn't much she could do, other than divorce him. She was still in love with him, the fool, and as much as I tried to talk her into leaving Ragnarr, she refused."

"What is 'divorce?'"

Hrefna turned to her. "Divorce means to end the marriage. The husband and wife go their separate ways and are free to remarry." At Selia's blank look, Hrefna studied her. "Is there no divorce where you come from?"

She shook her head. "No. Only death can end a marriage."

Hrefna pondered this. "Well, those are the ways of the White Christ. Not our ways." She raised her eyebrows pointedly as if to imply that Selia would be free to divorce Alrik if she chose to do so.

"Alrik and I were married at the house of my priest," Selia added.

"What?" Hrefna dropped her hands from the loom. "My nephew married you in front of a Christian priest?"

"Yes."

The woman blew out her breath. "Why on earth would he do that? He hates their followers."

At Selia's soft gasp, Hrefna immediately apologized. "I'm sorry, my dear. I simply can't for the life of me understand why Alrik would do something like that."

Her face hot with emotion, Selia spoke more sharply than she meant to. "He did kill my priest."

Hrefna nodded as though that were a given, but seemed distracted. "Unless," she mused, "he knew of the ways of your people and he wanted to make sure you couldn't divorce him." She appeared to be quite taken aback by this devious possibility.

Nonplussed, Selia pondered the unfamiliar concept of divorce. When she married Alrik, she had done so with the knowledge it would end only with the death of one of them.

Why was Hrefna so shocked?

"He must care for you more than I realized," Hrefna mused. "How long did you know each other before you wed?"

Selia's cheeks heated as she looked away. "A day," she said quietly.

Dropping her hands from the loom again, Hrefna's chuckle grew to a deep belly laugh that brought tears to her eyes.

Selia scowled, not at all pleased at being laughed at. "Why is that amusing?"

Hrefna caught her breath and wiped at her eyes with her sleeve. "Oh, my dear child. Alrik is in love with you, can't you see? He went about it like the big, stupid man he is, but it's clear to me now. The way he behaves around you-mooning like a besotted boy-and how angry he became toward Ingrid over you. Now it all makes sense."

It absolutely did *not* make sense, but Selia's heart swelled a bit at Hrefna's declaration that Alrik was in love with her. She tried unsuccessfully to hide her smile.

Hrefna watched her, all laughter gone. "You love him too, don't you?"

"Yes, I think I do." *Or I had until this awkward mess with Muirin.*

As Alrik's aunt returned to her loom, Selia resumed her work as well. "Finish your story, Hrefna," she suggested. "About your sister."

Hrefna startled briefly. "Of course, let me see . . . Evja told me Ragnarr would no longer touch her after he brought the slave girl home. He would not come to Evja's bed as a husband should to his wife. So out of desperation, she worked a spell in the hope of regaining Ragnarr's affections. It succeeded only once, and that is how she became with child.

"By the time I was called to the house of my sister, she was full into her confinement, with the slave girl slightly farther along. I couldn't stand to watch how Ragnarr treated that girl, as if she were the first woman in the world to carry a child. As if my sister wasn't also with child by him, and indeed hadn't birthed three healthy babes already. He spoiled Treasa, petted her and fawned over her, and he wouldn't let her out of his sight for fear some harm would come to her. I think he worried—perhaps with good reason—that Evja would try to end the girl's life."

Hrefna took a deep breath before continuing. "It became evident around this time that Ragnarr's mind was failing. He insisted to everyone that the slave girl was a goddess, and that their unborn child would be immortal. If anyone tried to argue with him, he became even more incensed, so we finally stopped trying. After I had been here for about a fortnight, he accused me of conspiring with Evja to delude him. He sent me away, telling me he would kill me if I ever returned to his house."

Although Selia had heard part of this tale from Ulfrik, the depth of Ragnarr's madness stunned her. She shivered despite the warmth of the day.

"That was the last time I saw my sister," Hrefna murmured. "The rest of the story I heard later from Dagrun and Geirr. The boys never spoke of it, and still have not to this day."

Hrefna worked the loom, visibly distressed. "When Alrik and Ulfrik were four years old, Ragnarr's concubine again found herself with child. She had twice lost babes between Ulfrik and this one, so of course Ragnarr was suspicious of foul play. Gudrun had married and was living in Bjorgvin with her husband. I think she felt relief to be out of Ragnarr's house. Jorulf was fifteen and big for his age, nearly the size of his father. Dagrun told me they frequently argued. The boy hated Treasa, and was furious at the way Ragnarr shamed my sister with his behavior.

"Ragnarr regarded Ulfrik with favoritism, as if the boy were his legitimate offspring and not a thrall's child. Dagrun has a big heart, and she told me she loved both of her younger brothers equally, although Jorulf and Gudrun didn't feel the same about Ulfrik as they did Alrik. This led to a very strained home life for everyone involved.

"Then Treasa began to bleed, and it became apparent she was losing her child. But the babe would not be expelled—only blood, for days on end. Treasa grew feverish and eventually took to her bed. As she weakened, Ragnarr was convinced a spell had been placed on her. He blamed Evja.

"Ragnarr had never freed Treasa, so she was still by law a thrall although he didn't treat her as such. Before she died, she begged Ragnarr to free their son, Ulfrik, as she feared for his safety. A slave's life is worth next to nothing, but to take the life of a free man or child is a serious crime. So when the slave girl died and Ragnarr freed her son, my sister could take no more. I wonder if she did plan to kill the boy. I'll never know."

Selia shuddered at how casually Hrefna could speak of a potential murder plot on a child. Poor Ulfrik. Did he know these grim details?

"Did Evja kill Treasa, as Ragnarr thought?"

Hrefna paused. "I don't know," she admitted. "Dagrun said she was not aware of such a thing. But she was only ten years old at the time, and of course viewed things as a child. Besides, it didn't matter if Evja killed Treasa or not, because Ragnarr was convinced she had. The day of Treasa's burial they argued bitterly. And the argument ended with him snapping my sister's neck."

Selia expelled a shaky breath. She had known how this brutal story would conclude. "And Jorulf?"

"He stepped in to try to save his mother. And when he could not, he drew his sword on his father, an insult which Ragnarr could not stomach . . . and so Ragnarr slew him as well."

Selia's hands trembled on the loom. "How could he kill his own child?"

"Because Ragnarr had gone completely mad. Dagrun and the boys witnessed everything. Dagrun said she had never seen such a look on Ragnarr's face as he killed her mother and brother. She thought in his bloodlust he would kill them all. So she took her younger brothers and ran. They escaped to their grandfather's house, and when Geirr discovered what his son had done, he took a party of men to find Ragnarr. They slew him here in this house."

Selia swallowed. Would she ever grow accustomed to the violent ways of this new land? Little wonder Finngalls could kill a foreigner without a second thought, if they took the lives of their own children when deemed necessary.

"Selia." Hrefna gained her wavering attention. "There are two reasons I'm telling you all of this. The first is simply for your own safety-you need to be very, very careful around Alrik when he's angry. We have all learned how to handle him. Or at least all of us have but Ingrid, who insists on taunting him like a caged bear. But you, child, you need to be aware of how dangerous it is to be near him when he's in his rage." She nodded toward Selia's shoulder.

"And," she continued, "you need to know when Alrik leaves, it is a good thing. Sometimes he chops wood or spars with Ulfrik, but when he leaves it's because he fears himself, of what he might do. I think his worst worry is that of turning into his father. He left because he feared he would kill Ingrid otherwise."

Selia pondered this for a moment. Perhaps Alrik's abrupt departure had not been the cowardly move she had taken it for after all. "Hrefna, do you think he will ever not be—" She found herself unable to say the word. As though to speak it would make it more real.

Not be a berserker.

"I honestly don't know," Hrefna replied. "I love Alrik like a son, but I realized long ago he was . . . damaged. There is something wrong with him, something beyond his control, and I feel sorry for him. I want more than anything for him to be happy."

Hrefna did understand. She loved Alrik as much as Selia did, perhaps even more. "I want him to be happy also," she whispered.

"I will say, Alrik has learned to restrain himself somewhat better as he's gotten older," Hrefna reflected. "He was quite a terror growing up. You should be glad you didn't know him then."

So Alrik's current behavior-which included nearly killing his daughter—was an improvement upon his behavior as a youth? Selia absently rubbed the rune carvings on her ring as she pondered this new information.

Hrefna noticed the gesture and gave her a puzzled look. Selia held out her hand for the woman's inspection. "Alrik gave me this ring. He said it would protect me from him."

Squinting at the tiny carvings, Hrefna spun the ring around on Selia's finger several times as she interpreted the runes. She met Selia's eyes with a bewilderment in hers.

"This is very powerful magic, Selia. It is a protection spell, clearly a death curse for anyone who attempts to harm the wearer of the ring."

Selia steadied herself against the post of the loom. Alrik had the ring specifically made for her as protection from his rages. He was willing to face death if unable to control himself. Furthermore, he had given it to her *after* he had learned of her shameful spells, even knowing she too was damaged and possibly brimming with dark magic.

"He must love you more than I even realized," Hrefna said.

Selia stared at the ring on her finger. If Alrik tried to hurt her he would die. Her heart rebelled at this thought, and it was all she could do to keep herself from pulling the ring off. That was why Ulfrik hadn't told her what the runes meant. He thought if she knew Alrik's life would be at risk, she would refuse to wear the ring.

Ulfrik, true to character, had discerned Selia's love for his brother even before she admitted her feelings to herself.

Chapter 19

Selia slept poorly that night in the big bed. She had so quickly grown accustomed to Alrik sleeping beside her, and now found she could no longer sleep well alone. Hrefna's assurance that he'd be gone a sennight at the longest did not help Selia.

It sounded like an eternity.

Ingrid was unharmed aside from some bruises and a tender spot on her head. She was staying with Bjorn Sturlason and his family, the blacksmith who lived on Alrik's property a mile or so into the woods. Ketill's youngest son, Bolli-who, along with Riki and Skagi was Ingrid's cousin on her mother's side-was Bjorn's apprentice. The boy was sixteen, just a year older than Ingrid, and the two were as close as siblings.

But even knowing Ingrid had suffered no permanent damage, the image remained in Selia's head of how Alrik had snatched her up and thrown her across the room. True, she was a hateful and evil-tempered girl, but no child deserved to be treated so by her own father.

She rubbed a hand over her belly. Although it was as flat as it had always been, she had a nagging suspicion she carried Alrik's child. She had not bled since her marriage, which by itself was not unusual as her cycles had never been regular. But the absence of her cycle seemed more concerning when she took into account the recent sensitivity of her nose and stomach, her ravenous hunger, and the heavy, aching fullness in her breasts.

Aside from the very real concern she might not survive

childbirth, there was another worry that plagued her. Most wives, upon realizing they carried their first child, would assume their husband would make a good father, and would protect his children from the evils of the world. But Alrik was a father already, and she had seen how he treated his daughter. He appeared to despise the girl. When he wasn't ignoring her, he was beating her.

How could Alrik teach a child right from wrong when he himself didn't seem to know?

Selia had taken Niall's affection for her for granted. Regardless of how he felt about her spells, Niall loved her. And she wasn't even his daughter by birth. Although strict, he had always been a kind and patient father, never raising a hand to her in anger. How could she have known not all fathers were like him?

Ingrid was without a doubt Alrik's child. Did he hate the girl because she was so like him? Or so like Ragnarr? Regardless, he treated his slaves better than he treated his own daughter.

And therein posed yet another problem-Muirin, the beautiful thrall who might be with child by Alrik. Hrefna had assured Selia he cared nothing for the girl, and the babe was most likely not his anyway. The word of a thrall could not be trusted, and Hrefna had seen Ulfrik sniffing around the girl more often than not. He seemed to have an affinity for the slaves, especially the Irish ones.

But the irony of the situation wasn't lost on Selia. She and the slave girl might both be carrying a child of Alrik's. As much as he tried otherwise, he seemed destined to repeat the sins of his father.

Selia gritted her teeth. She would not die a tragic death at the hands of her husband. Muirin must leave the farmstead; that was the only option at this point. And not return.

There was no light coming in from the smoke hole, and although it was the middle of the night, Selia knew she would not be able to go back to sleep. She dressed quickly, then slipped out to the barn.

There was a crick in Selia's back from sitting on the short, uncomfortable stool, and she was doing her best to stretch as she heard the barn door open. Muirin walked toward the sheep, feeling her way in the semi-darkness. She seemed confused when she couldn't locate the pail.

"Muirin," Selia said, causing the girl to scream and jump back in fright.

"M-mistress?" She squinted toward where Selia was sitting.

"Yes. I've been waiting for you for hours." She motioned for Muirin to come and sit next to her.

The slave's eyes grew wide at this. She stepped forward nevertheless, as one who knew disobedience was not an option. She was trembling as she sat down.

Selia watched her. "I'm not here to hurt you. I just need to know what happened between you and Alrik. That's all."

"Please." Muirin's voice was so soft, Selia had to lean forward to hear her. "If I'm late again, Mistress Hrefna will be very angry—"

Selia cut her off. "I've already milked them all." She waved a hand to the sheep. "So we have plenty of time."

The slave squirmed on the stool. "He . . . might not like me to talk to you."

"I can handle him," Selia said with more conviction than she felt. Muirin blinked at her as though this were the most foolish thing she had ever heard. Selia forged on. "I want the truth. Is Alrik the father of your child?"

The girl flushed. "I don't know, honestly I don't, Mistress. But Ulfrik said he is willing to claim it."

Of course he was. Should Selia expect anything less from him? He had been cleaning up after his brother for years.

But Muirin was hiding something—that was obvious. "Tell me how this happened," Selia insisted.

The girl chewed at her fingernail for a moment. "I was living in Bjorgvin. At the brothel. The master, Alrik . . . he bought me. I think he was lonely. He told me his wife had died and I reminded him of her. He brought me here. Everything was fine at first, but then . . ." Muirin stopped as if lost in the memory. Her luminous eyes glittered with tears as she looked at Selia. "Are you sure you want to know this?"

"Yes," she replied. *No,* her mind whispered.

Muirin swallowed. "He changed. He would hurt me . . . or just humiliate me. Usually when we were alone, but sometimes Ulfrik saw, too. Ulfrik said something to him about the way he was treating me . . . and the master got so angry. He accused Ulfrik of wanting me for himself. He said I belonged to him, and if his brother wanted me it could only happen if he was there, too. Because I was his property. It was as if he taunted him, to prove that Ulfrik was no better than he was."

Selia wrinkled her brow. "I don't understand."

The slave averted her gaze. "I had to lie with them both," she said. "At the same time. So you see why either one of them could be the father of my child."

A chilled sweat broke out over Selia's body. This was worse, much worse than she could ever have imagined. What had possessed her to come to the barn this morning? Some things were better left unknown.

"I'm sorry, Mistress," Muirin appealed. "You said you wanted to know."

"Yes, I did say that," she croaked. "Please, finish."

"After that night, the master didn't want me anymore. It was as though he was satisfied he had been able to dishonor his brother. He told Ulfrik he was done with me, that Ulfrik could have me as much as he wanted. Then soon after, they left to go a-viking . . . and you came back with them."

Selia closed her eyes and sat in silence for a moment. She felt dirty, covered in a filth she wouldn't be able to wash off. But there was one more question, the question that continued to gnaw at her. "Muirin . . . did you ever love him? Alrik?"

The girl paused and looked away. "Yes, perhaps at first. I thought I did."

The barn was suddenly stifling, thick with the musky odor of sheep. Selia stood, swallowing the bile that rose in her throat, but the slave laid a timid hand on her arm to stop her.

"Mistress, you must understand I am unable to refuse my master if he comes to me. Ever."

Selia understood the implication. If Alrik changed his mind and decided he wanted Muirin again after all, there would be nothing the girl could do about it.

With a shaky breath, Selia willed herself not to vomit.

Alrik remained gone for several more days. Selia burned for him, both wanting him and despising him, sometimes at the same time. How could she still care for a man such as Alrik? Yet more proof of her own flawed nature. As if she needed any.

Ulfrik had been avoiding her since Ingrid's announcement about Muirin. He had been her nearly constant companion on the ship as he helped her with her Norse, and Selia found she now missed her friend with a surprising intensity. Hadn't they shared a connection, an affinity of sorts? But perhaps she had been mistaken. Perhaps their conversations and laughter had been only a mild diversion for him, a way to pass the time as they sailed.

What did she really know about Ulfrik, anyway? Apparently much less than she thought she had. Although she could accept-barely-the fact of her husband's unnatural desires, she couldn't stomach the thought of his brother agreeing to the act Muirin had spoken of. But why? He was a man, no better than any other.

Yet she could not shake her disappointment in him. That he had been keeping his distance from her seemed a clear indication of guilt.

Despite the master's absence, the rhythms of the farmstead continued smoothly. Everyone, from Hrefna down to the lowliest thrall, carried on with their work, unperturbed. Alrik was frequently gone on raids, and when he was home they were all accustomed to him disappearing for days at a time. The farm did not need him to survive.

Although the slaves did most of the manual labor, no one was exempt from work. Ulfrik and Olaf were gone most of the day, busy overseeing fence repairs and checking on the livestock. Selia and Hrefna stayed at the house, spinning wool, weaving, and sewing. This took up an enormous amount of time. Hrefna was not only responsible for making the clothes for everyone in the house, but the sails for the dragonship as well.

In Ireland, most people possessed only one or two outfits of clothing. Here it was much different. The Finngalls seemed enamored with clothing, the men as well as the women. Hrefna had no less than seven gowns, each more colorful and beautifully trimmed than the next, and she changed her clothes daily. Alrik, too, had several complete changes of clothing in one of his trunks.

When Hrefna realized Selia had only one gown and one shift, she was shocked. Declaring such an oversight simply would not do, Hrefna made Selia's wardrobe a priority.

So the days passed rather quickly as Selia worked beside the woman. Selia told stories of her early life, of Ainnileas, Niall, and Eithne. Hrefna particularly liked to hear of Ainnileas' silly antics and frequent jests. But although she trusted Hrefna, she could not quite bring herself to reveal Niall was not her natural father.

Hrefna also shared confidences, of how much she missed her daughter Kolgrima as well as her grandchildren. A woman's lot included being apart from her own children.

To Selia, it seemed unusual to have only one child. All of the families she had known were big—many with half a dozen or more children. When she asked Hrefna about this, the woman smiled sadly.

"I had five more children after Kolgrima. But they all died, every one. They came too early no matter what I did, and they died before they could even take a breath."

Selia sucked in her own breath at this, and her hand fluttered over her belly for a moment before she could stop herself. She looked up at Hrefna to see if she had noticed, but the woman was staring at the loom, lost in her own grief.

"Oh, Hrefna. I am so sorry."

Hrefna nodded. "I finally consulted a cunning woman. She told me I was cursed, and there was no cure for it. No child from my womb would be birthed healthy. So she told me the ingredients for a tea to keep Olaf's seed from taking hold."

Selia did her best to hide her shock. She had never heard of such a thing. Wasn't it blasphemous, trying to control something which was surely in the realm of the divine?

But the Finngalls had no concept of sin. If their gods allowed them to divorce, perhaps they allowed them free will in this matter, too.

"You know, Selia," Hrefna said thoughtfully, "you might want to consider taking that tea yourself."

"What?" she sputtered.

"My dear child, you are very small. And Alrik's children are very large. His first wife was a good-sized woman, but even she had difficulty birthing his babes. The last one nearly killed her. Eydis so wanted to give him a son. I understand you love him, Selia. But I think that having a child by Alrik might not be in your best interests."

Selia was speechless.

Hrefna patted her hand, misinterpreting her hesitation. "Just consider it. That is all I ask."

"Hrefna," Selia whispered, blinking back tears, "I think I am already with child."

"Oh." Hrefna eyed her with a grave expression. "Does he know?"

She shook her head.

"Then it's not too late. There are things that can be done, if you like."

Selia didn't try to hide her shock this time. To contemplate such a thing . . . "No, Hrefna. I could not do that."

"I guessed as much. I just don't want to see any harm come to you. I like you, dear child."

Selia sank onto the bench, dropping her face in her hands. How had her life become so complicated? Not only was she not expected to live through delivering her babe, but her husband had most likely gotten a slave girl with child as well. Her husband who was, by his aunt's own admission, dangerously unstable. And currently missing.

Hrefna sat next to Selia and curved her arm around her shoulders, making soothing noises. That was all it took for the dam to break, and before she knew it she was sobbing against Hrefna's neck. The older woman held her until her sobs turned to hiccups, and then she wiped Selia's face on a corner of her gown.

Selia stared at the floor, sniffling. Lately, her emotions were so hard to control. What must Hrefna think of her? If Selia wanted to be viewed as a woman and not a silly child, surely this was not the way to do it.

"Hrefna," she mumbled, "do you think this will turn out like it did for Evja and Treasa?"

"What?" Hrefna took her by the chin, giving her a stern look. "Of course not. I told you Alrik cares nothing for that thrall."

Unconvinced, Selia persisted. "Does Muirin look like Eydis?"

"A bit, yes. But that means nothing. I don't know that Alrik ever really loved Eydis. I honestly never thought he was capable of loving anyone, except for perhaps his children."

Selia gaped at the woman. If what Alrik felt for Ingrid was love, she felt immensely sorry for anyone he hated.

Hrefna gestured with her free hand as though reading Selia's thoughts. "Not Ingrid so much. Their kinship has always been strained. They are too alike. No, I meant his younger daughters, Adis and Frida. They died with their mother. And whatever goodness there was left in Alrik seemed to have died with them."

"What happened to them?" Selia asked hesitantly.

"They were poisoned, I think. No one knows for sure. It happened last year when the men had gone a-viking. Ingrid was being even more difficult than usual, and her mother was at her wits' end. And Ulfrik's wife was here, too."

"Ulfrik's wife?" Selia echoed. "Ulfrik is married?"

"Why yes," Hrefna said, as though surprised she didn't know. "He was. He married Eydis' sister Hilda several years ago. He has his own farmstead-Geirr's old house-but he wanted Hilda to stay with her sister while he was gone, since Hilda was large with their first child."

Selia fumed. After spending nearly every waking hour with Ulfrik on the ship, one would think he might have mentioned the fact that he was married. But why did Hrefna speak of Ulfrik's wife as if she no longer existed? Had she and the babe died in childbirth?

Or had they died along with Eydis and her daughters?

"Ingrid was making everyone in the house miserable," Hrefna continued. "Finally, I could stand it no more, and I offered to take her to stay with Kolgrima for the remainder of the summer. She has kept Ingrid for us before. Ingrid is kinder to her than to anyone else, and that's saying quite a bit. Eydis and Hilda were greatly relieved at the thought of a break from Ingrid, I think. Ingrid and I set off for Kolgrima's farmstead, along with a few thralls. We had been there no more than a day or two when Bolli rode up with the news. The look on his face was such that I hope to never see again."

Hrefna quieted for a moment, lost in the memory, then glanced at Selia as if she had forgotten she was there. "They were dead . . . they were all dead. Eydis, Hilda, and the little girls. No one knew what happened-they had been fine one day and dead the next. I think that was the first time I had seen Ingrid cry since she was a small child."

Selia's eyes were brimming with tears as well. It didn't seem fair that one family should be shrouded with so much sadness, so much pain. "But why did you think they were poisoned?" she queried.

"It was the ale . . . it had to be the ale. By the time we got back two thralls had died as well. Thralls don't drink the same ale as we do," Hrefna explained. "They drink a weak brew, or water. The fine ale is reserved for the family. But the two thralls, thinking no one would be the wiser, had apparently helped themselves to the opened cask of ale and also died. I can think of no other explanation."

"Who would do such a thing?"

"It had to be one of the other thralls." Hrefna's voice hardened. "The thralls brew the ale. They have access to the alehouse, and they open each new cask as it's needed. One of them must have seen an opportunity and took it. But what I'll never understand is why the thrall waited until Alrik was gone to do it. Why kill women and children when it's the master you hate?"

Someone despised Alrik so much that they killed his family to punish him. They hated him enough not to kill him, but to watch him suffer-to watch the anguish of losing what he loved most slowly destroy him. The cold calculation of such an act sent a shiver up Selia's spine.

"When the men returned, it was the hardest thing I have ever had to do to tell them what had happened. I've never seen Alrik more enraged—he killed half a dozen thralls, at least, before Olaf and Ulfrik could stop him. He wanted to kill them all, slay every one of them and be done with it, but we were able to talk sense into him. It would have been much too expensive to replace so many thralls. So Olaf took them to Bjorgvin and sold them, and he bought new ones."

Selia took a shaky breath, sick with the tragedy of it all. The death of Eydis and her two young daughters, of Ulfrik's wife and unborn child. Not to mention all of the slaves-most likely innocent-killed at Alrik's hand. No wonder people still spoke of the curse of Ragnarr, for clearly there was a dark cloud of misfortune hovering over his house.

"I don't think he mourned much for Eydis. She was a good woman and very comely, yet they were not well suited to each other. But his girls . . . he did love them. He doesn't speak of them and he refuses to visit their graves, but I know it's because he cares too much. And when he looks at Ingrid . . . I think she knows he wonders why she survived but her sisters did not, and it makes her furious. It's why she taunts him so."

No wonder Ingrid was so hateful to everyone. She had lost her entire family except for the father who despised her. Selia didn't like the girl any more than she had before, but she understood her better now.

"Are Ingrid and Muirin friends?"

"Friends?" Hrefna laughed. "Of course not. Why would Ingrid be friends with a thrall? No, she only said what she did to get a rise out of her father. And to hurt you, of course. I love Ingrid as my own, but she is not easy to live with. It will take a very brave man—or a foolish one—to ever marry that girl."

As Selia struggled with her uncertainty, Hrefna placed her hands on her shoulders and regarded her with a stern expression. "Selia, do not concern yourself with Muirin. These things always have a way of resolving themselves. Ulfrik will claim the child, and we will forget about this entire mess soon enough."

Chapter 20

Suffering another sleepless night, Selia found it maddening to be so exhausted, yet to lie awake with her thoughts in turmoil. What if Alrik never returned? Although Hrefna had assured her this was typical for him-he was only hunting and would be back as soon as he had killed something-she was unconvinced. Could he be hurt, alone in the woods, slowly bleeding to death? Or was he with another woman, warm and snug in her bed? Both images were equally torturous.

The silence of the house was broken by the soft sound of the front door closing. She stilled, holding her breath to listen—had he finally come home? But several long moments went by. It wasn't Alrik.

But not Hrefna or Olaf either, for if they needed to use the privy they would have gone out the kitchen door. It must be Ulfrik who was awake in the middle of the night, no doubt returning from a visit to Muirin. His bench was in the main room, so he would use the front door when he found it necessary to sneak out. *Or in.*

Grumbling, Selia rolled over. Why hadn't Ulfrik trusted her enough to tell her about his wife and babe? If he had his own farmstead as Hrefna had claimed, then why on earth did he stay here at his brother's house instead of going home? And furthermore, why didn't he take his lover with him?

She flipped onto her back, her anger rising by the minute. Did he think he could just ignore her and she would forget they had ever been friends? Did the time they had spent together on the ship mean nothing to him? She was owed an explanation at the very least.

Selia flung the blankets aside, pulling her gown over her head with a curse. She didn't bother with shoes, but stormed barefoot into the main room. She stopped in front of Ulfrik's bench, hesitating for a moment. There was no movement behind his closed curtain. Perhaps it hadn't been him coming in the door, after all.

"Ulfrik," she whispered, "Are you awake?"

A few seconds of silence, then a rustling sound. He drew the curtain back and stared at her. "What are you doing out here?"

She frowned. "I need to speak with you."

"In the middle of the night?" As he sat up, the blanket fell into his lap. She averted her eyes from his bare chest as Ulfrik hoisted the blanket around his shoulders.

"Yes, now," she insisted. "You've been avoiding me since Ingrid said what she did about Muirin. You only come home to eat, then you leave without explanation. Why? I'm not a child, you know."

"I've never treated you like a child."

Was he trying to humor her? She clenched her fists. "I know everything," she hissed. "All of it."

He nodded, slowly. "Muirin told me you spoke to her."

She expelled a breath, deflated. Selia had assumed he had been keeping his distance from her so as to dodge an awkward conversation about who had fathered Muirin's child. "If you knew, then why have you been avoiding me?"

His eyes narrowed, and in the dim light he looked exactly like his brother. He spoke with more force than she was accustomed to hearing from him. "Because I'm not like Alrik-when I hurt someone I feel badly about it. And my brother just leaves as always, letting everyone else repair the mess he made. Muirin doesn't deserve this. Neither do you. But there is nothing I can do about it, nothing to make this right . . . and I don't like myself very much for it."

"Oh." She looked away, unable to suffer his unblinking gaze. What a fool she was. This had nothing to do with her, and everything to do with Ulfrik's own guilty conscience. "But if you care for Muirin, why not take her away from here? Hrefna said you have your own house."

He gazed at her for a long time before he spoke. "Yes, I have my grandfather's house. But I would rather not go back there. Did Hrefna also tell you that is where I lived with my wife?"

She nodded, flushing.

"Would you have me leave, then? Is that what you want?"

"No, of course not. I just thought–if you loved Muirin—"

"I don't. But I will take responsibility for her child. If it means that much to you, I will leave, and I will take her with me." His voice held hurt.

How thoughtless of her to suggest he take his lover to the home he had shared with his wife, who had died carrying their child. She should have realized the reason he remained here, at Alrik's house. The memories at his own home were too painful to bear.

Selia wanted to sink into the floor. Oh, why hadn't she just stayed in bed?

"I don't want you to leave, Ulfrik. I shouldn't have been angry with you. It's just that . . . I miss you."

"You have Hrefna now."

"But I still miss you," she said quietly. "You were my only friend on the ship. You were the only one who was kind to me. And now I've hurt your feelings."

He sighed. "I will always be your friend. But things are different here than they were on the ship. You don't need help with your Norse any longer. There is no reason for us to spend so much time together now. And if we do . . . well, people will think wrongly. Surely you understand."

Selia looked at him without answering. If she spoke, the hot tears that were building up in the back of her throat would spill out.

Ulfrik started to reach out for her, then thought better of it and dropped his hand into his lap. "You shouldn't even be out here now," he cautioned. "Go back to bed, Selia."

She stood there for several moments, reluctant to admit he was right. If someone-Hrefna or Olaf, or heaven forbid, Ingrid-saw them right now they would assume the worst. And if Alrik found out . . . well, she didn't even want to think about that. Her jealous husband was quick to jump to conclusions. Her decision to sneak out here to speak to Ulfrik had not only been foolish, but potentially dangerous for both of them.

"I'm sorry," Selia choked out, then hurried to her room, closing the door quietly behind her.

Selia slept later than usual the next morning. She stretched, slow and languid, and ignored the bustling sounds coming from the kitchen. She rolled over, promising herself she would arise in a few minutes.

She saw a pair of large male boots out of the corner of her eye and sat up with a start, all thoughts of sleep gone. Alrik was sitting at the little table, his long legs stretched out before him with his feet crossed at the ankles. He studied her with his piercing gaze, smiling his most charming smile, and Selia's heart fluttered inside her chest.

No. She was furious with him. He had gotten a slave with child, then left the farmstead without any explanation. She couldn't let him return as though nothing had happened. No self-respecting wife would allow that, and although *she* knew she had lost all self-respect when it came to Alrik Ragnarson, she would be damned if she was going to let him know it.

He crossed the room to sit next to her on the bed. The mattress gave under his weight, and Selia found herself tipping toward him. She moved farther away, shooting what she hoped was an icy glare in his direction.

"So you're still angry with me, little one?" He cupped her face, stroking her jaw with his thumb.

Despite herself, she felt her body grow warm with his touch. He was so close she could smell him-both the strong soap he had recently used, as well as the underlying male scent that was uniquely his. With fading resolve, she clambered out of bed to get away from him.

Careful to stay out of his reach, she stood before him. The chilly morning air rent through her thin shift, and Selia crossed her arms to hide her erect nipples.

Laughing, he crossed his own arms as he regarded her. "Are we playing a game then, Selia? You know I'll win."

"You conceited bastard," she spat in Irish.

He raised his eyebrows, not knowing what she said but obviously suspecting the worst.

She continued in Norse. "Alrik, why did you marry me?"

An impatient noise escaped him as he reached for her, but she stepped back. His gaze met hers, all humor gone from his face.

Selia spoke quickly. "I am your wife, not your concubine. I need to know if I should expect my husband to lie with the slaves, or only with me."

"The child isn't mine."

She gestured with an impatient hand. Whether the child was his or Ulfrik's didn't really matter now-it had all taken place before their marriage. What mattered was what happened from this moment on. Would he continue to bed the thralls? Was that the way of all Finngall men?

Although her Norse had vastly improved since she had married Alrik, it was still frustrating not to have the words to explain herself completely. Instead, she reached for his hand. "Alrik," she said as her tears spilled over, "I only need to know you will not do this again."

He closed his eyes for a moment with a sigh, then dropped his hand to his lap.

So this is my answer. She started to turn away from him, but he caught her wrist. "I married you, Selia—isn't that enough?"

She wiped her tears away. How could he think she would be satisfied to be married to a man who would continue to humiliate her? "No, it is not enough. I wish you had not married me. I would rather be your slave. It would not hurt as much as this."

He pulled her into a tight embrace. "You are my wife, Selia." His voice sounded hoarse in her ear.

"But you will grow tired of me."

"I won't." His lips found hers, hard and insistent, as if to prove that fact to her. She held herself stiffly, refusing to respond, despite the warmth that spread through her body at his touch.

Alrik's hand cupped the base of her skull, holding her head as he kissed her. His lips followed the trail of tears as they coursed over her chin toward her throat. He gripped her hair to force her head back slightly as his hot mouth brushed her skin.

Selia bit back a moan. *Bastard.* Did he think she could be placated with desire? Although she could not deny him her body, she could deny him her pleasure. She would die before she would let him know how much she wanted him.

He seemed to understand what she was doing, and he didn't care for it. He shook her a bit, scowling; held her wrists behind her back, causing her breasts to strain against the fabric of her shift. Then his mouth was on her, suckling at her sensitive nipples right through the fabric.

She felt her knees begin to buckle. She couldn't hold out for much longer. He teased her with his teeth, and a moan escaped her lips.

Alrik laughed in triumph, flipping her onto the bed with a wicked smile.

Their coupling was over quickly, as always when he was angry. Alrik found his release, rolling from her with a snarl. Selia sat up and tugged at her shift to cover her nudity. She met his gaze, careful to keep her face emotionless.

He appeared to be a bit ashamed of himself as he fastened his breeches. He stared at her for a long moment.

"Don't play games with me, Selia," he finally warned. "I'll always win."

She dressed without another word to Alrik, nearly running headlong into Ingrid as she hurried from the bedroom. The girl glared at her. Already furious, Selia had to restrain herself from slapping Ingrid's hateful face. The face that looked so much like Alrik's. She was no match for her husband in size or strength and would never be able to physically hurt him, but she sized up his insufferable daughter with a shrewd eye.

The girl seemed to sense this unexpected edge in Selia, and did what she did best—egg it on. Her eyes narrowed at Selia. "Whore," she mouthed, with a smile of pure evil.

In an instant, Selia's hand whipped through the air, landing on Ingrid's cheek with a resounding smack. The girl gaped at her, speechless. Selia watched with satisfaction as the pink outline of her handprint arose on Ingrid's face.

Ingrid lunged for her with a cry of fury, knocking her to the ground as she tried to claw at her face. Selia was vaguely aware of Hrefna's voice shouting at them to stop. Ingrid was stronger and heavier than she had anticipated, but Selia had spent most of her life wrestling with Ainnileas. She had learned long ago how to deal with a stronger opponent.

She grabbed a fistful of Ingrid's hair and pulled with a brutal twist. The girl screamed, grabbing for Selia's hand in an attempt to keep her hair from being ripped from her scalp. Selia jabbed her knee into the girl's ribs, knocking the breath from her.

Ingrid gasped and sputtered, and Selia took advantage of the moment by rolling on top of her. But suddenly, someone grabbed her from behind and lifted her off Ingrid.

Alrik held her still as she struggled and cursed against

his arm. Ingrid leapt to rush toward Selia, but was jerked back with a snap as Ulfrik grabbed her.

"Irish bitch!" she screamed, fighting to get away from Ulfrik.

"*Enough!*" Alrik bellowed. Ingrid shut her mouth but continued to glare at Selia with murderous eyes.

Hrefna hurried to Selia, eyeing her for any obvious wounds. "Are you all right? Ingrid, if you hurt her—"

The girl could not contain herself. "If *I* hurt *her*? That bitch attacked me, I tell you!"

"*Ingrid.*" Alrik released Selia to tower over his daughter threateningly. Ingrid stood tall, just as fierce, and Selia cringed despite herself as she waited for the inevitable blow.

But Alrik did not raise a hand to her. "You have been allowed to run wild for too long. You have been coddled and spoiled just to keep the peace in this house. I tell you now, that time is over. You are not a child. Indeed, you are old enough to be married although I would have to search far and wide to find a man foolish enough to marry you. But I swear this to you—if you raise a hand to my wife again, if you so much as speak to her with disrespect, I will find a husband for you. I will pay him to take you, if need be, to be rid of you once and for all."

The girl stared up at her father in disbelief. She looked around at her family, imploring them with her eyes to intervene on her behalf. No one made a move to help her. The look on Ingrid's face was pitiful to behold; equal parts anger, humiliation, and fear as she realized what the consequences would be if she erred once more.

Selia was unable to gloat. As much as she hated Ingrid, she felt an odd twinge of sympathy for her. She looked away, pulling the strands of Ingrid's hair, pale and insubstantial as a spider's web, from her fingers.

Alrik had been right earlier. He would always win.

Chapter 21

The night felt thick with unresolved tension. Selia remained cool toward Alrik, and he, in response, drank cup after cup of ale. Ingrid was still furious with everyone. She sat far in the corner, muttering to herself as she mended her gown where it had ripped in the fight.

Selia remained at the hearth, spinning wool with Hrefna, and did her best to ignore Alrik. When she accidentally met his gaze, she sat mesmerized for a few seconds as the firelight danced in their blue depths.

Then she forced herself to look away. She loved him, she wanted him, and nothing was going to change that fact. But the thought of him bedding another woman was so painful, it stole her breath.

Ulfrik quietly suggested a game of tafl. Alrik turned his gaze on his brother, glowering at him for a long moment before he grunted his assent. He turned his back on Selia to set up the board with Ulfrik, and although no one in the room made a sound, it was as though a collective sigh could be felt from the family.

Keir moved toward Alrik to refill his empty cup, but Ulfrik made eye contact with the slave and shook his head, almost imperceptibly. She went back to her corner, waiting.

Selia had never seen Ulfrik lose at tafl. Hrefna had told her he never lost unless he was either very drunk or trying to humor Alrik. Yet Ulfrik now played with such hesitancy, it seemed he'd changed his strategy as a way to calm the beast that raged inside his brother.

Alrik made another shortsighted move, and Ulfrik paused for a moment with his hand hovering over the board. But instead of taking the opening, Ulfrik moved his tafl piece as if oblivious of his brother's mistake.

Selia made a reproachful noise without meaning to, and Ulfrik looked up at her. Their gaze locked and she saw a flicker of surprise cross his face.

"What is it?" Hrefna asked, apparently noticing the odd exchange between them.

"Nothing," Selia shrugged. "I thought he would make a different move."

Alrik turned around to face her with a patronizing expression. "Don't interrupt."

"I'm sorry."

The game ended after just a few more moves. Alrik laughed, victorious. Perhaps Ulfrik had been right to throw the game. It was no different than when he sparred with his brother. It was no different than when she herself had taken Alrik into the woods to let him use her body to release his anger. It was all a means to an end; a more stable Alrik, which translated to a happier and more peaceful household.

He had vowed to Ingrid that the family would no longer coddle her and let her have her way, yet he had completely missed the irony of that statement. The family all coddled him much more than they did Ingrid. Each one of them tiptoed around him to keep him from exploding. Alrik was like a child who had been spoiled into thinking only his own selfish needs mattered. He had never been taught to respect the viewpoint of others.

How much of his behavior was due to his innate flaws, and how much was inadvertently encouraged by his family?

Alrik stood with a long, self-satisfied stretch, gloating over his win. His brother tipped his head toward him in an expression of gracious defeat. What a good liar Ulfrik was. Selia smirked at him over her spinning, but he kept his gaze averted.

"I'm going to bed." Alrik shot a pointed look at Selia over his shoulder, clearly expecting her to follow him. He staggered off to the bedroom, and Hrefna sighed in relief.

Selia began to put her spinning away when Ulfrik called, "Selia, do you want to play?"

She shot a teasing smile in his direction, detecting his embarrassment at having to lose to his brother. "Not if you allow me to win," she said.

"I won't."

Selia glanced at the bedroom door where she knew Alrik waited for her. If she wasn't still upset with him, she would have gone to him without hesitation. But now she wavered.

"Yes," she finally replied, "I will play with you."

Smiling, Ulfrik began to set up the board at the table. Selia gave him a puzzled look. It was customary to play tafl with the two opponents sitting across from each other, their knees nearly touching. The tafl board would then be balanced on the laps of the two men.

"You're too small," Ulfrik explained. "We'll play at the table so the pieces stay on the board."

Hrefna and Olaf gathered around the table as well. The woman's spinning lay forgotten on the hearth. Even Ingrid turned her body slightly to be able to watch, although she was careful to keep her face scornful.

The game took much longer than when Alrik or Olaf played, as both Selia and Ulfrik considered each move carefully. Early on, however, he made a move that was uncharacteristically thoughtless, and she frowned at him.

"Ulfrik," she chided in Irish. "I won't play with you if you insist on throwing the game. That's insulting."

He chuckled but didn't make any more foolish moves. His face was more animated than she had ever seen it, with flushed cheeks and eyes glowing in excitement. She grinned at him and he smiled right back. Their friendship seemed to have been magically restored with a single game of tafl, all his reservations about showing too much interest in her, gone.

"How long has it been since you had any real competition?" she asked in Irish.

He laughed. "You think very highly of yourself, don't you?"

"Let me answer that after I win."

Selia made her choice and moved the piece, but realized with Ulfrik's next move she had misjudged him. After another few moves he had beaten her.

She laughed in grudging admiration. "I'm going to start calling you Ulfrik the Devious." She hadn't dared to continue their nickname game since things had gone so badly after Mani, but it seemed safe now that Alrik was behind closed doors.

He chuckled, but didn't return the nickname with one of his own. He seemed thoughtful as he studied her. "You are a clever girl, Selia. You almost beat me."

She nudged him with a smile. "And I will beat you, next time," she said. "Remember that."

Chapter 22

She awoke in the morning with an ache in her neck from not having enough room in the bed. Alrik sprawled behind her, with a heavy arm thrown over her body and his obvious erection pressing into the small of her back. She stiffened, thinking he was awake, but his breath was deep and regular in her ear.

She lifted his arm to wriggle away, but suddenly his muscles tightened as the arm clamped down on her.

"Where do you think you're going?" he grumbled, his voice thick with sleep.

"I have to use the privy."

Alrik grunted his displeasure. He ran his hand over the swell of her hip and buried his nose in her hair. "Later."

Selia turned to look at him. "Alrik . . . please."

He frowned. "Come right back."

Throwing her gown on, she hurried from the room. She did use the privy, then took her time collecting some firewood while she was outside. She wandered into the kitchen, hoping that Hrefna would be there so she could offer to help the woman in some way. Then she would have an excuse for not going back to the bedroom.

The kitchen was deserted except for Alrik. He leaned against the wall, bare-chested, with his hair uncombed and a deep scowl on his face. "Did you fall in?"

She held out her armload of wood. "I was just helping Hrefna."

"That's what the thralls are for, Selia." He took the firewood from her, then dropped it onto the floor. Selia gasped at the mess, but before she could say a word he caught her arm and began pulling her back toward the bedroom.

They ran into Hrefna on the way, who paled at the look on her nephew's face. Alrik shook his head threateningly at the woman as he dragged Selia into the bedroom. He slammed the door behind them.

"Do you have anything else you need to do?" his voice dripped with sarcasm. "Milk the sheep, perhaps? Churn some butter?"

She narrowed her eyes and shook her head. Alrik sat on the edge of the bed, pulling her close, and leaned in to kiss her. She kept her mouth shut and held her body stiffly at his touch, and Alrik drew back in a blaze of fury.

"*Selia,*" he bellowed, shaking her so hard she bit her tongue. "Stop this now-I won't stand for it."

Her eyes welled up with tears as the metallic taste of blood filled her mouth. She didn't speak and refused to look at him.

Alrik growled in frustration and pushed her aside. He stood, then began to pace, which never boded well. "What do you want from me, Selia?" he demanded. "Do you want me to get rid of her? Fine-I'll send her away. Will that make you happy?"

"No," she whispered.

His face turned blood red as his fists clenched at his sides. "*Then what do you want?*" He pronounced each word slowly, through gritted teeth.

Alrik was much too angry to be reasoned with now. He exuded pure emotion; whatever capability he possessed for rational thought long gone.

Yet there might be a way to get her point across, although it would probably fan the flames of his rage to a dangerous level.

Selia compulsively twisted the ring on her finger. "Alrik," she said as he paced like a caged animal, "how would you feel if I . . . if I told you I let another man bed me?"

He snapped, rushing toward her in a blur of motion and lifting her off her feet. Selia gasped for breath as he shoved her up against the wall. His demented face was only inches from her own. Ring or no ring, he looked as though he might actually kill her.

"*Who have you been with?*"

"No one!" She squirmed against his grip.

"Ulfrik—is it Ulfrik? I'll gut him like pig—"

"No! Only you-I have only been with you." His expression was scornful but she pressed on. "How you feel right now is how I feel when I think of you bedding Muirin. But I cannot throw you against the wall."

She saw a flicker of understanding in his eyes. Her husband was selfishly preoccupied with his own desires, and unable or unwilling to see a viewpoint other than his own. So the only way to help him understand what she was feeling was to make him feel it for himself.

Alrik's hands shook as he set her down. His anger had dissipated somewhat, and he sank to the edge of the bed. "That's different."

She rubbed her arms, watching him. "No, it is not."

"You are my wife," he said with a bit more force. "You must submit to me."

"Yes," she agreed, walking over to him. Selia stroked his face as she looked into his eyes. "But do you want me to submit to you because I must? Or because I love you?"

Alrik's jaw dropped. Several seconds passed before he spoke. "Don't lie to me to get what you want, child." His voice held an edge of fear under the bravado.

Had no one ever told him they loved him? Hrefna? Eydis? His mother? Perhaps he had more insight into his own behavior than Selia realized. Perhaps he was aware of how his maniacal mood swings affected those around him.

Perhaps he didn't think he was worthy of love.

She took his face in both hands to force him to look at her. "I am not lying, and I am not a child. I love you, Alrik."

His lips came down upon hers hard, almost cruelly, as

if to punish her for what she had said. Then he drew back, watching for her reaction.

"I love you," she repeated, smiling at him.

"You are a witch, Selia Niallsdottir."

"No."

"You have put a spell on me."

"No, Alrik," she laughed.

"What other explanation is there? You have ruined me for any other woman. It's maddening-the only bed I want to be in is yours."

The vulnerability in his eyes was unmistakable now. Selia studied him with a furrowed brow as she realized she could hurt him, could cut him to the quick if she wanted to. Physically, Alrik was the strongest man she had ever known, yet there was a part of him as defenseless as a child. His statement that he desired only her was as close to a declaration of love as she was going to get.

He *did* love her. He just couldn't admit it without jeopardizing his ridiculous sense of manhood.

Before she could respond, they were interrupted by a loud knock. "Alrik," Ulfrik's voice came from the other side of the door. "There is a ship approaching. I don't recognize it."

Her husband's entire demeanor changed in the blink of an eye. He stood up, all hesitancy gone, then crossed the room in three strides to open the door. Ulfrik looked grim.

"How large?" Alrik demanded.

"Good sized. It's not a warship, or at least not one of ours. Possibly Irish."

Alrik flipped open the large chest at the foot of the bed, pulling out his mail shirt and iron helmet. He donned the shirt quickly, buckled his sword around his hips, then drew his battle axe out of the chest. "Is there time to send a rider to get Bjorn?"

"No," Ulfrik replied.

Alrik cursed under his breath. "Then we will meet them alone, brother."

Ulfrik nodded and left the room.

Why would an Irish ship be in Norse waters? The Irish hated the Finngalls, and a merchant ship would have gone well out of its way to avoid the bloodthirsty pirates. Selia had seen with her own eyes what the Finngalls could do to a merchant ship. Unless—

"Alrik," she said, grabbing his arm, "it could be my father's ship!"

He shook her hand away, glancing at her only briefly before leaning over to strap an extra dagger to his boot. "No, it's not." His voice was curt.

"But you do not know—"

He stood up. "It isn't your father's ship. You will go into the woods with Hrefna and Ingrid, and wait until we come for you."

She bristled. "I will not leave you."

"You will do as I say, Selia!" He clapped the helmet onto his head as he pulled her into the main room where the others were waiting. Male thralls also stood in the room, three that Hrefna trusted the most.

Alrik handed them daggers. He barked, "Go into the woods with the women, and protect them with your lives if necessary."

Dressed for battle, he appeared even larger than usual, and his voice had a quality to it that made him sound like a stranger.

Olaf and Ulfrik also wore their mail, and Selia felt a strange prickling on the back of her neck as she looked at the three heavily armed Finngalls. It was almost as though they had ceased to be the men she had grown to love, and had transformed before her eyes into Vikingers-soulless heathens bent on the slaughter of innocents.

But she had seen them in their battle raiment before. What was different now? Why was she feeling so peculiar? The smoke from the hearth was thick in the air and made it difficult to draw in a deep breath. She had become lightheaded, that was all.

No, there was something about the smoke . . . the smoke and the Finngalls. She felt a frustrated sense that this had all happened before, as if she should be able to remember something but could not. It was as if she tried to wrap her fingers around a shadow.

Ulfrik whispered something to Alrik. As her husband turned, his face was almost unrecognizable under the helmet. Only the braided beard was familiar. He took a step toward her and she stumbled back.

Her heart hammered in her chest at the icy glitter of his eyes behind his helmet. Even though she knew it was Alrik, she felt an overpowering urge to run from this man.

"Selia," he ordered, "go with Hrefna. *Now*."

She blinked. The dreamlike quality vanished, and Alrik was her husband again. The man she loved. What was wrong with her? She forced herself to stand by Hrefna and Ingrid, also armed with daggers. Hrefna appeared worried and grim, but Selia saw a definite gleam of excitement in Ingrid's eyes. Probably in anticipation of killing someone.

As the men left to face alone whatever fate would be dealt them, Hrefna led the group of women and slaves out the kitchen door and toward the woods. Selia followed the woman blindly, blinking back tears.

Ulfrik had told his brother the ship was large. How many men were on this ship? And how could three men, even well-armed and trained since childhood to kill, possibly expect to face them?

They were nearly to the tree line, and as they went up the hill Selia craned her neck to get one last glimpse of her husband. The ship moved through the water toward the dock, and she stopped short as she recognized the distinctive prow. The ship, wide and deep and a direct contrast to Alrik's long, shallow dragonship, had been designed to carry fine fabrics and other precious cargo through the treacherous open sea and safely back to Ireland.

"It *is* my father's ship!" she cried to Hrefna, and before the woman could turn, Selia was sprinting down the hill. She could hear Hrefna calling out for her to wait, but she didn't stop. She ran until she reached Alrik and the others, just as the ship was pulling into the dock.

"Alrik—"

He grabbed her arm. "Selia! I told you to go with Hrefna."

She squirmed and tried to pry his fingers away. "It is my father's ship," she insisted.

Alrik looked ready to explode.

Ulfrik stepped forward. "You are mistaken, Selia." He kept his eyes on the ship and didn't take his hand from the hilt of his sword.

Her eyes scanned the ship for her father. She recognized many of the men who had worked for Niall for as long as she could remember, but her father was nowhere in sight. And although the men had lashed the ship to the dock, no one appeared willing to step toward the small group of Finngalls who waited for them.

Except for one—a smaller, dark-headed figure who pushed through the men to stand alone on the dock.

Ainnileas.

Selia cried out as she saw her brother, and renewed her fight against Alrik's grip. "Alrik . . . let go," she begged. "It is Ainnileas . . ."

He looked down at her, stony-faced, then finally released her. She ran for her brother. Selia hugged him so tightly that after a moment he had to untangle her arms from around his neck so he could breathe.

He looked different than she remembered—older somehow, although they had been apart for less than two full moons.

"What are you doing here, Ainnileas?" she asked through her tears. She hadn't realized how incomplete she had felt without him. It was as though she had been missing a part of her body, a limb or an eye, and it had now been returned to her. She was whole again.

"I told you I would find you." His voice sounded deeper, almost like a man.

She laughed and went up on her toes to kiss his cheek. How had they been able to locate her? All Ainnileas and Niall knew was Alrik's name, yet they had found her.

She pulled back and her eyes scanned the ship. "Where is *Dadai*?"

A look of confusion crossed Ainnileas' face. He hesitated for a moment. "He . . . he is dead, Selia."

She stared, blinking in incomprehension, as her knees gave out from under her. She sank to the ground and Ainnileas knelt in front of her. Tears streamed down her cheeks as she looked at her brother. "No."

"I'm sorry," he said. "I thought you knew." He looked toward the small group of Finngalls standing on the grass, and Selia saw the accusation in his gaze. She gasped as though she had been punched in the stomach. Ainnileas was surprised she didn't know their father was dead.

Surprised the Finngalls hadn't told her.

Alrik and Ulfrik had insisted the ship was not her father's, even after she recognized it. How had they been so sure? There was only one explanation. They had already known her father was dead. Dead men could not sail.

"When, Ainnileas?" she whispered, afraid to hear the answer.

"The night you left."

A wail escaped her lips. She had a distinct memory of Alrik leaning over to whisper something to Ketill just before they had ridden away. Had Alrik ordered him to kill Niall?

"They killed him . . ." she choked out, unable to catch her breath.

"No."

Why was he lying? The truth was plain for her to see. She sobbed, struggling as he tried to comfort her, and a shadow fell over them on the dock. Alrik. He held his helmet under his arm as he watched the siblings with an uncomfortable look on his face.

"What did you do, Alrik?" she cried. She jumped to her feet, shoving him with every ounce of strength she had. He didn't move, which enraged her all the more, and she hit him in the ribs. Selia's hand glanced off the metal of his mail shirt, scraping away a layer of skin from her knuckles. "Why did you have to kill him?"

Ainnileas wrapped his arms around her from behind in an attempt to restrain her. "Selia," he said firmly in her ear, "they did not kill Father."

She sniffled, looking from Alrik to Ulfrik, who was now standing behind him. In fact, she realized, they were all standing there; Olaf, Hrefna, and Ingrid. She turned from them, suddenly hating them and their very foreignness, and buried her face in her brother's neck. "Then how did it happen?" she whispered.

He shook his head as if he were loath to remember it. "He was so angry when they took you. The one you scratched kept taunting Father, and laughing at him." Ainnileas' expression was hard. "And then, Father just fell over. His face turned purple and he couldn't speak. And then he was dead."

A small sob escaped Selia. *Dadai.* He had been forced to give his consent to his daughter's marriage to a wicked, dangerous heathen, and the pain and helpless fury he felt had killed him before the marriage had even been consummated. Alrik hadn't murdered him as he had the priest, but Niall was nevertheless a casualty of her Finngall husband.

She looked at Alrik, watching his face for signs of guilt, and saw none. Perhaps he was incapable of feeling genuine guilt or remorse. How practical for a warlord.

Selia wiped her tears on her sleeve before she spoke. "Why didn't you tell me?" she asked him quietly.

He closed his eyes for a moment. "To avoid *this*." He motioned to her and the scene she was making.

A bitter laugh escaped her. "Did you think I would not find out?"

Instead of answering her, Alrik confronted Ainnileas. "Why are you here, boy?"

Ainnileas hesitated. He understood more Norse than he spoke, so he wouldn't be able to answer the Finngall directly. "I needed to make sure you were all right," he said to Selia in Irish.

She translated for Alrik, although she refused to look at him.

His face grew dark as he glowered at Ainnileas. To his credit, her brother refused to be intimidated by the much larger man, and stood his ground with his arms crossed.

Alrik turned to Selia. "Tell your brother he is welcome to stay here for as long as he likes, but his ship must leave today." He scowled toward the ship full of Irishmen.

As Selia translated he added, "Tell him to forget whatever plan he had for stealing you away. You are my wife, and I will kill any man who attempts to take what is mine."

"Alrik!" she protested, but he cut her off.

"Tell him exactly what I said, Selia, or Ulfrik will do it."

Ainnileas flushed as she translated, and his jaw clenched so hard she could hear his teeth grinding. Alrik had been right, then-her brother did have some plan for her escape. What had he possibly been thinking?

"Tell this Finngall I will slaughter any man who leaves marks on my sister," he hissed in Irish, his eyes fixed on the thumbprint bruise still visible on Selia's collarbone.

She paled and glanced at Ulfrik, who was standing close enough to hear Ainnileas threaten to kill his brother. Ulfrik met her gaze but kept his face emotionless. The Hersir would not take such a threat lightly.

A cold sweat broke out over Selia's body as she gazed at Ainnileas. Although his body was growing from that of a boy into a man, he still looked like a frail child next to the huge Finngalls. Furthermore, he knew nothing of fighting. The only weapon her brother carried was a dagger at his hip, and she doubted he knew how to use it. His righteous anger would only serve to get him killed, but he was too pigheaded to realize it.

"Ainnileas." She spoke in a slow and careful tone, willing him to understand the gravity of the situation. "I don't want you to stay. You're going to get yourself hurt here, and I can't lose you too. Please, just go home."

He flashed his most charming smile at her, showing his dimples, and glanced toward Alrik and the others. "No, sister, I will accept the gracious hospitality of your husband. Please give him my thanks."

Chapter 23

When Selia awoke several hours later from a drugged sleep, she heard the boisterous strains of Ainnileas' whistle as he played an Irish melody. And not only was her new Finngall family tolerating it, they seemed to actually be *enjoying* it, if the clapping and laughter could be believed. Was she still dreaming? No. Her knuckles wouldn't be throbbing in pain if she was.

Hrefna had bandaged her hand and given her some sort of tea to drink, which she said would help with the shock of Niall's death. She had also tried to make Selia eat, but she had refused.

Maybe that was why the tea had affected Selia so strongly. One minute she was sitting on the bench, tucked in with furs as she sipped her tea and watched the uncomfortable attempts at communication between Ainnileas and the Finngalls, and the next she was waking up on the same bench, groggy and drooling, listening to her brother's whistle and Ingrid's laughter.

Ingrid? Surely Selia was mistaken. The only laugh she had ever heard out of that girl's mouth was an evil chortle, when she was gloating at someone else's expense. But the laugh came again—a female laugh, and not from Hrefna. It was an odd sort of embarrassed chuckle that could only come from someone who didn't laugh easily or often.

The room spun as she raised her throbbing head. Ainnileas stood on one of the benches placed on the other side of the room, blowing into his whistle and dancing along with the melody. Hrefna, Olaf, Ingrid, and even Alrik were gathered around him, looking up at him with expectant, smiling faces. Only Ulfrik was conspicuously missing from the group. Ainnileas made a silly face behind his whistle, clowning for his audience, and the family burst into laughter.

From the time they were small children, her brother had been known for his amiable nature and his sense of humor. He had the ability to charm his way out of the most uncomfortable situations. She had seen it happen dozens of times, both with their own friends as well as associates brought home by their father. But never, never would she have believed her brother capable of enchanting the Finngalls in the same way. Ainnileas, who barely knew any Norse, and who obviously wanted Alrik dead.

He reached the end of the song, finishing the melody with an explosive shriek of the whistle and a stomp of his foot. His crowd of admirers burst into applause. He bowed with a flourish, cheeks flushed and eyes bright.

"Again, Ainnileas!" Ingrid cried. Selia cringed at the way the girl's Norse accent butchered his name, but he shot her an indulgent smile. Ingrid blushed and dimpled right back at him, and Selia's jaw dropped. What sort of strange world had she awoken in?

She sat up and glared at her brother. "What do you think you're doing?" she asked him in Irish.

Everyone turned to look at her—everyone but Ingrid. She didn't take her eyes off Ainnileas.

He lifted his eyebrows in surprise. "You're awake," he said, bestowing his dazzling smile on her.

She refused his foolery. Her brother had always lived his life as if it were a game. He enjoyed the sport of getting what he wanted from almost anyone. Even the crew of Niall's ship-sea hardened men, all-had apparently been more than willing to sail through treacherous waters and into Finngall territory at the direction of young Ainnileas. She was very curious to know how he had managed that.

But Alrik was not a normal man, and she had seen her husband's mood shift from relative calm to a murderous rage in a span of seconds. How would he react when he realized Ainnileas was deceiving him? Although she didn't know what sort of game her brother played this time, she feared he would be dead when it was over.

Selia scowled at him and repeated her question. "What are you doing, Ainnileas?"

He laughed. "I so missed your grumpy face, sister." He turned back to his audience, speaking to them in Norse. "Selia can . . ." he pursed his lips, thinking for the word. He finally settled on "la la la," and looked at them with a questioning expression.

"Sing?" Ingrid offered helpfully, and he grinned at her.

"Yes, *sing.* Selia can sing. Very good." He raised his whistle to his lips as his eyes met Selia's.

"*No.*" She brought her hand down hard on the plank of the bench for emphasis. "I don't know what you're playing at but you need to stop it right now. This isn't a game, Ainnileas. *Dadai* is dead, and you're acting as though it's a *party.*" Her voice broke on the word and her eyes stung with tears.

No one but Ainnileas understood the Irish words, but Selia's tone was clear. Hrefna rushed to her, making soothing noises, and put her arm around her. "My dear child . . ."

Ainnileas jumped down from the bench to approach. He touched her shoulder gently. "I'm sorry, Selia." There was no guile in his voice now.

She gazed at him. He was the person she loved most in the world, and was therefore the only one who could jeopardize her love for Alrik. She could not be forced to choose between them. The threatened tears suddenly spilled forth, and she dropped her face into her hands to hide them.

Hrefna stood. "We need to give them some privacy." Her brisk tone allowed for no argument. She shot the men a pointed look and took Ingrid by the arm. "Come help me in the kitchen, Ingrid." The girl protested as she dragged her away.

Olaf went outside; Alrik rose to his feet more reluctantly. Selia met his gaze, but found the intensity of his eyes too much. She looked away, sniffling, exhausted, drained both physically and emotionally, bereft of energy to expend on Alrik right now. She had declared her love for him this morning, sure that nothing could sway her feelings.

But now her father was dead, and her husband was responsible.

Alrik turned to follow Olaf outside, and Ainnileas sat beside Selia. She closed her eyes and sank into his familiar form. Her brother held her for a long time, stroking her hair as she cried.

"I'm sorry," he repeated.

"You are a stupid boy." Selia mopped her face on a corner of her gown. "*Dadai* is gone and you're all I have left. Do you understand how dangerous it is for you here? If anything happened to you—"

"Nothing is going to happen to me."

"You don't know how Alrik is."

"He barely speaks a word of Irish," he pointed out with contempt.

"No, but his brother does. Ulfrik heard what you said."

Ainnileas shrugged as if unperturbed. "He won't say anything—he hates Alrik as much as I do."

She straightened in surprise. "*What?*"

"Watch the way he looks at him, Selia. It's obvious." He spoke in the patient tone one would use with a child. "When you were asleep, Alrik sent him off, I'm assuming to follow the ship and make sure it wouldn't return. I saw the look his brother gave him when Alrik had his back turned." Ainnileas paused for a moment, thinking. "Perhaps he'll even help me get you out of here."

She felt a crushing weight on her chest, as though she couldn't take a full breath. So her brother *was* planning to steal her away. But to have the impudence to assume he could understand the situation between Alrik and Ulfrik just from one look? It was pure madness to think Ulfrik would help him, putting his own life at risk in the process.

Selia closed her eyes and saw Father's Coinneach's surprised face as Alrik slit his throat. Except the priest's face became that of her brother's, with the light slowly fading from his beautiful eyes.

"What were you planning on doing?" She choked on the query.

"I assumed he would send the ship away." Ainnileas seemed nonchalant. "But we found a spot where the ship can hide, Selia. They will come back in three days' time and wait for us there."

"And how did you possibly think we could sneak away from Alrik?"

He snorted. "He certainly enjoys his ale, doesn't he? He's drunk right now in the middle of the day. So, three nights from now, he'll sleep a little more soundly than usual." He made a motion with his finger as if dropping something into a cup. "I'll set his ship on fire so he can't follow us."

The weight on Selia's chest intensified, and as she stood up she gripped the wall for support. "Ainnileas, listen to me. I will not go with you. This is my home now. Alrik is my husband."

Her brother leapt to his feet, eyes flashing. "*Your husband* is responsible for Father's death, Selia! And what is this?" He pulled roughly on the neckline of her gown to expose the bruise on her shoulder. "Do you expect me to sit idly by while that bastard hurts you? If I have to tie you up and carry you out of here over my shoulder, then so be it."

"I'm with child, Ainnileas!" She shoved him away. "I will not leave him. I will not raise my child without a father."

His anger dissolved into shock, and he blinked at her belly as he sank onto the bench. "It's all right. It's fine." He spoke in a whisper, as if talking to himself. "He won't mind."

"What are you talking about? Of course he'll mind."

He shook his head. "Not Alrik. Buadhach."

It was Selia's turn to be shocked. "*Buadhach?* Ainnileas, what have you done?"

He looked at her with hollow eyes. "I promised to bring you back to him. And he will pay the men triple their usual pay if I do."

The bile rose in her throat. So that was how a boy had persuaded a ship full of Irishmen to sail into hostile Norse waters; with the promise of riches from a desperate old man. But was Buadhach desperate enough to accept the fact his prospective bride was not only married to a Finngall warlord, but carried his child, too?

Doubtful.

"What will happen to you when I don't go back?" she whispered.

He shrugged. "You mean, after the men throw me overboard? I suppose I'll have a long swim home." He affected indifference, but Selia knew better.

"If you're not there in three days, they'll just leave without you," she argued.

"No, we planned for that. If I'm not there they'll sail east to trade, and come back on the return trip to try again."

She studied her brother. "I'm not going with them and neither are you. You must stay here until Alrik goes on another trip to Ireland."

"You mean a raid to Ireland." His voice held bitterness. "When your Finngall husband takes his next trip to butcher our people, can he drop me off at home first? No, Selia. I'll take my chances with Father's men. I buried your bride price in the barn after he died. I can pay the men. Maybe not triple, but it will be something."

Ainnileas sat and stared into space for quite some time, and Selia watched him warily. She knew her brother well. It was obvious he was hatching a new plan.

She grabbed his shoulder, forcing him to look at her.

"I'm happy here, Ainnileas. This is where I belong. I love Alrik, and I will not leave him. Now or ever. Whatever you're planning won't work, and it will probably get you killed. Please, just stop. I'm begging you to stop."

He gave her the shrewd look she knew so well, and her heart sank. "Of course, Selia. I understand. Let's just enjoy the time we have together and forget all about this."

The evening passed rather uneventfully. Ainnileas was on his best behavior throughout supper and afterward, yet Selia could not relax. She watched him, looking for any sign of his hatred for her husband. What if someone sensed his animosity and mentioned it to Alrik?

But her brother charmed them all equally, appearing to the inexperienced eye to be simply a bright, handsome, fun-loving boy.

She had no interest in tafl tonight, either to play or to watch. Alrik played with Olaf, drinking heavily, while Selia ignored him. Ainnileas and Ingrid watched the game, however, and she could not help her fury toward them both. She knew her brother was only trying to ingratiate himself toward Alrik. And Ingrid—stupid girl that she was—would have sat and watched a cup of water evaporate if a handsome foreigner told her it was interesting.

For someone who knew as much Norse as a toddling child, Ainnileas seemed to have quite a bit to talk about with Ingrid. They sat close together, whispering and laughing, his dark head setting off her pale blond locks. The way the girl embarrassed herself with him was absurd. Had she failed to notice she was much too big for Ainnileas? She was taller than he, with a sturdier build.

Selia knew her brother's interest in the girl was false-how could it be otherwise? Nevertheless it bothered her. She dropped her spinning into her lap as their laughter welled up once again. Her nerves could take no more.

Hrefna, always observant, eyed her for a moment, then reached for her hand. "Selia, come. I'll make you some more tea."

Sighing, Selia followed the woman into the kitchen. Hrefna set the water to boil and rummaged through the various pots that held a seemingly endless variety of herbs.

Hrefna placed her selections on the work table as she turned toward Selia with a sympathetic smile. "This has certainly been a terrible day for you, hasn't it?"

"Yes," she agreed, with some force. The most terrible day of her life. She met Hrefna's gaze for a moment, then looked away.

"Is there something you would like to ask me?"

Selia hesitated as Hrefna set the herbs to steep in the hot water, then blurted, "Alrik and Ulfrik knew my father was dead, and they did not tell me. Did you also know?" Selia cared for the woman, feeling a bond with her that she thought might approximate what a daughter would feel for her mother. Surely Hrefna had not lied to her as well.

"No, child, I didn't. Olaf just told me today what happened to your poor father. Do you think I would keep something like that from you?"

"No. I'm sorry."

Hrefna cupped her cheek gently. Another peal of laughter arose from the main room, and Selia shot a dark scowl toward the doorway.

"You don't like it that Ingrid is showing an interest in your brother?"

"No." Selia chewed at her lip, afraid to say more. Ingrid was Hrefna's niece, after all.

Hrefna set the cup of tea in front of her. "You have lived here long enough to understand what Ingrid is like. The only time we get a moment's peace is when she is staying at Bjorn's. But this," she inclined her head in the direction of the others, "this is wonderful. I have heard more laughter from Ingrid in the hours your brother has been here than I have heard from her in her entire life. Ainnileas is a lovely young man, and he has quite an influence on her."

Selia rolled her eyes, unconvinced, as Hrefna added, "I wouldn't be at all surprised if Alrik offered her to your brother in marriage."

Choking on her tea, Selia coughed and set the cup down. "No," she sputtered. How could she convince Hrefna this was a bad idea? "Ingrid is too young to be married."

"By law she could have been married three years ago. And I'm sure Alrik would have consented, if only he could have found a willing bridegroom."

Selia stared at Hrefna in dismay. How could she possibly tell the woman her hopes for Ingrid would be dashed as soon as Ainnileas decided the girl could no longer further his warped scheme?

If Alrik offered his daughter's hand to him, things would go from bad to worse in a heartbeat.

Chapter 24

Selia sniffled as she walked from the privy back toward the house. If only she had some chore that would keep her outside. Anything to avoid a further conversation with Hrefna-or worse yet, another sickening display of infatuation from Ingrid and Ainnileas.

She climbed up onto the retaining wall that circled the rear of the house and sat there for some time, kicking her heels against the stones. Everything was crumbling now; all she thought she could count on had been built on shadows and half-truths. Her foolish brother was either going to end up with his throat slit, or married to Ingrid. She wasn't quite sure which was worse.

And Alrik, the man she loved, had kept the news of her father's death from her. Not to protect her from grief, but to selfishly avoid her inevitable outburst of emotion.

But had he actually lied? Although he had hidden the truth, he wasn't the one who told her that her father was unharmed. That dubious honor went to his brother, when she had inquired about the safety of her family. Surely Ketill had told Ulfrik of Niall's death when they had spoken at the cove.

Ulfrik had lied to her. She kicked her heel hard into the wall, satisfied when she chipped a small stone out and it hit the ground.

As if on cue, Selia heard the faint sound of hoof beats in the distance. Shielding her eyes with her hand, she squinted into the setting sun. Ulfrik, returning from whatever errand the Hersir had sent him on. As he reined his horse to a walk, he glanced in her direction, then quickly looked away, steering the horse toward the barn.

Coward.

A male thrall followed him into the barn to tend to the horse, and Ulfrik emerged a moment later. She watched him approach. For two brothers who looked so alike, she could easily tell them apart even from a distance. Alrik moved with a swagger, the beautiful dance of muscle, tendon, and bone breathtaking to watch. Although Ulfrik's build was similar to his brother's, he carried himself very differently. If Alrik appeared to be godlike, then Ulfrik was . . . simply human.

He seemed guarded as he stopped a few feet in front of her. "What are you doing out here alone?"

She glared at him. "Well, if you've confirmed for your brother that the ship is gone, I can hardly run off, can I?"

Ulfrik ran his hands through his damp hair. Her sensitive nose picked up the scent of horse and fresh male sweat, which she found not unpleasant. But as a true Finngall, he would want a bath.

Indeed, his gaze flicked in the direction of the bathhouse before turning back to her with resignation. "If you have something to say to me, then just say it."

Selia readily showed her fury. "You lied to me, Ulfrik. You knew my father was dead, you knew it the night it happened, but you *lied* to me. I would expect something like that from Alrik, but not from you."

"Why?"

He took a step closer, and she blinked as she tried to refocus on him. The tea was beginning to work. "Because you're not like him. He doesn't know right from wrong, and you do."

Ulfrik's eyes flashed. "Are you sure about that? Are you sure he doesn't know right from wrong? Or maybe he uses that as an excuse to do whatever he wants, and we all just accept it."

He was livid. The man was known to guard his emotions the way a miser hoarded his treasure, yet he had flushed with anger, his hands clenched at his sides in a posture she had seen countless times from his brother.

Was there more to Ainnileas' suspicions than she had originally thought?

But she wasn't going to allow Ulfrik to deflect the conversation away from his own blame in this. "This does not concern Alrik."

"Of course it does, Selia. Think about why you have higher expectations for me than you have for your own husband. You continue to let him hurt you, yet you forgive him. I make one small mistake, and-"

"A small mistake!" she cried. "How can you call lying to me about my father's death a small mistake?" The tea *was* working; her words slurred a bit. Perhaps he wouldn't pick up on it.

But he scanned her face shrewdly. "Have you had more of Hrefna's tea?"

"Yes," she admitted.

"Then you need to get inside before you tumble from that wall." He stepped in to help her down. "We'll talk tomorrow." He placed his hands on her waist and was about to lift her, but Selia stopped him.

"Wait." She willed herself to concentrate as she looked at him. He was standing much too close to her; so close she could feel his body heat and smell his maleness. The expression on his face reminded her of Alrik. Why did he have to look so much like his brother? She shook her head in an attempt to clear it. "Tell me why you lied. I need to know."

Ulfrik's gaze was intense, wandering down to her mouth for a moment, just as Alrik's always did before he kissed her. But then he drew his breath in sharply and looked away. "That night, when Ketill told me about your father, I thought I might save you the pain of knowing he was dead." His jaw clenched. "I didn't tell you the truth because I didn't think you would live long enough to find out. I know what Alrik is, Selia. I know what he's capable of."

If she had wanted brutal honesty, there it was. Ulfrik

thought his brother would kill her before she had a chance to learn of Niall's death.

She nodded, the movement causing her head to spin. She suddenly felt very tired, and gave in to the need to close her eyes for a moment.

But when she opened them again, Ulfrik was in the middle of a sentence. Selia had the familiar feeling that she had jumped forward in time somehow, missing out on something important. Only the people who knew her very well could sense she had blacked out, but Ulfrik stopped talking and studied her.

"Are you all right? Is it the tea, or something else?" He glanced over his shoulder in the direction of the house.

Hrefna didn't know about Selia's spells. She would have to be told sooner or later, but Selia hadn't the nerve yet to have that conversation with her.

"I just want to go to sleep."

He helped her down from the wall. "Selia," he vowed, "if I had it to do over again, I would have told you."

She slept deeply, but awoke in the middle of the night with Alrik's hands on her body. The room was dark, and he seemed very drunk as he fumbled to pull her shift up. Selia stared into the blackness. After the strange encounter she had with Ulfrik earlier, she felt an irrational need to make sure it was indeed her husband who was currently sliding his large hand up her leg. She reached up, searching for Alrik's face, and sighed when she felt his braided beard.

Selia pulled him down to her, kissing him deeply despite his taste, like a vat of ale. He could make her forget about the events of the day, if only for a little while. She reached between them to unfasten his breeches, and as she felt the hardness of his manhood she also felt the edge of his teeth on her lips, and she knew he was smiling.

"Roll over," she whispered.

He complied with a chuckle.

Straddling him, she took both of his wrists and pressed them to the pillow above his head, then bent to kiss him again. He was too drunk to protest. She placed fluttering kisses down his neck, felt him shiver, then finally bit him on the shoulder.

Alrik groaned and tried to shift his hands from the pillow, but she interlaced her fingers with his and held him to the bed. He laughed but remained still. They both knew he could break free in a second, but clearly enjoyed her unusual behavior.

Selia leaned over him, brushing her nipple across his lips. He tried to catch her breast in his mouth but she pulled back. She teased him again, loving the unexpected exhilaration of being in control of this massive man.

It didn't last long. Alrik broke her hold on his hands easily, then with a firm clasp on her hips, he pushed her back and sheathed himself inside her. She cried out at the sensation, digging her fingernails into his arms as he began to move within her. She rode him hard, taking out her anger on his body. She threw her head back in the darkness as the waves of pleasure crashed over her, and the noise that came from her throat sounded like a sob.

Selia took in a shaky breath as Alrik's large body finally stilled beneath her. Drained, she moved to lie next to him in the bed, but instead he pulled her down on top of him, wrapping his arms around her. She relaxed into the warmth of his chest and listened to the thumping of his heart under her ear.

"Selia, my little one—I thought you would hate me." He slurred in his drunkenness, but she also picked up an odd tightness in his voice. If the Hersir were not speaking she would have sworn he was crying.

She tried to shift her body, but his arms clamped down to pin her to his chest. In the pitch blackness, the only way she could have determined if he shed tears would be to touch his face. He obviously wouldn't allow her such a liberty.

"I told you I love you, Alrik." She sighed. "I cannot make myself stop, even if I wanted to."

"Do you want to stop, then?"

She hesitated for a moment. "Sometimes when you are bad, I want to not love you so much. So you cannot hurt me."

He lay quietly for some time. "I have done many bad things in my life, little one."

"I know."

"You *don't* know." His voice sounded choked. "It never mattered before . . ." he trailed off for a moment, his hand stroking her hair. As he touched the dent in her skull, however, he shifted his hand away from it quickly. It had always made people nervous, and he seemed no exception.

"I can't change who I am, Selia. I can't change the things I've done. But I won't let you leave me." He held her so tightly she feared he would crush her.

His heart pounded now, directly under her ear, and she squirmed in his grip. "You are hurting me, Alrik," she protested, her voice muffled into his chest.

"I won't let you leave me," he repeated. "Tell me you won't leave me."

"I will not leave you," she assured.

He loosened his grip, and she felt the pressure of his lips on the top of her head as he kissed her. It was probably the closest thing she would get to an apology from him for not telling her about her father's death.

Alrik held her for a long time, and she listened as his racing heart slowed and his breathing deepened. His arms relaxed enough for her to shift her body a bit, and she reached for his face. She found his chin and he didn't move, so she slid her fingers up his cheek until she felt the damp tracks of his tears.

I am right.

Alrik Blood Axe had been crying.

Chapter 25

The next morning, Selia found Ulfrik unusually talkative as they broke their fast. He had stopped at Bjorn's house on his way back from ensuring the Irish ship had indeed sailed away from the coast of Norway. Ulfrik then had accepted Bjorn's invitation to take supper with him and his family. It had been half a year since he had seen Bolli Ketilson.

"Bolli wouldn't let me leave without sparring with him first." Ulfrik chuckled. "He is as big as his brothers, and better with a sword, I think. He said he is ready for his oath-taking as soon as you'll have him."

Alrik, suffering from a hangover, frowned at this. "Do you suggest I employ a wet-nurse to go with us on the fall trip?"

Ulfrik shrugged as he reached for more bread. "You and I were younger than Bolli on our first raid. We didn't need a wet nurse. Or at least, I didn't."

This only earned him a piercing stare from his brother.

Selia looked hesitantly from Alrik to Ulfrik. "What is a 'wet-nurse?'" she asked, unfamiliar with the Norse word.

Alrik massaged his temples. "I'm not in the habit of taking children along on the ship. A wet-nurse feeds a babe." He reached out and squeezed her breast, as if to demonstrate, and she smacked his hand away.

Her eyes darted toward Ainnileas, unsure how much of the conversation he was able to follow. If Alrik planned on going back to Ireland in the fall, then her brother could potentially go home with him. That was some time away, however; too long for Ainnileas to stay in Norway. It would give him more time to plot something, and more time to get hurt.

Not to mention how a long sea voyage would place him in a confined space with Alrik and thirty other Vikingers. She would be unable to intervene on her brother's behalf if he did or said something foolish, a likely endeavor for him.

She didn't know which was worse; sending him with Alrik or letting him take his chances with the Irish sailors of her father's ship. Ainnileas had joked about them throwing him overboard, but she had seen the look of fear in his eyes. The men had been assured a large reward for bringing her home safely to Buadhach, which of course they wouldn't receive if she stayed in Norway.

Would the promise of the silver Ainnileas had buried in the barn be enough to keep them from harming him?

Selia knew her brother well enough to sense his anger when he saw Alrik grope her breast. His breathing quickened a bit and his eyes grew dark. Furthermore, she was sure she had seen him exchange a glance with Ulfrik. But as usual, Ulfrik's face seemed expressionless to the point of boredom.

Hrefna had set up a bench for Ainnileas next to Ulfrik last night, on the far side of the room from where Ingrid slept. Clearly the woman was reluctant to allow the young foreigner to sleep close to Ingrid, regardless of how charming he was. Or perhaps because of it.

But this had allowed Ainnileas to have access to Ulfrik all night. He thought he had an ally in Ulfrik, a man he assumed hated Alrik as much as he; a risky assumption if incorrect.

Ingrid's face had grown red at her father's disparaging remarks about her cousin Bolli. But she stayed quiet. Either she was being mindful of Alrik's threat to send her away, or she was actually trying to impress Ainnileas with her calm demeanor. Males appreciated tranquility in a future wife.

"Why don't you have Bolli show you his skill before you decide?" Ingrid addressed her father but her eyes remained downcast.

Hrefna brightened and turned to Alrik. "We could have a gathering, just as we used to. You could watch the boy during the games to decide if he's ready for the oath-taking. And if he's not, then no harm done."

Alrik growled, "I have no patience for a gathering."

She continued on, undeterred. "We have plenty of ale, and cheese and butter. We could slaughter one of the bulls and a few pigs."

"Did you not hear me, woman?"

Hrefna smiled. "We could celebrate your marriage, Alrik. Ainnileas could play his whistle for everyone, and Selia could sing."

Selia sat up straighter and shook her head firmly. "No, I will not sing."

Ainnileas seemed to understand at least this much of the conversation, and he laughed aloud, nearly choking on his porridge. To her dismay everyone-except for Alrik, of course, whose frown only deepened-laughed right along with him. Not one of them knew why they were laughing, but Ainnileas' laugh was contagious.

She glared at her brother and attempted to kick him under the table. Her foot hit Olaf by mistake and his surprised grunt made everyone laugh harder.

Alrik stood and regarded his family contemptuously. "I'm going back to bed," he grumbled. "You fools can do whatever you want."

Hrefna didn't wait for her nephew to have a chance to change his mind. She sent Olaf away in one of the little boats, with a message for the war band of the gathering in ten day's time in celebration of their leader's marriage. Selia didn't have the heart to tell the woman that during the time she had spent sailing from Ireland to Norway, Alrik's men had seemed to despise her more and more by the day. Why would they possibly want to celebrate any event related to her?

Hrefna was beside herself with excitement as she and Selia left the house together. Selia had to quicken her steps to keep up with her.

"What is a gathering, Hrefna?"

Hrefna smiled. "A celebration that happens every summer. There is feasting and drinking, and contests of skill. It's a time for young people to meet and for old disputes to be settled. Everyone attends-the men, their wives, their children. And Kolgrima will come as well. I haven't seen my grandchildren in far too long."

"They could not attend last year?"

"There was no gathering last year. Alrik wouldn't hear of it after . . ." Hrefna paused. "Well, after."

Selia nodded. Of course he wouldn't have agreed to a gathering so soon after his first wife and younger daughters had died.

"But why wouldn't he want to have a gathering this year?" Selia asked.

Hrefna turned to her. "He is still so melancholy. We must help him, Selia. You and I. Alrik is a good leader in battle, and generous with the spoils of war. But there is more to being the Hersir than leading a war band. He has been neglecting his other duties. A gathering will right many wrongs in the eyes of his men."

Selia followed Hrefna into the dairy to count the inventory of cheese and butter, thinking the shelves looked as though they could easily get the family through the winter and well into spring. But Hrefna frowned and bit her lip. She didn't look pleased.

How many people could they expect? The thirty men, their wives, and several children apiece, plus the thralls that each family would bring along with them . . . that could equal a crowd of two hundred people. The size of an entire village. Selia felt a bit lightheaded herself at the idea of feeding a crowd that large for days on end.

She looked up at Hrefna's pale face, squeezing her hand. "We could send Ainnileas out on one of the small boats. He likes to fish. And maybe Alrik and Ulfrik will hunt."

"Yes." Hrefna gave a nod. "We will gorge them on meat and bread, and they'll never miss the rest."

"There are also seven vats of wine in the alehouse." Selia quashed the pang of guilt at the memory of the sailors murdered in the name of obtaining that wine. "If we get them drunk, they will not care about the food."

Hrefna laughed, beaming down at her. "My, you are a clever girl."

They walked to the barns to count the number of livestock that could reasonably be slaughtered. Selia was again struck at the sheer size of the longhouse as she saw it from a distance, and she turned to Hrefna.

"Is that why the house is so big? For the gatherings?" The dozens of unfilled sleeping benches in the large main room of the house would at least be put to use for a short time.

"No. Although it does help. Believe me, after everyone arrives, you won't be able to walk through the house without stepping on someone. We usually have the women and children sleep in the house, and set up tents outside for the men. They stay up half the night drinking, anyway."

Hrefna paused as if lost in thought for a moment. "In the time of Ragnarr, the house was filled with his men. That is the way most Hersirs live, surrounded by many of their own men. Typically the unmarried ones or the younger sons without land of their own. When Ragnarr was alive a dozen of his men also lived here."

Selia raised her eyebrows at this. Thank goodness Alrik had chosen not to continue the tradition. She had spent quite enough time surrounded by loud, sweaty, frequently drunken men while traveling with them, and had no desire to continue that on a daily basis.

"When Ragnarr killed my sister and nephew, Geirr came with his own men to slay Ragnarr," Hrefna said. "You see, each member of the Hersir's war band swears a blood-oath to protect him at all costs, even to the point of sacrificing his own life if necessary. A man who turns on his Hersir or who runs from battle is considered an oath breaker, and will be an outcast for the rest of his life. Geirr assumed he and his men would need to cut through Ragnarr's men to get to him."

Hrefna paused for a moment as she bent over to check on the hoof of one of the sheep. "But they didn't need to," she continued. "The men parted to let him through, and several of them even joined Geirr in cutting Ragnarr down."

"What about the oath?"

"Ragnarr's madness was a threat to the group as a whole. He had become dangerous, completely unstable. They recognized he wasn't the same leader they had sworn their oaths to. They knew he had to be stopped."

So that was why Alrik didn't want his men to live here. He could keep his mood swings in check-more or less-for short time periods while going a-viking with his men. His berserker nature would have an outlet in battle, giving him the physical release he needed. But for Alrik's violent tendencies to emerge at a time other than battle would be considered much less acceptable to his men. The beating of Skagi was just such an incident.

Selia scratched one of the sheep on the head and didn't look at Hrefna. "So Alrik is afraid if his men live here, they might kill him?"

"I think so, although he's never admitted it. We overlook his behavior more than an outsider would be able to. But there are times, usually in the winter, when he becomes so despondent, so hateful, no one can bear to be around him. I think he fears his men seeing him like that."

"I understand."

Hrefna hesitated. "My child, I'm not quite sure if you do. This, right now, is his best time. It gets much, much worse."

Chapter 26

Despite Selia's misgivings, Hrefna asked Ulfrik to take Ainnileas fishing in one of the little boats. Unwilling to send their guest out alone, she reasoned the only one who could communicate well with him would be Ulfrik. Which was exactly what Selia feared.

But since she could think of no reasonable objection to this plan, she was forced to watch silently as her brother and Ulfrik walked toward the dock to spend hours on end together, talking.

Or, knowing Ainnileas, plotting.

Ingrid pouted, angry she hadn't been invited on the fishing trip. Hrefna had needed her help in the house, after announcing the clothes of Alrik, Ulfrik, and Olaf simply wouldn't do for the gathering. While they sewed new clothing for the men, they might as well make a new set for Ainnileas so he wouldn't feel left out.

The girl perked up immediately, obviously excited at the idea of making a present for a handsome foreigner.

Thoughtfully, Selia watched Hrefna pull out bolt after bolt of fine wool cloth in the beautiful bright colors typical of the Finngalls. She had never seen people so in love with clothing, either men or women, but even for them this might be considered excessive. A sewing project such as this would prove huge, taking precious time that might be better used doing something else to prepare for the gathering. After all, every one of them already had several sets of beautifully-worked clothes that would be more than acceptable for the party.

All but her brother. His clothes were in the Irish style, much more subdued than those worn by the Finngalls, and were quite worse for wear from his time on the ship.

Selia studied Hrefna. Did the woman specifically want to make clothes for Ainnileas, but understood the only way she could do so without insulting his pride was to sew for everyone? She held back for a bit, not sure if she should be displeased for her brother.

But then Ingrid picked out a deep green bolt of cloth. She eyed it appreciatively, as though judging how the shade would look on Ainnileas.

Idiot girl. He hates green.

Selia chose the bright blue cloth, holding it out to her stepdaughter. "He likes blue," she said evenly. If Ainnileas were to get new clothes, she would at least ensure it was a color he liked.

The girl eyed her with suspicion, so Selia shrugged and turned away, ready to use the blue cloth for Alrik. It was a nice shade that would set off his eyes. But Ingrid grabbed it from her. She carried it over to the table without another glance at Selia.

"You are welcome," she snapped at the girl. Ingrid ignored her.

After much deliberation, Selia chose the red cloth for Alrik. Many of his clothes were red already, since the color suited him better than any other. But she would sew the breeches from the walnut-brown cloth to make it different from what he already had. Hrefna also had dozens of lengths of tablet-woven silk trim, and Selia found one in shades of red and yellow that would complement both the shirt and the breeches.

The patterns they would use to cut out the cloth were made from rough, undyed wool; the same material used for the clothing of the thralls.

Hrefna handed one to her. "Cut Alrik's out first," she instructed. "I'll need to use the pattern for Ulfrik when you're finished."

"What will we use for Ainnileas?" Ingrid asked.

Hrefna frowned, digging deeper into the chest, and pulled out a parcel from the bottom. "I knew there was a reason I saved these. I made them for the boys when I came to live with them. This one should work for Ainnileas." She shook out a pattern that seemed roughly the correct size. "They were always big for their age."

"How old were they?"

"Eight when I moved to the farmstead to care for them," Hrefna replied.

Selia swallowed as she looked down at her own belly. The tiny life that dwelled inside would outgrow her in a matter of a few years.

She spread out the red cloth. To save time she collected a length of deep blue cloth marked for Ulfrik, and laid it atop Alrik's cloth. She would pin them to the pattern together.

Hrefna put her hand on Selia's arm to stop her. "What are you doing?"

"I will cut Ulfrik's at the same time," she said with uncertainty. What had she done wrong?

Ingrid snorted, and Hrefna shot her niece a hard look. "Selia, it would not be appropriate for you to make clothes for Ulfrik. A wife makes the clothing of her husband, and if a man is unmarried, then a woman in his family makes his clothes. He would take it as a sign of interest from anyone else. Do you understand?"

"No." The rules of the Finngalls were so puzzling. Was she not in Ulfrik's family?

Hrefna paused. "Making clothes for a man can be . . . almost magic. It can bind him to you. A woman's thoughts and the words she speaks while she is making the clothes will influence the wearer. It is a very powerful gift."

Selia gasped. *That* was the real reason Hrefna had decided all the men needed new clothes—so her niece could ensnare Ainnileas. She stared at Hrefna for several moments in shock.

Storming over to Ingrid, Selia snatched the blue cloth from her. Ingrid screamed in rage.

"You—"Selia sputtered—"you will not use magic on my brother!"

The girl's eyes flashed as her hands clenched into fists. "Hrefna," she shrieked, "tell her to give that back to me!"

Selia hugged the cloth to her chest. "I will *not*." She turned to Alrik's aunt. "*I* am Ainnileas' family—*I* will make his clothes."

As Hrefna looked back and forth between them, Alrik emerged from the bedroom, shirtless and disheveled. Selia ran to him, clutching the cloth.

"It is a sad day when a man can't sleep in his own house," he grumbled to his aunt.

"It is also a sad day when a man drinks so heavily he can't arise from his bed until past noon," Hrefna pointed out.

He ignored her and turned to Selia with resignation. "What are you screaming about?"

Ingrid spoke first, glaring at Selia. "We are making new clothes for the gathering. And your wife will not let me make clothes for Ainnileas. She snatched the cloth from my hands."

"He is *my* brother," Selia insisted. "Ingrid should not do it."

Alrik raised an eyebrow at his aunt. They exchanged a long look, then Alrik sighed, shaking his head. "Let Ingrid do it."

Selia's jaw dropped. The girl crowed in triumph as she pulled the cloth away. "Thank you, Stepmother." Her voice dripped with sweetness.

Selia choked back a cry of rage as she stormed into the bedroom and slammed the door behind her. Infuriating Finngalls.

After a moment Alrik followed her into the bedroom, but she refused to acknowledge his presence. He had made it very clear her feelings meant nothing to him. How could he choose the wishes of his daughter-the daughter he hated-over those of his own wife? How could he have allowed such humiliation?

He sat on the edge of the bed, watching as she paced back and forth. Was he actually biting back a smile? She wanted to hit him.

"Selia." He reached out as she passed him. "Come here."

She smacked his hand away. "Don't you dare touch me, you Finngall bastard!" she yelled at him in Irish.

"'Bastard,'" he repeated, struggling slightly with the Irish pronunciation. "That seems to be a favorite word of yours. I'll have to ask Ulfrik what it means. I'm guessing, 'darling husband?'"

So he thought this a jest? Hrefna and Ingrid plotted to put some sort of Finngall spell over her brother, and Alrik found it amusing? She turned to him with gritted teeth.

"*Bastard,*" she said, this time in Norse. "It means bastard." Selia crossed her arms, waiting for him to explode, but instead he threw his head back and laughed.

"And what have I done to deserve such a title, my little Selia?"

"You would let Ingrid make clothes for Ainnileas. To make him *like* her," she seethed.

"I can see with my own eyes that he likes her. Why would you not allow her to show affection for him?"

"Because she is a terrible girl! Because I will not have her marry my brother!"

He pulled her into his lap. "No man has shown the slightest interest in Ingrid before now. Yet I must find a husband for her. What better match would there be than the brother of my wife?"

"They are children. They are too young to be married."

"So, you are not a child, but your twin brother is?" Alrik teased.

Furious, she turned away. She herself had been so besotted with the handsome Finngall, she had actually suggested *he* marry *her.* But this was different. Her brother's interest in Ingrid was simply a ruse, and there was no way to explain that to Alrik.

"Wouldn't you like to have your brother live here?" He tilted her chin so she was forced to look at him. "I would have a house built for them nearby so you could see him as often as you liked."

No. He has to leave. Ainnileas hated Alrik, and if he stayed here he would end up doing something foolish. "I do not want him to stay," she replied. "I am afraid you will hurt him."

"And why would you think that?"

She looked into her husband's face—so achingly beautiful, yet so dangerous. "Because you are a berserker." Her voice shook over the awful word.

His eyes narrowed but he didn't deny it. "Did Ulfrik tell you that?"

"No one had to tell me."

Alrik was quiet for some time, and she hesitated for a moment before forcing herself to continue. "Alrik, I love you, but I also love Ainnileas. If you ever hurt him . . ."

His face darkened as though he understood the unspoken implication. "You would choose your brother over me."

"I do not want to choose! Why do you not understand that?" She expelled an impatient huff. She had given up everything for this man, yet he still demanded more. Last night he had all but begged her not to leave, and now he seemed paradoxically determined to disprove her love for him.

Alrik's jaw clenched. "I knew you would do this. I knew you would try to manipulate me when you said you loved me."

'Manipulate' wasn't a word she was familiar with, but from the disdainful expression on his face he seemed to be accusing her of lying. She shoved at his chest, trying to squirm from his lap. "I do not know what that means."

"Of course you do, Selia. It's what women do best. You use your face and your body to get what you want. And if things don't go your way, you cry. Or you withhold yourself from me until I agree. You tell me you love me, then you tell me what you want me to do."

She gaped. Could he not see the behavior he described

was the only way she *could* get what she wanted? Otherwise she was completely powerless in their marriage.

"You have made me this way." She choked back tears. "You do not listen to me unless I have pleased you. You laugh at me and call me a child. You do whatever you want without thinking of me."

"So you *do* manipulate me on purpose."

"You are not listening, Alrik!"

"More trouble than you are worth." He smirked. "You women are all alike."

She clenched her hands into impotent fists. What should she expect from such a selfish man? He had no regard for the feelings of anyone else. It was little wonder no one could stand to be around him. "Why do you want me to hate you?"

He shot her an impatient look. "I don't want you to hate me."

"Yes, you do. Every time I tell you of my love, you do something bad."

He didn't answer. She pushed a lock of his hair from his face, staring at him until he made eye contact with her. Selia saw a flicker of fear cross his face before it was quickly masked.

"You are afraid," she guessed. "You think I will hurt you."

Alrik laughed. He pushed her aside as he stood up, towering over her in all his masculine glory. "And how could you possibly hurt me, little one?"

"I think you love me too, but you will not say it."

He grunted, turning to rummage through one of the chests. He pulled out a fresh shirt.

Watching him intently, she added, "You think it will make you weak if we are like Hrefna and Olaf—"

"Enough, Selia," he growled. "Stop talking, now."

"But—"

"I said that's enough!" He crossed the room, grabbing her shoulders. His angry face loomed inches from her own. "I wish you had never learned Norse—it was much easier when you kept your mouth shut."

Bastard. She kicked him hard in the shin, and Alrik hissed in surprise. "Well, I wish I had never met you—*that* would have been easier!"

The muscle in his jaw tightened dangerously. "Yes. It certainly would."

He shoved her aside as he stormed from the room.

Chapter 27

Ainnileas adapted easily to the family of Finngalls. As Selia had expected, within a few days it was as though they couldn't imagine a time when he hadn't been there. She watched with skepticism as her brother charmed them all. How long could he keep this up? What would happen when they saw through his ruse? Her task now would be to try keeping the foolish boy safe when it happened.

Ainnileas and Ulfrik continued to go out fishing together daily, and would bring back nets full of fish for the thralls to smoke for the gathering. Ulfrik, whose emotions were normally so subdued, now laughed and joked easily with her brother, bantering back and forth with him in Irish as though they had been friends for ages.

To make matters worse, Ulfrik was avoiding her again after their uncomfortable conversation behind the house. This bothered her more than she cared to admit, and the sight of him having such a good time with her brother was like salt in the wound. She had been replaced. Ulfrik now had a friend whose company he could enjoy without fearing he might get killed for it.

Alrik had gone hunting with Olaf the day she had fought with him. He left without saying goodbye, but she refused to worry about him. The tension in the house had eased with his departure, and Hrefna and Ingrid happily continued in their preparations for the gathering. The girl had rushed through the task of sewing Ainnileas' new set of clothes, and had been grinning like a fool ever since presenting him with the folded parcel.

Ingrid had done a sloppy job on the clothing and didn't have enough sense to be embarrassed by it. If Ainnileas possessed any prudence, he would realize the girl's poor skills as a seamstress were a direct indication of her unsuitability as a wife.

But no, he had been pleased with the gift, and wore his new Finngall outfit with pride, crooked stitches and all.

Selia took great care in the construction of Alrik's clothing. If his daughter thought she could ensnare Ainnileas in a Finngall spell done with careless, childish stitches, then certainly Selia could do her one better. As she sewed, she held an image in her mind of Alrik's beautiful smile, the one he bestowed on her so rarely. She imagined his anger and mistrust wiped clean. She repeated the words under her breath with each stitch. *Love me.* And if her mind wandered, as it sometimes did, she ripped out the tiny, perfect stitches she had just made and started again.

If this was what her husband called manipulation, then so be it. He had left her no other choice.

There was a noise outside that sounded like someone shouting from far away. Selia put down her sewing, cocking her head to listen. Hrefna sat up straighter and made eye contact with Selia.

The noise came again. Olaf's voice. The women leapt to their feet, racing for the kitchen door, with the others following behind. Selia threw open the door and clapped a hand over her mouth as she saw Olaf and Alrik emerging from the woods. Alrik had one arm slung across Olaf's shoulders and the other hand pressed into his side, where a dark stain of blood had seeped from his shirt and down his left leg, disappearing into his boot.

She sprinted to them. Several thralls ran to help as well, and as Selia reached them, two male thralls were taking Alrik under the arms. Olaf slumped to the ground, exhausted.

"What happened?" she cried.

Alrik was deathly pale, almost gray, and it took a moment for his eyes to focus on her. But it was Olaf who answered, his voice a hoarse whisper. "A boar."

Hrefna pushed forward through the small crowd, lifting her nephew's hand away to examine the wound. His shirt was encrusted with blood and stuck to his skin, and as she raised it a trickle of fresh blood dribbled down his hip.

There was a deep gash in his side just above his left hipbone, thick with blackened blood. Selia bit back a scream. How could a wound such as that be anything but life-threatening?

Yet Hrefna remained calm. She ordered the thralls to carry Alrik into the house, and to bring fresh water. "You know better than to hunt boar," she said to her husband in a stony voice.

Olaf looked miserable. "We had been tracking a deer when we came across fresh boar tracks. We decided to go after it instead."

They made their way down the hill, the thralls carrying Alrik between them. Selia turned to Olaf. "The boar did this?" she said, motioning to the wound.

Olaf nodded. "It charged me. Alrik shoved me aside and managed to spear the beast. But not before it gouged him."

Hrefna's eyes narrowed as she listened, and she muttered something under her breath. Was she angry at Alrik, Olaf, or both?

The thralls laid Alrik's semi-conscious form atop two tables the thralls pushed together. Hrefna took her scissors to cut the ruined shirt from his body. She set a wet cloth over the wound to soften the dried blood as Selia threaded a thick needle. After Hrefna carefully wiped away the blood, they leaned over to examine Alrik.

There was a gash as long as Selia's palm where the flesh had been laid open, which grew deeper until it ended in a sinister-looking puncture wound. Her own skin crawled when Hrefna stuck her finger inside the dark hole. Alrik grunted. Selia took his big hand in hers, as much for her own comfort as his.

To her surprise, his eyes fluttered open. He gave her a faint, wry smile before addressing his aunt. "Stop poking around in my gut, woman, and sew it up." The weakness in his voice belied the attempted bravado.

Hrefna's eyes flashed as she finished her examination. She reached for the needle Selia held out. "I should just let you bleed to death, you fool. Will you never learn? Would you make your wife a widow before-" She stopped herself, looking at Selia across Alrik's body before quickly averting her gaze. "Well, before you have even been married a year?" She jabbed the needle into his skin.

Selia paled. Hrefna had nearly given away her secret. Had anyone caught the slip? As casually as she could, she glanced at the others in the room. No one but Ulfrik was paying any mind. She saw the question in his eyes and turned away.

Alrik grunted again, either from the pain or because he was simply fed up with his aunt. "I think I would rather bleed to death than listen to your harping for another minute," he muttered, which brought more jabs from the needle.

"Wasn't it enough you almost got your brother killed the last time you went boar hunting, you stupid—"

"Enough, Hrefna," Olaf said. "This was an accident, as much my fault as his."

She glared at him until he reddened. "I will hear nothing from you, Olaf Egilson." Her voice held ice. "I know whose idea it was to go after the boar. I also know who *should* have had the good sense to say no."

Selia smoothed Alrik's damp hair away from his forehead. His eyes were closed again and the skin of his brow burned under her hand. Her belly tightened in fear. "He is very hot."

"I know, child." Hrefna looked grim. "I will make him some willow bark tea in a moment."

Unfamiliar with the word in Norse, still Selia knew what would be used for pain or fever in Ireland, and had seen the herb among the medicines in Hrefna's well-stocked shelves.

She ran to the kitchen. When she found what she sought, she returned to the main room, holding it out for Hrefna's inspection. "Is this willow bark?"

"Yes."

Quickly, Selia returned to the kitchen to make the tea. She could do something useful, at least—anything to take her mind from the fear that threatened to paralyze her. Alrik's wound looked severe, but sometimes worse than the wound itself was the fever that came afterward. Her hands shook as she stirred the fire to bring the water to boil faster.

There was a noise behind her, and she turned to see Ulfrik standing in the doorway. Selia blinked back her tears. She would not cry in front of Ulfrik.

"Hrefna said to put some feverfew in the tea as well," he said, using the Irish word for it so she would know what he meant.

She wasn't as knowledgeable of feverfew, and eyed the containers of herbs with uncertainty. Many of them looked very much alike and she didn't want to make a mistake. He reached over her to pull out the herb, and she blushed as he handed it to her. He took a step back but kept his gaze on her.

She expected him to leave once his duties as translator were complete, but he remained in the kitchen. What did he want? Selia turned to pour off some of the boiling water, but her hands were shaking so badly that she spilled several drops on her finger.

She jumped back with a curse. He took the pot from her hands to pour the water into the cup. "Are you with child, Selia?" he asked abruptly.

Busying herself with wrapping a wet rag around her finger so she wouldn't have to look at him, she mumbled, "I don't think that's any of your business."

He shrugged. "You're right, it's not. I just thought you might be, since your brother is in such a hurry to get you out of Norway. I take it Alrik doesn't know yet."

Ainnileas. That fool had done exactly as she had feared, and had tried to involve Ulfrik in his mad plot to steal her away. Ulfrik now had information about her brother that could prove deadly if Alrik found out.

"Please," she whispered, "don't tell Alrik."

"Don't tell him what? That you're carrying his babe, or that your brother wants him dead?"

She felt sick. She gripped the edge of the table to steady herself as he continued in a quiet voice. "Do you want to leave, Selia? Now would be the time to do it. He will be bedridden for a while, if he even survives this."

"Stop, Ulfrik."

"If he knows you're with child he'll never let you go. It will be too late when Ainnileas' ship returns—"

She cut him off. "My brother has no idea of what he speaks. I told him I wouldn't leave. You must promise me you won't say anything to Alrik. Please."

He met her pleading gaze for a long time before he spoke. "I don't want to see Ainnileas hurt any more than you do. But I can't allow you to get hurt either. Let me help you."

Selia's lip quivered as she stared at him. "No," she said quietly. "I will not leave Alrik."

Ulfrik said no more and silently stirred the tea. His face was blank, unreadable. "This is ready." He held out the cup to her, then strode across the room.

As he neared the doorway leading to the main room, he faced her. "Don't worry about Alrik, Selia—he'll be all right. He always is."

Chapter 28

Alrik's wound festered despite his aunt's tireless attentions. He lay in the bed, drifting in and out, mumbling incoherently as he burned and shivered.

Selia did not leave his side as he grew more and more ill. She made him as comfortable as she could, bathing his feverish body in cool water and refreshing the blankets as they grew damp with his sweat. She helped Hrefna change the poultices and strip the pus that oozed from the inflamed wound, and most of the time managed to restrain herself from vomiting.

Although Hrefna attempted to remain calm, it was clear she was becoming more desperate. The gathering was in four days' time, and Selia assumed it would be cancelled, or at least postponed, due to the accident. But Hrefna surprised her by refusing to do either. Instead, she concocted a foul mixture consisting of curdled sheep's milk, urine, and honey, then poured it over the wound.

She slaughtered a lamb, using the warm blood to draw runes on Alrik's body and on the floor surrounding the bed, while murmuring healing incantations. Normally suspicious of such things, Selia took great comfort in this. Her Christian prayers—whispered under her breath when she was alone with her husband—seemed hollow somehow.

Alrik would be furious if he knew she was praying to the White Christ on his behalf. God was probably no fonder of Alrik than he was of Him. So if Hrefna thought lamb's blood could save Alrik's life, then Selia was willing to slaughter the entire herd.

His aunt continued talking to him even though Selia was sure he couldn't hear her. "Your men will arrive soon for the gathering. Won't you feel foolish if you are lying in bed like an old woman when they get here? Be a man and rise to be the Hersir for your war band, Alrik! They need a strong leader, not a weakling who takes to his bed with a tiny scratch."

"Stop, Hrefna," she finally protested. Why did the woman continue to berate him while he was so helpless? It seemed wrong.

"I'm giving him something to focus on, child," Hrefna whispered. "Otherwise he might let himself slip away."

Slip away. Dead. Selia choked back a sob as Hrefna wrapped up the smelly remains of the poultice, then left the room, closing the door softly behind her.

Dead. She should prepare herself for the very real possibility that Alrik might die and leave her a widow. A widow carrying his child. She rubbed her hand over her belly as if she could offer comfort to the babe who grew inside and might soon be fatherless. How could she possibly raise an infant alone?

She supposed Hrefna would help her if she stayed here with the Finngalls. But would she even want to stay without Alrik? If she instead went home to Ireland with her brother, would he still try to marry her off to Buadhach?

Alrik stirred, becoming agitated the higher his fever climbed. She wrung out a cool cloth to place on his forehead. He said something unintelligible as his eyes stared into nothingness.

She put a hand to his hot cheek. "Shh."

"Selia . . ." He spoke so clearly that her heart leapt.

"I am here, Alrik."

But he wasn't looking at her; the Selia he was speaking to was in his fevered mind only. "I didn't know." His restless head would not be still on the pillow. "Odin gave you to me . . . you were only a child, how could I have known . . ."

He began to thrash about with more energy than Selia had seen from him during his illness, and nearly fell from the bed. She cried out, trying to restrain him. The noise and touch must have registered in his mind, because his wild gaze landed upon her as he sat up, gripping her shoulders.

"You look at me with those eyes. Always judging me."

She squirmed as his hands squeezed harder. "Stop, Alrik."

"I didn't know, Selia!" He let out an anguished sob as the strength drained from his body. He slumped back in the bed, and his eyes closed again. Although he continued muttering to himself, it was nothing more than the senseless ramblings of a fevered brain.

The sudden burst of energy had depleted him, and he now looked as pale and still as death. Even his breathing had slowed to the point that his chest seemed to barely rise. She watched for several minutes, counting between breaths. They got slightly farther apart each time.

She shook his arm. "Alrik." There was no response.

Selia sat on the edge of the bed next to him, lifting his hand to her cheek. It was strangely comforting, and she closed her eyes for a moment as she felt his hot skin on hers. "I love you." She placed a soft kiss on his palm and watched his face for some sort of reaction, no matter how small.

Nothing.

Alrik wanted a son. If he didn't have a male child to become Hersir after him, it would be up to one of his men to take his place, which would lead to infighting and needless bloodshed.

Three times Eydis had been confined to her bed, only to present her husband with a daughter. According to Hrefna, the only time she had delivered a son, in between Ingrid and the two younger girls, the child had been stillborn.

Selia placed Alrik's heavy hand on her belly. The fevered heat of his skin radiated through her gown and into her own body, as though she held a smoldering log against her. She put her hands over his, pressing in until she could feel the hard resistance of her womb, deep inside. "Alrik," she said again. "Your child—your *son*—grows inside me. Do you feel it?"

She watched him carefully, looking for a facial twitch or a change in his breathing, but there was none. "I need you, Alrik. The child needs you. Who will teach him how to be a Finngall? Ainnileas is not a warrior. You must wake up or your son will be a whistle-playing boy who does not know how to hold a sword."

Whatever hope she had that her words would find their way to him, giving him the strength he needed to pull himself out of the fever, dissolved as she watched his expressionless face. He had lost weight during the days of his illness, and his cheekbones were sharp, the sockets of his eyes sunken. His features looked as if carved out of stone. She had a compulsive urge to touch him, to feel the give of his skin and the muscle and bone beneath. To make sure he was still a living, breathing man, and not a statue. Or a corpse.

She sat for a few moments longer, then lay down next to him with her head in the crook of his arm. His body was so hot she began to sweat, and her tears and perspiration mingled with the dampness already on his chest. But Selia would have one more night in his arms, at least, before he died.

Hours later, she awoke in the dark room, chilled to the bone. Her clothes felt as clammy as if she had been caught in a sudden rain shower and had not changed out of them before climbing into bed. The candle had burned out, leaving the room in blackness, and she fumbled in blind confusion for the covers.

Alrik's skin underneath her cheek was as cool as marble. Stifling a scream, she reached in the direction of his face to feel for his breath. Instead she made contact with something soft and squishy-most likely his eye-and was rewarded with the sound of a grunt of pain, followed by a curse.

"Alrik!" Selia cried. "You are awake!"

"I am now," he grumbled.

A laugh so full of relief it tinged on hysteria bubbled up from her as she fumbled in the darkness, running her hands over his face and his damp hair, assuring herself that he was indeed alive.

He twisted his head impatiently. "What are you doing?"

With a hand on each side of his face, she lowered to kiss him. She made contact with the coarse hair of his beard first, and then found his mouth. "You are not dead."

"No," he agreed. "I'm not."

"I must tell Hrefna." Selia wriggled away and was out the door before he could protest.

The woman was asleep near the hearth, slumped over the table with her head in her arms. The embers of the fire lit up her red hair, making her seem very young from a distance. Her face, however, looked drawn and exhausted. Poor Hrefna. This ordeal had been just as difficult for her as it had been for Selia.

She touched Hrefna's shoulder and whispered her name.

Startled, Hrefna stared up at Selia with anguish in her eyes, no doubt fearing the worst.

"No, Hrefna," she said quickly. "He is awake!"

Although the fever had broken, Alrik was still frighteningly weak. The women fussed over him, fluffing his pillows and changing the damp bedding, and although Alrik protested, he didn't put a stop to it. When he found out the gathering was still happening as planned, however, he came out of the bed of his own accord in an attempt to reach Hrefna.

"Get over here, woman, so I can wring your neck," he yelled, but teetered and fell back onto the bed.

His aunt raised her eyebrows at him. "Is that any way to speak to the person who brought you back from the brink of death?"

"Just what were you going to do if I had died after all?" he demanded. "Have the party to celebrate?"

Hrefna laughed. "We would have had your funeral, you fool."

Alrik glared at her, grumbling under his breath, as a thrall brought in a tray of food. The strong smell of liver assaulted Selia's sensitive nose as the servant passed by. She clamped a hand over her mouth to keep the bile down. But it was too late, the damage had been done, and she streaked outside just in time.

When she returned, Alrik had finished the liver and was tucking into a bowl of what looked and smelled like blood pudding. Selia broke out in a trembling sweat but managed not to vomit again. She took a chair at the other side of the room, fanning herself with her hand.

He eyed her over the bowl for a moment, then turned to his aunt. Hrefna averted her gaze. Alrik snorted and looked back at Selia. "When were you going to tell me?"

She flushed. "I did tell you, last night."

"Last night?" He looked amused. "When I was insensate?"

"Yes. I told you not to die, because your son would become a silly boy like Ainnileas. He does not know how to fight," she explained. "He can only play his whistle."

Alrik burst into raspy laughter and stretched a hand out for Selia. She sat next to him on the bed. "You think it's a boy?" he asked.

She nodded. "Only a boy would make me so sick."

He laughed again, his beautiful smile making her knees go weak. Her blush deepened. Alrik sat up straighter, regarding her with interest.

He handed his aunt the empty bowl. "Hrefna, have the thralls prepare the bathhouse. I smell like a dead dog."

"That's not a good idea." She shared a frown between Alrik and Selia. "It's too far for you to walk, and I'm not sure if a . . . *bath* is safe for you so soon after your fever."

Alrik ignored her. He threw off the blankets and sat on the edge of the bed. He had a bit of color in his cheeks now, either from his repast of blood and liver or from the thought of having his way with Selia in the bathhouse. Attempting to stand, he wobbled a bit before sinking back on the bed.

"Go on." He waved Hrefna toward the door. "Let me know when the bath is ready."

Alrik won in the end, as usual. Hrefna insisted two thralls help him walk to the bathhouse, which he allowed, but the minute they were inside he dismissed them. He bolted the door, turning to Selia with an expectant look on his face.

But he was pale and out of breath. She led him to the chair and bade him sit so she could check his wound. She frowned as she lifted his shirt. "You are bleeding, Alrik."

"I'm not leaving without a bath."

There was no point in arguing with him. Selia watched him for signs of pain as she carefully pulled his shirt over his head, but his face remained stoic. He had to stand so she could untie his breeches, and as she pushed them down over his hips his desire for her became very evident.

Selia suppressed a giggle. "Hrefna said you must rest."

"Hrefna does not concern me," he replied as he climbed into the massive wooden tub. He sank into the hot water up to his shoulders and closed his eyes. "Come here, little one."

She shook her head as she undressed, taking down her hair to wash it before the gathering. She combed her fingers through the thick locks and caught Alrik staring at her.

"You're beautiful, Selia." He spoke in quiet tones as he reached out to finger a tendril of her hair. "I have never seen such a beautiful woman."

She smiled. Her husband was not one to give compliments easily. "So I am a woman now, not a girl?" she teased as she climbed into the tub. She sat across from him, arranging her legs so as not to bump his wound.

He shrugged. "You are carrying my child. I suppose that makes you a woman." Alrik reached for her, pulling her close. Selia carefully straddled his right leg, staying far from his wounded left side, and put her arms around his neck. She pressed her lips to his warm skin, felt the pulse beating there, and sent a prayer of thanks to the heavens—God, Odin—that her husband's life had been spared.

"I love you," she whispered into his neck.

"Good," he said, and she knew by the tone of his voice he was grinning. "Because you're going to have to do all the work. I can barely move."

Chapter 29

Ainnileas blew a few notes into his whistle, then called out to Selia from the other side of the room where he was consorting with Ingrid. "Sing with me, my sister," he said in Norse, causing Ingrid to giggle. The girl had taken it upon herself to teach Ainnileas her language, but she found his accent hilarious.

Or was Ingrid laughing because he had perhaps shared with her the embarrassing reason for Selia's reluctance to sing? She stabbed the needle through the cloth of the breeches she was sewing for Alrik, and refused to look up at her brother in his absurd Finngall outfit.

"No." She glanced over to where Alrik was reclining on one of the benches. He had slept for several hours after his bath, but had insisted on getting out of bed for supper. Hrefna had made him another large helping of liver and blood pudding, which he had downed with enthusiasm. Now he had his eyes closed again. "Alrik needs to rest."

"But *you* need to practice for the party," Ainnileas coaxed, this time in Irish.

She dropped the sewing into her lap with a sigh. At this rate she would be up all night trying to finish Alrik's outfit. "No," she snapped at her brother. "And I told you, I'm not singing at the gathering. Why would they want to hear Irish songs? No one would understand the words except for Ulfrik."

Ulfrik chimed in from where he had just finished a game of tafl with Olaf. "They don't understand what you're saying when you speak Irish, either," he pointed out, "so what's the difference if you're singing or talking?" Selia glared at him, and he shrugged. "Why don't we play a game of tafl, then? I remember the last time we played you promised to beat me."

She made a face. "And I will."

"If you beat me, your brother will stop pestering you to sing. I will personally flog him if he asks you again." Ainnileas laughed at this, and Ulfrik shot him an amused look. "But if I win, you will have to sing at a time of Ainnileas' choosing."

She chewed her lip, considering. What was Ulfrik up to?

"Selia hates to lose," Ainnileas informed Ulfrik, who did not seem surprised to hear this.

Ulfrik was an excellent tafl player, but he had been drinking rather heavily since supper. Selia studied him. His movements were slower, more purposeful, as always when he was intoxicated. She would have the advantage if she played him now. When she won, Ainnileas would have to finally shut up.

"All right." She put down her sewing. "One game."

Ulfrik brought the board to the table and began to set it up. The others gathered round to watch, and even Ingrid did not pretend to be indifferent. Selia looked over to where the girl sat shoulder to shoulder with Ainnileas, whispering and giggling. She gritted her teeth and helped Ulfrik arrange the pieces.

The game moved along at a snail's pace, for Ulfrik needed a long time to process each move. But although the alcohol had slowed him down somewhat, it didn't seem to have impaired his judgment as she thought it would. He made no mistakes. Near the end of the game, she began to suspect she might end up singing at the gathering after all.

Ulfrik made a particularly good move that took Selia by surprise, and she swallowed, wiping her sweaty palms on her thighs as she stared at the board. She looked up at her opponent, who leaned back, watching her in a very self-assured way. Apparently *he* also assumed she would be singing at the gathering.

Ainnileas snorted with laughter and Selia nearly threw one of the tafl pieces at him, but she forced herself to block everything else out as she studied the board. She mentally ran through all the possible moves she could make, followed by Ulfrik's most likely counter moves.

He drummed his fingers on the table, trying to annoy her so she would make a mistake. She slapped her hand over his to make him stop, and he grinned. "Make your move, Selia the Dawdler," he said as he drew his hand away.

Why was he choosing to joke with her now-an attempt to distract her, perhaps? Ulfrik had fooled her once before at tafl. But like most men, he had a weakness. And his was the way he underestimated her.

Selia moved her piece. For all intent it looked as though she had panicked and made a bad move, one that would eventually let Ulfrik's king gain access to her side of the board.

He moved his king a line closer, and Selia held back a smile. Ulfrik had fallen for her trap. When she counted the remaining lines on the board and calculated all the moves, she figured if Ulfrik moved his king to that particular spot, there was no way he could win.

It took two more moves for him to realize this as well. She eyed him with satisfaction as he stared down at the board, dumfounded.

"What?" Ainnileas barked impatiently.

Ulfrik cleared his throat, not taking his eyes off Selia. "She tricked me. I lost."

"You let her win," Ainnileas accused.

"No." Ulfrik shook his head as he took a long quaff of ale.

Selia stood, shooting a grin at her brother. "Would you like to know where you can put your whistle, Ainnileas?" she said sweetly in Irish.

Ulfrik choked on his ale, and as he coughed he spat it out all over the front of her dress.

She gasped. For a long moment she and Ulfrik stared at each other, too shocked to speak. Then she broke into laughter and everyone else joined in. Selia laughed so hard, tears ran down her face and she couldn't catch her breath.

"Sh—shush," she wheezed, "we will wake up Alrik."

"I'm already awake," he grumbled from his bench.

She wiped her eyes, still giggling. Perhaps he felt left out, all alone across the room while everyone else was having fun. She went to him and brushed the hair back from his forehead, surreptitiously checking for fever. "Did you see me beat Ulfrik at tafl?" she whispered.

"Yes."

Selia grinned at him. "Now I will not have to sing at the gathering."

"Hmm, that's unfortunate." Alrik spoke in a voice loud enough to be overheard. A strangely challenging expression settled on his face as his eyes met Ulfrik's. "I was looking forward to hearing you sing, little one."

Her smile faded as she regarded him. He was jealous; envious of the laughter she had just shared with Ulfrik, he now wanted to prove something to his brother.

He stroked her cheek, making her shiver. "One song," he coaxed.

"At the gathering?"

"No, now."

Selia gave him a hard look. To refuse would not only embarrass him, but would also bring him down a notch in whatever odd power struggle he engaged with his brother. Damn him for putting her in this position. Was she nothing more than a knob on the tafl board?

But she wouldn't scold him in front of the entire family, and Alrik knew it. She fumed silently for a moment longer, just to be certain he understood how upset she was, then stood and nodded at her brother.

Ainnileas whooped in triumph. He pulled out his whistle, leaping on one of the benches, then reached for her, as if he actually thought her willing to make a spectacle of herself up there with him.

She stubbornly remained on the floor. "Pick something short," she hissed.

He thought for a moment, then with a chuckle launched into "The Lamentation of Deirdre for the Sons of Usnach." Selia's jaw clenched, and she had a nearly overwhelming urge to leap upon the bench and strangle her brother. Not only was it the longest song they knew, but it was also the very song with which she had humiliated herself, a year ago. Ainnileas had chosen it for that reason, no doubt.

Infuriating boy.

She closed her eyes and began to sing. Since childhood, the tragic song had always been her favorite. Beautiful maiden Deirdre, betrothed to the much-older King Conchobar, did not love her affianced. While walking through a meadow, she met Naoise, a handsome young warrior who happened to be Conchobar's nephew. The two fell instantly in love, and Deirdre, against Naoise's better judgment, persuaded him to elope with her.

Selia blushed as she sang that verse. Thank goodness Alrik couldn't understand the words. Could it be her favorite song had inadvertently given her the courage to suggest he marry her? At least her own story would not end in tragedy like that of Deirdre, for old Buadhach was no match for her powerful Finngall husband.

But luck was not with Deirdre and Naoise, who, along with Naoise's two brothers, had traveled from Ireland to Scotland to avoid the pursuit of Conchobar's men. One day they received word that Conchobar had decided he did not want Deirdre after all, and requested Naoise return to him, where all would be forgiven.

Deirdre begged her husband not to go. But of course honor won out over the sound council of a woman. Naoise and his brothers were killed by the treachery of the king's men. Deirdre was captured and forced to marry Conchobar.

Selia shivered as she sang the most heartbreaking stanza of the song—

What, O Conchobar, of thee?
To me naught but tears and lamentations
Hast thou meted out;
This is my life, so long as life shall last,
Thy love for me is as a flame put out.
He who was the fairest under heaven,
He who was most beloved;
Thou hast torn him from me.
Immeasurable is the injury;
I see him not until I die.

She blinked back hot tears. Had anyone noticed? It was silly to be so moved by a song she had sung so often. But the last time she had sung it she had been but an inexperienced child. Now, the thought of losing her husband the way Deirdre lost Naoise nearly took her breath away.

The song concluded with Deirdre's violent suicide. She was the most beautiful woman in Ireland, and her beauty inflamed Conchobar to kill his own nephews. Deirdre opened the door of her carriage as it traveled at high speed, and dashed her head against a rock.

At the final note, Selia took a deep breath and opened her eyes. She saw Ulfrik first, whose face was flushed with either alcohol or emotion. Since he would be the only one who actually understood the words of the song, perhaps the tragic tale had affected him.

The rest of the family sat in open-mouthed amazement, staring at her. She blushed, averting her gaze.

Hrefna broke the silence first. "By the gods, dear child, you have a voice the likes of which I have never heard. Why is it that you didn't want to sing for us?"

Ainnileas laughed. Selia's frown dared him to speak. He winked instead.

Niall had been a sociable man, and had frequently brought home dinner guests. And after dinner he would request his daughter sing for their guests, a task with which she usually complied without hesitation.

On the night they shared dinner with their nearest neighbors, Osgar the blacksmith, and his son, Naithi, disaster struck. Ainnileas leaned close and whispered that the widowed blacksmith was going to ask Niall for Selia's hand. She pinched him, sure he was teasing, but afterward couldn't remove the thought from her mind. Which, of course, was exactly why her brother had said it.

Selia winced when her father suggested she sing "The Lamentation of Deirdre." Such a lengthy song. Her belly tightened with apprehension. Every time she looked at Osgar she felt ill. Why had Eithne used such a heavy hand when spicing the mutton? The meat lay like a stone in her gullet.

As Selia stood to sing, the blacksmith stared at her with a flushed, lovestruck look on his craggy face. Her skin crawled and she looked away, but met the gaze of handsome, green-eyed Naithi, who had a similar expression on his own features.

She closed her eyes and sang, trying to block everything else out. But her churning stomach was difficult to ignore, and she prayed to make it through the song without having to run outside. She took a deep breath, concentrating on reaching a particularly high note, then smiled in relief. But she made the mistake of opening her eyes. Osgar was smiling at her, revealing a mouthful of decayed teeth. Her mind supplied the disturbing image of his rotten mouth on hers, at which point Selia's belly lurched again and she vomited—

At the feet of the handsome Naithi.

Now she fiddled with the folds of her skirt, flushing so deeply it felt as though her face was on fire. "I become flustered, sometimes," she muttered, which caused another outburst of laughter from her brother. He made a sound in his throat like a cat retching up a hairball, and she could take no more. She turned on him, snatching a cup of ale from the table, and threw it at his head as hard as she could.

Ainnileas ducked, laughing, as the ale splashed against the wall behind him. "I hate you," she hissed at him.

Selia snatched up her discarded sewing and rushed to her bedroom.

Chapter 30

Alrik came in a bit later, limping to the bed. He sat for a moment, watching her sew, and when she looked at him she saw a glint of amusement in his eyes. Obviously Ainnileas had told her humiliating story to everyone. She jabbed the needle into the cloth as though it was her brother's traitorous face.

"Come here, Selia." Alrik held his hand out to her.

"You will have nothing to wear to the gathering if I do not finish this," she retorted.

He smirked, pointing toward the chest they both knew was full of clothes. She sighed, dropping her sewing, and went to him.

She had removed her damp gown that smelled of ale and had been sewing in her shift. Alrik eyed her breasts appreciatively where they pushed against the fabric. He wrapped his hands around her waist and seemed pleased that his fingers no longer met. Although Selia's belly had not yet begun to protrude, her waist had noticeably widened.

"Did you care for Naithi?" He pronounced the Irish name with difficulty.

"Naithi? The blacksmith's son?"

"Who else?" Alrik's voice was cross.

Surely he wasn't jealous?

The idea of him envying the boy was absurd. Alrik was as handsome as one of his heathen gods, and a powerful Hersir as well. Yet here he was, concerned about the possibility his wife might be in love with a skinny lad who lived across the ocean.

"No." Selia bit her lip to keep from laughing. "Until I met you that day in Dubhlinn, I did not care for anyone. I thought boys were foolish."

He chuckled and seemed satisfied. "Well, if the way you snubbed us in the market is any indication of how you treated them, I'm surprised anyone had the courage to try again."

What was his meaning? Perhaps she had misunderstood him. "In the market?"

"Yes, when you bumped into us." At her blank look, he formed a mischievous smile. "Ulfrik is used to women ignoring him, but I'm not."

"Alrik, I met you on the hill. And I never saw Ulfrik until you took me away."

Selia watched the blood drain from his face. Since leaving Bjorgvin, she hadn't had one of her bird spells, but she had had many of her staring spells, where she would blank out for just a moment or two. There was no warning when they came upon her, so there was no way to hide them. She was usually able to claim distraction or simple daydreaming, if anyone noticed.

Alrik had never mentioned the times Selia's eyes would occasionally glaze over, so she assumed he didn't notice. But if what he said was true about that day in Dubhlinn, he had bumped into her in the market while she was incapacitated by a spell. He had then followed her up the hill when she had gone to see the dragonships.

It wasn't a simple chance meeting as she had thought.

Selia studied her husband thoughtfully. "Alrik, when you came to me the next day in the woods, you were surprised I spoke any Norse."

"Yes."

"Then how did you think you could ask me to go with you?"

He paused for a moment. "I wasn't going to ask you. I was going to take you. I wanted to take you the day I saw you in the market." His eyes burned into hers, and she couldn't look away. "You set up such a craving inside me. I had to have you."

"But you didn't take me," she whispered.

"No." He swallowed. "I didn't want you to fear me. You do something to me, Selia. I lose all reason when I look at you. You drive me mad with desire, yet at the same time I want to protect you. I want to protect you from me."

Alrik's face flushed dark, as though he immediately regretted his words. It was the closest he had ever come to admitting he loved her.

He set her aside to unlace his boots, grunting and cursing as he tried to pull them off, getting angrier by the minute.

As she watched him she realized he was embarrassed, not because he couldn't remove his boots, but from nearly confessing he loved her. She knelt down to assist him. "Do you need help with your breeches, too?" she teased in an attempt to lighten his mood.

But his anger stayed firmly in place. "Selia," he said abruptly, "I don't want you to spend so much time with Ulfrik. No more tafl."

"What?" Her smile faded. "Why?"

"It doesn't matter why. Because I said so."

Her lip quivered as she stood up. "Have I done something wrong?"

Alrik stared at her for several moments. "If it had been Ulfrik you met in Dubhlinn—instead of me—would you have gone with him?"

Selia gaped in surprise. Did he actually believe she was interested in his brother, or was this simply his way of picking a fight with her after his near-admission of love, a way to deflect the conversation away from what he perceived as a weakness?

"No," she replied. "I told you—you are the only one I have ever wanted."

"But you do care for Ulfrik," he probed. "I see the way you look at him. I see the way you laugh with him."

"He is my friend, Alrik." She felt her face flush with temper. "He is kind to me."

"He is kind to you," her husband mocked. "Yes, he is *so* kind, and he wants nothing in return. I tell you Selia, you don't know anything about my brother. If I gave the word, he would ravish you just as he did Muirin—"

She cried out, covering her ears. "Stop! Why are you saying such things?"

"Because they're true!" His anger had escalated to a dangerous level. "No man can look at you and think of friendship, and Ulfrik is no better than anyone else."

"Alrik, *stop.*" She cradled his face in her palms and looked directly into his wild eyes. She could feel the tension in his body as it shook with rage; could sense the beast inside him, pacing to get out. She stroked his face gently as though calming a nervous animal.

"I only want you," she reassured him. "Only you."

If he wasn't limited by his injury, this would be the point when he would either push her aside to go chop wood, or throw her down onto the bed and use her body as an outlet for his anger. But he could do neither, and they both knew it. The frustration of unaccustomed physical weakness was almost too much for him to bear.

"I want you to stay away from Ulfrik. Do you understand?" There was still venom in Alrik's voice, even though his body sagged with exhaustion, his cheeks wan.

This moment had been bound to come-it was actually a surprise it hadn't happened sooner. But that didn't make it any easier. "Yes," she said, keeping her eyes lowered so he wouldn't see the emotion behind them.

"You can play tafl with me if you like. I'm a good player."

Selia nodded, pushing him backward onto the bed. "Lie down now." He didn't resist, allowing her to lift his legs one at a time so he wouldn't hurt himself. But he pouted all the while, like a petulant child after a tantrum.

"You can be cross at me tomorrow," she said. "Now it is time to sleep."

"Humph," Alrik grunted.

She lay down next to him with her head pillowed on his shoulder, stroking the bare skin of his chest through the neckline of his shirt. Without conscious thought, she hummed a melody to soothe him, and after a few moments felt her own eyes grow heavy.

"Do all the Irish know that song?" he asked, disturbing her reverie.

Selia startled. The song she had been humming was "The Lamentation of Deirdre." Of course it had been in her head since she had sung it so recently. "Yes, I think so."

"I knew I had heard it before." His voice slurred as he sank into slumber, mumbling, "I think Ulfrik's mother used to sing it to him."

Chapter 31

Hrefna worked her way through the noisy crowd of the gathering toward Selia, carrying Kolgrima's youngest daughter, Signy, on her hip. The babe was gnawing on a drool-soaked wooden ring as Hrefna stopped in front of her.

"Take her for a moment, while I check on the food," she said, handing her over.

The tot gave Selia a confused expression, and Hrefna laughed. "It will give you some practice."

Selia stared at the babe. What was she expected to do with her? She was ashamed to admit she knew next to nothing about children, having had neither younger siblings nor cousins growing up. She had shared this concern with Hrefna, that she feared she might accidentally damage her own babe somehow, after it was born. Infant heads were so wobbly and their skulls so fragile. Wasn't her own skull proof of that?

Hence the practice with Signy, a healthy, chubby child so thick with padding she looked as though she would bounce if Selia dropped her.

Weaving her way through the crowd of mostly women and children, she walked toward the docks where the men were gathered to watch the swimming races. Although Ainnileas was unable to participate in most of the Finngall contests-sword sparring, archery, and wrestling not being among his talents-he was a very good swimmer, and had surprised her by agreeing to join in the races.

She was out of breath by the time she reached the docks, and she shifted the heavy babe to her other hip. Surely the child's mother would want her back soon—if Signy's weight were any indication, she was a frequent feeder. She scanned the crowd, searching for the flame-haired woman who looked like a younger version of Hrefna, to no avail. Selia was stuck with the child.

The race had already started but the swimmers were too far away for her to see where Ainnileas was. She could make out a dozen heads bobbing in the sea, but from this distance she couldn't pick out his dark hair.

The babe made a fussing sound, and Selia jiggled her the way she had seen other women do. But the fussing intensified, and several of the men standing on the shore turned, looking annoyed. When they saw it was the Hersir's wife, they hid their scowls.

She made a face at one of their broad backs. "They hate me already, and you're not helping," she whispered to the red-faced tot as she bounced her up and down on her hip.

Signy only cried louder.

"That babe is as big as you are," Alrik chuckled behind her. She turned to find him walking toward her with barely a limp. It was amazing that a man who had been on his deathbed merely days ago could look as he did now, the very picture of health. The red shirt and brown breeches she had made for him fit nicely, just snug enough to show off his powerful form, and she smiled as she took in the sight of him.

He had been in a fine mood since the men had arrived, especially considering he was under strict orders from his aunt not to participate in any of the games. Although his side was healing well, a bloody fluid would leak from the wound whenever he strained himself. Hrefna had threatened to have him tied to the bed if he even contemplated joining in the festivities.

Alrik had given her a look that said he would like to see her try, but so far he had followed her instructions. And although his men seemed worried about his wound, they joked of how his incapacitation was in their favor as it meant someone else would actually have a chance to win at the games. This seemed to please Alrik a great deal. It was difficult to tell if his current good spirits were due to the well-wishes of his men, or simply a result of one of his random mood swings.

"Where did you wander off to a moment ago?" he asked Selia, squinting at the heads bobbing in the water. "I turned and you were gone."

She glanced up at him, trying to judge his intent. He had been more watchful of her than usual since the crowd had arrived. "I had to use the privy," she explained, "but there was a line, so I went into the woods."

He faced her, now unsmiling. "You either need to stay where I can see you or tell me where you're going."

Was he still under the assumption she would run away the first chance she got? Hadn't they moved past that? The babe fussed and Selia shifted her to her other hip. "Why do you not trust me, Alrik?"

Signy screeched, swinging her dimpled arms wildly, and threw her wooden ring into the dirt. Alrik scooped the child out of her arms. "I trust *you,* Selia," he said, lifting Signy over his head. "But I don't necessarily trust every man here."

The startled Signy stopped crying and stared down at Alrik for several moments. He smiled, lowering her almost to his face, then quickly back up again. The tiny girl laughed. She opened her mouth in a wide, toothless grin, and tried to grab his nose.

Selia blinked at them. The idea of the Hersir playing with a babe was contrary to everything she knew about him. He was the most fiercely masculine man she had ever met, scornful of anything he perceived as weak or womanish. Yet here he was, being kind to an infant. How could a man who was an admitted butcher of the innocent now hold this child with such gentleness? Just when she thought she understood him, he seemed to do something completely unexpected.

He shifted Signy to his right hip. Her eyes lit up as she spotted the hilt of the sword he had insisted on wearing, despite Hrefna's protests. Signy leaned toward his left side, reaching for it, and Alrik winced but didn't discourage her. "You little Valkyrie—if you were a boy I would start your training immediately."

Signy took hold of the sword's hilt in her chubby hands, pulling herself toward it with her mouth opened wide. Selia looked away. How many children had Alrik killed with that very sword? And how many more, currently safe and warm in their mothers' womb or suckling at their breast, were destined to die by his hand during some future raid on her homeland?

Shivering, she firmly shut the door on those thoughts. She had to be more vigilant or she would give herself nightmares again.

"There she is," Kolgrima called, striding up behind them. Signy squealed with delight and reached for her mother. Alrik handed her over. Kolgrima was several years older than Alrik and a grandmother herself, yet she was still a remarkably beautiful woman.

"My father is looking for you," she said to Alrik. "Two of the boys are arguing over Rannveig Ingjaldsdottir."

Frowning, he followed Kolgrima back through the crowd in search of Olaf. He gave Selia a pointed look over his shoulder that made it clear she was expected to be there when he returned.

She turned back to watch the races. What had he meant when he said he didn't trust every man here? True, not all of them were his own men. Some were the sons or foster children of the members of his war band, not yet ready or willing to be sworn themselves. Some were distant relatives, either by blood or marriage. And a good many were thralls, since every family had brought several slaves along with them to help shoulder the work. But every man at the gathering, whether sworn to Alrik or not, understood very well who the Hersir's wife was. They knew better than to even glance in her direction. Skagi's face was a constant reminder to everyone of how unstable Alrik was when it came to his wife.

Unless his comment was in regard to someone else.

Could he be referring to Ulfrik? Or, heaven forbid, Ainnileas? Had Alrik learned of her brother's mad plan for her escape, and his own brother's willingness to help get Selia out of Norway?

Or perhaps he didn't *know*, but nevertheless believed something was off about Ulfrik's behavior. Alrik knew his brother just as well as Selia knew Ainnileas, and might therefore have a sense of what he was contemplating. That could account for Alrik's outburst of jealous anger several nights ago.

Shouting erupted from some of the men in front of Selia, and a general sense of anticipation that indicated the race was coming to a finish. She ducked through the men, scanning the bay for Ainnileas.

The race had taken the swimmers across the bay to the cliff opposite the farmstead, then back again, and now they were more than halfway to the dock. Her heart leapt as she saw a dark head among the lighter ones, toward the front. She clasped her hands together, restraining herself from calling to him in encouragement, unsure if the Finngalls would consider it rude to cheer for a foreigner.

Apparently Ingrid did not share Selia's concerns, for her voice could be heard shouting above the general din of the crowd. "Hurry, Ainnileas!"

Peering around one man's fat belly, she saw her stepdaughter some distance away, standing with one of Kolgrima's daughters. Bergdis had also fallen in love with Selia's handsome brother on sight, and had been trailing him around like a large puppy since her family's arrival at the gathering. But rather than being jealous, Ingrid seemed confident Ainnileas' affections wouldn't be compromised. In addition to being stout and quite plain, her cousin had a lazy eye that would occasionally wander away to focus on something else while she was talking. It seemed to make Ainnileas uneasy.

Selia chewed at her lip as she took in Ingrid's careful attention to her appearance. Before Ainnileas had arrived, her hair looked as though it hadn't been washed or combed in ages. Indeed, the girl screamed if her aunt even approached her with a comb and a look of determination. Now her hair hung clean and shiny down her back in a glittering wave of pale silk. Hrefna had made a new gown for her, of a bright blue that matched her eyes, and it was fitted snugly to highlight her figure. A woman's gown, not a child's. Her white skin was scrubbed clean, and her red cheeks and lips were bursting with youthful good health.

Ingrid *was* beautiful, every bit as beautiful as her father, and when she smiled or laughed all eyes turned to her. Hrefna and Alrik's fear that no one would want to marry the girl seemed groundless. If the admiring glances she was getting from the male Finngalls were any indication, she would have several marriage proposals before the gathering was over.

But Ingrid had eyes only for Ainnileas, and he for her. At first Selia had convinced herself that her brother was using Ingrid for some warped reason, but lately she had come to the sickening realization his feelings for the girl were genuine. Whether she liked it or not, her horrid stepdaughter might someday soon become her brother's horrid wife.

The swimmers were coming closer now, and Selia cheered her brother on as they neared the shore. It was a close race, with three or four swimmers within a few strokes of each other, the rest some distance behind them. It looked as though Ainnileas might not win, but his position in the race, toward the front, was encouraging.

The first swimmer to pull himself from the water was Ulfrik. The crowd broke into cheers and whistles as he leaned over with his hands on his knees, gasping for breath. Like all the swimmers he wore only his breeches, and seawater streamed down from his hair and over his torso. Once, she would have gone to him without hesitation to offer her congratulations, but now she stood planted to the ground and pretended not to see him when he tried to make eye contact with her. If her avoidance of him hurt his feelings, she knew he wouldn't show it.

Two swimmers emerged next; a young man married to one of the daughters of Alrik's men, and Ainnileas. Selia ran to her brother to give him a hug, wiping cold droplets of water from her cheek with a laugh. "You did it, Ainnileas!"

He shrugged as he tried to catch his breath. "I suppose third place is acceptable." He wasn't looking at his sister, but instead seemed to be focused on something over her shoulder.

Selia cringed as she turned to see Ingrid and Bergdis coming toward them.

Ingrid squeezed his arm. "You did wonderfully, Ainnileas." She left her hand on him just a second too long, and he met the girl's eyes with a knowing smile.

Selia stared at them. The look Ingrid had just exchanged with her brother was familiar, one she had probably given Alrik many times, and he to her. It was a look of desire, full of promise and expectation. If Ingrid and Ainnileas weren't already bedding each other, they would soon enough.

Ulfrik strode over, clapping her brother on the back, and Ainnileas grinned up at him. Their camaraderie seemed genuine as well. Selia shifted uncomfortably. That natural, easy friendship would never be possible again for her and Ulfrik.

She meant to congratulate Ulfrik politely before moving on, but instead found herself staring at him, unable to look away. She had never seen him without a shirt on, at least not up close and in broad daylight, and she now gaped at the sight of dozens of scars on his body. They looked like slash marks of varying lengths, most of them old and faded.

One though, a large and ragged scar, appeared to be the remnant of a wound that had gone completely through his shoulder and out his back. "Ulfrik," she gasped, "what happened to you?" Without thinking, she reached up to touch his shoulder, running her fingers over the thickened, silvery scar.

He met her gaze and Selia dropped her hand. "That one was from a boar attack when I was twelve."

She shuddered. It looked as though the wound had been much worse than Alrik's. So that was what Hrefna had meant about Alrik nearly getting his brother killed the last time they had hunted boar.

"And the rest." She nodded to his torso. "They are from battle?"

"Some. But they're mostly from sparring with Alrik. I didn't have a mail shirt when we were children."

A vision arose in her mind of Ulfrik as a small child, holding a shield in front of himself as his brother attacked. Why hadn't someone stopped it-Hrefna or Olaf, or Geirr, the boys' grandfather? Surely they could see the damage being done.

Selia's voice shook. "They should not have let him hurt you like that."

Ulfrik looked down at her with eyes that seemed accustomed to hiding pain. He finally spoke to her in Irish. "If Alrik doesn't hurt me, he'll hurt someone else. They knew it then and they know it now."

The truth of his words couldn't diffuse her anger at him being used in such a manner.

But before she could respond, his gaze flickered away at something over her head.

"He's coming, Selia." Ulfrik's voice held a warning note. Had he guessed the reason for her recent evasive behavior, or had the Hersir ordered him to stay away from his wife as well?

She blanched as she turned to see Alrik striding down the hill through the throng of people, his height making him easily visible in the crowd. She could not let him see her speaking with his brother. Ulfrik was half naked, and she stood much too close to him in an attempt to hear him over the din of conversations around them.

With her heart pounding in her ears, she moved to the other side of Ainnileas and stared at the ground.

She felt Ulfrik's gaze on her but she couldn't bring herself to look at him. Why had Alrik put her in this awful position? She wiped her sweaty palms on her gown, and willed her heart to calm. It felt as though it would beat out of her chest.

"Selia." Ainnileas' voice suddenly sounded very far away. He seemed surrounded by a hazy light that hurt her eyes.

"Are you all right?" Ulfrik asked. He also seemed bathed in the light and she had to squint to see him. His mouth moved in a slower time than the words he spoke, their tone jumbled, distorted.

No . . . not here. She must hide from all these people. The house was so far away; it would be impossible to make it there in time. Where could she go?

A sickening whoosh of fetid air rushed past her head. It sounded as though scores of birds cawed above the crowd. She ducked to avoid one as it flew at her face. How could she possibly protect her brother from all those birds?

Selia reached out for him. "Close your eyes," she managed to choke out.

Then she was moving, being pulled through the crowd. She looked down at her feet. Were they hers or someone else's? A large, male hand held on to hers. Not her brother's, as he was hurrying along on the other side of her, a grim look to his face.

His mouth moved as he spoke, but she couldn't hear him above the cawing of the birds.

Alrik made his way down to the shore. Selia was typically easy to spot—her dark curls stood out among the sea of blonds and redheads—but she was nowhere to be found. He had specifically told her to stay where he could see her, yet she had wandered off again. Why did she insist on disobeying him?

He approached Ingrid, who was in conversation with one of Hrefna's granddaughters, the plain one whose name he could never remember. "Have you seen Selia?" He ground his teeth at Ingrid, daring her to point out how he had no control over his own wife.

She looked at him with barely masked hostility. "She went into the woods with her brother and Ulfrik. Ainnileas said she was sick." She shook her head in disgust. "I don't know why she needed his help to vomit."

Alrik stilled as the images rushed into his head, the images that would take over his mind if he didn't make a conscious effort to block them out. Ulfrik. Touching Selia. *Inside* her. Had they planned this all along, as they whispered and laughed on the ship-to wait until his guard was down, and then run off together? Were they laughing at him right now?

Or had his traitorous brother told Selia and Ainnileas the unthinkable, and they now plotted their revenge against him?

His field of vision went dark for a moment. He saw his own hand plunge a dagger into Ulfrik's belly, gutting him like a deer as his brother's hot blood spilled into the dirt. Ulfrik's eyes, scared, cowardly, as the life drained from his body and Selia screamed.

Alrik would make her watch her lover die.

It was all he could do to string words into a coherent sentence. "You're sure Ulfrik was with them?"

Ingrid smiled. "Of course I'm sure. He was pulling your wife along by the hand."

Chapter 32

Ainnileas leaned over his sister, stroking her hair. "It's all right, Selia . . . it's all right." He knew his voice rarely registered in her mind when she was under a spell, but it somehow made him feel better to speak to her. And as he had done more times than he could remember, he murmured his comforting words in the language they had made up together as children.

As accustomed as he was to his sister's spells, they still raised his hackles. How could they not? Selia's eyes would stare into nothingness and she would spout horrible things that made his blood run cold. She called the spells 'bird spells,' which had always brought to mind a large black bird with its talons wrapped around her. An evil creature that stalked her from the shadows, waiting for its next opportunity to tear her to shreds.

And there was nothing he could do to stop the spell as it overtook her. Ainnileas could not protect his sister from the cruel darkness of her mind.

Selia spoke only nonsense when she was under the grip of a spell; confusing, chaotic ramblings he assumed was the legacy of their lives before the time of Niall. She would speak of blood and smoke and pain. Sometimes she would look directly at him, eyes wild and dark, as she warned him to run from a bad man, or from the birds she was convinced wanted to peck his eyes out.

But it was when she called for their mother that his throat would constrict with unshed tears. He could feel his sister's despair as clearly as if it were happening to him.

Selia's voice began to rise as it sometimes did during a spell, and he tried to hush her. Although Ulfrik had assured him that he knew about her spells and did not think badly of her for it, Ainnileas wasn't sure how the rest of the Finngalls at the gathering would react if they stumbled upon this strange scene in the woods.

"Cassan." Selia's wide eyes stared through him. "Run. Run away . . ."

He shushed her, but Ulfrik perked up from where he was leaning against a tree. "What is she saying?" he asked. "She told me you were the only one who could understand her when she was like this."

Ainnileas hesitated. He trusted the man, to be sure, but he had never shared the details of his sister's spells with anyone, not even Niall. Before he could answer, Selia cried out again.

"Cassan, run! He has a knife!"

Ulfrik knelt next to him. "What is 'Cassan?'"

Ainnileas chewed on his lip. He knew his sister had shared with Ulfrik how they had been foundlings. "Cassan is what she calls me when she's under a spell. It must have been my name. Before."

"How could she remember—"

Ulfrik was interrupted by Selia's piercing scream as her wild eyes landed on him. "No! Stay away from him!" She lunged at him, swinging at his face, and he had to hold her wrists to stop the blows. She struggled and screamed even louder.

Ainnileas' jaw dropped. She had *seen* Ulfrik. She typically lost herself to such a degree that she didn't interact with anyone, even Ainnileas; but somehow Ulfrik had triggered a reaction in her. His sister's terror crept over him, cold and desperate. It was hard to separate her emotions from his own when they were felt with such intensity.

He shook his head firmly as Ulfrik tried to pull her away from him. "She's trying to protect me from you. You should go. You're making it worse."

There was a noise behind them, and they both turned as Alrik crashed through the trees. His face contorted with rage as he saw Ulfrik holding on to Selia. His eyes burned into his brother's and his fingers twitched around the hilt of his sword. "Get your hands off my wife," he snarled. "Do you think she is some thrall you can rut with when my back is turned?"

Ulfrik leapt into a defensive position, keeping his eyes on Alrik's sword hand. Naked save for his wet breeches, he didn't have so much as a dagger with him. He would be completely vulnerable if his brother chose to attack.

"Would you rather I had let this happen with a hundred people to witness?" He motioned toward Selia.

"Better than a hundred people witnessing you pull my wife into the woods," Alrik sneered. "Just how am I supposed to explain that?"

Ulfrik gave his brother a thin, almost taunting smile. "I don't know, Alrik. Use your imagination."

Alrik cried out in rage as he pulled his sword from its scabbard. Ainnileas stood in front of Selia, blocking her with his body, as the Finngalls circled each other.

"I'm unarmed," Ulfrik said. His eyes were a bright, glittering blue. Ainnileas could see no fear on his face, only a strange sort of defiant anticipation. "Will you dishonor yourself by killing an unarmed man?"

Alrik laughed. He threw his sword to the ground, then unfastened his dagger from his belt and tossed it on top of the sword. "I don't need a weapon to kill a little thrall bastard like you."

Ainnileas heard a sound from his sister behind him, and turned to find her looking around the forest in confusion. She gasped as her gaze landed on the two Finngalls, and Ainnileas pulled her behind the log she had been sitting on. She was so disoriented she barely struggled.

Alrik leapt toward his brother, taking a swing at him, and Ulfrik ducked. Alrik sprang up again with an explosive uppercut that landed squarely under Ulfrik's jaw, causing him to stumble backward. He took advantage of his brother's momentary lack of balance and lunged for him in an attempt to knock him to the ground.

Ulfrik, however, brought his right knee up as he fell, and as Alrik landed on him the knee jabbed into his wounded left side. Alrik made a horrible noise, like a dying animal. His face turned chalk white as his body sagged onto that of his brother.

Selia screamed, struggling to rise, but Ainnileas restrained her. She fought him to no avail, weakened from her spell. He held her behind the log without much effort.

The brothers rolled in the dirt, cursing and beating each other. Alrik appeared to be in a good deal of pain from his wound, and a rapidly-spreading dark spot had bloomed on his shirt. Ulfrik had the advantage now. He rolled on top of his brother, wrapping his hands around his throat.

Selia screamed, begging them to stop, and Ainnileas clapped a hand over her mouth. In a few more moments that Finngall bastard would be dead and this entire nightmare would be over. His sister would be safe. They could go home.

But Selia sank her teeth into his hand, and as he drew back she elbowed him in the gut. Ainnileas doubled over in pain. She jumped over the log, trying to shove Ulfrik off her husband.

"Stop," she begged in Irish. "You're going to kill him!"

Ulfrik's face appeared demented, and she stumbled backward as he stared up at her. "I'm doing you a favor, Selia," he ground out.

Alrik's own face was purple. His eyes bulged from his head as he clawed at his brother's hands in a desperate attempt to breathe. He looked as though he only had seconds left.

Selia ran to the pile of weapons on the ground, grabbing the dagger. Ainnileas gasped. What was she doing?

"Selia, no!" he shouted, but she ignored him. She caught hold of Ulfrik's hair to jerk his head back. As she pressed the dagger to his throat, his surprised eyes rolled in her direction.

"Let go of him, Ulfrik." She spoke in a hard, threatening voice that Ainnileas had never heard before.

"You would kill me? He's a monster—"

"*Let go!*"

Ulfrik slowly removed his hands from his brother's throat. "You have no idea who you married," he spat. "If you did, you would have thanked me."

Coughing, Alrik sat up with a hand to his throat. He couldn't have understood the heated exchange in Irish between his wife and his brother, but he looked back and forth between them with smoldering rage. "I want you gone, Ulfrik. Out of my house," he rasped. "If I ever see you again the ravens will glut on your flesh."

Ulfrik's voice held bitterness. "As long as I have your permission to leave, Hersir."

"Oh, you have it, Oath Breaker."

He gave Alrik a curt nod and stood. "I'll be gone tonight, then."

Ulfrik walked away without a second glance.

Ainnileas was still standing behind the log, and hesitated as his eyes followed Ulfrik. "I cannot believe you did that," he whispered to Selia.

She turned, still clutching the dagger. She appeared crazed. "You need to leave too, Ainnileas! Go with him until your ship returns for you."

He gaped. "Selia-"

"No!" she cried. "I can't even look at you right now. When will you understand that Alrik is my husband? The father of my child? Whatever hatred you have for him matters nothing to me. If you are so willing to watch him die, then you have no business being a guest in his house. Go, now."

Ainnileas stared at her-his sister, his twin. How could she push him away after everything he had tried to do for her? He had crossed an ocean to save her, yet she would choose this wicked Finngall over her own brother.

Selia was beyond help now. There was nothing he could do.

"I do understand," he called over his shoulder as he walked away. "I understand that you're a fool."

"Alrik," Selia choked out. She dropped the dagger and knelt beside him. "You are bleeding."

He pushed her hand away as she reached toward him. "Don't touch me."

"Alrik, please—"

He rose, his face blistering with fury, snatched his dagger and sword from the ground, and stalked away without another word.

Selia remained in the woods for a long time. She cried until she had no tears left, then she stared into space, unable to move. It was all she could do to make herself breathe. How had everything gone so wrong? Not only had she nearly killed Ulfrik and completely alienated her own brother, but somehow, even after saving Alrik's life, he still despised her.

He would surely divorce her after this. He had been uncomfortable about her spells already, but as he stalked away he had made it very clear he wanted nothing more to do with her. And just because she couldn't divorce *him,* it didn't mean he couldn't divorce *her.* The Christian rule against divorce wouldn't have any power over a Finngall Hersir.

It was over; her life was finished. She couldn't live without Alrik any more than a body could live without its heart. She would lie here in the woods and wait for death to come for her. She rubbed her hand across her abdomen. *Poor little child, to never have a chance to be born.* Her own soul was damned to eternal fire already, but what would happen to the babe? Would God take pity on her unborn, or would it burn along with its mother? A wail escaped her and she buried her face in her hands.

There was a rustle of leaves, and she jumped as she felt an arm go around her. *Hrefna*. Alrik's aunt pulled her against her bosom as Selia burst into fresh sobs.

"Shhh, child." Hrefna rocked her like she would one of her grandchildren. "Where did he hurt you?"

Selia was crying so hard she could barely speak. "He . . . didn't . . . hurt me," she managed to choke out.

Hrefna leaned back to look at her. "Well, what happened then? Alrik's bleeding, Ulfrik's bleeding, and you're crying." She paused for a moment. "Did Ulfrik try to—" She gestured mutely.

"No!" How could Hrefna think such a thing? "But everyone hates me now. Even Ainnileas," she sniffled. "Alrik will divorce me, Hrefna. I'll die without him."

The woman took her by the shoulders. "Stop, child. You're getting worked up over nothing. I learned many years ago that no matter how angry Alrik gets, it will fade. Whatever happened between you two will be nothing by tomorrow, mark my words."

Selia shook her head. "No, he hates me." Her voice trailed off to a whisper. "I am full of dark magic."

Hrefna's lips twitched as if to force back a laugh. "My dear, I don't think I've ever met anyone *less* full of dark magic than you."

Selia averted her gaze. If Hrefna wasn't going to take her seriously, then she would rather be left alone.

But Hrefna grasped Selia by the chin and looked into her face thoughtfully. "Does this have something to do with how your eyes glaze over?" she asked. At Selia's gasp, she smiled gently. "You and I spend the entire day together, Selia. No one 'daydreams' that much."

What must Hrefna think of her? "I'm sorry," she whispered.

"What is there to be sorry for? You cannot help it any more than you can help this," she said, her fingers parting Selia's hair to carefully press the divot in her skull.

She stared at the woman uncomprehendingly. What was she talking about?

Hrefna raised her eyebrows. "You have no idea, do you?"

"No idea of what?"

"Oh, my poor child. All this time." Hrefna stroked Selia's hair. "My brother suffered from a similar condition to yours when we were children, after he fell from a tree and struck his head. For years his eyes would sometimes glaze over, like yours do. Sometimes his body would thrash about. I was terrified every time that happened."

Selia's breath caught in her throat. "It was because he hurt his head?"

"Yes. I have even heard of men coming back from battle with the same symptoms after a grievous head injury."

Selia began to shake, and she wrapped her arms around her knees, holding on. Could it be-could it *possibly* be-that her spells were the simple result of whatever had caused the dent in her skull? Not a punishment from God, or a sign that wickedness dwelled inside her. For her entire life she had lived in shame of her secret. Could everything she had been lead to believe be wrong, a mistake?

Her throat was so dry she could barely speak. "Hrefna, sometimes . . . I see things that are not there, and *smell* things that are not there. Could that also be from this?" she asked, touching her head.

The woman shrugged. "My brother said he would see a strange light just before his muscles began to twitch. It was how he knew it was about to happen."

Selia clapped a hand over her mouth and began to sob. Her body was wracked with a strange combination of fury and relief, and she could neither speak nor think coherently for quite some time. Hrefna held her until her sobs quieted.

Spent, she lay against Hrefna's shoulder. She felt empty, almost weightless; as though she could drift off into the heavens if she wasn't careful.

"Alrik is a foolish, superstitious man, and if he has made you feel ashamed for what you cannot help, then he will have me to answer to," Hrefna vowed. "I'll speak to him tomorrow after everyone has gone. But for now, we must get back to the gathering. Bolli will swear allegiance to Alrik tonight, and it would not look well for the Hersir's wife to be absent from the ceremony."

Chapter 33

Selia sat on one of the benches in the main room of the house, pressed close to Bergdis. The girl was sweating profusely and doing her best to avoid looking at or touching Selia, which was difficult considering the tight quarters. It was anyone's guess what sort of lies Ingrid had told her cousin about her new stepmother.

Ulfrik and Ainnileas were absent from the crowd that had packed in nearly shoulder to shoulder. Nor had she seen them outside. What right did she have to be upset about Ainnileas' departure? She had sent him away, after all.

Alrik hadn't spoken to her since the awful incident in the woods. When she returned to the farmstead, his fierce gaze landed on her only briefly before turning away in apparent contempt. He hated her and he didn't want her here. But what Alrik hated more than anything was to be embarrassed, and so he would wait until they were alone to tell her he was divorcing her.

Selia's first impulse was to run back to the woods, but Hrefna gave her a pointed look from across the room that told her to stand her ground.

The house was overflowing with people in anticipation of the ceremony, and the air was thick with stagnant body heat as well as the smoke from the hearth. She swallowed. Her mouth was watering as it did right before she would vomit. She closed her eyes and kept her breathing shallow, willing the bile to stay down.

"Are you going to be sick again?" Bergdis asked. She pulled her gown away from where it touched Selia's knee.

She shook her head, as much to convince herself as Bergdis. The girl wasn't nearly as hateful as her cousin, so Selia attempted to smile at her. "I'm fine. Have you seen my brother?"

Bergdis stilled. "No."

Selia's eyes narrowed suspiciously. The two girls had been as thick as thieves for the past few days, following Ainnileas around shamelessly. Why wasn't Bergdis with them now?

"Where is Ingrid?"

The girl's face turned white, then blood red. "I don't know," she said with forced nonchalance.

So Ainnileas and Ingrid had sent her away for the chance to be alone together. Stupid, *stupid* Ainnileas, risking the wrath of the Hersir over such a dubious prize as Ingrid. Alrik would kill him if he thought the boy was deflowering his daughter behind a bush somewhere, regardless of whether or not he considered him a potential husband for her. And Ainnileas had the nerve to call *her* a fool. She closed her eyes and focused hard on her breathing.

Dozens of thralls had been working their way through the crowd, replenishing empty cups of ale and wine, and Selia was surprised to hear a familiar, Irish-accented whisper. "Would you like some wine, Mistress?"

She opened her eyes to see Muirin standing in front of her. The girl flushed crimson, and Selia was again struck by her flawless beauty. But never again could she look at Muirin without thinking of her in bed with both Alrik and Ulfrik— the shameful act was burned into her mind as though she had witnessed it herself.

Had the thrall been opposed to it? Had she encouraged it? Had she any say in the matter at all?

Selia frowned. Muirin had to have been in agreement; otherwise Ulfrik wouldn't have accepted his brother's invitation. He wasn't the type to force himself on a woman, slave or no. Perhaps Muirin wasn't the innocent victim she made herself out to be. Perhaps she encouraged the Hersir in other ways as well.

Muirin's lovely green eyes, long and slightly slanted like those of a cat, met Selia's regard for a moment before she lowered her gaze to the floor. The girl's condition was impossible to hide now, and Selia glanced uncomfortably at the bulge under her dress.

The slave flushed deeper, shifting from one foot to the other. "I can bring you some ale if you would rather—"

"This is fine." She accepted the cup of wine from Muirin to make her go away. The girl bobbed her head in deference before fleeing back toward the kitchen.

Selia drank deeply of the wine in hopes it would steady her nerves. If Ulfrik truly was leaving the farmstead, he would more than likely take Muirin with him. He wouldn't leave the child here if he wasn't permitted to return. She would miss him, but their bond had been damaged beyond repair this afternoon.

With Ulfrik and Muirin both gone, she and Alrik would have little left to fight over. Selia brightened a bit. Without all the distractions of late she might be able to salvage whatever feelings her husband still had for her.

Another thrall disturbed her reverie by attempting to pour more wine into her empty cup. The movement caused the cup to slip from her fingers, rolling under one of the tables. The thrall stared at it, then back to Selia, blinking like an owl. "I will get you another," the woman said, and was off toward the kitchen before Selia could stop her.

The thrall came back with a fresh cup of wine. Her gaze traveled over Selia from head to toe with a surprising directness as she handed it to her.

"Thank you." Selia took a sip.

The thrall didn't go on her way. What on earth did she want? "I'm sorry," the woman said, in clear, perfect Irish. "I shouldn't stare at the mistress of the house."

Selia smiled at the lovely sound of her native language. "It's all right," she said.

The slave looked startled, and she hurried off without another word. What a strange woman.

"Well," Bergdis huffed, "I suppose they think you're the only one who wants any wine."

Bolli's young voice shook with emotion as he stood in front of Alrik, and began his formal oath to the Hersir. "I am Bolli, son of Ketill, and grandson of Bruni. I have come to offer my oath to you, Alrik Ragnarson."

Alrik sat in a chair, facing both Bolli and the crush of witnesses. He had changed out of his bloody, dusty clothes and combed his hair. He now looked the part of a mighty Hersir, even though his face and neck still carried the bruised evidence of his fight with his brother. Alrik held his sword under his arm, with the hilt of it on his knee, toward Bolli. Selia noticed his thumb twitching as he gripped it.

Although to the casual observer the Hersir appeared calm, she knew he was still furious and would like more than anything to drive the sword through the belly of an enemy.

Or his brother.

Alrik leveled his intense gaze on Bolli, and to the boy's credit he did not look away. "Will you come into my war band, Bolli Ketilson, to serve me as warrior?" His voice was low and raspy from the throttling he had received at the hands of Ulfrik.

"I will, Hersir," Bolli vowed.

"Speak your oath then."

Bolli's throat moved visibly as he swallowed. He knelt before the Hersir, putting his right hand under the hilt of Alrik's sword. "I, Bolli Ketilson, make this oath, that I shall answer the call of battle, and shall never flee from the field. I shall strike the enemy down without quarter to bring honor to my Hersir and my war band. I shall follow my Hersir without hesitation or fear, protecting him with my life. If he should fall in battle, I swear on my own life to avenge him. By Odin Allfather and mighty Thorr, may this sword upon which my hand rests run me through if I fail to keep my oath."

Alrik looked down at Bolli's bent head. Although the boy was large for his age, and his strength and skill had been proven during the games of the gathering, he was still only sixteen years old. As of yesterday Alrik had been adamant that he would not accept Bolli's oath this year.

Everything had changed this afternoon. With Ulfrik now gone, the Hersir could not afford to turn down a strong and willing addition to his war band.

"I have heard your oath, Bolli Ketilson. Hear you now my vow to you. I shall gift you with gold and silver, sharing the plunder of battle as you merit. Never shall you feel hunger or thirst while my belly is full or my thirst is slaked. My sword shall stand between you and your enemies, cutting down any who dare raise a hand against you, and if you should fall I shall avenge you with my last breath. May Odin Allfather, god of oaths, hear my words, and may mighty Thorr hallow this vow."

Alrik stood and handed his sword to Olaf. Selia noticed a flicker of pain cross her husband's features. It was gone as quickly as it came, and it could easily have been mistaken for a trick of the light if she hadn't been aware of the fresh assault to his wounded side.

Olaf handed him another sword, then Alrik turned back to Bolli. "Rise, Bolli Ketilson, and join your war band." He presented the boy with the sword, and an eruption of shouting and cheers arose from the witnesses.

Bolli smiled as he accepted his gift. His gaze flickered over to where Selia and Bergdis were sitting, where he obviously expected to find his cousin Ingrid. He tried to mask his disappointment when he realized she wasn't there. But Bolli was young and had not yet perfected the masculine art of hiding one's weakness at all costs. Although he attempted to appear unconcerned, Selia could see the hurt written across his features.

She willed Alrik to look in her direction as well. Surely Hrefna was right; surely he wouldn't stay angry at her forever. But he seemed to have forgotten all about her presence. He grabbed one of the thralls as she passed by, leaning over to whisper something into her ear. With a sickening start, she realized it was Muirin.

Alrik did look across the room then, as he held onto the beautiful slave girl who was his property. He leveled his gaze on Selia with a wicked smile.

Selia ran, pushing her way through the crowd. Her stomach cramped as though she had been stabbed with a knife, and she prayed she wouldn't vomit before she reached the woods. How could Alrik do this to her? How could he brazenly commit the one sin she was unwilling to forgive? He'd made sure she had been looking. He *wanted* to hurt her. He wanted to hurt his brother as well, and by bedding Muirin he could do both in one fell swoop.

She made it to the tree line as another excruciating cramp gripped her. Falling to her knees, she vomited, choking and barely able to breathe.

Muffled laughter filtered through the woods, likely young lovers searching for a trysting spot. Selia forced herself to rise. She couldn't let anyone see the Hersir's wife in such a humiliating position. She stumbled deeper into the trees until she finally collapsed in a small clearing. *Something is wrong.*

The pain was now in her back just as much as her belly, and she doubled over in agony. There was something warm and wet between her legs. Had she vomited so violently that she urinated on herself?

What if it was blood? *No . . . please God . . .*

As she writhed in pain, she felt an arm go around her and she cracked opened her eyes to see the female thrall who had served her wine.

"Deirdre," the woman murmured, pushing a damp strand of hair from Selia's face.

She looked up in a fog of pain. "Please," she panted, "Get Hrefna. I think something is wrong with the babe—"

As another pain ripped through her, she screamed and grabbed the thrall's arm. "Help . . . me . . . ."

The woman hesitated for a moment, then reached under Selia's gown to gently probe between her legs. When she pulled her hand out again her fingers were bloody, and Selia wailed.

"Hush now." The thrall put both arms around her. "There is nothing that can be done. It's just as well his child dies in your belly."

Several seconds passed before her words registered with Selia. How dare this woman—a slave, at that—speak to her so about her child? She tried to push the thrall away, but was incapacitated with an intense wave of pain. She felt as though she had been shoved outside her body and was actually floating above it. She saw herself writhing on the ground, screaming, being comforted by a stranger.

Deirdre, a small voice whispered in her head. *Deirdre.*

Was the woman a stranger? Although Selia had not remembered seeing her before today, she seemed somehow familiar. She looked up at the thrall, almost too exhausted to speak. "Why did you call me Deirdre?"

"Because it is your name. Do you not know me at all, child?"

She stared into the thrall's sorrowful brown eyes. Did she know this woman? It was hard to judge the age of a thrall, but she guessed her to be several years older than Alrik. Her short, curly brown hair was lightly streaked with gray. Her delicate features might have once been beautiful, but her face held a pinched expression, and deep frown lines marred her forehead.

The woman was thin almost to the point of emaciation, with narrow shoulders and tiny, childlike hands-a build too fragile for the manual labor that was expected of a slave.

"No," she rasped, turning away.

But the thrall leaned forward to brush Selia's sweaty curls from her face where they had escaped from the confines of her fillet. And then Selia smelled her.

It was the most wonderful smell in the world, the musky crook of this woman's arm; the scent of warm milk and soft skin, and the murmured breath of midnight whispers.

Selia leaned against the woman and breathed it in.

Mamai.

"You are my mother," Selia whispered haltingly.

"Yes, Deirdre," the thrall murmured. "I am your mother. For all these years I thought you dead, and now I find you are married to the very man who would have murdered you-"

Selia cut her off with another cry of agony, and her eyes rolled up to the woman. Surely the haze of pain was making her hear things. Alrik had not tried to kill her. Hadn't he given her the ring to avoid that possibility entirely?

There was a rustling of footsteps from behind them in the forest, and then Ainnileas knelt beside her. He took her by the shoulders and pulled her away from the woman. "Selia, what ails you?"

"What are you doing with her, Grainne?" Another familiar voice spoke, this time in Norse.

Selia looked up to see Ingrid staring at the thrall.

Grainne ignored the girl and gazed at Ainnileas. "Cassan," she breathed, reaching out to touch him. "You are so like your father."

Ainnileas paled. He tried to pull Selia to her feet but she doubled over as more pain gripped her. He put an arm under her knees, lifting her, and began to carry her toward the house.

"Wait," Selia panted. "She is our mother."

He stopped. "No. Our mother is dead."

"Ainnileas?" There was a hint of panic in Ingrid's voice. She couldn't understand the Irish words, but anyone other than a simpleton could tell that something of great importance was happening.

"Do not trust this girl," Grainne warned Ainnileas, with an abrupt gesture in Ingrid's direction. "She carries the blood of the devil in her veins—her beauty masks a soul as black as night."

Ainnileas stood frozen as he gaped at the woman. Ingrid was clearly frustrated at her inability to follow the conversation. She made an exasperated noise and ran toward the house, no doubt to tattle to the slave's master.

As Selia moaned in her brother's arms, Grainne grabbed him with a face so fierce, he took a step backward. "Listen to me carefully, we don't have much time. You are both in danger. Alrik Ragnarson is the wickedest man who has ever walked the earth!"

Ainnileas snapped, "I don't care about Alrik. Tell me why you think you're our mother."

"I know my own children! I have seen your faces in my mind every day for the past sixteen years. I thought Deirdre was dead, but I hoped beyond hope you had survived, Cassan."

"What happened, then?" he asked with suspicion. "Why did you leave us?"

Grainne paused to catch her breath. "The devil raided our village and burned it to the ground. He murdered your father. He raped me!"

Ainnileas sank to the ground with Selia in his arms, and she cried out, wracked with another violent wave of pain. "You're wrong," she gasped, as the pain passed. "It wasn't Alrik!"

"I would not mistake the man who attacked me and tried to kill my child." Grainne's voice was bitter. "He hit you with the hilt of his sword. He would have run you through if his brother hadn't stopped him."

Selia screamed again, but the agony she felt was not the physical pain of her belly, but from the knowledge that this thrall-her mother-somehow spoke the truth. Alrik, the man she loved more than life itself, the man she had been willing to give up everything for, had destroyed her birth family and had nearly murdered her by caving in her skull with his sword.

And then he had married her.

Everything, *everything* had been built on a lie. Not even death could feel worse than this.

Alrik followed his daughter through the woods, with Olaf, Hrefna, and Ketill hurrying behind him. Ingrid was a foolish girl and prone to exaggeration, and this jaunt into the forest was surely a waste of his time. If Selia and Ingrid didn't hate each other so, he would be more suspicious of some sort of feminine ploy they were in on together, something to distract him from his anger. If this was simply his wife's dramatic way of getting his attention, she would regret it.

He heard a scream from up ahead, a sound so agonized it couldn't possibly be false. He pushed past Ingrid and broke into a run.

He burst into a small clearing and saw Selia lying in her brother's arms, with Ketill's thrall hovering over them both. As Ainnileas' gaze met his, the boy leapt to his feet, flipping Selia from his lap in the process. He rushed toward Alrik with his dagger drawn. Ainnileas snarled something unintelligible in Irish, ending with '*bastard*.' Alrik had heard that word often enough from his wife to know what it meant.

It was a clumsy attack, and he blocked Ainnileas' arm as he lunged. He took hold of the boy's wrist, spinning him around to hold the knife to his own throat, then squeezed the thin bones until Ainnileas cried out in pain. The wrist under Alrik's hand felt as fragile as Selia's, and it took every ounce of self-control he had not to snap it. The little whelp needed to be taught a lesson in respect.

"Stop!" Ingrid shouted, grabbing her father's arm. The thrall jumped up as well but was restrained by Ketill.

"Take this boy, Olaf," Alrik barked. He shoved him over to Olaf, who had to sit on Ainnileas to control him.

Hrefna knelt next to Selia's body, writhing on the leaves. His wife rambled brokenly in Irish, and as her eyes rolled up to meet Alrik's her screams intensified. Hrefna gripped her tightly to keep her from crawling away.

Alrik also began to kneel, but the thrall broke free from her master and leapt in front of Alrik as though to block him from his wife. He shoved the woman toward Ketill, and she stumbled and landed at his feet.

"Restrain your thrall, Ketill," Alrik warned, "or I'll do it for you."

The woman laughed hoarsely, an odd sound that caused all eyes to turn to her. "You don't even remember who I am, do you, Alrik Ragnarson?" she choked out. "I have wished you dead every day of my life for the past sixteen years, but you forgot who I was the moment you were through with my body."

The thrall was obviously mad. Ketill gave the woman a stern shake. He whispered something in her ear but it only made her laugh harder.

Alrik leveled his gaze onto Ketill's. "Keep her away from my wife." Seeing that Ketill had a firm grip on the thrall, he knelt on the ground next to Hrefna. His aunt's face looked grim as she pressed on Selia's belly.

"Is she losing the child?" he asked.

Hrefna bit her lip and wouldn't look at him. "We need to get her to the house so I can examine her."

His aunt had reacted with a surprising fury when Ingrid had described Selia's agonized screaming in the woods. "If your wife bleeds out the babe, you have no one to blame but yourself after what you have put Selia through today," she had vowed.

Now he could see it for himself. His child was dying.

The blood that seeped from Selia's body and soaked into the ground was the life force of his son.

Alrik swallowed as he looked down at his wife where she thrashed and sobbed on the ground. The sight of her in so much pain made his chest tighten uncomfortably. He reached out to touch her face but she smacked his hand away, screeching in Irish.

He moved to lift her, but a piercing scream shot from Selia's lips, no longer a cry of pain, but of rage. She fought him like a madwoman, punching and clawing, even trying to bite him.

"What's the matter with you?" he demanded as he struggled with her, trying to hold her still without hurting her further.

She laughed then, the same crazed-sounding laugh that he had heard from the thrall. "How—how could you *marry* me—"

"She knows what you did," the woman said with satisfaction in her voice.

He felt the blood drain from his face as his gaze traveled slowly over the thrall. His mind's eye saw a younger version of the woman in a small Irish cottage, her pretty face dazed as he threw her across a narrow room.

No.

How could this be happening—how could Selia's mother be here, now? Alrik only knew her as Ketill's thrall, and until this moment hadn't realized his wife's mother was still alive, much less living over the next ridge.

But someone had realized it.

Ulfrik.

That traitorous bastard had something to do with this. He had sworn he wouldn't reveal Alrik's secret, but that hadn't stopped him from finding another, more devious route to achieve his goal. His brother wanted Selia; Alrik had seen it in his eyes at the market in Dubhlinn. Only once, then he had masked it from then on. It amused Alrik to allow his brother to spend time with her on the ship, knowing the torment he must be feeling to be so near to something that could never be his.

How could he have known Ulfrik would turn on him?

Alrik turned back to his wife. The expression of loathing on her face was like a knife in his gut. His hands shook like a desperate little boy's as he held on to her. "You are still my wife. You were given to me—"

"No!" she cut him off. "I am *not* your wife—I divorce you!"

He leapt to his feet, pulling Selia up with him. He leaned close to her face, shaking her once for good measure. "You know you can't divorce me. You're *mine.*"

"You tried to kill me . . ."

"I love you!" Alrik's voice cracked over the words. Desperate *and* weak. "I need you, Selia."

Her face appeared crazed as she screamed at him in Irish. Without warning, she pulled the dagger from Alrik's belt, drawing it down sharply toward his abdomen. He shifted his body just in time and the tip of the dagger sank into his forearm.

Hrefna cried out as a line of blood oozed from the gash in his sleeve.

Alrik roared, ripping the dagger from his flesh. Selia had tried to kill him. He had let his guard down, allowed himself to care for her, allowed himself to *love* her.

And this was what he got for it. Repulsion.

Humiliation.

As the familiar darkness flooded his consciousness, it was all he could do to keep from going under, to let it take him. He fought it, harder than he ever had, even as his hands wrapped around his wife's neck. It would be so easy. One quick snap and it would all be over.

The ring.

He could feel the rapid beat of Selia's pulse under his hands, like a frightened animal. The blood from his wound flowed over his fingers and onto Selia's skin, standing out in stark contrast against her white throat. As though he had slit it.

It would be so easy . . .

Alrik could hear a commotion of people yelling at him, but their voices sounded very far away. Why wasn't Selia struggling? It wasn't like her to go to her death without a fight. This was wrong, all wrong. He blinked and forced his hands to relax their hold.

The darkness screamed at him, furious at being deprived of the kill.

Selia hit him weakly. "Do it," she sobbed. His eyes flickered toward her ring. She tugged it from her finger, then threw it at him. "*Do it!*"

Alrik stared down into her beautiful face; a face that would never look at him with love again. She hated him enough to die to be free of him. She hated him enough to provoke him to kill her.

Hrefna had been right-he had no one to blame but himself.

He had created this nightmare, but he wouldn't let the darkness make him kill the only woman he had ever loved. The darkness wouldn't win this time. He took a step away and Selia sank to her knees, sobbing.

Alrik walked into the forest and didn't look back.

Chapter 34

Deirdre floated, hazy and weightless. Where was Mamai? Why didn't she come?

The woman carried her. Sometimes it was dark, and Deirdre would focus on the small twinkling lights in the black sky. Then she would drift away again to the space that had no pain.

Sometimes when she closed her eyes she was pursued by a bad man who carried a large knife, like the one Dadai had taken out of the chest. The bad man who had hurt Mamai when he burst through the door and spilled the porridge.

His angry eyes scared her.

But even scarier than the bad man were the birds. Deidre hated the ugly black birds. Once when she opened her eyes she saw a little boy lying very still on the ground, with a black bird pecking at his face.

Her brother screamed. Deidre tried to call out to him, to tell him to close his eyes so the bird could not get at them, but the words would not come.

The woman hushed them. They moved past the boy and the bird flew away, flapping its wings close enough to Deirdre's head that she could feel the motion and smell the odor coming from its sharp beak. She screamed for Mamai.

Nothing came out but crying.

Selia lay in the bed she had shared with Alrik, staring at the wall, fighting off the aftereffects of yet another bad dream. She had given up trying to understand why they came to her, if they truly were memories of a nightmarish childhood.

She could still smell her husband's scent on the sheets where his blond head had lain on the pillow next to her just three nights ago. He had slept with his arm around her that night, his hand thrown over her belly as if protecting the child that grew inside. Her eyes burned with tears at the memory, but none fell. There were no tears left in her to shed.

Alrik was gone. He had walked into the woods that horrible day, and no one knew where he was. Hrefna was worried about him. She must be wondering if her nephew was all right, wandering alone, so soon after his own brush with death. But she didn't voice her concerns, and Selia didn't allow herself to ask about him. Alrik wasn't her responsibility any longer.

Ainnileas and Grainne would come in to sit with her occasionally. Ainnileas always looked pale and serious. He had broken off his association with Ingrid but refused to speak of it any further. He was hurting, a deep, jagged wound that Selia was intimately familiar with, but she had no words of comfort for her brother now. There was no room inside her for anything other than her own misery.

Grainne would sit by the bed, silent and still, staring at her. It seemed as though she wanted to say something but couldn't bring herself to do so. It was unnerving.

Selia still found it unbelievable her mother was alive. For so long she had believed the unnamed woman buried in the woods behind their house in Ireland was her dead mother. Grainne said the woman was a neighbor who had run to warn them the Finngalls were raiding the village. Her name had been Ionait. With her husband murdered, Deirdre lifeless from the blow from Alrik's sword hilt, and she herself in the clutches of Alrik, Grainne had begged Ionait to take the children and run away. She had thought Deirdre dead, but couldn't bear to leave the tiny body to the ravens. And that was the last she had seen of her children.

Did her mother hate her? Selia had married the man who had destroyed Grainne's life. She had carried his child. But worse, she had loved him, and maybe to her mother that was most unforgivable.

At Hrefna's bidding, Olaf had bought the slave from Ketill and freed her. Ketill was unhappy with this, as Grainne had been his favorite thrall, but Hrefna was insistent. The man seemed to know better than to argue with her.

According to Ainnileas, the plan was for him, Selia, and Grainne to move to Ulfrik's empty house as soon as Selia was well enough to travel. They would go home to Ireland when Ainnileas' ship returned. Ulfrik would stay with Ketill until his own houseguests were gone.

There was a hesitant knock on the door, then Hrefna's head appeared. "Selia, are you awake?"

She didn't have the energy to laugh. She was nearly always awake now, regardless of the time of day or night. Whenever she closed her eyes she would find herself back in the woods, the agony of the memory so intense it took her breath away. Blood and pain had heralded Alrik Ragnarson into her life as well as out of it.

When she did manage to drift off to sleep, it was fitful. Sometimes she dreamed Alrik chased her, but his eyes were missing and he ran blindly, holding out his hand to search for her. He loved her. He needed her. When she stopped to help him, however, he would laugh and pull out his sword as he stared down at her with wide, empty eye sockets. He had tricked her once again.

It was better to just stay awake.

Selia didn't answer, but Hrefna entered carrying a tray of food. By the smell of it, it was blood pudding again. She gagged. Hrefna had forced her to eat large quantities of certain foods that she insisted would build her strength back. Blood pudding was the most frequent offender.

The bleeding had been incomplete; no tissue expelled. Hrefna continued to insist if the remains of the child didn't come out on their own, they must be removed to ensure they didn't rot inside her. The only way to accomplish this was for Selia to imbibe herbs rumored to act as an expulsive, which she flatly refused to do. If she died, so be it. What did it matter now, anyway?

She sat up as Hrefna adjusted the pillows behind her. She placed the tray upon Selia's lap, then made herself comfortable in the chair next to the bed.

Selia shuddered, staring down at the foul concoction in the bowl. "I feel fine, Hrefna. I do not need this."

"You're as pale as death, child. Eat it."

Selia stirred the congealed substance. "If I eat it, can I leave? Ainnileas said Ulfrik's house is ready for us."

It was true; Olaf had taken several thralls to the house to oversee cleaning and repairs, and to stock it with supplies. Ainnileas and Grainne were simply waiting for Selia to be well enough to travel. However, she knew if it were up to Hrefna, she would be imprisoned here on forced bed rest even longer.

Hrefna hesitated. "I wish you would reconsider. Just give it some time."

Selia pinned her with a long look, causing Hrefna to avert her gaze. They'd had this conversation already, and Hrefna had made her position clear that she wanted Selia to stay. She insisted Alrik loved her, and she him; although the current situation might seem hopeless, the marriage was not beyond redemption.

Even if Selia wanted to stay, she knew she could not. She had unwittingly plunged a knife into her mother's heart by marrying Alrik. Staying with him now, knowing what he had done, would be inexcusable.

How could Hrefna not understand how necessary it was to leave a man who had single-handedly destroyed her family? The woman could talk endlessly about Alrik's flawed nature, but some acts could simply never be forgiven.

And so they were at an impasse. Although Hrefna claimed to love her like a daughter, she clearly loved Alrik more. This only added to Selia's raw feeling of betrayal.

Now she turned to Hrefna and stressed, "I want to leave today." Alrik could come home at any time, and she had to avoid seeing him again at all costs.

With a resigned sigh, Hrefna nodded and left the room, closing the door softly behind her.

Ulfrik's house was modest, consisting of one long, narrow room with sleeping benches on two sides and a hearth in the middle, holes cut in the ceiling to let out the smoke. Ragnarr had been raised in this house, as well as Alrik and Ulfrik for several years. To Selia, it seemed to carry a melancholy air, as if the walls retained the sorrows of its previous occupants.

One corner of the room was curtained off for bathing, the only modicum of privacy afforded by the small dwelling. Although she had been raised in a house not much bigger than this one, the close quarters were difficult to adjust to after the luxury of Alrik's longhouse.

She pined for solitude, a place to be alone with her thoughts without the watchful eyes of her mother and brother upon her. It was as though they both secretly suspected she was still in love with Alrik, and were looking for the evidence in her behavior.

How could she explain to them? If she felt like crying, or if she had no appetite, it wasn't because she still loved Alrik but rather due to everything she had lost. So she copied Ulfrik's example and kept her face impassive even as her insides churned with emotion.

It didn't help to see the kinship between Ainnileas and Grainne grow stronger by the day. Although their mother's smile was sad when she regarded her son, she seemed almost unable to look away, or to keep her hands from him. She was always touching his face or his arm. According to Grainne, Ainnileas—or 'Cassan,' as she called him—bore a striking resemblance to their father. Only Ainnileas' curly hair set him apart from Faolan.

"I met your father when we were little more than babes," Grainne said with a sad smile. "He was the most beautiful boy, with the smile of an angel. My father was a blacksmith, and Faolan would come to have him sharpen something or other. He asked for my hand when we were fourteen, but my father refused."

"Why?" Ainnileas asked.

"He was the son of a traveling bard. My father wanted more for me. So I was betrothed to another man from the village and we were set to marry. But Faolan came to me early one day as I was milking, and we left together."

Grainne's gaze lit on Selia, and she studied her for several moments before she spoke. "He loved you both more than you will ever know, but he had a special bond with you, Deirdre. You were so small when you were born, and no one but Faolan expected you to live. He would hold you on his chest and sing to you, for hours."

Her mother's eyes were hard, almost accusing, as though she held Selia responsible for Faolan's death.

Selia looked away. How was she expected to respond to this? Should she apologize for the way her husband had murdered the only man Grainne had ever loved?

But Ainnileas diverted the conversation to something less painful, and the woman once again brought her attention to her adored and blameless son. Her Cassan.

The name set Selia's teeth on edge. Why didn't Ainnileas put his foot down and tell her that wasn't his name any longer? But he humored his mother, which only served to highlight Selia's selfishness in refusing to answer to the name Deirdre. Yet refuse she did.

Hadn't she been required to give up enough already, without having to give up her name as well? Couldn't she choose one thing for herself instead of everyone assuming they knew what was best for her?

The worst times were when Ainnileas left the house to go fishing or to check the snares for game. That left her alone without Ainnileas as a buffer between Selia and their mother. And there was nothing she could talk to her mother about without the conversation involving Alrik in some way. It lay between them like a festering wound, growing uglier by the day. At those times she would leave the house with an excuse of gathering firewood or filling up the water bucket, just to get away from her mother's accusing eyes.

Selia sat with Ainnileas and Grainne during meals. She pushed the food around on her platter and pretended to eat as well. She didn't trust Grainne not to put something in her food, and she had lost weight. Her gown was loose and the skin of her hands seemed to be stretched over the bones.

Twice, Ainnileas had actually grabbed her by the hair, attempting to shove food down her throat. In an effort to avoid another force feeding, Selia had begun to take a bite or two at each meal for appearances' sake but only pretended to eat the rest. She suspected her mother knew about this, although Grainne would only watch, saying nothing.

After supper every night, Selia often wandered outside, picking up a few sticks of firewood to make it seem as though she performed some useful function. Sometimes she would find a patch of berries and gorge herself on them until she felt sick. Sometimes she stood at the top of the cliff and stared out at the sea churning white and angry below. The wind whipped at her gown and her hair, and if she closed her eyes she almost felt as though she were flying. Flying far away.

But inevitably Ainnileas would see her and would come out to scold her. What if her foot slipped? What if she got too close to the edge and the earth gave way under her?

She would allow him to steer her back into the house, and retire to bed, feigning exhaustion. Even though Selia still suffered from a terrible insomnia, the semi-privacy of her bench was preferable to the uncomfortable silences the three lapsed into whenever she was present for the conversation.

When they thought she was asleep, Ainnileas and Grainne would talk well into the night, laughing occasionally as their mother told stories of things the twins had done when they were babes. Selia had been a precocious child, bossy and talkative, while Ainnileas had been more of a follower, trailing after his sister with his thumb in his mouth, content to do her bidding.

Sometimes Grainne would cry and Ainnileas would comfort her. Once, after several cups of ale, Grainne sobbed that Faolan had done something unforgivable the night the twins were born. The fact that Deirdre-Selia-still lived was proof of his sin. When Ainnileas tried to question her, Grainne refused to answer, saying what was done could not be undone.

Selia lay awake for quite some time, pondering this. What could her father have done? And how could her survival have had anything to do with it?

From eavesdropping on the conversations between her mother and brother, she gathered quite a bit of information. After Grainne's rape and abduction from Ireland, she had been about to be sold to a slave trader in Bjorgvin along with several dozen others. Ketill Brunason, however, had taken a liking to her. He paid Alrik well for her, and brought her home to be a nursemaid to his three young sons.

Ketill's wife had died of a fever after giving birth to Bolli. The farmstead was a poor one. Although he was not unkind to Grainne, her life there was hard. The man owned very few thralls, so raising the children was only one of Grainne's many responsibilities. And although she grew to care for the three boys, she could not forget about the children she had lost.

The bitter hatred she felt for Alrik Ragnarson-Ketill's brother-in-law, no less-grew in her heart, year after year, and she vowed to kill him if she ever got the chance. The opportunity to make good on her vow only occurred once in the past sixteen years, and she had failed.

Grainne grew quiet then and would speak of that topic no more.

Ketill arrived unexpectedly one morning, several sennights after the small family had moved into Ulfrik's house. As he set a rucksack of fresh supplies down on the table, he stared at Selia, visibly shocked at her appearance.

Ketill's expression made her conscious of her tangled hair and wrinkled, stained clothing. She wore the lavender-colored gown Eithne had made for her, the gown that had once been beautiful but had been ruined during the traumatic trip from Ireland to Norway. Hrefna had not understood why she had insisted on leaving everything Alrik had given her-jewelry, clothing-but Selia was adamant. She could not have any reminders of him.

Ketill asked Grainne to accompany him on a stroll. The woman exchanged a long look with him before nodding in agreement. As they walked away, Selia began unloading the supplies. For a man who owned a poor farmstead, he had certainly brought quite a rich variety of foods with him. For his former slave, no less. Did Grainne think she was fooling anyone? Clearly they were lovers.

Selia used the time to bathe while she was alone in the house. The woolen curtain provided little privacy, so she had been hesitant to remove her gown when her mother was home. She used cold water, washing quickly, but her hair was snarled and her bath took longer than she anticipated. She was still rinsing the soap from her hair when she heard the door latch clatter.

"Selia?" It was Grainne. She had finally stopped trying to call her Deirdre.

"I'm bathing." She tried to hide the panic in her voice. "I'll be right out."

"Have you seen my—"

Grainne drew the curtain back and stopped, mid-sentence, with her mouth open. Her eyes bulged at the sight of Selia's abdomen.

"Get out!" Selia grabbed for her shift.

"You little *liar*," her mother rasped. "Why have you kept this from me? Did you have Hrefna lie to me as well? Were the two of you conspiring together until it was too late to do anything about it?"

"Too late to kill it, you mean? You obviously didn't use enough the first time."

Grainne stared. "What?"

"I'm not stupid. I know you poisoned my wine at the gathering." Selia pulled her gown over her head. "But I'm too far along for you to do anything now. Unless you want to kill me, too."

Grainne screamed in rage and shoved her into the wall. "I *should* kill you! You willingly carry his devil child even after—"

"It's an innocent babe. Your grandchild!" Selia pushed Grainne away.

"Do you think that matters?" Grainne's laugh was that of a madwoman. "Any fruit of that seed is rotten to the core. No child of Alrik Ragnarson can be suffered to live."

The air seemed to leave the room as a sickening realization dawned on Selia. Her mother *was* mad, willing to kill her own daughter to end Alrik's bloodline. If that were the case, then why would the woman have had any qualms about killing the family of the man she hated?

Selia's voice shook as she spoke. "You did it. You killed Alrik's wife and daughters."

Grainne made a small noise in the back of her throat and tried to dart away, but Selia grabbed her arm, digging her fingers in. "You killed innocent women and children."

"He was supposed to drink it too!" Grainne cried, shaking free.

"It *was* the ale, then." Selia could only gape in shock.

Hrefna had been correct. But the cask of ale Grainne had poisoned-meant for Alrik and Ingrid as well-had been opened while Alrik was on a raid and Ingrid was away from the farmstead. The revenge her mother sought had been incomplete.

Grainne's thin body sagged in exhaustion. "He took my family from me. He took everything from me."

Selia shrank from the woman she was loath to call mother. "How does that make you any better than he is?" she whispered.

Chapter 35

Ulfrik's house was built high on a cliff, and to get to the sea one needed to walk around on the right side where the slope was gentle and even. But Selia had found a rough path on the left side of the cliff, where she could climb down to a small area of beach not visible from the house.

She hurried there now and sat against the rocks for hours. The days weren't as long now as they had been earlier in the summer, and she could again judge the time of day by the position of the sun in the sky. She would wait until the afternoon to go back to the house, when Ainnileas would be home with whatever he had gathered from the snares. And she wouldn't be alone with Grainne, now or ever again.

Selia rested her head on her knees, as exhaustion came upon her hard and fast. Should she tell her brother what Grainne had done? What would his reaction be? Since the woman had wormed her way into Ainnileas' heart, Selia's kinship with her brother had become strained and uncomfortable. Maybe Ainnileas would agree with Grainne's warped reasoning that her actions had been justifiable.

One thing was certain, however. Selia could not go back to Ireland with Grainne. Even if the woman didn't intend to kill her during her confinement, it wouldn't stop her from trying to harm the child after it was born. And Grainne would live with Ainnileas, of course.

Which left Selia adrift.

Regardless of whether she stayed in Norway or returned to Ireland, she had no one she could trust.

Sometime later, she opened her eyes and realized she must have fallen asleep. The sun had moved past the edge of the cliff, and now the small area of beach was in shadows. She shivered underneath the cloak that was thrown over her.

Cloak?

Selia's body jerked as she saw Ulfrik sitting next to her.

"I thought you would sleep until the tide carried you off," he said. His sober voice belied the smile she could see in his eyes.

She studied him. Were they friends again? The last time she had seen Ulfrik she had held a dagger to his throat. "What are you doing here?" she asked. "I thought you hated me."

"I don't hate you, Selia. Ketill said you looked unwell, and I came to check on you."

She snorted and looked away. "*Unwell*," she mocked. How dare Ketill Brunason pass judgment on her appearance? "You can tell him I'm very well, thank you."

Ulfrik was quiet for a while. "I used to come down here too," he said finally, "when I was a child." Nodding his head at the secluded beach, he added, "Alrik would laugh at me because I missed my mother, so I would hide from him."

She imagined a small version of Ulfrik, climbing down to the cove to cry for a woman who had sung Irish songs to him. Selia wasn't the only one who had lost everything.

She turned to him. "I'm so sorry for what I did to you, Ulfrik. You—you saved my life. When I was a tiny child."

"Yes."

She hesitated. "Am I the reason they call you 'child lover?'"

"Yes."

Selia swallowed. "Thank you."

He laid a hand on her shoulder, giving it a cautious squeeze. The small gesture of kindness caused tears to well up in her eyes, and as she brushed them away she moved closer to him. She meant only to hug him, but he was warm and solid, and she found herself settling into the crook of his arm. They sat for several moments, not speaking. Selia could hear the beat of his heart against her ear, strong and steady.

"I'm still with child, Ulfrik." She sniffled. "Everyone thought I bled the babe out, but I didn't. I've felt the quickening."

He stilled, but the sound of his heartbeat accelerated. "Does anyone else know?"

"No one but Grainne."

"Not Hrefna? Not Ainnileas?"

"No."

"Are you sure Grainne didn't tell Ketill?"

Why was he questioning her so insistently? "My mother only found out today, after Ketill left. She was furious. I think she's going to try to kill it."

"What? Why would you think that?"

"Because she already tried once, at the gathering. She put poison in my wine. She must have figured out who I was. She didn't want her daughter to bear Alrik's child." Selia was careful not to say more, knowing Ulfrik's ability to deduce the truth of a situation from only a word or two. What would he do if he learned Grainne had killed his own wife and unborn child?

"She admitted this to you?"

"Not exactly. But I know she did it." The tears were falling in earnest now and she didn't even attempt to hide them from Ulfrik.

He shifted his body to look down at her. "If that is true, you can't leave with her when Ainnileas' ship returns."

His blue eyes met hers, and she blinked, flushing. Why did he have to look so much like Alrik? It was difficult to sit close to him without being reminded of how she had loved his brother.

Ulfrik was virile and strong, and he desired her, too. Selia could no longer delude herself. She *smelled* it on him, the same way she had been able to smell it on Alrik. The scent of a man changed when he was aroused.

Ulfrik pressed his hand to her face, wiping a tear away with his raspy thumb. It was a gesture Alrik had done many times before, and his brother's touch shook Selia to the very core. A small, faint sound escaped her lips. *How mortifying.*

Had he heard it? She stammered and tried to pull away, but his fingers slid around to the back of her neck. Their eyes locked for a moment.

"Please," he whispered. Then his lips were on hers.

She had always known Ulfrik to be a gentle man, but his kiss was as fervent as that of Alrik's. His hot mouth branded her as if claiming her for his own. Her body flooded with need as Ulfrik's tongue sought hers. She melted into him, unresisting, allowing his mouth and hands free reign. It felt so wonderful to be held, touched, caressed. So wonderful to not think about the pain she had lately endured—

Then Ulfrik pressed her backward onto the sand. He was on top of her, holding her firmly with his hand under her head. His mouth plundered hers as his manhood pushed against her thigh.

"Selia . . ." Ulfrik rasped. A ragged, tortured question. He would not move further until she consented.

She took in a shuddering breath as she looked up at him. What was she *doing*? This was Ulfrik, her husband's brother. She pushed his chest, and he pulled back slightly, his expression vulnerable, naked; raw. What she saw in his eyes terrified her.

She averted her gaze and squirmed to get away. "Get off me."

"Selia—"

"No."

He released her. Selia's first impulse was to run, but where could she go? Back to the house, where her mother wanted to kill her and her brother would recognize her for the whore she was? Into the wild woods of Norway? As if she could expect assistance from any of the Finngalls. No one in this land cared whether she lived or died, except for perhaps Hrefna.

And Ulfrik.

She scuttled several feet away from him, sitting with her back against the cliff, burying her face in her knees as her tears spilled over. What was she supposed to do now?

Ulfrik struggled to regain his composure. It had taken every ounce of strength he possessed to let go of her. The heady sweetness of her mouth had drained him of whatever self-control he claimed, and the feel of her body under his had nearly sent him past the point of no return. He shuddered to think what he might have done.

He watched Selia cry for a moment. The sight of her in such distress was like a physical pain, deep in his chest, but as he moved closer to comfort her she shrank against the rocks as though his very presence terrified her.

"Stay away from me." Her voice was muffled and thick with tears.

He cursed himself. Had he hurt her? He had almost forced himself on her. The overwhelming need to touch her had proved to be too much, but he had meant only to kiss her, not to pounce on her like an animal. *No better than Alrik.*

"I'm sorry." His voice sounded hoarse to his ears, and he cleared his throat. "Did I hurt you?"

Selia's only response was to cry harder. She looked so small, huddled as she was, almost like a child. What had come over him to grab her like that? Now she was frightened, and it was his fault.

"I swear I didn't mean to hurt you—"

"You didn't hurt me. Just go away."

Then did she cry because she was ashamed of herself for what they had done? Or worse, because she was still in love with his brother and had only used Ulfrik as the closest substitute she was likely to get?

He swallowed. "I want to come with you to Ireland. We'll take a different ship from Grainne. I'll care for you. Even if you still have feelings for Alrik, it's all right."

She stared at him with a red, tearstained face, but didn't try to deny his assertion that she still loved his brother. Ulfrik kept his expression unreadable even as his heart felt pierced inside his chest by her tiny, sharp fingers.

"No. You're like a brother to me."

"I'm not your brother, Selia!" He spoke more harshly than he meant to, making her flinch. He forced himself to take a deep breath. "I can make you happy. Let me try." *I love you.*

She didn't speak for a moment as she mopped her face with her sleeve. "What about Muirin? And her child?"

He gritted his teeth at the name. "I'm through with Muirin."

Selia made a choking noise. "So the child is Alrik's."

Regardless of his words, he seemed to hurt her further. He shook his head. "No. That's not what I meant." He watched her face as she studied him, and he could imagine the thoughts churning in her mind. He needed his wits about him. But he always found the seductive curve of Selia's mouth so distracting, her eyes so haunting, and as a result it was difficult to keep his own mind sharp when he looked at her.

Hastily, he changed the subject. "I saw Ainnileas on my way to the house. I've asked for your hand, Selia. I want to marry you." *Even if you are still in love with my brother.*

She stared at him. "You know I cannot remarry unless Alrik dies." Then her face drained of color and she clapped a shaking hand over her mouth. Her eyes grew huge.

Yes, he is dead, he longed to tell her. What satisfaction he would feel from that statement. *The bastard is dead and you're free.*

"He's not dead. But when he does die . . ." Ulfrik saw the understanding on her face and knew he had said too much. He should have waited until she was safely out of Norway to have this discussion with her.

"What's wrong with him?" she demanded.

"Nothing."

"Ulfrik!"

He sighed. "You know how he drinks."

Selia bit her lip. "Because of me? He's drinking himself to death because of me?" She was terrible at masking her emotions, and Ulfrik clearly saw the fear and worry written on her face. Worry for a man who, above all, had the blackest heart in the entire world.

"How can you still love him?" He didn't bother trying to hide the bitterness in his voice. "After everything he's done to you?"

"He is the father of my child."

"What does that matter? I'll raise the child as my own just as Niall raised you."

Selia didn't answer, and Ulfrik studied her face with increasing concern. Her eyes were ringed with purplish smudges and there were hollows under her cheekbones. He had attributed her gaunt appearance to the despair over losing the child, but now knew that was not the case. Was she pining for Alrik, then?

Or was she not eating because she feared her mother would poison her food as she believed she had poisoned her wine? Selia had been living with the knowledge of her continued confinement for quite some time, and was probably terrified at every meal that Grainne had discovered her secret and would take matters into her own hands.

"Selia, let me help you. I'll protect the child from your mother. You can't go back to the house and you have nowhere else to go." This was blatant manipulation, but it couldn't be helped. "Come with me now to Bjorgvin. We'll take a ship from there."

For a few heartbeats she appeared to be considering this offer. But then she gave him a shrewd look. "Why would you do that, Ulfrik? Why would you leave a child that might be yours, to raise one you know is not? Why would you be with me knowing I still care for your brother?"

"Because I love you." His voice shook as he spoke. He had never said those words to anyone.

Selia huffed and turned away. When she looked back up at him, her silvery gaze was piercing. "I need to know something, and you must tell me the truth. You and Ketill are friends and you've been to his farm countless times. Did you know Grainne was my mother?"

"Why does this matter?"

"It matters to me. Did you know?"

He sighed. "Yes."

The expression on her face was one of pure devastation. "You orchestrated this, didn't you? So I would find out at the gathering."

He made a move toward her but she pressed back against the rocks. "Selia, please. There was no other way."

"Why didn't you just tell me?"

"I wanted to-believe me, I wanted to." He shrugged helplessly. Alrik would have killed Muirin and her unborn child if he told Selia the truth. He had figured a way to protect the babe's life and still reveal Alrik's secret.

Who would have imagined such a debacle? "You had to get away from him, Selia. He's dangerous. You know he would have killed you eventually. I did what I had to do to keep you safe."

"Did you conspire with Grainne to kill my child?"

"*What*?"

"Did you?" Selia leapt to her feet. "You told me Alrik would never let me leave if he knew of the babe. How can it be a coincidence that I nearly lost my child the day I found out about my mother? I knew something wasn't right-how would she have known my condition? Where would she have gotten the herbs she needed if she didn't realize who I was until she was already at the gathering? *You* planned this so you could take me away from Alrik!"

He stood up as well, moving toward her. "You're wrong. I would never do anything to hurt you."

Selia was cornered against the cliff. "Get out of my way, Ulfrik."

"No, listen to me first—"

She darted around him but he grabbed her arm. She tried to shake loose. "Let go of me!"

"Your mother didn't poison your wine. It was Muirin."

Selia stopped struggling. She looked as though he had slapped her in the face.

"I knew nothing of it until afterward, or I would have stopped her. I never would have let her hurt you. Muirin realized I was in love with you. She wanted you to leave but she knew Alrik wouldn't let you take his child away. The timing was coincidence, I swear it."

Selia cried out in rage, "Lies—more lies! How can I believe anything you say?"

"I'm not lying."

"Then why did you let me believe it was my mother?"

"Because Alrik will kill Muirin if he finds out what she did. And the child with her."

She tried to pry his fingers from her arm. "*Let go of me.*"

Ulfrik released her and she stumbled backward a few steps. "Selia, everything I've done has been for you. To protect you."

"Protect me? All you've done is ruin my life, Ulfrik! He *loved* me." Her voice grew tight with emotion. "And he was happy with me, but you couldn't stand it. And now you expect me to be grateful to you for destroying him?"

"Selia-"

"Stay away from me. I don't want or need your protection."

The sharp little fingers that were wrapped around Ulfrik's heart sliced deeper, ripping and tearing, until the bloody thing was rent from his body in a brutal jerk. A gruesome slaughter, as bad as anything he had experienced in battle.

The taste of Selia's lips was still on his as he watched her run away.

Chapter 36

Selia scrubbed the tears from her face with her sleeve as she stormed up the beach and through the woods. She wouldn't go back to Ulfrik's house, the sanctuary he had so kindly offered to them while they were waiting for Ainnileas' ship to return.

The perfect place to corner her while she was alone and vulnerable with grief.

Ulfrik wasn't the master tafl player for nothing.

She had allowed him to kiss her, to touch her. And she had found some level of pleasure in his touch. She had encouraged him. What was wrong with her? Only a whore would do such a thing. She felt sick but there was nothing in her stomach to come up.

Whore. Her lips felt bruised from Ulfrik's kisses. She could still smell his scent on her. She headed for the spring that bubbled behind the house to wash herself, and as she rounded the path she plowed headlong into her mother.

Grainne dropped most of the sticks from the pile of firewood she had been collecting and narrowed her eyes, raking them over Selia from head to toe. "Well, I see you didn't waste any time with the brother. Should I be surprised?"

"You have no idea of what you speak," Selia hissed through gritted teeth. Her hand itched to slap Grainne's face, and she clenched it tightly to avoid doing so.

"Don't I?" Grainne sneered.

She flushed. "Get away from me. I have nothing to say to you."

"I still have plenty to say to *you*, traitor child."

The woman was deranged. Selia pushed past her, but Grainne grabbed a fistful of Selia's hair, jerking her back.

"Get off me!" Selia screamed.

But Grainne looped hair around her hand, over and over until she held Selia so tightly she couldn't move. Grainne grasped a stick, sturdy and sharp, in her other hand. "You weren't supposed to live." Her voice made gooseflesh pop up on Selia's arms. "All of this happened because you didn't die when you should have."

Selia tried to push her away but Grainne twisted harder, forcing another scream as tears sprang to her eyes.

Grainne only laughed. "You'll cry for yourself, won't you? And you'll cry for the devil whose seed you carry. But have you shed one tear for your own father, the man who died because of you?"

"It's not my fault—how can you blame me for that?" she panted.

"Oh, but it is. Know this, child. *It is your fault*. Your soul is as putrid as that of the devil you lust after, and I knew it from the beginning but I didn't want to believe it—"

"Selia!" Ainnileas' voice came from the direction of the house. "Selia!"

"I'm here!" she choked out. And in the span of a second Grainne released her hair, then disappeared into the woods. As if she had never been there.

Selia was still reeling as her brother burst through the trees. He looked around, blinking, when he saw she was alone. "Why were you screaming?"

She rushed up to him. "She's mad, Ainnileas, completely mad!"

"What are you talking about?"

"Grainne. She tried to kill me. She would have done it if she hadn't heard you coming."

"*What*?"

"She had a stick—"

"A stick?" His expression made it clear what he thought about a small, frail woman armed with a stick.

"It's not amusing! She almost killed me." Selia sniffled. "And if you think I'm getting on a ship with that woman, you're as mad as she is."

"So that's what this is about." Ainnileas looked disgusted. "You'll find any excuse to stay here. It won't work, Selia. Besides, Alrik is nearly dead. I've already spoken with Ulfrik, and he's asked for your hand. I'm sure you'll agree he's preferable to Buadhach."

She shoved him. "*No,*" she fumed. "I'm already married!"

"You are divorced." He had to use the Norse word, since the concept didn't exist in Irish. "You married a heathen, and you divorced him. You are free to remarry, and I am responsible for finding a suitable husband for you. Ulfrik is a good man. He's agreed to be baptized to make the marriage legitimate. And he paid as much for you as Alrik did even though you're not a virgin."

"I won't have him. You must return the bride price." Her voice trembled as she glared at her brother.

He shook his head. "I can't. We need it to get home if you're not going to marry Buadhach."

She had been sold—bought and paid for. Ulfrik had simply been claiming his property down at the cove. "No!" she shouted, pushing her brother hard enough to make him stumble backward.

"It's done, Selia—it's over!" Ainnileas shouted. "When will you learn to do as you're told? If you had listened to Father he would still be alive."

Selia felt the blood drain from her face. For the second time today she had been blamed for the death of a father. She swallowed. "Return the bride price," she ordered harshly. "Or throw it into the sea-I don't care which. But I'd marry the devil himself before I would step one foot on a ship with you or with Ulfrik Ragnarson."

She walked for hours as twilight came and went, and the moon rose in the sky. Her body ached with exhaustion but she forced herself to keep going. She kept the coastline in sight, knowing it was the only landmark that could be trusted, since every hill and valley she crossed looked the same.

After a while she felt a strange sense of weightlessness, as if her body had indeed died and only her ghost was now floating across the ground. A ghost on her way to begin an eternity with the devil. But at least it was eternity of her own choosing.

She heard the babbling of a stream nearby and veered into the woods until she found it. Selia knelt at its bank, gulping handfuls of water until her thirst was slaked, then rested for a moment as she stared at her watery reflection in the moonlight. She looked terrible, with sunken eyes and her hair a wild bird's nest around her shoulders. Something about her gaunt face reminded her of Grainne's, and she shuddered.

The woman's bond with Ketill was clearly deeper than master and slave. Grainne's voice would soften whenever she spoke of him, and she had seen the way her mother had looked at him when he was at the house this morning.

Ketill had kept her enslaved to him for sixteen years. He had surely done things in battle just as atrocious as any other Finngall. How could Grainne love him, yet deny her daughter's right to love Alrik?

How could the woman fail to understand it could just as easily have been Ketill, or any other nameless, faceless Finngall who had killed her husband and raped her? But it *had* been Alrik, and Grainne had latched on that to such an extent, she could see nothing else. To the point where it had driven her mad enough to try to kill her own daughter.

Selia looked again at the cool stream. It was wide, but not so deep she could drown in it. She stripped off her filthy gown and shift, then walked out into the water. She sat down to allow the stream to bubble over her legs and belly; splashed water onto her face and gave it a vigorous scrub, washing away the memory of Ulfrik's lips on hers.

The babe kicked, a small, fluttering movement that reminded her of the feeling of a minnow held in her hand. She smiled, cupping the curve of her belly. He was strong; too strong to be stilled by the poison that had been slipped into her drink. She would protect this child and watch him grow into a man. Her son would be a Finngall.

Selia lay back, holding her breath as the cool water gurgled over her face and hair. As she sat up, she felt strangely empty, as though the water had scrubbed her soul clean. She dressed with a renewed lightness to her heart, then headed for home.

She entered through the kitchen door, surprising Muirin so greatly that the girl cried out and dropped the cooking pot she had been scrubbing.

Muirin flushed purple and sank into a curtsey made awkward by her enormous belly. "Mistress," she whispered under her breath.

Selia picked up the pot and handed it to her, as it appeared the thrall wouldn't be able to rise again if she tried to squat. What was Muirin doing in the house? Hrefna had done her best to keep her in the barn or the field-as far from Selia as possible. But with her absence, Muirin must have again been given free run of the place. Had that included Alrik's bed?

Selia cocked her head curiously. "Have you been sleeping with my husband?"

A choked gasp came from Muirin's throat. "No . . . no. He tried. But he was . . . unable."

She gave the girl a sharp look. Unable—like Old Buadhach was unable? How was that even possible? Alrik was always able, sometimes exhaustingly so. Had something happened to him, then?

"Where is he?" she demanded.

Muirin's eyes darted toward the bedroom. "He stays in there, all the time."

"Where is Hrefna? And Olaf?"

"Asleep."

Good, they were alone. She leaned in close to the girl. "I know what you did, Muirin. Ulfrik told me."

The thrall's beautiful face turned chalk white, and her mouth opened but no sound came out. So Ulfrik had been telling the truth, this time at least.

"But you failed. My child is stronger than your poison." Selia drew her gown tight against her belly to show her the rounded outline. "And when I tell Alrik what you did he'll kill you."

Muirin backed against the wall and began to cry. "Please, Mistress," she stammered, "take pity on my child and wait until after it's born."

"You showed my child no pity."

"Please . . . I beg you . . ."

Selia let her cry for several moments until she was satisfied of the girl's terror. "There *is* something you can do for me, Muirin. If you do exactly as I say, I won't tell Alrik of your treachery. But if you don't, I'll make sure you die the day your child is born. I'll kill you myself if I must."

As Selia entered Alrik's bedroom, she nearly took a step backward, assaulted by an odor that hit her like a physical slap; a smell of unwashed man, stale alcohol, and urine. He was at the little table in the corner, asleep with his head lolled back against the wall. There was a cask of ale next to him. The cup in his hand had tipped over, its former contents now a dark stain on his breeches.

The candle on the table was burnt down nearly to a nub, and she stood frozen as the flickering light danced over Alrik's inert form. His hair clung to his skull in lank, greasy strands, and his clothes were filthy. The stench of urine was overwhelming. Had he become so drunk he had urinated on himself? No, the smell was coming from a muddy puddle in the furthest corner of the room.

Selia stared. Even more disturbing than his drastically unkempt appearance was how *small* he appeared. It was a physical impossibility for a man to shrink, yet it was as though all of the Hersir's bravado and arrogance had shriveled away, leaving only an empty shell that vaguely resembled him.

Selia swallowed hard, then returned to the kitchen for a large basin of water and a cake of soap. Muirin was gone, obviously not wanting any other uncomfortable encounters with the mistress of the house.

She shut the bedroom door, then lit another candle. Selia stripped the filthy blankets from the bed. She pulled clean linen out of one of the trunks, as well as fresh clothes for Alrik when he woke up. After finishing the bed, she wet a rag, wringing it out slowly, and washed Alrik's face. His cheekbones felt as sharp as knife blades under her fingers.

When she wiped a line of drool from Alrik's chin, he startled awake.

He blinked, disoriented, and rubbed a hand across his mouth. His eyes focused on her and he stopped mid-movement. He sat for several moments, gaping at her as if she were a ghost.

"Alrik," she whispered, "I have come back, if you will have me." Selia gently pried the cup from his fingers, then set it on the table.

Alrik's eyes flickered dully. "I know you're not real." His voice was thick, as though it had been some time since he had spoken.

She leaned in to kiss his forehead. "I am real."

He seemed afraid to touch her, and sat with his arms down at his sides as he stared at her. "Why do you torment me?"

Selia cupped his face in her palms. Obviously he was too drunk to have a conversation of any substance. "Alrik, listen to me. I have left my family and come back to you. I have walked all the way from your grandfather's house, and I am very tired. Let's sleep now and we will talk in the morning."

His hesitant hands slid up her body, fingers clenching around her upper arms. Selia winced as they made contact with the spot where Ulfrik had gripped her tightly as they argued this afternoon, which now seemed ages ago.

"Selia?"

At her smile, he snatched her up in a hug that expelled the air from her lungs. He made an odd noise, a small, strangled yelp, and she tried to draw back. Was his wound not completely healed-had she bumped it? But a second later, she realized he was crying. Not just crying, but *sobbing.*

She stood, blinking at the sight of her husband crying like a child. She had never seen a man cry before. Alrik's body wracked with sobs of such intensity that it was difficult for her to remain standing, but she planted her feet farther apart and held on to him. She stroked his hair like a mother comforting her young.

After a while his sobs slackened a bit, then finally stopped. He continued to grip her, though, with his face buried in her bodice.

"Why did you come back?" he rasped.

Selia paused. How could she answer that? She had willingly returned to a man who had not only destroyed her family, but had tried to murder her as a child. A man who was arrogant, selfish, and prone to violent rages. A man directly responsible for the spells that had plagued her for as long as she could remember. Most people would consider her decision to return to her husband as foolish at best, and at worst, a wish for death.

"I came back because I love you, Alrik. There is bad in you but there is also good. And I love the good more than I hate the bad."

He lifted a bloodshot gaze. "I'm sorry," he slurred, "for what I did to you. There is no way to make it right. I'm so sorry."

She nodded, stroking his hair, as he lowered his head to her breast again. "I love you so much, Selia. Every day it was torture to not come after you."

"Why did you not come for me then?"

Alrik sat back in the chair. He spoke slowly in his drunkenness. "Because I thought you hated me. Even if I forced you to come back I knew there was nothing I could do to make you love me again."

She looked into the beautiful blue eyes that had lost their light. "I tried to hate you. But I could not, and I hated myself for it. I longed for you every night."

Now he smiled at her, but it was small and faint, nothing like the cocky smile of the Alrik she knew. She reached for his hand to place it on her abdomen. "And every night as I felt your son kick inside me, I longed to tell you."

His eyes grew large. "The child lives?"

"Yes. Feel for yourself."

"But . . . Hrefna said you lost too much blood for the child to have survived."

"And yet he does."

He cupped the small, hard swell of her belly. "You truly are charmed, little one. You are unbreakable."

Selia placed a soft kiss on his lips and ran her fingers down his torso, finally stopping at his crotch. She squeezed gently and he leapt to life under her hand. *Hardly unable.*

Alrik drew his breath in. He hesitated for a moment as he looked down at his appearance, as though knowing how he must appear to her.

She shook her head as she unfastened his breeches. "I do not care," she said, lifting her gown to straddle him in the chair. She closed her eyes and lowered herself onto him with a sigh.

Alrik groaned and his hands clenched around her hips. "My Selia," he choked out.

As she rode him, his body tightened and arched with restrained passion. She could sense the frustrated beast pacing inside him. Why wouldn't he let go?

Selia leaned in to kiss the spot she loved best on his body, where the ropy muscles of his shoulder and neck met. She drew her tongue slowly up his neck, then bit him where the tendon stood out. "Please, Alrik," she whispered into his ear, "I need you."

Alrik made a noise deep in his throat, a kind of growl. He stood, still inside her, then backed her against the wall, thrusting so deeply that Selia cried out. She smiled with satisfaction as she gazed into his face, wild with lust, his bright eyes burning into hers.

The sad shell of a man was gone, as was the husband who had so tenderly expressed his love for her moments ago. Now she faced the beast, fierce and uncontrollable. Selia's body began to quiver as waves of pleasure crashed over her, threatening to drown her. She closed her eyes and held on.

She might have blacked out for a moment, whether from the intensity of her release or from one of her spells. But when she came back to herself, Alrik had shuddered to completion and held himself still, breathing hard as he stared down at her. The wild blaze in his eyes was fading.

"Did I hurt you?" The concerned look on his face faintly reminded her of Ulfrik.

She shivered at how she had actually thought him honorable. If she hadn't seen through Ulfrik's lies, they would have been in Bjorgvin by now, ready to take the first ship to Ireland in the morning. And Alrik would still be here alone, drowning in his own misery.

Selia pushed a lank strand of hair out of her husband's face. "No," she replied.

"I will never hurt you again, little one," Alrik vowed.

Selia nuzzled closer, certain she had made the right decision. She was home, and nothing could make her leave again. "I know," she whispered.

Bonus: An Excerpt from Book two of the *Sons of Odin Series:*
A Flame Put Out, Coming Soon from Soul Mate Publishing

Selia's saga continues as she struggles with the harsh
reality of existence as the wife of a Viking berserker. A
devastating loss pulls Alrik deeper into madness, while a
secret Selia desperately wants to keep hidden comes to light,
threatening everything she holds dear. Is Selia's love for
Alrik enough to keep her in Norway? Or will the protection
offered by Alrik's brother Ulfrik finally sway her to leave?

Prologue

Ireland, 860 AD

Grainne heard the children whispering. It was just after dawn, too early for them to be awake. She shushed them over her shoulder as she stirred the kettle of porridge, but had trouble keeping her face stern as Cassan grinned at her.

Deirdre climbed down from the bench she shared with her brother. She toddled over, with Cassan following as he always did. "'San is hungry, Mamai," she lisped.

She regarded her little daughter. "Is that so? And what is it he wants, then?"

"Cakes," Deirdre replied with a serious expression, referring to the oatcakes and honey Grainne would sometimes make as a special treat.

"Well. If Cassan wants oatcakes, we will have to send Dadai into the forest to chase down a bee and steal his honey."

Deirdre pouted, as though doubting her father would be willing to undertake such a task. But she stomped off to the barn to ask him, with Cassan toddling several steps behind.

Grainne shook her head as she watched them go. The twins had been born too early, and although Cassan was somewhat small at birth, Deirdre had been tiny, barely longer than her father's hand. Her cries were so weak she sounded more like a kitten than a human child, and her mouth was too small to properly suckle. No one had expected the fragile infant to live.

But live she did. Faolan had made sure of that, despite Grainne's misgivings. Shivering, she crossed herself at the memory.

Little Deirdre not only survived, but quickly exceeded her brother's development. She uttered her first intelligible word before she could walk. By the time she had reached a year, she could speak in sentences, and at two she remembered every word spoken.

The child's uncanny precociousness made Grainne uneasy. What if someone put the chain of events together and realized what Faolan had done? But he scoffed at her worries.

Even the village priest believed Deirdre's abilities were a gift from God. He came to their house nearly every evening after supper, reciting scriptures to the child in Latin. And she soaked it all in, her face solemn with concentration. The priest thought someday little Deirdre might become a nun.

Grainne and Faolan didn't speak of the irony of that plan.

Cassan barely said a word other than the unintelligible jargon he spoke with his sister. Grainne would sometimes lie awake at night, listening to them chatter to each other in the dark. And hated it.

Her son was good natured with an even temper, a direct contrast to his sister's more stubborn nature. He allowed Deirdre to take the lead in all things, content to follow and do her bidding. Although Grainne worried about Cassan's meekness, Faolan found great amusement in this and said it would prepare the boy for his eventual marriage.

The door opened and Deirdre entered, pulling her father by the hand. Cassan was several steps behind with his thumb in his mouth. "Dadai will find the bee," Deirdre informed her.

Faolan shrugged helplessly with a smile, and Grainne's heart nearly burst with the beauty of it. She had loved him since they were children, thinking him the most handsome boy in all of Ireland. A man such as Faolan could have had any woman who struck his fancy, but he had chosen her.

He handed her the pail of milk he had been carrying, cocking an amused eyebrow. "Am I truly to go hunting for honey, then? Or is Deirdre—"

Suddenly a woman's scream sounded outside, calling for Faolan. Both Grainne and Faolan jumped as Ionait, the widow who lived at the neighboring farm with her son, rushed in from the mist beyond, darting through the open doorway.

"Finngalls," she gasped, clutching her chest. "They are here! Aodhan is fighting them!"

Grainne could hear faint shouting and the clanging of metal. Ionait sobbed and backed toward the door, but Faolan blocked her way.

"Stay here," he ordered, in a voice Grainne had never heard him use before.

He flipped open the leather chest that sat near their bench, pulling out an ancient-looking sword. He was a farmer, not a warrior, and much handier with the pitchfork or scythe. But Grainne knew her husband would not leave his family unprotected while he ran to the barn. His grandfather's sword would have to do.

Time seemed to stand still as Faolan gazed down at the faces of his children, before exchanging a long look with Grainne. "Bolt the door," he said. Then he was gone, out into the early morning mist.

She heard his raised voice, followed by incomprehensible noises that reminded her of the snarling of wolves. Was that the language of the Finngalls? They were close then, so close, and she ran to bolt the door.

There was a scream from outside-a male scream-and then silence. "Faolan?" she whispered hoarsely.

If the Finngalls were still out there, the door would be no match for their weapons. Grainne waited, each second an eternity. What if Faolan had killed the Finngalls, but was now outside, wounded?

She took a deep breath, slid the latch over, and opened the door. The thick mist hid all from her sight, and she hesitated. Should she search for Faolan or stay with the children, who were crying behind her?

A noise, footsteps just a few yards in front of her, made her heart leapt.

"Faolan?" she whispered again.

It wasn't Faolan. The devil himself emerged from the mist, a Finngall as large as two men, wearing a mail shirt and iron helmet. He carried a battle-axe on his shoulder, stained red with blood. When he spotted her, the smile forming on his lips seemed the most chilling expression Grainne had ever seen.

Too late she tried to shut the door, but the Finngall pushed into it with such force that she fell. The children and Ionait sobbed hysterically, and the devil growled something to them in his wolf language. Grainne turned, crawling on her hands and knees, desperate to protect her children.

The Finngall picked her up by the neck to toss her upon the table. Bowls of porridge flew from its surface and hit the wall with a clatter.

The giant laughed at her screams as he laid his axe next to her on the table. Her gaze fixed on the black hairs glued to the blood that smeared it, and she stared, numb and still. Faolan.

She felt nothing as he lifted her gown. Her body was as cold as that of her dead husband.

But the children's screams intensified, and she turned hollow eyes in their direction. "Run," she choked out to Ionait. "Take the children!"

Ionait seemed frozen in fear, clutching the twins to her breast. Deirdre struggled to break free of Ionait's grip, but Cassan only stared, pale and open mouthed, wailing.

Grainne's attacker pulled off his helmet to wipe his sweaty brow with one massive forearm. She stared at his face, memorizing every line and plane. Without the helmet, she realized he was very young. For all his size, this Finngall devil was barely more than a boy. Yet his eyes were empty and cold, devoid of any human emotion.

Deirdre suddenly broke free from Ionait and rushed toward the giant devil, biting his leg hard enough to draw blood. He bellowed as he turned his unholy gaze on the toddler. As he reached for the axe, Grainne flung her hand to the side, pushing it to the floor.

He stretched his big hand out to grab Deirdre, and Grainne wrapped her arms around one of his to slow him down. "Ionait, run—now!" she screamed at the woman.

Ionait sobbed as her eyes darted to the door. She couldn't reach it without getting within an arm's length of the Finngall. As she inched across the room, clutching the children, another gigantic Finngall demon entered the house. Foreign words tumbled from them as they both cursed each other.

The devil suddenly broke from her desperate grip, catching her by the hair, slinging her across the room.

Grainne's temple hit the hearth and the edges of her vision went dark. A burning log from the hearth rolled to the corner, then blazed bright as the willow branch wall caught fire. The flames crackled upward, hot and quick; smoke filled the room.

She stared, dazed.

A voice in her head that sounded like Faolan's urged her to get the children away from more danger, and she forced herself to her feet. The two Finngalls were still shouting at each other, and the bigger one shoved the other aside to make him stumble.

Then, in a motion so fluid and quick Grainne barely had time to react, the devil pulled his sword from its scabbard, bringing the hilt forcefully down upon the small curly head of her daughter, as though squashing a bug.

Grainne screamed as Deirdre's tiny body collapsed in the smoke. Her head bounced against the dirt floor, and her wide, sightless eyes stared into nothingness. The devil flicked the sword up and over in his hand, catching it so the blade now faced downward, then raised his arm to run the child through with it.

The second Finngall yelled and ran toward the devil with his shield before him as if to block the blow. But he used the shield as a weapon, bringing the metal edge of it down upon the hand of the devil. The room echoed with the sound of metal cracking bone.

The devil dropped the sword and stared at his mangled hand for a moment. With a roar, he overturned the table to pick up the axe that had fallen under it. The second Finngall lunged for him. They rolled on the floor, snarling at each other like wolves.

Grainne crawled to the body of her child. Deirdre was pale and still, limp, and Grainne sobbed as she clutched the tiny form to her breast.

Suddenly the second Finngall spoke to her in strangely-accented Irish. "Run," he panted, "before he kills the other one."

Grainne and Ionait turned to flee, each holding a child. The devil grabbed Grainne's ankle, pulling her to the floor, and she had to twist her torso as she fell to avoid crushing the body of her little daughter.

"Take her, Ionait!" she begged. If the devil meant to carry Grainne off into slavery, she would not leave the tiny body to be burned inside the house, or thrown to the ravens.

Ionait seemed to understand, for she grabbed Deirdre's floppy body and pulled it clear of the Finngalls. As the woman hurried into the mist, Grainne saw Cassan's terrified face peering over Ionait's shoulder.

"Mamai," he cried, holding out a tiny hand to her.

Chapter 1

Norway, 876 AD

Selia awoke to the faint, melancholy strain of a bird chirping. The silk bedding was soft against her cheek, and Alrik's familiar body was warm and solid behind her. She nestled closer, loath to open her eyes. All would be right with the world if she could just stay here, with her husband's arm covering her like a shield, the past events nothing more than an unpleasant dream.

Or for that matter, the events of yesterday.

Alrik's fingers grazed her arm, pausing near her shoulder. "Did I do this to you last night?"

She lifted her arm to look. There was a faint bruise, an outline of fingers and thumb from where Ulfrik had grabbed her in the heat of their argument. It stood out against the white of her skin like a brand, proof of her would-be sin for the entire world to see.

Out of her mind with misery, she had nearly succumbed to Ulfrik's persuasion. Her husband's brother knew how to play upon her fragile emotions, attempting to maneuver her as carefully as he would the pieces on a tafl board. Though she had spurned him, still she had come uncomfortably close to allowing him liberties.

Selia would carry that secret to her grave.

Now she simply answered, "Yes."

Alrik swallowed, visibly distressed. "You haven't been back a day and I've already hurt you."

"It is all right." She snuggled up to his chest. "You know how easily I bruise. And it was worth it."

He laughed, such a wonderful sound. How she had missed it. "Well, be that as it may, I'll have to be more careful now. For the sake of the child." His hand cupped the swell of her abdomen as he smiled down at the life that grew inside her. His face was achingly beautiful despite the red-rimmed eyes and unkempt hair.

Selia caressed his cheek. "I love you, Alrik." Her voice came out in a whisper.

His gaze met hers. "Even after all I have done to you."

"Yes. I knew I should stop loving you. But I could not."

He appeared to ponder this for a moment. "I have caused you so much pain. There is no way to make it right." He shook his head. "You should have stayed away, Selia. I destroy everything I touch. You and the child would have been better off—"

"No," she replied firmly. "I cannot be without you, Alrik." She turned his chin to force him to look at her. "You cannot make me leave again."

His smile made her heart flutter. As he bent to kiss her, there was a knock at the bedroom door.

"I hope you're decent, because I'm coming in," Hrefna called.

Alrik sat up. "Stay out of my bedroom, woman, or you're going to see more than you bargained for," he commanded in the booming voice he used when giving orders to his men.

But Hrefna entered anyway, grinning from ear to ear, and Selia pulled the blanket up just in time to cover her nudity. The woman ignored Alrik, rushing over instead to envelop Selia in a hug. She made a choked noise that was between a laugh and a sob. "I knew you would come back, child," she vowed, "even though Alrik didn't believe me." She shot her nephew a gloating look, and he snorted at her.

Selia blinked back tears as she embraced Hrefna. This woman was more a mother to her than Grainne could ever hope to be. She had missed her terribly, nearly as much as she had missed Alrik.

Hrefna held her at arm's length, her brow pinching together as she took in Selia's appearance. "Have you been ill, dear? You look much too thin. I know I sent plenty of provisions with Olaf, and when Ketill stopped by yesterday morning he said he had supplies for your family as well."

So Ketill had known the appalling state his Hersir was in, but had not thought to mention it to Selia. Obviously he had told Ulfrik, though. And Ulfrik had taken full advantage of the situation.

The thought of Ulfrik made Selia's stomach tighten into a knot of fury. She willed her face to stay expressionless. "There was enough food," she said. "I . . . I was ill, yes." She drew the covers tight against her belly to show the rounded outline. "I am still with child."

Hrefna reached out in wonder to touch her. "How can this be?"

"Because he is strong," Alrik asserted. "My son is a warrior."

"Humph," Hrefna scoffed. "Warrior or not, your wife lost so much blood she nearly died herself. I can't understand how the child still lives."

Alrik scowled at her. "She has the protection of Odin. Is it so hard to imagine the child does too?"

Selia looked away in discomfort. This sounded a bit too much like Ragnarr's delusions.

Hrefna seemed unnerved as she studied them both. "Well," she said after a moment. "Let's get some food into you then, Selia. It doesn't appear Odin has been feeding you properly."

Alrik's frown deepened at his aunt's sarcasm. She turned to him. "And you need a bath, my boy." Hrefna wrinkled her nose in distaste. "It smells like a barn in here. You simply can't go around pissing on the floor."

Selia walked out the kitchen door, humming softly under her breath. She had eaten and bathed. Hrefna had spent more than an hour combing out the knots in her hair, then styling it for her. Selia felt pretty again. She looked the way the mistress of a household such as Alrik's should look, and not like some undernourished thrall dressed in rags, with burrs in her hair.

She turned into the woods to look for her ring, plagued by the vague memory of throwing it at Alrik the day everything had gone so horribly wrong. The likelihood of finding the exact spot in the woods where the incident had occurred was slim, and of actually finding the ring even slimmer, but she still wanted to try. Was it soft sentiment that drove her to look for the band of silver, or the harder reality of knowing the runes would keep her safe?

After searching unsuccessfully for some time, she gave up—the ring was gone. Maybe Alrik could have another one made for her. She turned to go back to the house, but as she approached a large boulder she heard the sound of someone crying. She peeked around the other side. And recognized the pale, unkempt hair of Ingrid.

The girl had her head buried in her arms but was not doing a very good job of muffling her sobs. Selia hesitated. Ingrid would be furious if she knew anyone had seen her like this. And it wasn't as though Selia could do anything to help her, even if she wanted to. The girl hated her with a passion.

She took a step backward to slip away, but the hem of her gown caught on a bush, rustling as she pulled it free. Ingrid's head shot up. The look on her face changed from despair to rage as she met Selia's eyes.

"You!" she shouted. "Get away from me, you Irish bitch!"

Selia's eyes widened at her stepdaughter's ire but didn't return the insult. The girl had obviously loved Ainnileas and was hurting. Maybe just as much as Selia herself had hurt after losing Alrik. That kind of misery was punishment enough. She turned to leave.

"Wait," Ingrid sniffled. Selia looked back at her. "Did he . . . did Ainnileas say anything about me?"

She studied Ingrid's tearstained face, but didn't answer immediately. Ainnileas had not spoken of the girl, not even once, but that meant nothing. For as long as Selia could remember, whenever her brother was upset about something he would withdraw. His typical lighthearted banter would be silenced for a time, then he would return to himself once he had worked through whatever was bothering him.

Ainnileas had been unnaturally reserved the entire time they had stayed at Ulfrik's house. And Selia had been too caught up in her own sorrow to notice or care.

But Ingrid deserved an answer. "He was very sad," Selia said slowly, "but he did not speak of why."

Ingrid's sudden laugh rose into hysteria. Selia gasped as the girl pounded her fist into her own stomach. She continued to hit herself until Selia knelt to grab her arm.

"Ingrid, stop."

The girl pushed her backward. "Leave me alone!"

Selia stared as realization dawned on her. "Are you with child?" she whispered. She was sure the pair had lain together.

What would happen if Ingrid were with child?

And what would Alrik do to Ainnileas?

Lightning Source UK Ltd.
Milton Keynes UK
UKHW020658191221
395919UK00007B/127